RISK OF LOVE AND MAGIC

A CALIFORNIA MALCOLM NOVEL

Patricia Rice

The Risk of Love and Magic

Publication team: Beta reader: Lisa Waters

Proofreader: Jennifer Stevenson

Formatter: Vonda McIntrye

Cover design by Killion Group

Book View Café Publishing Cooperative

P.O. Box 1624, Cedar Crest, NM 87008-1624

http://bookviewcafe.com

978-1-61138- -370-6 ebook

978-1-61138-371-3 trade paper

Other Book View Cafe books by Patricia Rice:

California Malcolm series:
The Trouble With Air and Magic

Rebellious Sons:
Notorious Atherton

Family Genius Mysteries:
Evil Genius
Undercover Genius

Praise for the California Malcolm series:

"Patricia Rice writes stories with so much attention to detail the characters truly seem to come to life."—Booklist starred review—*Lure of Song and Magic*

"Rice brings you great characters, a dynamite plot and plenty of magic and she accomplishes the whole thing without a shoot-out. Don't miss it." –RT Reviews 4 ½ stars— *Lure of Song and Magic*

One

Magnus Oswin jimmied his shoulders under the Camaro to bolt in the new electronic engine he'd designed. Brains and power—a Special Forces car if he ever saw one. A loud country tune wailed on the classic muscle car's speaker system.

The musical tribute to baseball bats and windshields abruptly cut off.

HELP ME, the car cried.

Magnus sat up so fast that he whacked his head against the undercarriage. Rubbing the bruise, he slid the platform from under the car and grabbed the cell phone he'd synched with the car's new Bluetooth.

Unknown was all the caller ID displayed. But he knew who it was. He'd spent weeks of sleepless nights attempting to track the mysterious Librarian's entreaties.

He was a mechanic, not a computer technician. But even his computer genius brother Conan couldn't trace these pleas.

Magnus tried dialing back but only reached a disconnect message. He thought about shoving the phone in his pocket and forgetting about it, but he couldn't. Whether she was liar, traitor, or bait, the Librarian was his key to getting his hands on General Adams—his latest obsession.

No man tricked him, locked him up, and attempted to steal his hard work without paying the consequences. The general had to be insane to have even considered something as whacko as hijacking a military experiment. Insane men should not be allowed access to military channels—even generals who'd disappeared into the desert and fallen off the radar.

Growling, he closed the garage door and set the security locks through the car's dashboard—his latest experiment. It needed more work, but the Librarian was higher on his agenda.

He carried the phone past his brother's flashy Mercedes sports coupe and into the ground floor space of Conan's beach house. Unlike his brother, Magnus had never needed much of a roof over his head. The beach house was a nice perk, but he would be content to live in a tent if that's what it took to find the general.

The Librarian's pleas were scraping his nerves raw. She'd helped save a bunch of people, including himself, from the general's plots. If she needed help, they owed it to her to provide it.

Magnus entered the spacious open area that was Conan's office. His younger brother glanced up from one of his many monitors.

"Librarian?" Conan asked, turning his screen around so Magnus could see the same message texting across the screen.

"Still no coordinates on the messages?" Magnus asked, handing over his phone so the call could be traced.

"Her computer may be stationary, but the calls are bouncing off satellites. I'm getting closer to finding an epicenter with each call, but as we all know, the desert is a big place."

Dorrie—Dorothea Franklin—arrived bearing a tray of sandwiches from the local deli. "Francesca just called. She's receiving fragmented numbers that strike her as frantic, but she can't decipher them." She dropped a paper of coded numbers on the desk.

Half Chinese, half Irish, with wild black curls she hadn't bothered taming today, Conan's fiancée was related to a family with admittedly weird abilities.

"Receiving?" Magnus asked warily. "By phone, text, or ether?"

"Ether," she retorted, meaning Francesca's psychic claims.

Magnus ignored the psychic fantasy and studied Dorrie's numbers as Conan fed them into his computer. They had a pattern. "We need military code software. These aren't coordinates," Magnus told them. "What are the chances this is some play to exchange a hostage for the 'copter?"

"Paranoia doesn't suit you," Dorrie told him. "It's confusing your chi."

Snorting in amusement at his fiancée's comment, Conan hit the keyboard. "I'm on the code." Looking more like a long-haired, blond surfer than a computer whiz, Conan tapped his keyboard faster than seemed humanly possible, accessing dozens of websites that he probably had no business knowing existed.

"How would the Librarian know military code if the general isn't feeding it to her?" Magnus demanded. "What if she's leading us into a trap?" He examined the food, found a sandwich not dripping bean sprouts and greenery, and sampled it before nearly gulping it whole and looking for another.

"You may be big tall manly man, but you need to eat your veggies. Sprouts and spinach are good for you," Dorrie pointed out, before settling cross-legged on a floor pillow to munch her lunch.

She was too damned observant, but he shrugged off the criticism. He had been quarterback on his college team. He wasn't small. He'd inhale anything. But he preferred meat. He helped himself to another.

"The Librarian is smart," Dorrie continued. "If she's figured out that we have ex-military working to find her, she'll use anything she can. I don't like the sound of it if she's growing frantic. She's never asked for help for herself before. The General may suspect that she's been aiding us."

Magnus felt his gut grind. He'd left Special Forces because he didn't feel capable of carrying the world on his shoulders. His fiancée's death had proved that he lacked good judgment. He didn't want to be responsible for saving the Librarian, but he didn't want to be responsible for her death either.

Crap.

Scarfing the second sandwich, he helped himself to a laptop, took the couch, and connected with several old Marine buddies. His big fingers didn't fit the keys as expertly as Conan's, but coordination, he could do.

Dorrie sipped her drink and murmured, "My, I like watching strong silent men work. Scintillating conversation."

"Got it," Magnus said without satisfaction some hours later, staring at the laptop screen. "Psychic mumbo-jumbo doesn't mean squat."

Returned from a design consultation and wearing her hair tamed into a knot at her nape, Dorrie took the machine away from him. "Psychic readings aren't always spelled out, you realize."

Conan was already studying the de-coded message Magnus had sent to his e-mail. "Starwood. Dollar Lake. We use psychics and secret code and we get a hiking trail?"

"Hiking trail?" Magnus Googled the names and came up with reviews of trails. "No Starwood related to Dollar Lake. If someone has the Librarian tied to a tree, she could scream to one of these industrious hikers texting from a damned mountain."

"Starwood." Dorrie pounced on an iPad. "Starwood. I know that name. Have you sent the message to the whole family?"

"Done." Conan hit a button. "Including Pippa and Oz, although they're probably out stargazing or doing yoga at this hour."

"Oz takes his phone to bed with him, and Pippa's waiting for final arrangements on our wedding. They'll answer." Dorrie went back to poking the iPad. "All I'm getting is hotels," she complained a few minutes later.

"I'll guarantee there are no four diamond hotels in Dollar Lake," Conan muttered from his desk.

Magnus rubbed his crooked nose in frustration, then kept typing, digging deeper, not joining the discussion. He studied the terrain around Dollar Lake but saw no indication of permanent habitation. It was a national forest, deep in the mountains outside of San Bernardino. They could fly low over most of it, but without a direction, it would be useless. Campers could be hidden in the trees and they'd never know.

Would crazy hikers name a particular grove of trees *Starwood*?

"Francesca says try scrambling the words or letters. She can't promise she got the numbers in correct order," Dorrie reported, clicking off her phone. "Psychic reception is not a science."

Conan shut down his computer in disgust and stood up, stretching his back. "This is nuts. Let's go get some Thai and think about it."

Magnus didn't move. "Bring some back for me."

He tuned out the protests. This was the best clue they'd had. The general could be moving the Librarian from location to location. If he didn't act now, he'd lose this chance. Whatever the source, the code had been translatable. It had to mean something.

After the room emptied, Magnus realized Conan's computer was still beeping with messages. He moved into the desk chair to read them. Dorrie's extensive psychic—or psychopathic— family offered numerous suggestions, including astrological instructions.

Magnus assumed Conan's trained investigators could follow up the more logical clues, but given their prior experiences with the Librarian, his bet was that the answer would be illogical.

Stomach growling, his muscles feeling the lack of exercise, Magnus was about to hunt down his own food when a text pinged from their older brother Dylan, commonly known as Oz. They all hated their first names, but Dylan had grabbed the Oz moniker first.

PIPPA'S MOM SAYS WOODSTAR IS THE NAME OF A REHAB FACILITY.

Magnus punched his phone to Oz's number. "Put her on," he commanded when Oz answered.

"There's a reason I sent that text to Conan and not to you," Oz complained. "Do you even have a life? You do realize it's after ten and most reasonable people would wait until morning to call? Gloria Jean is probably in bed."

"Dammit, Dylan, the general could be moving her as we speak. Did you ask Gloria where this place is? Is it even in California?"

"She doesn't know anything except that she heard it discussed way back when she was disabled and in the rehab hospital, which is in California, so one assumes Woodstar would be here. She thought the place might be a drug rehab or for the mentally impaired. That's all she can recall."

"If I can't find more, I'll call in the morning." Magnus hung up without the niceties. He was on a mission—the place he felt most comfortable.

A *mental* institution would explain a lot. The general couldn't have found a more painful way to torment him.

He'd be better off handing anything he learned over to someone who understood crazy people better than he did. He was likely to drive an unstable Librarian over the edge—as he had Diane.

Hoping "Dollar Lake" indicated the institution was in California but checking other Dollar lakes, mountains, and rivers just in case, Magnus dug into his research.

Conan and Dorrie arrived with steaming boxes of food. Magnus lifted a hand in greeting and grabbed a spring roll.

"Let's hope you find the Librarian before the wedding," Dorrie said, opening a box of vegetables and unwrapping the chopstick paper. She stuck his fingers with a stick until he took the utensils. "We were counting on you being present in mind as well as in person."

"Of course. I'll bring the shackles. He's all yours." Magnus plied chopsticks to the veggies and typed with one hand, not looking up from the keyboard.

"You can take the laptop downstairs," Conan suggested helpfully.

"Yeah, right." With a grudging sigh, Magnus sent his searches to his cloud account, stuck a machine under his arm, and gathered up his food. "I'll leave you lovebirds alone. I don't suppose you're honeymooning in Siberia over the next few months."

"Sorry, old boy, gotta work. You're the one free to camp in the woods." Conan escorted Dorrie from the room, leaving Magnus to carry his load to his own empty space downstairs.

Plugged into his online communities, Magnus didn't notice he was alone. He was comfortable with machinery, although he preferred engines that roared to silent computers. People were his downfall.

By dawn, after a brief catnap, he thought he had the code worked out. Sending his findings to his brothers, he threw together a backpack, lowered the Camaro from its lift, and cruised into the dawn.

Two

Nadine Malcolm finished inputting the data sheets she'd been assigned, then shoved her cheap black-framed glasses up her nose. With a surreptitious sideways glance, she verified that the guard was busy poisoning his health with sugar and coffee. Swiftly, she hit a series of keys.

The guard turned around before she could do more. The repetitive message she'd stored would automatically go out to the phone numbers she'd recorded. She didn't hold out much hope that any of the recipients would follow up, but she could annoy the tar out of them if they didn't. She'd left politeness behind in a faraway time and place.

She innocently fiddled with her too-long Orphan Annie curls and flipped a page, pretending she was checking her work.

Once she handed in the data sheets, she focused on the code numbers she was mentally sending into the universe. She needed to hold them in her head until she snagged an opportunity to type them into her cloud cache for physical sending.

"Thirty-four, twenty-two," she told the guard in genial tones as they traversed the cold tile corridors to the cafeteria. "Eleven-eighty."

"Yeah, and H-E-double hockey sticks back atcha," the guard grumped, following her to the cafeteria where she could get a plate of cardboard eggs.

The amusement of playing this role had worn thin since learning Vera was no longer safely in the college boarding house where she belonged. Buttering her toast, Nadine debated cutting herself with a plastic knife. Would they take her to a real hospital in a real town? She'd have a better chance of escaping closer to civilization than this remote outpost.

As an experiment, she tried breaking the plastic knife while she forked her dry eggs, but she couldn't produce an edge sharp enough to even poke out an eye. If she poked any eyes, it would be the evil eye of her own personal Nurse Ratchet.

The vibrations in the universe seemed exceptionally intense today. Or maybe she was just on edge because of Vera and picking up more disturbances than usual. With no means of finding out, she blocked out the distraction by repeating the code numbers in her head, just in case anyone was listening. She knew there were others out there who could receive her psychic transmissions, but she didn't know if they paid attention.

Usually, rumbling in her universe meant the general was coming. She might want to escape this asylum—but not into his dangerous spider trap.

Tucking the broken plastic knife into the aluminum foil that had wrapped her tray, Nadine amused her audience by wrapping the foil around her orange curls. She stuck a plastic fork like a feather into the foil turban.

"Eight hundred," she told the guard, rising from the heavy bench. They didn't allow patients near chairs that could be used as weapons or shields. She was average-sized chubby, not a weightlifter. A physical fight for escape wasn't happening.

The skinny scarecrow of a guard scratched his crotch and led her down the fluorescent-lit tile corridor to the reception desk in the lobby. "Bingo," she told the nurse waiting with her meds and a paper cup of juice.

"We're all winners, dear," Nurse Ratchet said with that gleam in her eye that Nadine wanted to punch out.

She figured the witch was sleeping with the General and getting paid well to do so.

"Burp." Nadine took the pills and dropped them into her orange juice, then dumped the concoction on Wretched Ratchet's pristine white SAS walking shoes.

"You bitch, you did that on purpose!" Wretched grabbed a towel to wipe the leather.

"Ta-ta," Nadine agreed. She'd used similar diversionary tactics when she'd first been brought here, with every intention of escaping.

Her prior attempts had merely taught her the location of every guard post in the building—and exhausted her chances. They made her sleep during the day now so that her waking hours were in the dark, when she was their sole focus. She wasn't a nature lover. They probably thought she'd be afraid of the mountain at night.

She had run out of waiting time if they'd taken Vera. She'd finally reached the point where she'd risk bears, cougars, and rabid squirrels to escape this loony bin.

She shouldn't let distant vibrations raise her hopes, but she was in a mood to fight for her freedom.

If she stabbed Wretched in the eye, would they take her to jail?

Wait a minute...

Whoever was driving up the road boiled like a thunderstorm. Power like that was worthy of a diversion.

In the cool October morning, Magnus studied Woodstar Villas Assisted Living on Dollar Lane. Psychic messages weren't all they cracked up to be if he was in the right place. Lake—Lane. Starwood—Woodstar.

The "villas" were in the middle of an evergreen forest in the mountains beyond San Bernardino, up a creek so narrow that no one in their right mind would find it— appropriate, if the Librarian was psycho. At least he didn't have to hike to it.

He was almost disappointed. The place looked normal—a sprawling stucco building half-hidden behind a stucco wall—hence the Villa name. It was, however, well off the beaten path. They weren't advertising their presence.

It was a little after eight in the morning. Magnus didn't know if his brothers were out of bed to receive his texts. He was too far into the mountains for them to reach him quickly, even if they were awake. He just liked to keep back-up alerted.

He glanced down at his jeans and the rumpled flannel shirt he'd pulled over his t-shirt. He probably should have suited up. Maybe not. That would have just put people on their toes.

A metal security gate was his first obstacle. He could unlock the code with his experimental system, but he didn't want to start a fight at this stage of the game. Leaning out of the Camaro's window, he flashed a fake ID at the guardhouse. If this was the right place, and he had to do something obnoxious, he'd rather not leave a trail. He announced the name of the CEO he'd looked up online.

"Do you have an appointment?" the bored guard asked.

"Of course. I should be on your list. I'm running late, but he's expecting me," he lied glibly, with skills learned at his TV-producer brother's right hand.

"He ain't here yet," the guard confirmed. "I'll call up to the house and see what they want me to do."

Crap. Magnus waved in agreement and studied the situation. If he knew the Librarian was actually here, he could return with storm troopers.

He knew no such thing.

He climbed out and leaned against the pillar next to the gate while checking his phone for messages. He sent a couple of photos to Conan, just in case. Electronic lock with manual backup on the gate. His car could open it.

"They said to come up and wait in the lobby," the guard yelled at him.

Well, hell, that took all the fun out of it. He'd rather blow up gates than figure out how to get past whoever was in charge to look for someone he didn't know. What *had* he been thinking?

Oh, right, he hadn't. As Diane had once told him, he acted instead of thinking. In his past life, that had often made a difference between life and death.

In this case, it was likely to be more complicated. Magnus drove the power car to the parking lot and contemplated his next move, but he was no strategist. He needed a way of communicating with the Librarian to see if he was at least in the right place.

Maybe if she were truly psychic, she'd know he was here. He mentally laughed all the way to the entrance.

The double front doors were barred. He announced his arrival into an intercom and waited for a guard to slide back the bolt. He needed Oz here to feed him lines.

The doors opened. Before Magnus could cross the threshold, a whirlwind in an aluminum foil hat, enormous black-framed glasses, and springy orange hair grabbed the Taser from a security guard. Shooting the guard with her one cartridge, she rapidly switched to stun and rammed the gun against a mean-looking nurse in her way. The nurse screamed in shock and toppled.

Startled, Magnus stepped aside rather than risk being hit. Little Orphan Annie shoved past and flew down the sidewalk.

He swung around to observe her progress, wondering if she planned to run right past the security gate and into the forest.

"Nadine, get your ass back here!" thundered the buxom nurse in orange-stained shoes trying to scramble from the floor. The guard was still twitching. "Catch her, you idiots!" She gestured at a uniformed guard racing up and...

Magnus looked around. Him? He and the bumpkin were the only protection for a mentally disabled patient against a mountain forest?

The Oswin Zorro instinct kicked in. He was off and running without giving it a second thought. He was closer and more in shape than the stumbling guard. He dashed down the walk and caught up with the aluminum-foil lunatic just as she reached his car. *His* car. There was a parking lot full of cars. Why his?

She barely came past his shoulder and was half his width, but she snatched the key from his hand as if he were a marshmallow. She opened the door with the key's electronic switch, hopped in the driver's seat, and had the car running before he could reach inside and yank her out.

"No time," she shouted. "Get in or I'll run over you."

The stout guard tripped over his shoelaces and stumbled into Magnus's back. "She's a nutter," the guy muttered. "Let me at her."

"I'm the *Librarian* and you found me," she retorted, revving the engine.

"You're a librarian nutter," Magnus concluded, thoughts racing along with his car engine.

It would be just his luck that his key to the general would be insane. He didn't like coincidence, but he wasn't taking any chances of losing his only clue. He shoved her from under the steering wheel and across the bucket seat.

With one hand, Magnus propelled the slow guard out of his way, He slammed the door and spun gravel backing out. "I'll bring you right back if you're lying."

"Not lying. Saw you with the Asian guy. Thirty-four, twenty-two, eleven, eighty, eight-hundred, right?"

The code, the freaking code that had kept him up all night. "Not quite in that order," he griped. "How did you see me with Bo?" Magnus asked warily, ramming the gas pedal before the gates could close. The Camaro hit warp speed in sixty seconds. Did they have cops on mountains?

"Don't know," she said. "I see things. Your friend—Bo?—sends out powerful vibrations. You *were* here to get me, weren't you? Which Oswin are you?"

She *saw* things. He and Bo had been buried in an underground tunnel. No one had *seen* them except their captors. Magnus rolled his eyes. "I so do not need another psycho in my life. Please tell me you're actually sane and you're just a little rattled right now."

"I'm sane and just a little rattled right now, and you didn't answer my questions. Maybe if I ask them one at a time—you did come for me, didn't you?"

Of average height and sturdy bone structure, she looked about sixteen wearing those ridiculously huge glasses to hide long-lashed green eyes. The foil hat over Orphan Annie orange curls wasn't helping her case any. Dark shadows left her eyes haunted, and beneath the mop of hair, her almost elfin features seemed gray—like Tinkerbelle fading away because no one believed in her. Her lips were pale, bitten, and unadorned by cosmetics. Very definitely an inmate.

"If you're really the Librarian, we got your messages." *He* was the one a little rattled. How could an inmate in an asylum possibly have known who he was? "We've been looking for you. You didn't exactly make it easy."

"Good." She took off her glasses, tucked them in a pocket beneath her Tweety-bird sweat shirt, and nodded her foil-wrapped head. "You have smart people working for you. I need your help. Could we please go to UC Irvine? You can drop me off at the park and be on your way. Better hide the Camaro later, though. They'll have film of the plate."

"No registration yet. It's a junk vehicle." But it was very visible. He heeded the warning.

He'd installed seat belts when he'd redone the interior. She actually put on hers, exhibiting some degree of sanity given the way he was taking the curves on the narrow road. "I'll report the car stolen and leave it somewhere." It hurt to abandon his prize project, but he could hope no one would steal a rusted out hulk before the police "found" it again.

"Don't ditch it near the campus," she ordered in panic. "The general will know exactly where I went if you do. Can you have someone meet you in the desert or somewhere later?"

He glanced at the elfin-featured redhead in a cartoon sweatshirt, readjusted his thinking, and took a left on the highway, sending the car climbing the mountain. "Hi, my name is Magnus Oswin. May I have the pleasure of knowing who just became my boss?"

"Magnus Maximus!" she cried in delight, her mood instantly swinging. "It's a pleasure, indeed. I'm Nadine Malcolm. You know me as the Librarian. How did you get the code? Your friend Bo again?"

"Maximus?" he inquired warily, wondering if he ought to turn around and take her back right now.

"Magnus the Great. Norwegian or Swedish. I don't remember. I'll just call you Max. Maggie doesn't suit."

Maggie? He'd creamed the last moron to call him that—back in sixth grade.

She leaned forward anxiously to study road signs. "Take the side road at the next intersection."

"You're wearing aluminum foil. Don't give me orders or call me Max," he said grumpily, hitting his Bluetooth button and ordering it to call Conan.

"Do you have a pen knife?" Instead of taking off the metallic hat, she held out her hand, palm up, as if expecting him to hand over a weapon.

"You think I'd give it to you?" he asked incredulously, swinging down the side road and praying he wouldn't end up in a bear cave.

"Then I can't take off the hat," she said impatiently.

Conan's voice interrupted from the speaker. "Yo, bro."

"I've got the Librarian and she's whacko," Magnus told the speaker. "I need to hide the Camaro. I'm heading for the desert."

"Desert later, Irvine, now!" she yelled at him, rummaging through his glove box.

"Desert, first," Magnus countered. He gave his location. "Play GPS and tell me the nearest town."

"Morongo Valley," Conan replied, evidently calling up a map on his computer. "Bound to be a big facility like a school that you can find easily. We can meet there."

"That's *hours* out of our way," Nutty Nadine cried, emerging from the box with a screwdriver. "We don't have hours to spare."

"Want me to meet you with the team or with butterfly nets?" Conan asked dryly.

"Nobody! Don't tell anybody!" she shouted frantically, practically bouncing in her seat. "Just drop me off and I'll hitchhike."

"Morongo Valley," Magnus said, ignoring her orders, "just you and Dorrie, if she's bored. Butterfly nets might be good. Give me coordinates when you have them." He punched off the phone.

"You can't drag anyone else into this! The more people who know, the easier it will be for the general to find me," his partner in crime insisted frantically.

Her big green eyes were even wider without the black-framed glasses, Magnus decided when she turned her pleading look in his direction. Pointed chin, high cheekbones, and radiating intensity like a neutron bomb.

"If you don't want the general to know where you're going, then this is the way to do it. Take my word." Magnus kept his internal compass on east and followed the narrow, nearly-dirt path past the timber line and down towards the rocky desert.

"If you won't take my word that the general will find us, why should I take yours?" she cried in frustration. "I have to find my sister, and I can't afford to waste hours while you do things your way. Just let me out at the next intersection."

She looked ready to jump. The aluminum foil hat and screwdriver weren't helping her case any.

"When was the last time you hitchhiked?" he demanded. "Do you have any idea what kind of yahoos hide up in these hills?"

"People hitchhike all the time," she insisted. "I just have to avoid any rangers in case Nurse Wretched has called the law. But I'm betting she calls the general first, and it takes time to get through his shields." She tugged down the car's visor and made a face at the cracked, dull mirror on the other side.

"Only crazy people hitchhike," he retorted. "If you're that crazy, I'll take you back to Nurse Wretched where you'll be safer."

"I'm not crazy. I'm just dangerous because I know too much. And see too much. And I quit drinking the Kool-Aid." She flung the tinfoil hat into the back seat and started jimmying at her temple with the screwdriver.

Appalled as she stabbed herself in the head, Magnus screeched the car to a halt. He reached over and jerked the tool out of her hand. In those few seconds, she'd managed to break through her luminous skin. Blood streamed down her fair cheek. "That's it. You're going back now. I didn't break you out of there to watch you kill yourself."

He didn't think he'd calm his pulse anytime soon. One suicide was one too many. A second would kill him. He flung the screwdriver out the window.

Big green eyes framed in ridiculously long brown lashes glared at him from behind the sunburst of curls. "Microchip. I'm not the crazy. I'm starting to suspect the general is." She turned back to the mirror and began prying at the nick with her fingernails.

Microchip? Feeling sick to his stomach, Magnus caught her chin and turned her to look at him. His big hand practically encompassed the entire side of her face. In the sunlight, he could see a dark patch right beneath the hairline.

"Tracking device," she said defiantly. "Want me to put the foil back on?"

Fighting back nausea, he produced a penknife, sterilized it with flame from his lighter, and with a quick slash, pried back the skin. Blood gushed. He grabbed tissues from the backseat. She pried the chip loose and flung it out the window.

"Go," she ordered. "I won't bleed to death. I've done this before."

Magnus rubbed at the frown lines on his brow but kicked the engine in again. She'd shaken him to his not-easily shaken core. He needed explanations to ground him back in reality. "I haven't slept all night, and I'm starving and apparently unable to translate Librarian-ese. What Kool-Aid and does it have anything to do with microchips?"

"Yes, and I'm not explaining until I have my baby sister safe." She held the tissues to her head to stanch the blood and refused to look at him.

After what he'd just seen, he didn't have the heart to argue. A madman had implanted a microchip in her head? Like one would a dog? Then leashed her to a mental institution. He'd seen some horrific sights in the service, but this took the crazy to new levels.

"Does your time table allow for food?" he asked, almost politely. "It will take Conan time to travel over here."

She shrank further into the seat. "I've eaten. Please, just let me out somewhere. The general is my stepfather, and I know whereof I speak. He'll seriously hunt us down. I can't afford to lose any time."

Magnus processed that nugget of information. The general had planted a microchip in his own kid's head? "Do you know where he is?" he asked, trying not to sound as if he'd like to grind the man's bones.

"No one ever knows where he is. I've always known he was paranoid. Now I'm convinced he's delusional. He keeps track of everyone and lets no one know where to find him. He could be in Irvine right now, tying my sister up and hauling her off. I just can't wait any longer."

"Tell me where to find your sister, and I'll send Conan's team to protect her. What the hell do you think you can do to save her from a maniac?"

"I can read his mind," she said simply.

Three

Nadine waited for the explosion of disbelief. She hadn't told very many people about the mind reading gig. She wasn't good at it, and it wasn't a credible topic except among the general's inner circles. Mostly, it produced severe headaches and confusion—like she would admit *that* to a man who thought her insane.

She waited for her driver to turn around and take her back to the funny farm.

Instead, Marvelous Max silently digested her statement and followed the directional signs to Morongo.

She had expected this Oswin brother to be ruthlessly efficient, and he'd proved that. She really hadn't expected him to be...so very large. This was one of those huge old muscle cars, but his broad shoulders still seemed to take up all the space. The hands deftly guiding the vehicle around curves and over potholes were large enough to throttle her, which he would probably like to do.

"You're a mind reader?" he finally said as they joined the sparse flow of traffic on the state route.

He had a marvelous deep bass voice that ought to hide any inflection, but she read voices too. His disbelief came through loud and clear. "No, I said I could read my *stepfather's* mind. I cannot read yours, most of the time, anyway. You advertised your presence pretty clearly when you reached the Villa, thank you. I did sort of read Bo's, but he was projecting wildly, and I'd been keeping my mind open, just in case. It's not as if I had a lot to fill it."

Mad Max rubbed his hand over his crew cut dark hair. She hated short hair. It reminded her too much of the military, which reminded her too much of the general. Of course, her stepbrothers wore their hair long, so she ought to hate long hair too.

"Maybe I am insane," she said with a sigh, littering the countryside by flinging the bloody tissue out the window. "But you must have picked up my code somehow. I haven't been able to send it to my message center, so I've just been repeating it in my head, hoping someone would hear."

"If you were hoping someone would hear your head, you could have been a little more clear and just used the address," he said dryly.

"I tried that. It didn't work. I think we have too many words in our brains which get mixed up with mental messages. Images and numbers are different, but not as easy to translate." Surreptitiously, she studied his profile. Like all the Oswins she'd seen in photos, he had strong, square features and a cleft chin, not precisely handsome but rugged. His nose had a bump in it, as if it had been broken at some time. His eyebrows were thick and sat on a masculine ridge that kept his long lashes from being indecently feminine.

"You knew how to reach us," he argued without giving her a second look. "Why didn't you just text?"

"Since they caught me sending those texts to Oz, everything I type into the computer gets recorded. I had to use code to *physically* send anything. I cut and pasted the 'help me' message from another document and sent it from a cloud cache that the doofuses are too ignorant to know about, but I don't luck out and come across useful phrases very often. My days of easy access to computers ended when your brother found his kid. The general really went off the radar then."

Maximus didn't look happy. He radiated disbelief. Nadine didn't care. She had one purpose and one purpose only at this moment—save Vera.

Conan rang back. At the punch of a button, his voice emerged from the car's speakers. "I've got a man who lives near Morongo. He can meet you at the schoolyard when you get there and provide you with a new vehicle." He gave driving instructions to a street that should be easily visible. "Do we need to send a protection squad?" he asked.

The Maximator glanced in her direction. Nadine shook her head negatively. "I don't want to meet *anyone*," she said as insistently as she knew how.

"I can respect that," he said gravely. "Negative, good buddy," he told his brother. "We're staying off the radar."

"Conan is the one who's trying to find my computer, isn't he?" Nadine asked when Magnus turned off the phone. She hoped to prevent him asking the questions she could hear bouncing inside his skull. This Oswin had very noisy thought processes.

"That's what Conan does. If you could give him clues that might lead to your stepfather, we'd be appreciative."

"Negative, good buddy," she parroted. "It will only get someone killed. Once I find my sister, I'll find a computer and take down his network. We'll be good then." Sort of. Maybe. With a lot of luck—which she seldom had. She was speaking through her non-existent hat, but bravado was all she had.

He sent her a dubious look as if he could read *her* brain waves.

"Taking down the general's network won't stop a maniac," he warned. "You planning on finding new identities for yourself and your sister?"

She shrugged. "Already have." She tried not to admire the two-day-old scruff on his very large, very square jaw. She might be a geeky, inexperienced nerd, but she was still female and not immune to masculine pheromones. She needed to get away before she fell under his spell. She was apparently too receptive to suggestion.

He pulled off at a gas station with a mini-mart. "You need first aid, and the car needs gas. Do I need to tie you up to keep you from running?"

She stared at him. "Tie me up? Are you serious?"

"You're a danger to yourself and your sister and probably a lot of other people. As far as the cops know, you're an escaped lunatic. I don't think anyone would stop me," he said with a shrug.

"Where do you get off calling *me* a danger to anyone?" she cried in protest as he pulled up to the pump. "I'd need a semi-automatic and a machete before I could even *look* threatening."

She thought the corner of his mouth quirked upward until he straightened it and glared down at her. If she'd known he was coming today, she'd have worn the Hulk shirt that said *Don't Make Me Angry* instead of a stupid Tweety Bird.

"I don't understand what you can do or how," he told her as if she really were stupid, "but I'm well aware that you're not harmless. I want the general. You're my key to getting him. You want your sister. I'm your key to finding her. Truce?"

She kept her arms crossed and glared at him from beneath an orange curl she didn't bother brushing out of her eyes. "Fine then. Have it your way."

He climbed out to fill the tank. He took his electronic key with him. She hated electronic ignitions. Why on earth would a car this old have a fancy new... Duh. Maximus Magnifico was some kind of mechanical genius, which was why the general had wanted him.

She didn't have time for playing games. She wanted to find Vera, and it would be far faster from here than heading into the desert. Besides, she didn't need any more intimidating alpha males telling her what to do. She surveyed the lot, looking for a friendly trucker. They all looked surly. The price of gas must have gone up again.

She spotted a preppy-looking teen climbing out of a Kia with Orange County plates. It was Sunday. What were the chances that he was returning to school after a weekend at home?

She wished she really could read minds, but unless someone was screaming inside their head, the best she could do was read body language and physical clues. Even if someone sent thoughts in her direction, she generally picked up *vibrations* more than words—unless they were psychic. That seldom happened.

She'd actually *felt* Mad Max at the gate, probably because he'd been thinking about her messages and steaming with suppressed frustration. A mind as powerful as his could explode under pressure. Probably best to get out of his way.

"I'm getting ice cream," she said, climbing out of the front seat.

"You don't have money," Maxico reminded her. "I'll be there in a minute. Find some Band-aides and Neosporin."

"I'll use the restroom while I'm waiting." She strode off before he could argue with that, too. She'd rather admired the determined way the Oswin brothers had tried to track her down and had followed the few clues she'd sent them. Now that she was out, she really didn't need to risk all that potent focus on her. Vera came first, over anything and everyone, including herself.

When they were safely in Guatemala or somewhere, then she'd have time to regret not having a chance to know the family she'd never see again.

Magnus didn't possess Conan's nose for trouble, but gut instinct told him Nadine couldn't be trusted. Once she disappeared inside the mini-mart, he kept a close eye on the vehicles in the lot, particularly the truckers. But he had to feed a card into the meter and remove the pump and screw up the gas tank, and he didn't have eyes in the back of his head.

By the time he walked inside the shop, she was gone.

Knowing his size intimidated, he tried not to scowl and curse aloud as he approached the young Latino boy at the register. Nadine was hard to miss, and the boy offered a brief description of the college kid she'd conned into giving her a ride. Magnus passed on a twenty and stalked outside, mentally castigating himself.

That's what he got for dealing with lunatics. The damned woman's head would probably rot off from that screwdriver trick.

He'd lost the damned Librarian, the key to everything. He kicked the concrete gas tank pad with his boot.

He couldn't take the chance of having the Camaro traced. He still had to go on to Morongo Valley to trade it off. And he damned well knew he was going the opposite direction from Nadine. He called Conan as he raced down the highway and passed on a description of the kid and his car.

"Almost no chance in hell in finding a Kia in freeway traffic," Conan informed him. "And the mountains prevent a good look from a helicopter. I'll see what I can do, but our best bet is to figure out where Vera...Malcolm?...was staying. I don't think either of them are on my genealogy charts. Where in hell did the general find them?"

Magnus didn't possess Conan's fascination with the family tree that connected the Oswins with the Malcolm family and their weird abilities. He just wanted to stop the general, and he'd let his one and only clue escape. "Apparently, General Adams married their mother. I assume their father was the Malcolm, and one assumes he's dead or otherwise not in the picture. She said she'd already established fake ID, so I'm betting Vera didn't use her name at school. Needle in a haystack time."

"I'll get the student lists, check for missing person reports, see what I can find and send a 'copter up for the Kia, just in case. Pity we can't send out an APB for Tweety Bird. How long do you think she'll last with the kid driver before he flings her out of the vehicle?"

Magnus thought about the way the aluminum-foiled lunatic grabbed opportunity and played it as hard as she could. He shook his head. "She may be crazy, but she's smart crazy. As long as the kid does what she wants, she'll lay low. I think."

She'd been a pale ball of nervous energy. Magnus fretted all the way into town. He made the trade-off, sacrificing his intelligent power car for a beat-up Taurus, then fretted all the way back up the mountain again.

He'd had the key to the general in his hand. Why the devil had he let her escape?

The pain in the big green eyes behind those hideous glasses haunted him all the way into Irvine. The way she'd driven a screwdriver into her head twisted his gut.

He was a damned sucker for victims. After they found this one, he'd better write off women forever.

Nadine knew she wasn't exactly invisible. She had clown-orange hair, wore a bright yellow sweatshirt, and sported a shoplifted bandage on her temple. She couldn't go directly to the campus.

She told her driver to let her out at the Metro stop in Anaheim. She'd only had a few years of relative freedom when she'd gone to UCLA as a kid—back when she'd been drinking the Kool-Aid and thought she was helping her country. But she'd learned the route to Disney even if she'd never had time or money to go.

Since those days, she'd siphoned the price of a decent house into a bank account that the general didn't know about, but she had no good way to access it without a computer. She was still stone cold broke.

Nadine filed onto the next westbound train with the rest of the passengers and stayed one step ahead of the conductor until the next stop. The OC stations were still operating mostly on the honor system. Maybe she could send them a check from Guatemala to cover all her stolen fares.

She'd never had anyone to rely on but herself, so she didn't exactly *miss* having Maximus at her side. But she assumed he would have had better means of transportation than waiting for trains. She itched to fly to the campus.

And Maximus had been a lovely distraction when she'd needed one. She might be the only twenty-three-year-old virgin on the planet, but it wasn't from lack of interest on her part, just lack of opportunity. Magnus Oswin had walked straight out of every woman's romantic fantasy. Except for the short hair, of course.

Just thinking about what he might be hiding under that rumpled flannel shirt provided a level of distraction as she appropriated a ratty army jacket left behind on a seat. She wished she'd had more opportunity to see Magnus in motion so she could fantasize better while train jumping.

In Irvine, she stole an ancient bicycle that was more wreck than transportation and pedaled onward. It had to be mid-afternoon by now.

By the time she reached the campus, she was gasping for breath and glad she didn't need her glasses for biking or they'd slide off her sweaty nose. Mental institutions didn't offer good exercise facilities, and she'd gained weight doing nothing.

She'd get angry and lose her focus if she thought about those months of enforced incarceration, so she let Fantasy Magnus play in her head as she biked to the center of campus. She didn't think a bike was traceable, but she would take no chances. She wiped off her prints and left it for the next desperate person to steal. Slipping into crowds, she jogged off down a side street. The day was growing warmer and the jacket was out of place, but it hid Tweety Bird.

She hid in an alley, nervously fingered the glasses in her pocket, and surveyed the boarding house where Vera had been living. She saw nothing suspicious. Curtains blew in the windows. A tabby cat slept on the porch. One of the students climbed into a car and drove off.

The general's demented sons and grandsons didn't appear to be sitting on any roofs with telescopic rifles. She'd taken psychology along with her computer classes. She thought the general's sons must have inherited some combination of sociopathic genes from both parents. She'd like to crack open their heads and lay their brains out on a microscope slide to see.

She had to take the risk. As if she belonged here, she trotted up the back steps, opened the door that Vera had said never stayed locked, and took a dark interior stairway up to the room where she'd seen her sister last.

The door was unlocked. Vera would never have left it that way. Entering the sunny spacious room, Nadine felt all her senses close up and shudder.

The room still contained material traces of her sister, but not her essence—except the waves of fear.

Tears running down her cheeks, Nadine clutched a pink stuffed bunny Vera had kept since childhood, emptied her head, and called on the universe.

The universe, as usual, didn't answer.

Four

"I surrender," a weary voice whispered from the cell phone.

Magnus slumped in the front seat of the rusted Taurus and tried to force his gut to unclench. "I'm near the campus park. How do you want me to find you?"

"Are you planning on throttling me? If so, I want to be fed first, in a public place. Bring a hoodie to Gina's on Campus Drive."

"Damn, you're a bossy tyrant. You want me to steal a hoodie or find it under a bush behind a bench next to the bus stop?" he growled. He was starving. He could *eat* a hoodie.

She hung up on him. Not a people person was the Librarian.

That gave him food for ugly thought while he looked around for clothing stores or people wearing hoodies. It was seventy degrees and sunny. Hoodies did not proliferate around here until evening.

He saw a couple of female students walking past in sunhats and had a *duh* moment. She wanted to hide her hair and bandage! He yanked a fifty out of his wallet and tried not to look like a pervert when he walked up to the women holding the bill stretched in both hands. "Look, I'm desperate. I promised my girlfriend a sunhat. I forgot to get it. Can one of you sell me yours?"

They held a whispered consultation, snatched his bill, and handed him both hats, then ran off giggling. Obviously, sunhats weren't worth fifty bucks.

Fifty was cheap if it led him to the Librarian and her stepfather. Using his phone as GPS, he located the pizza place, studying it from the outside before walking in.

No frizzy orange hair or bright yellow Tweety-bird greeted him. Hoping he hadn't been set up, Magnus found a table in back. Not knowing if Nadine was a health nut or just a plain nut, he ordered the house special and a vegetarian whole wheat pizza, plus beer. She could drink water if she didn't like beer.

His gut didn't unclench until he saw her enter wearing a bulky green army jacket. Damn, she'd wanted the hoodie not just to hide her bandage but the bright yellow shirt.

She scowled at the flirty sunhats he'd placed on the table. Magnus held up a finger indicating that she wait, walked up to the cashier where they kept a stack of school t-shirts, and bought a black one. He returned and wordlessly handed it to her.

Apparently she understood gestures better than words. Her unexpected grin drew his gaze to her lush lips. Before he could admire more, she grabbed the shirt and darted back to the restroom. When she returned, she had her springy hair and bandage hidden under the smaller sunhat, her glasses tucked into her collar, and she sported the too-large black shirt over the Tweety-bird sweatshirt. She carried the army jacket under her arm. Her clothing still looked insane, but her smile had Magnus shifting in his seat.

At least she'd managed to disguise her breasts so he wasn't too distracted. He'd been without sex for a little too long if he was noticing lunatics in Tweety-bird shirts.

"Prepared for anything," she announced.

"Creative," he acknowledged dryly, waiting as the server dropped the pizzas on the table.

Nadine helped herself to both pizzas and the beer. "Thank you. It's been a long time since breakfast."

"What happened?" Magnus asked the minute the waiter left. "Did you find your sister?"

Her eyes closed in what looked like bliss as she finished chewing, but he was already realizing that nothing she did reflected the chaos boiling inside of her. So he waited expectantly.

When she opened her eyes, she'd switched gears again and glared at him. "Do you really think I'd be here if I'd found her?"

"No, but I'd hoped you'd be so appreciative of my breaking you out of hell that you'd actually offer to help me." He tore off a hunk of pizza and chewed with anger as much as hunger.

"I *am* appreciative. That's why I won't help you find the general. No good can come of trying to physically capture a man with his connections. Once I disable his network and shut down all his systems, he'll be harmless."

"If your sister really has gone missing, we can't disable anything if his network will lead us to her," Max pointed out. "I'm assuming that's what you want. How do you expect us to find Vera if you won't give us access to the general?"

She seemed to grow pale before his eyes—paler, since she had a redhead's porcelain skin. She clutched something wrapped in the army jacket that he hoped wasn't a gun while she gathered herself together.

"We don't know that the general found her," she replied stubbornly. "I could feel her fear, but it wasn't specific. Vera left a lot of her stuff in the room, as if she planned on returning. She could have been spooked and ran for other reasons."

Magnus let the "feel her fear" line pass. Pippa and Dorrie said weird things like that often enough that he believed they felt things he couldn't. Not surprising given his lack of people skills. He'd been called emotionally dense. "So what do you expect to do now?" he asked with caution, not wanting to set her off again.

"I need access to computer equipment. I could probably get it on my own, but I know my limits. I need food and shelter as well as computers. Give me those, and I'll be out of your hair in twenty-four hours."

"You have as much as admitted that you're a walking target, even without the microchip. The general is bound to know you've escaped by now. If he's hunting for you, I can't take you anywhere near my family without marking them as a target for a madman." Max sipped his beer and pondered the problem.

"Your family is already on his shit list, but you're right. There's no reason to involve anyone else. If you have credit cards, we can buy a new computer and hole up in a motel. Once I have a computer, I'll have money, and I can pay you back."

She looked at him so hopefully that he almost agreed. She actually sounded sane. Except a man who planted microchips in his kids' heads wasn't sane, and anyone thinking she could outrun a wily varmint like the general wasn't working with a full deck.

"I'm doing no such thing unless you agree to tell me everything you know," he insisted. "I have to protect *my* family, too. Knowledge is power."

She ate her pizza and let her gaze wander the room. Magnus got itchy just watching her plot. He waited until they'd nearly consumed the pizzas, then slapped a hand over her wrist.

"Let's pretend I can read minds, too. I'm not letting you out of my sight. You're a danger to yourself, your sister, my family, and anyone else with whom you come in contact— if the general really is what you say he is. I have the experience and the contacts you need. You have to trust someone, sometime. Make it me."

"You're an obsessive, just like he is," she said. "You're intense, you're military, you're focused on the goal without any knowledge or concern for the means to that goal. Give me one good reason why I should trust you?" she asked defiantly.

Wearing that hat and shirt, she should have looked like a pouting teenager. But without the geeky glasses, her eyes held wells of painful wisdom, and her mouth—was full, curved, and all stubborn woman. Magnus had to respect the mind and courage that had helped Oz find his kid.

"You don't trust the entire armed forces of this country because of one crazed man? Is the general still in the military or retired?" Magnus had never asked anyone to trust him before. He was a loner, probably one of the reasons he was ex-military. And probably another reason she shouldn't trust him.

"Retired." She sank back against the seat, looking exhausted. "I haven't slept in twenty-four hours. I can't think straight. I just want a computer so I can find my sister. Do we have to make this difficult?"

"You think I've slept since you started sending those damned 'Help Me' messages? I'll find a motel, but I'm warning you now, I'm not letting you out of my sight, for your own good as well as my mental health." He stood up, grabbed her arm, and hauled her to her feet.

She stumbled, and he adjusted his frustrated grip as he escorted her out the door. She didn't object to his manhandling. Magnus figured that meant she was completely wiped.

Once he'd installed her in the rattletrap Taurus, he rang Conan. "I need fake ID. I've got the cash for one night in a cheap motel, but I don't want anyone tracing my name on credit cards. The general has that ability, doesn't he?" Magnus addressed that last at his weary passenger.

"That and more if he puts his mind to it," Nadine agreed. "Without me, he's handicapped. His understanding of computers relies on hired help. His sons only pay attention when it benefits them."

"Not taking any chances," Magnus said into the phone. "What have you got?"

"I'll drop off a card and ID in the morning at the surf shop up the street from my place" Conan said. "Ted knows you and will hand them over, unopened. Will that work?"

"That works. We'll find a motel between Irvine and your place. We need a computer, too. I can't pay cash for that, and I think it needs to be completely wiped."

"That's easy. I'll clean a drive on one of my spares and give it to Ted with the cards. I take it you've found your runaway?"

"Yeah, and we're both beat. This line may not be safe much longer. May need to throw in a new phone while you're at it." Magnus didn't worry about overburdening Conan's bank account. His brother had just landed a lucrative contract, and Magnus could pay him back. Money wasn't their problem. Security was.

Conan agreed. When he signed off, Magnus started the engine, giving his passenger a surreptitious look. The Librarian had her head back and her eyes closed, but he didn't fool himself into thinking she was asleep.

"Aren't fake IDs illegal?" she asked with her eyes still closed.

"Conan has top dog security clearance and permission from authorities in cases like this. I don't do illegal," Magnus assured her, uncertain of her conversational direction.

"I ought to give you credit at being good at what you do," she said reluctantly. "I'm just not used to trusting anyone. I don't want to be manipulated again."

"Given what little I know of your background so far, that's understandable. We'll simply have to work around our mutual distrust. It's not as if I'm likely to trust someone who could be certifiably insane." He was afraid to look up a cheap motel chain if the general had a chance of tracing his phone calls, even though he'd disconnected the GPS hours ago. Magnus simply steered toward the airport and hoped for the best.

"By now, I probably am insane, or extremely neurotic." Nadine produced a ragged pink stuffed toy from the jacket's capacious pocket and rubbed it on her cheek. "Let's just concentrate on Vera."

"Is that hers?" Magnus asked, trying not to imagine all the weird reasons she was stroking a toy.

"Our mother gave it to her for her birthday when she was five. I don't think she would have left it behind if she wasn't planning on going back. Or unless she didn't have time to go back for it. I was hoping it would help me reach her," she said sadly.

All right, another lunacy he'd let pass. "She may have outgrown it. She may have just gone to the beach with her boyfriend. We need to watch the apartment."

She shrugged and tucked the toy back in her pocket. "She was afraid. That's all I know. She has no Malcolm abilities and can't send me mental messages. She's just a smart kid who wants to be a teacher. She's a good actress but life in the public eye is hazardous for her health. The general won't believe us. He swears she's hiding her talents from him."

"Let's start there. Why would the general care what *talents* she has?" Spotting a sign for a low-end hotel chain, Magnus took the next exit. He hadn't lived in California for years, but the John Wayne airport area was navigable.

"Don't you get it yet? We're all human guinea pigs in his effort to memorialize the work of Feng Po-po, his first wife. He swears a Malcolm killed her with *dim mak*, and he's determined to use us all as weapons in her name."

Magnus would have said *certifiable,* except he'd heard Conan's fiancée swear she could kill with her mind. And according to Nadine, the general believed Dorrie could do it.

Five

Nadine wanted to empty her head and simply luxuriate in the motel's tiled shower with all the pretty smelling products, but she nearly fell asleep on her feet. She'd been living on the edge for so long, she didn't know how to relax.

She didn't even know who she was anymore.

Drying her hair, wishing for a good pair of scissors or at least a round brush to straighten some of the kinks, she stared at her face in the foggy mirror. She hadn't seen herself in months. The picture wasn't pretty, even with her glasses off. She was fat and slovenly and looked like a Disney cartoon—not the kind of woman a hunk like Magnus would notice.

She was smart. She didn't need to be pretty. She didn't need a man—much. Just because she was sharing a cheap motel room with a glorious specimen of masculinity didn't mean she needed to have dirty thoughts. She was pretty damned certain Maximus Magnus would run in the opposite direction so fast his head would spin if he thought a butterball like her was interested.

With her spongy mass of frizz almost dry, she donned the overlarge t-shirt he'd bought for her. Had he actually chosen the largest size he could find for a reason or because he'd just grabbed the first shirt he found? Mysterious Max intrigued her far more than she should allow—probably because she needed something else to think about besides all the things that could have happened to Vera.

Warily, she entered the darkened bedroom. The big bully had moved one of the beds in front of both door and window to prevent her escape. Freaking control freak, just as she'd figured. He was sprawled on top of the covers, fully dressed, and snoring.

With a sigh, she crawled between the sheets of the second bed. So much for any romantic thoughts. But one of these days... even a neurotic nutcase could dream.

Having spent the night tossing and turning in the unfamiliar environment, Nadine didn't feel particularly refreshed as they ate at the free breakfast bar the next morning. Magnus studied the muted news screen in the lobby while she scanned the day-old newspaper she'd found on one of the tables.

Computers were her connection to reality. She was suffering from major electronic withdrawal. Impatiently, she scarfed up a bowl of nasty cereal, ate through an apple, and waited for Maximus to finish consuming half the buffet.

"Are you planning on leaving food for the next person?" she inquired politely.

"Three cars in the parking lot," he responded, finishing off his apple.

She refrained from rolling her eyes at his means of communication. Sadly, she actually understood him. "They all got up earlier than we did and left all this lovely food? Yeah, it would be a shame to waste it." She stuffed two apples into her jacket pocket.

He took two of the plastic-wrapped pastries.

Since they had no luggage, it was just a matter of tucking Vera's bunny into the army jacket, climbing into the Taurus, and heading out into rush hour traffic. Praying that all she needed was a computer, Nadine clenched her hands in her lap and watched the tsunami of automobiles rushing toward L.A.

She'd never owned a car. She'd hardly ever been out of her college dorm or home office enough to travel. The speeding flow of traffic terrified her. Magnus drove with one hand, as if they were on an empty highway and not traveling eighty miles an hour on a collision course with ten thousand other cars.

She closed her eyes so she didn't have to see the wall of semis they were about to hit. It didn't help.

She'd learned to keep her mouth shut at an early age, but gradually, it dawned on her that she might be free to speak her mind. She didn't know how long this freedom would last, so she might as well experience it while she could.

"Is there any way we could take a slower route?" she asked, trying not to sound frightened. He glanced at her in surprise, and she nearly expired of fear. "Watch the road!"

"You don't get out much, got it." With nail-biting rapidity, he zigzagged across the lanes to the next ramp and pulled off the freeway. "Better?" he asked as he merged into bumper-to-bumper traffic on a six-lane.

"Probably not, but I can breathe again," she admitted, releasing the pink bunny in her pocket. "I was not designed for the fast lane."

"Could you have even driven the Camaro you intended to steal from me?" he asked in amusement.

"I'd have figured it out. I'm very good with machines." She tried to sound casual but feared it came out stiff and just a little defensive. The freedom to speak came with a lot of pitfalls.

Now that the adrenalin rush of escape was over, she felt lost and incapable of planning beyond the next step. She hated that.

"You might be good with machines," he agreed, "but driving is about second-guessing the other drivers and knowing when to get out of their way. I don't think you're that good a mind-reader." He turned down a side road and began navigating increasingly narrower streets, crossing major ones and leaving the traffic behind.

"I'd need a lot more experience," she said, studying the quieter streets they passed. "I'd like to learn to drive, should I get out of this alive."

"You think the general will kill you?" he asked in amazement, darting her another of those nerve-racking looks. His light gray eyes against his dark, weathered face seemed to cut through her like laser beams.

"If he can't capture me again, yes, of course. I know too much." She'd accepted her fate the moment she'd decided to run. "He tolerated me as long as I believed in his purpose and followed his orders. I became a traitor to his cause the instant I rebelled."

"And you thought your purpose was...?"

"Protecting the country from terrorists, of course. I saw it as a non-violent shield of psychics who could penetrate the enemies' thoughts, see potential targets without drones, and develop machinery that the enemy couldn't possibly duplicate. The general already has an entire industry of technicians at work. He's not a poor man, just obsessive."

"He's searching for psychics even though he believes Malcolms killed his wife? I thought he *married* a Malcolm?"

"He married Mom because of me and Vera." Nadine compressed her childhood hurt deep inside and wrapped it up tightly before speaking. "Once I figured out where to look, I learned that he and Feng Po-po tracked our weird family tree for years. They hired a few Malcolms to work in their labs. I think they blackmailed a few more. They weren't above kidnapping when necessary. He helped your brother's nanny steal his kid, planning on keeping an eye on him to see if he developed any particular genius he could use. That's when I broke."

Magnus cursed, stopped for a red light, and turned to study her. "How could he possibly know who has any kind of *genius*?"

She shrugged. "With kids, it's a simple matter of sending in a psychologist with a series of tests that Feng Po-po designed. School administrators love tests. She'd feed them some relevant information about student behavior from the tests—and come away with charts on the kids she was really interested in. That's how the general found me and Vera—at school—after tracing our dad's genealogy and reading Po-po's tests."

"And he struck gold in you but not your sister?"

"Yep. Our dad died in the service when we were little, and we were thrilled to have a dad again. Mom had been working her fingers to the bone trying to balance her career and us on a teacher's salary. In that last year, she was doing it on unemployment checks. Then the general came along, and suddenly, we were rich. We had a swimming pool and nice clothes and a kindly old man who spoke fondly of our dad. I bent over backward to please him."

Nadine supposed she owed Mad Max some sort of explanation, but she didn't owe him enough to slice open her soul and bleed over the heartbreak of treachery and deception. By now, she was pretty sure the general had lied about everything, including knowing her father. She hadn't totally processed the treachery yet. One crisis at a time was all she could manage.

"When did you learn that he actually hated Malcolms?"

Of all the obvious questions he could have asked, he had to go for the difficult. "You're creepy, you know that?" She leaned her head back against the seat, not wanting to deal with the vat of fear seething inside.

"Interrogation was part of my military training," he told her. "Go ahead and hate me, if you like. But I know men like the general. I can help better if I know more about him."

"Get two computers, and I'll give you access to any files I can still find while I hunt Vera. I really don't want to talk about this."

"Your call." He drove down a street that offered a view of the ocean. "Conan's in Santa Monica. We'll stop, pick up the credit cards and a computer. Any preferences to where we go from there?"

"A park bench works for me if your new phone has a hot spot we can use. Otherwise, we need a place with Wi-Fi." Nadine relaxed a little at the thought of having the world under her fingers again—and this time, with more freedom than she'd known in her life. Kind of scary, actually, but she would only take that thought one step at a time. "I'd love to be able to watch the ocean a bit. I've never more than glimpsed it."

"If you're accessing the general's files, we'll probably need to stay on the move. Conan will make certain we have what we need." He shot her another unfathomable look. "You've lived in California all your life and have never walked in the surf?"

"We lived inland. I was only fourteen when I graduated high school. I wasn't exactly old enough to go carousing with the seniors on weekends. And I got my masters in a little over three years. No time for partying then, either. I was too young and too nerdy for frat boy parties anyway."

He whistled and eyed her with new respect and just a hint of interest—for her mind if not her body. "How old are you anyway?"

"Twenty-three. Want to make something of it?" She really wasn't interested in fighting with him, but she wanted to test her new-found freedom to say what she liked.

"It explains a *lot*. A masters? In what, am I allowed to ask?" He took the coast highway north.

The traffic was abominable but the glimpses of surf and sand kept her entertained better than the conversation. She'd never even seen the Santa Monica pier. "I want to ride the Ferris wheel," she said as they drove past. She'd *heard* of all the fun possibilities in the world outside her sheltered one. She'd studied those that interested her. But it was hard to know where to start without any experience to guide her.

"When this is all over, I'll take you on every ride your heart desires. Are you avoiding my question?"

She didn't believe his promise. But she could do it on her own—if she survived.

"No, I'm not avoiding anything. My degree just isn't very relevant. I'm a computer engineer with enough courses for a masters in psychology. I'd have gone for a doctorate except the general insisted I had enough education, and he needed me at home. He was paying my tuition, so I couldn't argue."

"Way out of my league," he said in admiration, turning up a hilly side street that led to jaw-droppingly gorgeous mansions. "I earned a BS in mechanical engineering by the skin of my teeth."

"Because you're better at doing than at taking tests," she suggested. "School isn't for everyone."

"Books are a dead bore," he agreed. He pointed at a two-story contemporary beach home. "That's Conan's place where I'm currently staying. If you ever need us, go there."

Nadine already knew the address, but she memorized the looks of the location, and the streets he drove down as he steered toward the surf store. "You're lucky to live in such a lovely place. Did Bo get back together with his wife and kids?"

He was busy looking for parking and didn't glance her way. "They're working at it. He still has some time left in the service before he can get out and help his dad. How much do you know about all of us?"

She shrugged. "Only bits and pieces after they started monitoring my computer time. I know the general heavily investigated Dorothea's family since they knew Feng Po-po, so I know more about them from before my incarceration."

"Dorrie's marrying Conan next week. We've been ordered to solve your problem so we can attend the wedding. Dorrie's family is dying to meet the Librarian who helped them. Her grandmother knew Po-po, and Dorrie knows a little about the general's sons since two of them and his grandson tried to murder her."

He shot her a quizzical look, evidently unwilling to pry but wanting to know. Nadine shifted uncomfortably in her seat.

"Let's not put a polite face on it. My step-family *killed* Dorrie's mother. I doubt she'll want me present, but thanks for the offer. Am I coming in with you?" she asked as he found a space near the surf shop and shut off the engine.

"Best if you do. I'm thinking of leaving the Taurus here and finding a rental with our new IDs." He climbed out and opened the door for her. "And if you're a Malcolm, you'll be welcome with the women. It's the Oswins you'll have to persuade. We don't want a walking target anywhere near family."

That would be her. Nadine followed him to the shop, feeling more lonely than she'd ever felt in an already solitary life.

Six

Magnus shoved his new ID and credit cards into his pocket, picked up the computer Conan had left for him, and watched the four-eyed female wander the surf shop, fingering fabrics.

She needed clothes. So did he. Bright pink tank tops with Hoby written on them were not his favorite fashion, but they'd blend in here on the coast. Echoing his distaste, she rejected all the spandex but accepted the sunglasses he bought for her without even checking how they looked in a mirror.

He took her elbow and steered her down the street in search of a thrift store. This was Santa Monica. There might be thrift stores somewhere, but not near the beach. He located a boutique and led her in.

"Find a dress. We'll shop later." He pointed at a rack of colorful sundresses.

She eyed the flirty-hemmed florals, glanced at him in disbelief, and made her way to the back of the store. There she rummaged through shelves with her nose turned up in distaste. Eventually, she produced a skinny blue sleeveless shirt with a collar and a pair of cut-offs with rhinestone-encrusted pockets. And a pair of flip-flops with big flowers on them.

"I need underwear," she told him, dropping her stack on the counter. "But let's hit the computer first."

She ignored the pretty shiny things adorning the counter and shook her head at the offer of a scarf to match the shirt. Magnus didn't have a lot of experience with buying clothes for women, but her complete disinterest in the pricey boutique surprised him. He'd thought women lived to shop.

He'd been expecting enthusiasm and praise for his generous offer, he realized. Stupid of him. Nadine obviously had different priorities.

Intrigued despite himself, he led the way to a quiet bench overlooking the ocean. Nadine seemed much more interested in the view than she had been in the boutique. Letting her pace back and forth, Magnus set up his phone and hot spot, and booked a rental car at the nearest outlet. Then he held out the laptop to his companion. "I'm calling a taxi. You have until it arrives."

Still wearing the army jacket against the early morning breeze, she flashed him the delighted smile he'd expected earlier, settled onto the bench, donned her black-framed glasses, and went to work with the proficiency of a well-programmed robot.

The faster she worked, the more she frowned.

Busy with his phone, Magnus didn't disturb her. When the taxi arrived, he grabbed her elbow and towed her away while she continued to type with one hand.

"You have officially lost your right to call me obsessive," he declared after giving the driver the rental office address. "ADD much?"

She offered an inelegant snort, checked the bars on his Wi-Fi, and shut the laptop. "They need a diagnosis of TMA, Too Much Attention. Vera hasn't touched her social media in a week. She's not responding to my IMs. Mail to her box is bouncing. She's gone off the radar."

She spoke in a neutral voice that Magnus interpreted as trained to hide her fear. The damned general had turned her into the perfect military machine.

"I don't suppose it's too much to hope that she's another computer genius and that you can reach her by some mysterious internet connection?"

Nadine shrugged. Despite the army jacket, he caught the movement. The army green made her long orange hair stand out even more. He wanted to stroke a curl to see if it was as soft and springy as it looked.

"Vera knows what I've taught her," Nadine replied, not noticing his fascination, "but no, she's no expert. She hates technology. She's a people person—and that's what scares me."

"You think she made friends with the wrong person—one of the general's minions maybe?" Magnus hated the twisting pain in his gut at the realization that he might not only have to bring down an old man, but find a young girl.

"It's a rough world out here. The wrong person doesn't have to be a minion," Nadine said sadly. "Don't get me wrong. Vera isn't stupid. Once she realized the level of our stepfather's paranoia, she agreed to run when I told her. That was back when I could sneak in and use the office computers. She chose a college. We bought her a new identity and got her signed up."

"So much for avoiding illegality," he pointed out.

"Everything I do is illegal as far as I'm aware. I thought I had government clearance, but I didn't, so why bother now?" She glared out the taxi window.

"Back to Vera..."

Nadine took a deep breath and continued. "She stole away without the general even realizing she was unhappy. She's a great actress. She's totally squeamish, but she even removed the microchip and hid her trail after she left. The general screamed bloody murder and sent his sons all over creation hunting for her, but until now, she's successfully eluded them. I should have made her go back East, but I didn't want her that far away," she said with a hint of gloom.

"Besides, for an actress, the best film and theater experience is in L.A." Magnus rubbed the bridge of his nose and tried to imagine two young girls outsmarting a military-trained general with an army of minions at his command. It didn't compute well, but he'd seen Nadine in action. The general might have a point—her brain was a formidable weapon even if the rest of her was dandelion fluff.

He rented a white sedan indistinguishable from any others on the road. Not knowing how long they'd be living on credit cards, he was hesitant to stay in pricey ocean inns, but Nadine's internet voodoo produced a B&B near San Diego that wasn't too exorbitant. He used the credit card and an ATM at the car rental office to collect cash so their path wouldn't be obvious if the card was discovered.

"Could you teach me to drive?" Nadine asked some hours later, as they traversed the freeway past the marine base.

"I doubt we'll have time, and you need a permit to drive on public roads. Even if you had escaped with ID, you wouldn't want your permit application popping up on the general's radar."

He could almost hear the disappointment in her silence. He felt like he'd kicked a cat. She was only a means to an end, and he shouldn't care, but... She was a naïve twenty-three and she'd helped others instead of herself. He'd have to keep in mind that she wasn't a tool to be used.

While Magnus arranged for a balcony view room at the B&B, Nadine hid under her hat, jacket, and sunglasses.

Ocean Beach wasn't particularly picturesque, but it was cheap.

Taking a chance that she wouldn't run this time, Magnus left Nadine in their room, under the surveillance of the pink toy. She had her ugly glasses on again, and was intently pounding away at the laptop.

He drove into town to buy another computer for his own use and called Conan while he was out. "Her sister's dropped off the map. Found anything?"

"Birth certificates. Their father is a Malcolm but isn't on my genealogy chart. I found his military record. Their *mother* actually traces back to the Oswin/Ives line. She was a bio-scientist who went in for teaching instead of the big bucks. Find the name Vera was registered under, and I'll search school records. No one has reported any missing students. I'll work through her housing unit and classes, look for people who know her."

"Thanks." Magnus gave him the alias he'd pried out of Nadine earlier. "Nadine's good at hiding her feelings, but she's really worried. It's hard to make her focus on the general with her sister missing."

"Do we call in Dorrie's family yet?"

"I'll ask. She doesn't like talking about the general. I'll keep you updated. Cloud account the same?"

"Yeah, I'll move it again tomorrow and let you know where. Note this password and ID."

Magnus memorized the information rather than write it down. Assured now that they could exchange information without being traced, Magnus returned to the B&B. Nadine had propped herself on the balcony and draped a towel over her head and the laptop screen so she could read through the sun's glare. Surf crashed on the rocks below. Her fascination with the ocean was presumably the reason she was out here.

"Any progress?" he asked, setting a fast-food lunch on the table.

"I think I've tracked Vera's computer. Whoever was using it shut down before I could send a message. Not certain if that was accidental or if they're shutting me out." She removed the towel and grabbed the large soft drink, half draining it.

"You said something about access to funds. Where are they and can Vera— or whoever has her computer— empty them?" Magnus opened the paper around his burger and studied her expression, but she revealed nothing.

"Vera wouldn't bother the funds unless she thought the general was about to find them." She returned the towel to her head, apparently disapproving of the direction of his thoughts. She typed rapidly and continued, "The funds are untouched. If you give me an account number, I can have money transferred to cover my expenses."

Nadine wasn't completely a helpless victim then.

"I'll ask Conan to set up something," he replied. "I'm a mechanic, remember? Give me a car or a helicopter, and I'll fix whatever you want. Banks and computers aren't my thing." He ate contentedly, not caring if she thought him a beefwit. In one of her downswings, Diane had dubbed him with that epithet. He'd learned his lesson about dealing with crazy women.

"A do-er, got it," she said with her usual shrug, "but still a thinker or we'd not have made it this far. So don't give me the dumb jock baloney."

While Magnus studied on that interesting remark, Nadine typed some more, then uttered a triumphant cry. "She used the credit card for groceries in Hemet. Why would anyone in their right minds go to Hemet?"

"Maybe she joined a motorcycle gang." Magnus finished his hamburger waiting for her to reach the obvious conclusion.

"Or someone stole her card," she finally said, her mood deflating as she threw off the towel, took off her glasses, and reached for her drink. "Damn."

"Or she gave the card to someone in hopes of leading anyone tracking her in the wrong direction." Magnus doubted that suggestion, but for some idiot reason, he hated seeing that brief flash of triumph disappear. "Conan wants to ask Dorrie's family to help us. They'll ask nosy questions, but they might be helpful. Is that okay?"

"Keep them away from the general," she responded without looking up. "He thinks they're responsible for Po-po's death, and he hates them with a passion. I think if he could find someone strong enough to breach their defenses, he'd kill them all."

After that dire warning, the Librarian ate in grim silence, frying her pale white nose under the bright California sun. Magnus grabbed her sunhat and plopped it on her head. "Redheads crisp out here."

She'd donned her new shirt and shorts so her shrug was more

expressive. “Sunburn is the least of my worries.”

“You said you’d let me into the general’s files,” he reminded her, setting up his new laptop now that he’d finished lunch. “If he’s got Vera, would that information show up anywhere?”

“His files are compiled by minions. Anything recent would be in there only if someone computer-oriented added it. If they know computers and have an ounce of sense, they’ve moved the files to someplace I won’t know. Jo-jo is more into personal intimidation than keyboards.”

“Jo-jo?” Magnus turned his laptop around so she could show him where to search.

“General Joseph Adams. We used to call him Jo-jo when we were kids. My mother could never remember names and was always making up nonsense names that stuck in her head better. She may have grown tired of hearing of the saintly Po-po and called him Jo-jo just to irritate him.”

“Like you call me Magnus Maximus?”

“Yeah, to irritate you.” She shot him a beaming smile then darted back under her towel again.

“Because that’s how you remember names,” he corrected. He poked through her computer while she worked on his, but she’d erased her history already. He should introduce her to Homeland Security. They could use a few geniuses, although they probably already had enough paranoids.

“I’m giving Conan this credit card info,” Magnus warned her. “He has trained detectives who can trace it and question the businesses where it’s used.”

“I won’t close the card account yet,” she agreed. “I can get into the Malcolm genealogy website, but it looks like Jo-jo has found another computer guru this past year. The files haven’t been touched since I left. They’re sending new ones to a different server. I can access the archives if you want to read them, but there’s no hint of what’s happening now. So far, I haven’t been able to locate any of his new network servers.”

She shoved his laptop across the table and retrieved her own. Magnus was aware of her gaze falling on him as he plugged away at the keyboard. He didn’t know what she expected him to do or say.

He managed a “thanks,” before returning to typing.

“You’re sending those links and passwords to Conan and not

reading the material yourself, aren't you?" she asked.

"He has software that processes keywords," Magnus said, unoffended by her inference that he was a stupid slacker. "I'll scan your index for relevance, but you've just said the files won't tell me anything. I respect your intelligence, so why should I duplicate your effort? Conan will send me addresses, habits, any connections he can find in these documents. If we need power and influence to smoke out the general, we call Oz. That's how our family works."

"You'd rather grab an assault rifle and go after him, wouldn't you?" she asked, returning to typing. "Good thing your brothers can keep you out of trouble."

Magnus snorted but didn't bother contradicting her. He'd tried to flatten the general's guard hut with a helicopter, then held one of his grandsons like a punching bag so Bo could beat the crap out of him. Both his brothers and their significant others had stood back and watched.

Not wanting to pull the geeky towel trick, he took his phone inside where he could read the screen. Moments later, a noise from the balcony jerked his head around.

Nadine was squeezing the pink toy and shaking violently, giving every appearance of a woman having an epileptic seizure.

He almost had a heart attack watching her spasm uncontrollably. Magnus dropped the phone, dashed out, and lifted her from the chair before she could topple. Holding her against his chest, he headed for the bed.

She stopped trembling. In seconds, he had a struggling, panicked female in his arms, swatting him as hard as she could.

Even in his struggle to hold her, he noticed she hid real breasts under her loose clothing. And no armored bra.

"Don't *do* that," she said, whacking his biceps with a little more control now that she'd returned to coherency.

Assuming she wasn't reading his mind and telling him to stop noticing her breasts—he lowered her feet to the floor. Apparently he found insanity attractive, because he didn't mind checking her out. She was a nice armful.

He continued to steady her while she found her balance. "You're really white," he informed her with concern.

"As if I'd seen a ghost, right. I get that a lot." She stepped from his hold and placed a hand on the table to steady herself. "Just don't startle me like that again."

"Can't promise that," he told her flatly. "Someone has a seizure, I'm trained to follow procedures."

"Not a seizure, not the kind you're thinking anyway." She sank back in a chair, closed her eyes, and rubbed her temples. "I was seeing a schoolroom. Kids of different ages working in groups. I *felt* Vera. I didn't see her."

Magnus clenched his fingers into fists and tried to keep his voice below a bellow. "You were having a psychic episode?" He tried to disguise his disbelief.

She shot him a scathing look. "I've transferred some of my funds to the identity I created for myself when we set up Vera's alias. A credit card will be overnighted here. I'll be out of your hair then. I appreciate that you came looking for me, even if it was the puzzle that interested you, not me."

She walked out of their shared suite, slamming the door behind her.

Seven

Torn between collapsing on the bed and crying, and slamming out of the room, Nadine chose the latter. One fit a day was sufficient. She would not let the oaf know how his cold disbelief hurt, not when she was in this fragile state. Real visions left her physically weak and emotionally vulnerable, and she just wasn't going there.

She wiped away an angry tear and stomped down the stairs.

She could walk to the beach and dip her toes in the surf. That might be the only thing the general couldn't track her doing. Unless, of course, the beach had security cameras aimed at satellites, and Jo-jo's new guru was as good as she was.

Counting on a lack of surveillance equipment, she donned her new sunglasses and hid her hair under her hat.

Not acknowledging the landlady's greeting, Nadine stomped down a path of feathery greenery and brilliant bougainvillea. She was almost running by the time she reached the street. She turned in the direction of the surf and hunted for a way down to the water. The rocky bluff didn't look promising.

While she walked, she tried to recall every detail of her vision, but it was like recalling a dream. Bits stayed with her—like Vera's fear. But the rest... Cursing, she walked faster.

Magnus caught up with her before she found a way down to the water. He grabbed her arm and steered her toward an alley.

"Beach access," he told her before she could shake him off.

He was bigger than the general and far more muscular to have swept her off her feet so easily. At five-five and with too many extra pounds, she wasn't exactly a lightweight. He ought to be physically intimidating, but in Mad Max's presence, she only felt safe, as if she had a giant jock bodyguard.

She didn't want to feel safe with the big oaf.

She shook off his grip but followed him down the gravel path. Aging timbers led the way down to a rocky shore.

Surf crashed against rocks, boulders, and patches of sand. In near delirium at finally reaching this one dream, Nadine raced toward the rolling waves. Cold water slapped over her new flip-flops, and she squealed, hopping up and down like a kid until she got used to it. A wave hit high, splashing her legs and wetting her jean shorts.

For just this one moment, she was real. She didn't have to think, to plot, to do anything more than absorb the sun on her hair and the surf on her toes. The salt water erased all thought of the general and his minions.

Flinging her arms in the air, she danced in circles, startling a gull. She laughed until she cried, finally finding a release for all the jumbled emotion she usually had to conceal. She didn't stop until she stubbed a toe against a rock and stumbled in pain.

"Impressive," Magnus said from above the tide line. "Do you do encores or do I need to splint your toe?"

"Killjoy." Nadine climbed out of the water to sit on a rock and examine her toe. There was something weirdly satisfying about sitting beside the big lug while sopping wet. "I think I remember playing in the surf when I was really little. All those memories disappeared with our family albums."

He crouched down and moved her toe back and forth. She wanted to snatch her foot back, but at the same time, she wanted more of his hand on her ankle. The man was dangerous to her peace of mind in more ways than one.

She had to remember they had different goals. Hers was to find Vera and run for safety. His was... She wasn't entirely certain but it seemed to involve finding the general and probably throttling him. That was a stupidly dangerous goal when shutting down his networks would safely paralyze everything he owned and destroy his spider web.

"What happened to the family albums?" he asked.

"They burned in a house fire when I was about nine." She froze at an unwelcome thought. "Mom agreed to marry Jo-jo not long after that. *That's* how he did it."

"Hysterical, paranoid, or a useful insight?" Max inquired gravely, helping her to stand.

"All three." Grumpily, she let him hold her arm if it made him feel better to do so. She wasn't used to anyone looking after her. "I was a kid then and just delighted to have a dad. It's all kind of fuzzy, but Mom was out of work, and things were really tight. She cried a lot."

Anger shook her as those feelings of long-ago anxiety came tumbling back and matched the fear she'd learned since. "I recognize his tactics now! He burned us out so we had nowhere else to go—no memories to keep us going. The bastard. He probably got her fired, too, so she was helpless."

She tramped toward the stairs, steaming. "What precisely is it you want to do with the general if you find him?" she demanded.

"He stole military secrets. I'll bring him to justice," he replied without hesitation.

"You can't and you won't and it's dangerous to even try," she warned. "He and his sons are venomous spiders hiding in dark places. Best just to spray their web."

"Sorry, not enough. I want him and his thugs behind bars before they kill anyone else. I understand that if they're your family, you're reluctant to help."

"I thought they were family," she said gloomily. "Jo-jo really was the only dad I knew, and he provided all the material things a kid could ever want. I've tried to find excuses for him." That felt right. Her mother hadn't loved the bastard. Jo-jo had *forced* her to marry him, even if she hadn't realized it at the time. "But I just spent months in a loony bin because of him and his miserable sons. I'm not his tool anymore. If I can access his network, I'll take it down. Once I find Vera and we're somewhere safe, I'll help you find him."

"Thank you," Maximus Grandus said. "Some sanity has returned. I feared you might be suffering from Stockholm syndrome." He caught her waist and carried her the rest of the way up the stairs.

Nadine swatted him again, although she was aware his muscled biceps suffered no more harm than if it had been bit by a fly. "Quit hauling me around. I'm standing on my own two feet for the first time in my life. Let me get used to it."

"Yes, ma'am." He set her down on the street at the top of the stairs. She felt inexplicably cold where he'd been pressed against her side—and slightly off balance. She tilted her head and tried knocking water out of her ears.

"We need more clothes," he told her while striding down the alley. "There's a thrift shop a few blocks inland. Are you planning any more fits or do you want to see what they have?"

"I don't *plan* fits." She hurried to keep up with him. "I've pretty much regimented all the rest of my life, because I can't control the part that I don't understand. Visions are freaky and unsettling. If what I saw was real, Vera might have been highly emotional and trying to reach me mentally. She doesn't usually do that because she's bad at it."

"How do you know that?" he asked.

"Because the general made us practice until our heads hurt and we quit telling him anything. We pretended his experiments didn't work."

"So he gave up on mental telepathy but you kept practicing?"

Nadine sent him a suspicious look at his apparent complacence. "Not that you believe me, but yes. That's how I learned it was easier to receive numbers and images than words. Sometimes touching something personal like a toy bunny forges a connection. Vera was sending me an image. Something is desperately wrong. I just don't know what."

She tucked away his reference to Stockholm syndrome to look up later. She ought to know how it worked, but she seemed to have blocked it—the way she'd blocked a lot of her childhood. The mind could only take so much—particularly one like hers crowded with so many other issues.

"You saw a schoolroom," he prompted her.

"I don't know where. There were tables and desks and whiteboards and kids working. No address. Nothing visible out the high windows. No identifiers. Vera was taking education classes at school. Maybe she was substitute teaching. I don't know her regular routine anymore. I couldn't communicate well from a mental institution."

Nadine stalked into the thrift store. Racks of clothing and shelves of junk emitted a musty odor, but she'd never seen a store like this. Fascinated, she skimmed through the clothing, locating a size larger than she used to wear and hoping for the best. Delighted at discovering a bright orange tank top for a few dollars, she kept hunting until she'd located a large gauzy blue shirt and loose jeans. And a pair of white shorts and a green hoodie! It wouldn't matter if the jeans didn't fit right if the loose tops covered them.

Arms full, she cruised the perimeter. Scissors. Round brush still in the packaging. Purple beads.

"Why did no one tell me places like this exist?" she asked deliriously, piling up treasures on the counter. "I detest malls, but this is perfect! I'll just do without underwear."

She practically felt Magnus Max's gaze dip to her breasts. She definitely felt her nipples tighten.

He dropped jeans and various shirts on the counter. "There are other stores around," he said in that gravelly deep voice that had the ability to pierce her innards. "Socks and shoes might be useful. Toothbrushes and razors because a B&B won't provide them. I'm starting to feel like a porcupine."

She studied his studly villain appearance: stubborn square jaw, strong cheekbones, planed jaw bristling with manly beard, and the damned crew-cut. "You could grow a beard as a disguise and I'd call you Black Bart," she offered. "But if you have to be practical..." She tried to give him a disapproving look, hoping he'd back off.

Sloppy, nerdy her was becoming entirely too aware of jock pilot him.

He slapped cash on the counter and carried her sacks outside, forcing her to follow. "No beard," he said. "No Black Bart. If you won't go all goofy over racks of pink princess outfits, we can Google up a Target and drive inland, pick up the necessities and maybe a pizza for dinner."

"Goofy?" Letting him stride ahead of her, she stopped in front of a salon. She could whack her own hair with her new scissors as she'd been doing since college, but just once... wouldn't it be nice to have it professionally done?

She hated asking Mad Max for anything more. Maybe tomorrow, when she had her own card. Wickedly, she stepped inside, just to see how long it would take him to discover she wasn't trailing behind him.

She made an appointment for the next morning. Max was waiting for her outside when she emerged.

"You could have signaled," he said, waiting patiently for her to precede him down the street this time.

"You wouldn't have noticed if I'd smacked you on the back of the head with a palm tree." She wanted to investigate all the fascinating little boutiques they passed. She apparently hesitated too long admiring the work of a tattoo artist—Max caught her arm and moved her onward.

Maybe she should keep dallying so he'd keep holding on to her. Except she needed to focus on Vera, not the improbable.

"The more time we spend in public, the more likely we are to be noticed. I don't think the general will take your escape lightly. All it takes is one Facebook photo..." He let the sentence dangle ominously.

She hurried onward but the reminder only made her angrier. "I've *never* had a life," she protested bitterly. "Once I find Vera and get out of here, I'm going to be a shopkeeper. I'll make my own hours and go shopping anytime I like. Or go bowling. Or to a fair."

"You've never done any of that?" he asked with frank curiosity, studying her through those clear gray eyes that gave her shivers.

"Jo-jo's idea of fun was target practice and karate. Want me to chop a board in two?"

"No, thank you. You're better off knowing how to kick an assailant in the nuts. Muggers normally don't carry boards."

"Yeah, my thought exactly. And mostly, the real thieves are hidden behind computers anyway. Or carry guns. I wouldn't stand a chance against a gun, even if I owned one. So I'm thinking it's best not to go places where people carry guns." Nadine wondered if they'd be safe in Costa Rica. She would look up crime statistics.

"Better yet, don't flash gold in places where people carry guns. And don't do drugs or rob banks."

She jabbed a bony elbow into his side. "You're not amusing." She'd never talked to a man the way she did with this one, but Magnus Maximus begged for retaliation.

"I'm just trying to figure out if you have any idea that gun control is a serious political issue or if you're simply making up maxims out of the clear blue sky of your head." He opened the passenger door of their rental car to help her in.

"Politics are irrelevant since I've never been allowed to vote. I caught the occasional on-line news snippet, but finding Malcolms was Jo-jo's obsession. Keeping up with his business files was pretty much a 24/7 job. And see, I even know slang."

"From college, six years ago." He started the engine and pulled out of the B&B's driveway. "You're like someone who's spent her whole life in a museum or a time warp. You're not quite real."

She sank into her seat rather than acknowledge the truth of that.

"What was the last film you saw?" he asked.

"Other than the film the newscast promises at eleven?" she asked with just a touch of sarcasm. "What part of 24/7 don't you understand?"

"Pretty much all of it. No one can work in front of a computer all day and all night, all of their life. You had to get out sometime, at least before they locked you up."

Nadine crunched her frizzy hair between her fingers but didn't bother ripping it out as she had for a time as a teenager. "Don't try to analyze what you don't understand. I'm a geek. I like computers. I thought I was saving the world while not making a fool of myself having fits in public. End of story."

"Loco," he said succinctly.

"You don't think I haven't considered that?" she asked angrily. "Why do you think I minored in psychology?"

Eight

While La Loca shopped for underwear in Target, Magnus picked up his own necessities. While he walked the aisles, he called Conan to try to persuade him that Dorrie or her family would do a far better job of housing Nadine.

Conan laughed. "We're planning a *wedding*, big bro. Have you seen women planning a wedding? Her ancient grandmother is toddling around Oz's place as we speak, rearranging the furniture for good luck or good spirits or gourmet *chee* or whatever. Even Pippa has been reduced to hiding in her studio. Dorrie's cousins would be eternally grateful if you'd give them tasks that would take them off the map. Want me to send you the Chinese twins and see if they can sniff her out?"

"No, she doesn't want them involved, says the general hates Dorrie's family. I still want to send Nadine to Francesca. Those two can play telepath and drive each other nuts. Better yet, send *me* to Francesca. She has a pilot's license and can fly me to the moon."

Conan snorted. "I'm not entirely certain Francesca is female, but I'll talk to her. Her family owes the Librarian almost as much as we do. I doubt that she has a place where you can hide though."

Magnus twitched his shoulders with discomfort. He was getting too damned *close* to Nadine, to the extent that he almost understood her insanity. He scanned the store in search of her as he talked. "Have you learned anything about the sister?"

"The student registered under the name you gave me hasn't been in class for a week. I'm working on friends and neighbors," Conan replied grimly.

Damn. Magnus didn't want to tell Nadine that.

"I'm useless without her direction. Keep on it." Magnus signed off, mentally cursing. How did he tell Nadine that they'd verified Vera had gone off the map? Was she likely to go ballistic again?

And that was only one of his many problems. A kid he didn't know and who may have wandered off on her own wasn't as immediate as his current dilemma. Being full red-blooded male, he couldn't help notice that Nadine was sexily female. She had curves in all the right places. He didn't need a full rack, just a juicy handful, and she filled the bill.

They were living together. It was natural to think about sex—except she was scarcely more than a naïve teenager with apparent tendencies to imprint on those who looked out for her.

And she was crazy. He had a bad record with crazies. He had to put her somewhere safer than with him.

He stopped in the health care aisle to pick up shaving soap and razor. As an added precaution, he threw in condoms because he was trained to be prepared. And then he checked out before Nadine so she wouldn't notice.

He'd given her a stack of cash, but he waited by the registers in case she needed more. She'd filled a basket but managed to stay within the exact dollar amount he gave her. She had to be a walking calculator to perform that feat.

He tried his best not to notice what she was buying, although the scissors she'd purchased earlier had worried him. Diane had threatened herself with scissors once. He hadn't believe the threat. He paid more attention with Nadine. At least Nadine had the sense to keep her hair concealed beneath the hat and her glasses hidden in a pocket so she wasn't quite as noticeable.

"Want a pizza?" he asked, taking most of her bags and heaving them over his shoulder. He led her out into the suburban shopping strip with its choice of fast foods.

"Please. I've lived on sawdust for a year. Can we take it back to the hotel? I've thought of a few more places online that I can check. And if those don't work, I warn you, I'll start hacking," she said, following him into the neighboring pizza joint.

"I figured you already had. See what damage you can do from my phone while I order at the counter. Any preferences on pizza?" Magnus gestured at the overhead menu. He'd lived on pizza for years and considered it a basic food group.

She studied the menu and heaved a heartfelt sigh. "Better make mine a salad. I did nothing but get flabby this past year."

Magnus glanced down at her in incredulity. Her clothes didn't reveal cleavage, but he could see nice high C-cups. Her jeans revealed soft hips a man with big hands like his could dig into. She was dangerously close to perfect. "Flabby? In what world?"

She glared back. "Flabby. Chunky. Overweight. And I want salad."

"My God, I finally find a woman who doesn't look like a spike, and she thinks she's fat. Never, in ten million years, never will I understand the female mind. You're all loco." He stalked up to the counter and ordered one pizza with everything on it, doubled the salad so he could pretend he was eating healthy, too, and added cookies.

By the time Magnus gave his order, Nadine had taken a booth, donned her computer glasses, and was punching the keyboard of his high-tech phone. She glanced up at his approach and eyed him warily. "You really don't think I'm fat? I've never been thin."

"You're not meant to be a swizzle stick." He dropped their Target bags into a booth. "Not any more than I'm meant to be a pencil. I'm big-boned. You're well-rounded. What matters is if we're healthy. And quit fishing for compliments. Have you made any progress?"

"Compliments?" She stared at him as if he'd suddenly grown two heads and one of them was green. "I look like a four-eyed orangutan. I don't expect compliments! All I said was that I needed to lose weight. You're the one with some personal neurosis about size. And yes and no on the progress."

"Four-eyed orangutan! *Orangutan?* I'm taking you to the zoo when this is done. Have you ever seen an orangutan? First thing you'll notice—their hair doesn't curl. And my weight is muscle. With exercise, yours can be, too. No neurosis there. What did you find?"

Magnus ground his molars at the weight argument. His late fiancée had always ended up turning that one against him. He liked Nadine's curves, but he wasn't saying that aloud and giving her any more ideas than she already had. He was having difficulty keeping his eyes from following those rhinestone-studded jean shorts molded to her rounded ass.

He took a deep gulp from his water bottle and kept his mouth firmly shut while she made hash of his phone. He'd never seen anyone type so fast with two thumbs.

"Vera buys teaching supplies from a particular online store," she said, blessedly dropping the argument. "Her account was used last week, but the shipping address isn't hers." She held up the phone to show him.

He grabbed the phone and raised his eyebrows. "Damn, but you're good at this." He copied the address, and texted it to Conan, relieved to be back on a sensible path and to not have to tell her that Vera had really disappeared. "We'll let my brother send one of his men to check out the address. She may have just been making a contribution to some school. Or we could have ourselves a thief," he added, so she didn't get her hopes too high.

"What kind of thief buys school supplies? Even I'm not that simple," she said with scorn, taking back the phone. She was buried deep in the internet when their food arrived.

Nadine could barely contain her excitement by the time they carried their meal and purchases back to the B&B. Vera was alive and out there. Her sister was charging to obscure accounts with a different credit card but using the same user name and password she always used.

Nadine wanted to leave right now and find the shipping address, but it was hours north of here, well above L.A., and the Oswins were far better at detective work than she was.

She wished she could say the same about her own objectives.

So far, the general's new internet guru had changed every server and ID that she'd stored in her hidden cloud storage. She couldn't touch him. She needed a better plan than a massive FAIL.

So she sat at the small table on the B&B's balcony and ate salad across from a gorgeous hunk who thought she was an idiot. And loco. And not fat.

Magnus ate salad and pushed half the pizza toward her. Real food instead of loony bin paste was too tempting. She ate a piece of pizza and finished her salad. She resisted the cookie. She didn't need sugar when she could barely sit still from impatience.

She bounced her leg, played with her hair, and wished for a bike so she could work out some of her frustration. "Do you dance?" she finally asked.

He finished his pizza and regarded her gravely. "Not that I've noticed."

She laughed at his wary non-answer and flung a paper napkin at him. "I never learned. I've never been to a concert. I played Pandora on the computer whenever I had a chance, but I have no idea what music is popular. A sign at the beauty shop said there's a musician at the beach café tonight."

"And you want to go." He considered it, checked the sky, and shrugged. "It's in walking distance. Can't see how it would hurt anything except maybe our ears."

"I don't imagine a café has dancing, but won't you need to know how to dance for the wedding?" she asked with curiosity. Maybe she needed to spend more time looking up Magnus the Mystery Man.

"I had lessons when I was a kid. I just don't go looking for opportunities," he said. "Remember we're trying to be inconspicuous. Don't land yourself on YouTube."

Delighted that he'd agree to give her an opportunity to see a little more of the world, Nadine dashed back into the bedroom to sort through her new acquisitions. She showered and used her new brush and hair goop to straighten her distinctively orange curls. Then she clipped her hair back in a French braid. The night air was cool so she donned jeans with yellow embroidery on the hem and a long-sleeved gold jersey.

She admired the effect in the mirror but decided her waist was too pudgy. She pulled the green hoodie over the top. The sunhat was stupid at night, so she left it off. She didn't need glasses unless she had to read a menu in dim light, and they'd just eaten. Cocking her head, she tried to decide if she'd look like herself if captured by a camera.

"You look gorgeous, and the general would have to be blind not to recognize you. We'll just stick to shadows." Watching her preen, Magnus shrugged on a blue plaid flannel shirt over his muscle-revealing black t-shirt. "Let's reconnoiter."

Gorgeous? Nadine narrowed her eyes to study his expression. She hadn't taken him for a charming liar, but there were times...

He took the stairs down and left her trailing behind—again. Not charming. Still uncertain about liar. Looked good in jeans though.

It wasn't quite dark as they strolled toward the little row of businesses along the main beach. The café's patio had overhead heaters to warm the overflow crowd. Acoustic guitar strummed over the gentle pounding of surf. Nadine knew that relaxed people weren't as likely to thrust their angst into the ether to give her headaches. If she could just keep from having any more fits...

She'd only partially lied about working 24/7 all her life. Most of it, she'd spent terrified of making a spectacle of herself in public. Work had been her haven.

But after months of being deprived of anything close to a life, she wanted to *live*. And in some way, Magnus made it easier to face the world.

She attempted to soak up every sensation, the muted conversation of the crowd, the smoke from the fire in the outdoor fireplace, the mellow notes of the musician—and the big man holding a hand to her waist and guiding her expertly to a table in the shadows.

She felt like a butterfly struggling to shed her chrysalis.

She let Maximus Grandus order fancy coffees. Her college nights had been spent sitting at a computer and drinking what was plainly raw sewage compared to the brew handed to her here.

She sank into the lovely music, tapping her hands on the table to the beat. Her toes drummed time. She swayed to the lilting songs. To her disappointment, no one danced. She wanted to watch and learn. If she lived, maybe she could find a DVD to teach her. She was dying to get up and move.

The musician slipped into a slow song. She finished her coffee and regretfully realized the beautiful evening had to end. Mad Max had been patient with her need for escape, but she couldn't expect him to stay here all night. There were still half a dozen more places she could hunt for Vera. The internet was riddled with hiding holes.

As if understanding the geek was back, Magnus took her hand and helped her from the seat. Women turned to watch him, but he didn't seem to be aware of it. Nadine wanted to stick her tongue out at all the elegant, slender young things—not a mature reaction, she realized. She should be allowed one episode of teenage irrationality. This was her moment to walk off with the prom king. She grinned at her own silliness.

He led her away from the patio, down the steps to a secluded shadow on the beach where the haunting music lingered.

To her startlement, he swung her around to face him, held one hand behind her back and the other in the air.

"Waltz," he said gravely. "Simple steps. Place your left hand on my shoulder and just follow me."

How had he known? In amazement, Nadine gingerly placed her hand on his hard, muscled shoulder. The sensation nearly froze her.

To the lilting tune from the café, she shuffled in the sand, trying to follow him. Off balance at being held this close to a man without beating him with her fists, Nadine couldn't immediately relax. But the night and the music and maybe the special coffee worked their magic, and her feet miraculously caught the pattern he was teaching her.

She was just starting to loosen up and thrill with the movement when Magnus swept her backward with the final notes of the song.

He was leaning over her, his hand braced on her back, his mouth not inches away, his gaze staring into hers. *Thrill* didn't even come close to describing the sensation paralyzing her.

"Not the time or place," he said with what sounded like genuine regret as he stood her back up. "Maybe after we find your sister."

Not the time or place for what? Had he really meant to *kiss* her? "Maybe after you kill the general?" she asked lightly, trying to cover how badly the moment had shaken her and that she was not quite herself. The Nadine she knew wouldn't have asked such a leading question. Or recognized that he might actually be talking about... kissing. She hoped.

"So, maybe we're not the right people either. Let's go," he said abruptly, catching her hand and dragging her back to the stairs, ruining the moment with their reality.

The musician announced a break, and Nadine saw no point in lingering. Uncertain whether she was sad or glad that Magnus had more sense than she did, she trudged back toward the B&B.

His phone rang before they reached the house.

He answered, uttered a curse, punched a link, and held up the screen so she could see.

The nightly news was showing an old photo of Nadine with Vera, saying they'd been kidnapped and asking for the public's help in finding them.

They dived for their computers the instant they reached their room. Magnus didn't waste time wondering what the hell he'd been thinking by almost kissing La Loca. He hadn't been thinking. He'd been *doing,* as usual. To him, sex was sex. Not to his companion, though. He knew better.

Rather than think about what he'd almost done, or how damned *good* she'd felt and smelled in his arms, he called up more links to news reports. He consulted with Conan while Nadine wept and rattled her keyboard. Evidently, she hadn't expected the general to call the cops— or hunt the sister who had left years ago.

"How long has Vera been off the general's radar?" Magnus asked as he studied an image of the two girls as young teens. Vera had dark straight hair she wore in bangs. She was smaller than Nadine and wasn't wearing glasses in the photos. The image definitely wasn't of a college age woman.

"Two years. We smuggled her out after high school graduation. She's been on her own for *two years*! How could he do this?" She typed more furiously, calling up more news clips.

"You said she's a wannabe actress. She should know how to disguise herself," Magnus said, trying to be reassuring. "I'm going down to the drugstore to get you some hair dye and bigger sunglasses. I take it those aren't reading glasses?"

"No." She scrunched up her little nose and looked up at him. "Mild astigmatism. I need them for the computer or in dim light. Can I be a blonde?"

"Your hair might end up green. Best just to take it a few shades darker."

"How do you know?"

Magnus shrugged. He didn't like talking about Diane, but Nadine deserved answers. "Had a girlfriend who used to change her hair every month."

"An ex-girlfriend?" she asked warily, studying him from behind the ugly glasses.

"Late girlfriend. She's dead." Before she could ask more, Magnus strode out, hoping to hit the drugstore before it closed.

Hoping to escape the need to explain.

She was still at the computer when he returned. When she glanced up, he saw pity in her eyes. The damned Librarian had been dredging internet archives again. Diane's death had hit all the Alaskan newspapers. His name had been mentioned.

He hated having his life or his psyche dissected, and he hated seeing pity in anyone's eyes. That's why he didn't talk about Diane.

"Did you find Diane's body?" she asked. "Is that why you go mean sometimes?"

In disgruntlement, he threw his purchases on her bed. "Yes, I found her body, in the bathtub. She considerately left the water on and the drain open in an insane gesture of cleaning up for herself after we'd argued about the mess she'd made of the bedroom."

"She was the nut, not you," Nadine reminded him, unsympathetically.

"Manic-depressive, I'm told, but she refused treatment. I'm the idiot who didn't recognize the symptoms and make her get help." Irritated, he pointed at the packages. "We'll leave here first thing in the morning. Conan's looking for a place where we can hide out. The address you gave us is a school. Conan has a guy watching it. A photo of your sister may help him. I don't suppose you have anything more recent than the one the TV is showing?"

"Sent it to you already." As if she'd completely blanked his gruesome explanation of Diane's death, she stood up and examined his purchases, trying on the wrap-around sunglasses and making faces. "I hope we're going somewhere sunny to justify these. I'm not exactly movie star material."

"How many movie stars have you seen?" he asked grumpily, returning to his computer.

"None," she agreed. "But they're always wearing sunglasses in the images online. The photos I sent you are ones Vera posted on Facebook from her drama class's theater production. She played several roles and wore several wigs. She could look like anything now. The general won't have any new photos to pass around. He quit playing dad after Mom died."

"How did your mother die?" Magnus had to ask, because it might take him closer to the general.

"The same way your girlfriend did." She stalked into the bathroom carrying the hair dye and scissors.

After that ambiguous and ominous statement, the scissors worried him. Diane had slit her wrists, but she'd used a kitchen knife.

Nadine's mother had slit her wrists? Or committed suicide by other means? Magnus propped his head on his palm and pushed to block the black thoughts.

Depression might be genetic, but Nadine didn't strike him as depressed.

Of course, like Nadine, Diane had foolishly appealed to his Zorro complex. He'd thought she needed his help and that he was good for her. He had been clueless about Diane's emotional state. He'd just considered her mood swings to be part of who she was and accepted the bad with the good.

He refused to accept responsibility for Nadine's emotional state. He would keep her physically safe, if possible, but that was his limit.

She emerged half an hour later with damp dark hair trimmed almost to her ears. He hated it.

"I guess my eyebrows and lashes are dark enough," she said doubtfully, staring into the mirror. "I don't know if making them blacker would help."

"You'd have to hide the natural arch of your brow and the length of your lashes, then wear a ton of make-up to hide the fullness of your lips. Just wear the shades unless you want to go Muslim."

She turned and raised her sinfully expressive reddish brown arches at him. "You noticed my *lashes*?"

"Hard to miss." Magnus refused to meet her eyes but zoomed in on one of the TV images full screen so she could see. "You and your sister both have large green eyes framed with heavy lashes. You hide yours with glasses."

Those lashes had swept her cheeks and hidden her expression when he'd almost kissed her. But her lips had been pouty and ready—then. He really needed to get a grip.

"Right. I need to let this dye set. If you want to go on to bed, I'll work with the lights off." She settled cross-legged on her bed. "I've remembered the names of some more of Vera's friends. She hasn't been doing social media under her name since she left for college, for obvious reasons, but her friends might have more photos under her assumed name. This could take me a while. Hacking Facebook is like stepping into a rattlesnake nest."

"I don't get much sleep when I'm on a project." Magnus turned back to his work on the general's grandsons. Adams had had four sons. Dorrie had killed one and gotten another locked away. She may have killed one of the grandsons, as well, although the doctors had claimed it was a brain tumor. Conan's mild-mannered wife-to-be was the kind of deadly weapon the general had accused of killing Po-po.

That left two more sons and half a dozen grandsons to track. He could wield his contacts to find files on a military man who had sent his sons and possibly his grandsons in his footsteps.

Magnus heard the hair dryer switch off some time later. Unlike his brother Conan, he was attune to his surroundings at all times.

Insanely, he was particularly attuned to Nadine.

She slipped silently into the darkened bedroom where he was bent over the desk with a lamp shining on his keyboard. He tried not to look up, but he couldn't resist.

Her insistence that she was fat, and her surprise every time he offered a candid compliment, kept him intrigued by the workings of the female mind. Did women *really* think he was looking at the sparkle on their jeans?

She was too much in shadow to see clearly. "Turn the light on," he told her.

She hesitated, then only turned the bathroom light on behind her. She was wearing a long blue nightshirt that clung in all the right places.

"My hair, Maximus," she reminded him, pointing at her head to force his gaze upward. "Am I invisible yet?"

He studied what she'd done. She'd chopped off all her quirky curls and straightened what was left into short tendrils on her nape and forehead that emphasized her narrow chin and big eyes. "You've turned yourself into Tinkerbelle," he said, almost in disappointment. "I liked your hair long."

"Tinkerbelle has blond hair, not brown," she corrected, studying her reflection. "I've always wondered what I would look like if I had normal hair."

"Not like yourself. A geek should look intelligent, not like a lost waif. It's a good look, but it's not you." He couldn't explain better than that.

She sent him one of those enigmatic looks that women had perfected.

"Maybe I don't want to be a geek. Maybe I should be a beautician. I could set my own hours then."

"If you can change your hair that much, you'd probably be good at it—until you slit the throat of the first hag who criticized your work." He turned off his computer and stood, unable to cope with the vibrations she emanated. "Go on to bed. I'm taking a shower."

"Maybe Dorrie will teach me *dim mak*," she said ominously.

"Maybe you could slay men with your eyes," he agreed, before shutting the door between them.

Nine

Slay men with her eyes! If only she could.

Magnus hadn't seemed to appreciate her new pixie look. It had taken a mess of product and a hot dryer to straighten the curls.

Why should she care what he liked? It was her head and her life.

Liar. She'd wanted him to kiss her. She'd wanted to feel like a female and not some tool to be used. There for a little while—at the beach, when they'd danced—she'd almost thought it would happen, that she might actually attract a man's interest.

At this rate, she could die a virgin. Did she have to seduce the damned man? Not happening. She was an introvert for a reason.

She crawled between the sheets and pulled the blankets up so she could have the windows open and hear the surf.

She heard him return from the bathroom. He'd turned out all the lights but she thought he was wearing a t-shirt and boxers. They didn't make him look any more approachable.

"I'm sorry about your fiancée," she whispered. She hadn't intended to say that, but the weird part of her brain had thought it a good idea.

"She wanted more than I could give," he said, climbing into his own bed. "Her friends said she was probably manic depressive. I didn't know. Maybe I could have done something if I had understood, if I'd got her some help."

"Not unless she wanted to change. Manic depressives are capable of logical thought. They can ask for help. But those highs are like drug highs—very addictive in their own way. Suicide damages more than just the person committing it, but the illness apparently prevents them from thinking beyond themselves." She'd had lots of time to study suicide.

"I forgot you took psych. How old were you when your mother died?"

His voice was distant. She tried to read it, but he could just be being polite. Or digesting what she'd told him. She wanted it to be the latter.

"Sixteen. Vera was thirteen. She left no note. We were absolutely shattered. I still can't believe she did it. I wish I had the last journals she wrote, but the general took them away. Since then, I've developed a thousand suspicions but no proof. At the time, we just thought he was being good to take care of us even though we weren't his kids. We tried our very best to be the best kids he could have."

"Bastard didn't appreciate what he had," Magnus said dismissively. "I take back what I said earlier. Your new hair makes your eyes seem to take up half your face. A blind idiot like him probably won't recognize you. Good night."

Nadine lay there stunned, trying to accept this new perspective.

Magnus didn't seem much concerned with her stepfather's opinions and probably not his survival. He expected her to feel the same way. And she should. She knew the general's ruthlessness. And she knew he hadn't really seen her as a person, which probably did make him a blind idiot.

But she'd spent most of her life as an invisible robot, trying to please her stepfather. This new perspective was exciting. Maybe, just maybe, she might be as important as the general—in this new and alternate universe she was now inhabiting.

For the first time in her life, Nadine was free to wonder what would happen if the general died.

If anything had happened to Vera, she might be ready to help Magnus make certain that he did.

"We need to be on the road," Magnus roared, prowling the perimeter of their small suite the next morning.

"*You* need to be on the road. I don't see the advantage of exposing myself to more people than necessary," Nadine countered, amazed at the amount of courage she'd gained since Mad Max had entered her life. When her response didn't cause him to shout the roof down or fling her over his shoulder, she dared to continue. "We need information, and we don't have it."

"I waited until your credit card arrived. What are we waiting for now?" he demanded.

At least he was listening. Score one for the commando.

"For a destination," she said firmly. "I like the anonymity. Our landlady doesn't mind if we have breakfast sent up instead of dining with her. This is a crowded beach town with strangers everywhere, so the locals don't notice me. I canceled my hair appointment because of your paranoia, but I'm not driving aimlessly all about."

Okay, so seeing her photo flashed all over the news had made her jittery and hiding made her happy. She didn't see a problem with that.

"You like the Wi-Fi," he translated, partially accurately. "You're stuck in Librarian mode, but it doesn't work so well without the general's active files."

Nadine scowled at his perceptivity. "His new guru has abandoned all the servers with which I'm familiar," she admitted. "I can't even find his computer."

"Today's the last day we can stay here," he reminded her. "The room is reserved for tomorrow. You can't hide here any longer."

Nadine refused to admit defeat, although having to appear in public again was beyond daunting. "The general has gone down a mole hole. We'll need to lure him out, but I can't even begin to figure out how until Vera is safe. Surely your brother will have word from his team soon."

"Not if your sister was simply sending supplies to that school. We have no reason to believe she's anywhere near it. You haven't found any other purchases or Facebook friends, have you?" He stopped at each window to examine their surroundings as he paced.

"Not yet. She's savvy and knows the general might trace her, so she's lying low, just like I told her. I wish I could meet your Francesca. Maybe between the two of us we could mentally reach her." Frustrated, Nadine sent another probe into the internet universe—just about as useful as mental telepathy at this point.

Mad Max's laptop sounded a warning alert. He dropped into the desk chair—he'd usurped the desk, leaving her the couch or the table. He hit a few buttons and Conan's face filled the Skype screen. Even Nadine looked up to see what that portended.

"We've got a 'maybe' sighting on Vera," Conan announced.

Dorrie's face came into view. "Nadine, my family is desperate to meet you. If you can't get past the annoying Oswins, we'll come tie Magnus up."

Fascinated, Nadine pushed her glasses up her nose and crouched at desk height, peering under the large biceps blocking her. This was her biggest glimpse into the world of people the general had tracked, the distant family she'd never known. She didn't know how to relate, except for the matter at hand.

"Tell me about Vera first," she asked. "Then I'll decide whether to push him over the edge."

Magnus knuckled her head, presumably to remind her that he was right there. It was amazingly reassuring knowing that he wouldn't shout at her impolite comments.

A new face appeared on the screen. This person had spiky dark red hair—the rich deep color Nadine had always admired. Combined with cutting high cheekbones, and expressively wide lips, her face screamed movie star, but Nadine wouldn't recognize a star if they named her.

"We want you to stay with us but it's too dangerous," the redhead announced. "Oz has found a place not too far away. It has good internet so you can order groceries, if you want, instead of going out."

"Hiding is what Pippa would do." A big man who looked like a more polished Magnus with longer hair appeared in the screen. "We could just put you in her hide-out but then Pippa couldn't hide there. I'm Oz, and I owe you for returning Donal to me. I thought a little more accessible hiding place would allow you to get out and about."

"Vera?" Nadine asked insistently, a little overwhelmed by these strangers she'd once tried to help.

"Nadine's TMA," Magnus said helpfully. "Stay focused, folks. What have you got on Vera?"

"TMA?" Conan reappeared, apparently turning the computer to prevent family from crowding around.

"Too Much Attention. Borderline Asperger's, probably. Vera?" Nadine asked again.

"Autistic!" she heard someone in the background shout. "That explains the mind-reading."

Nadine wanted to pull what was left of her hair but she followed Mad Max's example and tried to wait patiently. Magnus set her in front of him, letting her perch on the edge of his chair between his legs. The powerful muscles of his thighs almost distracted her. The man could crack bones with those thighs. She tried not to snuggle too far back and learn what she was missing.

"Our guy on the scene spotted a teacher at the school who might fit that photo you sent us of Vera wearing a blond wig. He's staying away until we have more info and permission from you to go forward."

Nadine squeezed her nose between her palms and tried to think while Magnus's voluble family chattered in the background and her mind spun with fear and excitement.

"Give her a minute," Magnus said in his grave tone. "You say you have a place where we can stay? Where we could take Vera?"

"Down by the coast. Place is filled with rentals and weekend palaces. Strangers won't be noticed like they would be up here at Oz's place. It's only about half an hour away. One of Oz's clients is filming in Australia and agreed to let us use it. Gated community. Alarm system. No questions asked," Conan said. "I'll take it if you don't want it."

Magnus snorted. Nadine interrupted. "Please, let us take it until we can get Vera there. We might need help in reaching her. She won't speak to strangers, and I don't want her to be scared off. I'll have to send her a warning of some sort."

"And when we're done, the two of you can have it for a honeymoon hideaway," Magnus suggested.

"Honeymoon hideaway, I love it!" Dorrie said in the background. "Can we have the butler back?"

"Butler?" Magnus asked warily.

"The place comes fully staffed. We have to send them on a paid vacation before you arrive," Oz answered, peering over Conan's shoulder. "I don't think the staff will object."

"I was thinking more of a cottage in the desert sort of thing," Magnus grumbled, "not one of your movie productions."

Nadine elbowed him. She tried to imagine a palace on the coast with butlers but the distraction created by his family blanked her mind.

"Nadine deserves the best. You can go crawl under a car like a rattlesnake if you'd rather," Oz offered.

Nadine snickered, but the man behind her didn't flinch or get mad. She eagerly drank in the family dynamic. She'd spent her life tip-toeing around family. This free-for-all was an eye-opening experience.

Dorrie shoved her way past the men. She had green eyes, too, Nadine noticed, which stood out rather noticeably against her Oriental coloring.

"Francesca wants to meet you. She's my cousin, the pilot who helped us find Bo, and a telepath, too. She thinks maybe if the two of you work together, you might reach Vera without alerting anyone."

"Having one of my men *call* Vera would be more effective," Conan said dryly.

"No!" Nadine nearly shouted. "She was taught to run if a stranger called her. She probably won't have a phone anyway, or not one whose number you can trace. When can I meet Francesca?"

"You do realize your method of communication is ridiculous in this day and age?" Magnus asked impassively.

Nadine pinched the bridge of her nose and nodded. This way led to madness was what he wasn't saying.

Undeterred, Magnus continued. "It will take us nearly six hours to drive up there. This is Saturday. The traffic through L.A. should at least be moving. We'll be there this evening."

Nadine wanted to hug him for understanding. Instead, all she could do was bounce excitedly. "Thank you! And if there's anything I can do to help with the wedding, just name it. I appreciate how much time I'm taking away from the preparations."

The red-haired Pippa leaned over Conan's shoulder. "My mother and I are having fun with that. Dorrie has her wedding dress, and she and her grandmother have feng shui'd the entire house. The others just plan on showing up. Having you and your sister attend would be a treat. You're family!"

"I'm not family," Nadine pointed out regretfully. "We just occupy the same family tree somewhere back in the dark ages."

"That's all it takes. See you soon." Pippa backed away.

Magnus wrote down the directions to their new safe house and signed off.

Nadine fell back against the bed, exhausted by the emotional, confusing interaction. She needed to calm down or she was likely to have another fit.

She couldn't calm down. They might have found Vera! And the Malcolm women wanted them for family? Not if she and Vera had to flee to Nicaragua.

Priorities, she had to prioritize her worries. "I don't suppose we could drive past that school before we settle into our luxury hideaway?"

"It's Saturday. What are the chances we'll see her? It's a few hours out of the way. Your call, though." Magnus began packing up his laptop.

Nadine sighed. "You're right, but I hate it. I want to walk up to the school and search the grounds, sneak into their office and look for employment records, stand on the roof and shout. So what I want is probably not the best choice."

"Oz pretty much did all that and worse when Donal went missing. That's why we know the routine. You've helped us. Now we help you. We should have bought a suitcase for our things." He glanced around at the new clothes scattered about.

His steadiness blessedly calmed her as her own screaming emotions couldn't. She could Zen out on his solidity—at least while Magnus was working for her and not against her.

"We can pick up a tote on the way. There's not so much that we can't carry it down now." Nadine hurriedly folded all her new attire, fished a Target bag out of the trash, and began dumping her personal items into it.

When she glanced up, Magnus was dumping a box of condoms into the plastic bag he'd retrieved from the trash.

Condoms. He'd thought about having sex. With her? Please, lord, let it be with her. If she knew Vera was safe, she really wanted to celebrate. What better way than to move forward into the life she'd never had—with this man who gave her courage she hadn't known she possessed.

The possibility that Magnus was thinking of having sex with her so fuzzed her brain that she meekly followed all his instructions, gathered her precious belongings, and trailed down to the car without a word.

"It may not be Vera," he warned as he pulled the car out of the lot, apparently misunderstanding her silence.

"I know, but it's one hope more than I had yesterday. And meeting Francesca will add another." She squeezed the pink bunny while pondering the possibilities. "Vera isn't a great receiver, but if she's worried and trying to reach me, she'll be more open than usual. I've never worked with anyone else or from such distances, but I don't know what else to do. It's kind of exciting knowing someone else who might have the same weirdness as I do."

At his silence, she darted a look in his direction. He was frowning. "What? You still don't believe in telepathy?"

"Anything is possible. Physics proves that. I just don't believe it's practical. Why didn't you set up some kind of cloud communication where you could reach each other?"

"We do IMs when necessary, but not often. Interception is always possible. I wanted Vera to make a clean break in case I couldn't. Even before I was locked up, I was constantly monitored. The temptation to check on Vera would have been too great. She needed to leave and start a new life without me holding her back."

"What set you off back then? Why not let the general pay her way through college like he did for you?"

"You're fishing again," she said, leaning her head back against the seat and sorting through her memories, looking for the safe ones.

"Can you blame me?"

"No, I suppose not." How could she think of having sex with a person she didn't fully trust? Easy, she admitted. She was desperate. And he was more man than she'd ever dared to dream of—except for that rigid militaristic streak. Surely that wouldn't apply to sex.

"Vera wasn't under Jo-jo's thumb the way I was. She had the opportunity to develop a suspicious mind," she continued. "She snooped. She led on the general's grandsons, got inside some of his facilities. Up until then, we'd only been allowed in offices with computers. She got inside the engineering labs."

She could practically hear Max's bushy eyebrows whiz up his face.

"Adams Engineering? The ones who supposedly would be building the experimental helicopter for the army?"

"Yep, that and others. The general's connections are vast. He has all sorts of military contracts in many different fields. You can see why I thought I was working for the good of the country, even if his obsession with my father's family was a little weird."

"What did your sister discover?"

"That some of the people working for the general did so under duress. He kept them locked in the basement of the lab."

He drove silently, apparently playing with that appalling notion. Finally, he spoke. "Conan and Dorrie tried to look into one of those labs near L.A., back when they were hunting for me and Bo. Dorrie didn't like what she called *vibrations*, but security ran them off before they could investigate. I don't suppose that would be the one your sister visited?"

"Probably not. I don't really know how many labs he has, but I'm pretty sure he closed the one Vera found after we found a way to disable the computerized security system."

"And let the victims out?"

There was that perceptive streak again. Nadine sighed. "Yeah," she agreed. "And the general knew it had to be us. Things got pretty nasty after that."

Ten

Fretting over how "nasty" the general could be to two young women after they let his captive scientists free, Magnus tried questioning Nadine as they drove up the coast. She clammed up, donned her black-framed glasses, and turned her formidable attention on his cell phone rather than answer.

He claimed no understanding of women, so he wasn't about to hurt his brain attempting to figure out one who swung hot and cold, lucid and insane, bold and timid, all within the space of minutes. She'd had an unsettling childhood and possessed a dangerous brain. He'd stick with that.

Stymied in his interrogation, Magnus caught himself stupidly wondering if there would be any place to dance in their next stop. They'd been on the same page then. She'd actually smiled when they'd danced. She had a glorious smile that almost convinced him that she could be normal—under different circumstances.

But the Librarian wasn't normal and never would be. She didn't fool him with her nonchalance. Her sister had wanted the lab workers free, and Nadine had performed one of her magic acts.

She had undermined a paranoid general and let his pet engineers free. Didn't she know that people had *died* for less?

Beside him, his pixie-haired companion exclaimed in shock. Or maybe disgust. Magnus waited to see what she'd discovered now. The landscape was bleak up in these hills. The general couldn't very well sneak up behind them, so Magnus wasn't inclined to panic. Yet.

"The ratfink claims we were living with him and working in his office when we disappeared! He's describing your car as one his security guard saw cruising by his house before our *disappearance.* I can't believe the bold-faced lies! How does he get away with it?" she exclaimed.

"People who lie for a living have no conscience," Magnus said with a shrug. "The ability to form moral judgment is lodged in an actual part of the brain, and in some people it's underdeveloped, possibly due to some chemistry imbalance. Lying doesn't cause them a twinge of concern or even affect lie detector tests. The worst case scenarios are sociopaths."

"I *know* that," she grumbled. "But sociopaths are other people's fathers. It's hard to apply that label to someone you've known and respected. It requires separating a child's emotions from an adult's logic. Give me time to cope. In the meantime, the cops will impound your car now, if they've found it."

"Conan reported it stolen, but we've always known it would draw the general's fire. He'll know we're behind your escape. But he'll have some difficulty proving it to the law with that story."

Max hoped the cops didn't mess with his Camaro project too much—or let the general near it. He didn't want to be responsible for a paranoid terrorist getting his hands on the experimental components.

"Don't speed," she whispered unexpectedly. "What happens if the police pull us over?"

"I'd get a ticket, not you." He slowed down, although he hadn't been going faster than traffic. That she hadn't objected to freeway driving spoke of her desperation to reach Vera. "Don't blow anyone up or get drunk in public places and the cops will never notice you."

"Humor, har-har," she muttered, thumbing through his phone. "What if I sent the police an anonymous message essentially telling them that the general is a big fat liar?"

Magnus considered the implications. "They won't believe an anonymous message without evidence. You'd either have to reveal Vera's former whereabouts and her fake ID, or you'd have to reveal yourself."

She grew quiet, and he glanced worriedly in her direction when her fingers stopped tapping the phone. He was still trying to get used to the short hair that revealed her vulnerable nape. He didn't want her to be vulnerable.

He wanted her to be the mysterious, invincible Librarian who had saved him. He needed to straighten out his head. She was just another confused female—who really did need rescuing.

"I can give them information about me that only I would know," she said, having given the problem some thought, "to prove the message comes from me. And then I can tell them about Woodstar. Would they look?"

"They might," he agreed. "But it's going to be tough convincing them that a retired general is an unmitigated liar. Are you ready to start revealing him for what he is?"

"I wish I knew for certain that he really isn't protecting the country," she murmured unhappily. "I believed in him for so long...."

"Look at it this way—do the ends justify the means? Should he be allowed to plow over the rights of every person he comes across in order to achieve whatever nebulous power he thinks he can wield?"

"It's not *nebulous*," she said. "He wields *tremendous* power. And he really did love Po-po and wants her name to be commemorated by proving that psychic warfare is possible. And if there were enough of us, it might be possible. But there aren't."

"So he's amassing other weapons besides Malcolms, experimental ones," Magnus concluded.

"He's building weapons, yes, but they're military contracts and hardly a secret. It's just he uses extraordinary means to develop them. He may never prove Po-po's theory that psychics can be weapons, but we do have uses. He'd love to get his hands on you. He's convinced your engineering brilliance is abnormal."

Magnus itched just thinking about it. Adams had made him an offer when he'd hijacked the helicopter. That proved the general was off level by a full bubble. Magnus realized now that he'd come pretty close to being one of the engineers held under duress. His gut burned in a fervent need for retaliation.

"I'm not psychic," Magnus corrected. "What happens to the people who refuse to be coerced into working for him?" he asked, knowing he probably would have killed the general— if the general hadn't killed him first.

She clasped her hands around the phone and didn't look at him. "I don't know."

That's what he'd figured. "As far as I know, no one has come forward to file a complaint." He left her to consider the implications. He couldn't force her to turn in the general. She had to do it willingly.

That didn't prevent him from going after the bastard with any tidbit that she fed him.

"I have to get Vera to safety before I can start digging him out of his mole hole," she asserted.

Magnus hid his wince. So, he could bait the general now or pray they'd find Vera soon.

"Jo-jo would use Vera against me if he could," she continued, reinforcing his thoughts. "I surrendered any chance at independence when I gave Vera her freedom. I'm not reneging on that choice now."

That level of responsibility for another human being prevented him from doing what he knew needed to be done, dammit.

They grabbed lunch at a drive-through, ate it on a pull-out on a bluff along the coast where Nadine could bask in the view. She replaced the geek glasses with the big sunglasses and really did look like a film star. There was no telephone reception out here, so Magnus watched in reluctant appreciation as she paced up and down, exploring every nook and cranny of the overlook. She was wearing the blue capris she'd bought yesterday, with a loose, gauzy orange blouse over a tank top, taunting him with glimpses of curves. She had great legs despite her claim that she never got any exercise.

She'd used some of his cash at one of their gas stops to buy a map. Finding a place out of the wind, she spread it open. "Where is the town where we think Vera might be?"

Magnus pointed at Victorville, on the eastern side of the mountains, near the Mojave. "Odd that she'd end up near the desert where the general hides."

"Not odd, and the general doesn't hide there, so quit trying to sneak information. He hid you in one of his bunkers, but it's not even a main one." She glared at the map. "California is an impossible state to get around. This is where we're going, isn't it?" She pointed to a dot along the coast.

"Yep. Oz is here." He pointed to another dot up the road from the coast but in mountainous area. "No direct route to the desert from there. We have mud slides on this side of the mountain, snow in winter on the peaks, and fires on the desert side, so finding safe places to build highways is a challenge."

She sighed and folded the map. "I hope Francesca is waiting for us. I don't know what we'll do if telepathy doesn't work."

Magnus gritted his teeth and tried not to remind her that telepathy wasn't real communication and that the general was the key.

Nadine held her breath as they navigated the steep descent

from the scrubby bluffs to the coastal highway. She wanted to leap out and examine every wildflower they sped by, all the interesting boulders and rock formations, and take pictures to preserve the ocean view in hopes she could access them later, whatever the future had in store.

Instead, she sat on her hands, bit her tongue, and let Magnus fly past all the fascinations she'd never seen or explored. He was obviously familiar with the terrain and took it for granted. She didn't mind appearing an idiot and demanding they stop, but she didn't want to miss any chance to meet Francesca.

She knew she was placing far too much hope on an experiment that had failed numerous times. Vera simply wasn't a good receptor. They'd come to accept that. But now, it was vital.

She kept her anonymous sunglasses on as they drove through a small town consisting of pricey boutiques and restaurants. Nadine hoped there were grocery stores nearby. She was hungry and tired of fast food.

Magnus had no difficulty in finding the gated community. He handed over his information to the security guards, and they passed him through without question. She breathed a sigh of relief as the gate closed behind them, but the relief was short lived.

She stared in dismay at the mansions they crawled past. Someone had mentioned *palaces*. That's exactly what these were. Money temples, the general had called them—conspicuous consumption run amuck. She supposed screen stars hid in here. Oz worked in TV, she remembered.

The nondescript Ford they were in must look like a servant's vehicle. They circled around until they figured out where the house numbers were hidden. Nadine concealed her gasp as they turned up a drive to a glass and steel castle. If the ground floor garage counted, it towered four stories above the coast. Down here on the street, the view was blocked by other mansions. Up there on the top...

"I don't like this," Magnus grumbled as they stopped to pick up keys and remotes from a security box to which he'd been given the code. "It's too conspicuous."

Nadine agreed, but probably on different levels than he meant. "Hide in plain sight?" she suggested. "Do I have to wear jewels to walk past all those windows?"

He sent her one of those heavy-lidded looks that shot her

hormones to all the right places.

"Wear clothing, at least. Wonder how many of the neighbors are voyeurs who scope each other out?" he asked, following her thought and teasing her cluelessness.

"Oh, thanks for that image. Now I'll have to wear a burka." She sank deeper in her seat and glared at a second sprawling structure at the end of the drive with a house sitting on top of a second garage. A carriage house?

Magnus keyed the remote and the garage opened on an army of classic cars. "No room at the inn," he concluded.

"We'll just pretend we're the new butler and maid and park at the kitchen door." She eyed a red Ferrari in awe.

They parked behind a hedge and Nadine carried her Target bag to the side door, hoping Maximus had a key and that they wouldn't set off any security alarms.

The enormous stainless steel and granite kitchen echoed, striking Nadine as a deserted space station. "I could stand here and pick up the vibrations of the universe," she said in awe. "May I pitch a tent in the kitchen?"

Magnus issued one of his you're-nuts snorts, took her arm, and steered her into the next room.

"I'm not sure I trust you with this much space," he concluded gruffly. "Promise not to bungee jump off the balcony?"

She gazed up at the atrium balcony spilling foliage in the filtered sunlight from the enormous front windows. "Hang glide, maybe?"

He actually laughed at that, which warmed her better than hot chocolate. When Maximus Grandus relaxed, he was awesome.

She halted in the atrium to study a marble statue taller than she was. It adorned a two-story, ceiling-to-floor waterfall fountain. When she realized the statue was a stylized nude couple wrapped around each other, she blushed, and hurried ahead.

Behind her, Max chuckled. "I need to take you to museums?" he called as she took the soaring stairs upward.

"Please," she said honestly. "Just don't catch me by surprise like that."

"With statues or naked?"

She blushed again. "I've led a sheltered life," she replied, aiming for haughty but probably fooling no one.

"So I've gathered." He started opening doors on the second floor. "Bedrooms. Find one that looks unused, I guess."

She looked for one with a view, settling on one decorated in pale blues, greens, and sand so it brought the outdoors in. It looked as if the decorator had done her job but no one had ever moved in. No personal effects or clothing made this a home. The balcony was a bonus.

Her first night alone—no guards outside the door, no Magnus watching to see that she didn't take flight.

She wasn't entirely certain she had any idea how to be alone.

Uneasy with that realization, she peered around the door into the hall to see which room Magnus took—the one across from hers, naturally.

Strangely comforted knowing he was nearby, she emptied her meager belongings into a drawer, set Vera's pink bunny on the bed, and wished for a bread crumb trail to lead her back to the kitchen.

The security intercom buzzed.

Nadine hurried into the hall, looking for a way to answer it. Magnus appeared, opened a panel cover, and hit one of the many switches behind it. She stuck her tongue out at him. He raised a quizzical eyebrow but told the garbled voice from the security gate to send someone in.

"How did you know where they hid the speaker?" she demanded as they descended the stairs.

"I looked. That panel was the obvious choice. Francesca just arrived. She brought dinner. I hope you like Chinese."

"Just because she's of Chinese origin doesn't mean she'll bring Chinese."

"It does when I told Dorrie to send some." He hit the foyer ahead of her.

"You're a smartass, Maximus!" she shouted after him.

Giddy with her new freedom and by Francesca's arrival, Nadine dashed down the rest of the stone stairs to the grandiose foyer. Magnus already had the door open.

No one entered, but in her mind, a sudden image of the general loomed—wearing his uniform, shouting, and looking livid.

Nadine grabbed her temples and sank to her knees.

Eleven

When Nadine fell to her knees, holding her temples, Magnus flung Francesca a suspicious look but kept his hands to himself. He'd learned not to grab La Loca in one of her fits.

Instinctively, he crouched down, shielding her from the intruder. He placed himself in a position to catch her in case she toppled and bit back his curses so he wouldn't interfere with whatever was happening inside her head.

Utter relief washed over him when she didn't repeat the seizure routine.

This time, she recovered in seconds, catching his arm to steady herself before she glared up at Francesca.

Magnus had met the helicopter pilot, Dorrie's cousin, before. She was tall and elegant, wearing her shiny black hair pulled back in a simple cream ribbon matching her silk shirt and slacks. She carried a sack of still-steaming cartons of food, but she maintained an expressionless composure while Magnus helped Nadine to her feet.

Uneasy, but not having a clue about what was happening here, he remained silent and watchful as the two women gauged each other. Even with her hair dyed brown, Nadine was the more colorful of the two in her orange gauze shirt, yellow tank top, and blue jean capris. She was shorter than Francesca and less sure of herself—and still she balled her fingers into her fists and stuck her chin out pugnaciously.

"What did you do that for?" Nadine demanded.

Francesca shrugged. "That creep has been in my head like that ever since my cousin Bo encountered him. If you were raised by that bastard, we can't trust you."

Catching the gist of the argument and not particularly wanting to hear more craziness, Magnus swiped the food from Francesca's hand and stomped toward the kitchen. "Whatever you just did, cut it out. Nadine was the one who helped me and Bo out of that hole, and you're the one who can leave if you won't trust her."

He surprised himself in saying that. He liked to remain objective, but his rescuer complex had kicked in. He'd seen Nadine's genuine fear and distress and heard her stories. She was the victim here.

"I need that man out of my head," Francesca insisted without an ounce of remorse. "Why aren't we going after him instead of some kid who is probably playing hooky to go to the beach with her boyfriend?"

Nadine halted so fast that Magnus hadn't realized she wasn't still behind him until he heard her speak.

"Vera is not just a kid. She's an exceptionally intelligent and motivated teacher who understands people far better than I ever will. She's lived under *that man's* thumb most of her life and is terrified of him. She will not do anything to endanger me or to reveal herself to the general. If she's disappeared, it's because she felt threatened."

Magnus raised an admiring eyebrow as Nadine stalked past him, into the kitchen. Maybe she didn't precisely need rescuing—just a keeper.

He glanced back at Francesca, who didn't appear properly chastised. "We get the innocent to safety first," he told her. "That's proper hostage procedure."

Nadine began opening cabinets, not acknowledging the *hostage* comment. Magnus engaged in a brief stare-off with Dorrie's pilot cousin. Once upon a time Francesca would have been just his type—ultra chic, mechanically adept, gorgeous, and able to look out for herself.

Diane had been like that, he'd thought, but obviously, his judgment was skewed. Francesca held no appeal for him now. Apparently, his new type was blatantly crazy and terrified, a stubborn, independent ball of orange fluff. He'd be adopting kittens next.

Disgruntled, he began setting boxes of Chinese on the long contemporary inlaid wood table and let the women settle their differences.

"You picked up the whole image I sent you?" Francesca asked, hunting through drawers for silverware.

"If you mean did I see the general in full uniform and engaging in one of his tirades, yes. I shut down after that." Nadine slapped some dishes on the table.

Magnus winced. He remembered the general that way the one

time he'd met the old buzzard. He'd been behind bars and unable to plow a fist into the bastard's jaw. *That* was the image Francesca had been projecting? Bo had been there, too. She'd actually *seen* that image in Bo's head?

This psychic business was damned peculiar. And useless.

"It was extremely rude to broadcast that loudly if you know what you're doing," Nadine stated matter-of-factly.

Francesca made a dismissive gesture and scattered forks and napkins around the table. "It's not as if I know anyone else besides my grandmother who is receptive. Generally, I'm the one on the receiving end."

Magnus grabbed a box, settled on a stool, and began dishing food onto a plate, trying to pretend this was normal dinner conversation. Nadine's silence, closed eyes, and faintly constipated expression warned it was anything but.

Francesca froze and frowned.

Rolling his eyes, Magnus scooped up whatever delicious concoction Dorrie had chosen for them and started eating.

Francesca continued frowning and spooning up soup as she tried to catch whatever image Nadine was "sending."

"I can see someone who looks like the photo that Conan sent me of Vera. I can't tell what she's doing." Francesca tilted her head and closed her eyes. "No, that's all I'm getting."

"That's a start." Nadine set a cold beer in front of him.

How had she noticed his preference for beer when he hadn't been drinking any?

"But it's too easy when we're in the same room and know we're sending images," Nadine continued. "We're both receptors and Vera isn't. The chances of reaching her are slim unless she's half asleep or in a hole and sensory deprived."

As he and Bo had been, Magnus conceded. That Bo had been able to project their location had been a freaky miracle. The psychic business was for crazy people like Adams—an interesting option, but a well-engineered drone would work better.

"Vera has always been a lark who goes to bed early," Nadine said, pouring wine for herself and Francesca. "Perhaps if we wait until dark and send a message every fifteen minutes, there will be some chance she'll notice and realize we're trying to reach her."

Magnus glanced around to see where she'd found the wine. On

the far side of the Sub-Zero was an immense wine rack. The lady might be a few bulbs short of a chandelier, but she was a keen observer. And lacked normal social boundaries—like asking permission to appropriate expensive drinks.

"What message do you want to send?" Francesca asked.

Nadine wrinkled her nose. She didn't have a redhead's freckles, Magnus noted. From lack of sun?

"I've been thinking about that. If she's in a place where she can follow the news, then she must know that I've escaped, and the general is after us."

Francesca nodded and sipped her wine. "Nice wine. What is it?"

Magnus glanced at the towering wine rack. "Probably a hundred dollars a bottle, so let's not ding Oz's budget too badly."

Both women shrugged and poured more. Well, he'd wanted independent women. Obedience didn't come with the territory.

"I want to send Vera a simple password to a basic Dropbox account so we can communicate," Nadine continued. "We used to share one when she was in high school, but the general thought we were keeping secrets and made me take it down."

"Were you keeping secrets?" Magnus asked, because he couldn't help himself.

"Of course," both women replied and laughed.

That would teach him to keep his mouth shut.

They put away the leftovers and Magnus made coffee while the women explored the house. Francesca was insisting on appropriate feng shui for their experiment while Nadine was more concerned about the sound of ocean waves, warmth, and cushions for some yoga position she claimed helped open up her mind.

If he wanted to learn what made them tick, scientific research required that he just shut up and watch. Up to a point.

They chose the balcony off Nadine's bedroom, then decorated it with appropriate plants and gewgaws from the rest of the house. As the sun began to hover above the waves, they settled on yoga mats.

Magnus found a wicker chair in the shadows of the room and stayed out of sight. He was out of his element and needed an oily rag and a spark plug to clean.

Admittedly, the ocean waves were relaxing. The soft murmur of voices dissipated when the women concentrated on the paper with the password written on it—image and numbers. Magnus put up his feet and leaned back and closed his eyes.

He hadn't been this relaxed in days. Weeks. Maybe years. The tide burbled out in a gentle rhythm. The women spoke in harmony. He kept one ear open for anything out of synch.

The next thing he knew, he startled awake with a snore. Anxiously, he checked on Nadine. She and Francesca were finishing off the bottle of wine on the balcony—while perched on the rail three stories above the street.

Nadine—naturally—was blowing bubbles with a giant wand. Where the hell had she found bubbles? Laughing, she swung her arm wide, wafting iridescent soap into the night—and nearly toppling off the edge.

Not crazy, just drunk.

Magnus strode onto the balcony. Ignoring a startled Francesca, he grabbed Nadine by the waist and carried her into the en suite bathroom, where he dumped her into the shower stall and turned on the water. "You're sticking to one glass of wine until you develop a head for it."

Nadine sent him a sultry smile and began unfastening her shirt. Caught off guard, Magnus almost stayed to watch. Almost. The water had plastered the gauze and knit to her breasts, which apparently hadn't been confined in one of the bras she'd insisted on buying. His prick rose straight up for the occasion.

Even more irked, he slammed out of the bathroom and watched Francesca carry off the wine bottle. She gave him a happy wave and a wink and sauntered down the hall. How many bottles had they emptied?

What the hell was happening to him? He knew Nadine was another crazy, too mixed-up to know what she was doing. He had no business looking at an emotionally disturbed and possibly mentally unstable female as he just had.

He had the urge to dive into the waves from three stories up just to see if he could straighten out his head—or his hormones.

Instead, he grabbed the sheet of paper containing the password they'd been trying to convey and located Nadine's laptop on the balcony. They'd apparently been celebrating something, and he hoped he'd find out what in here. He clicked on her Dropbox and looked for messages from the beyond.

He opened the box's only contents— a recently received

document. An address and a time appeared with no other information. Had they *really* contacted Vera?

He could grab his keys, hop in the car, and be on the other side of the mountain in time to case this joint before the given time. He reached in his pockets to confirm he had the keys.

And Nadine started to sing in the shower.

Damn, damn, and triple damn. He couldn't leave La Loca loose on her own.

He couldn't take her out in public.

For once in his life, he had to think first and act later. *Fuck.*

Well past disgruntled, Magnus forwarded the message to Conan. He refused to question the mumbo jumbo that had produced the mysterious address. He just wanted this over while he still maintained his sanity.

As if in reward for his good behavior, Nadine emerged from the bathroom wearing nothing.

Twelve

Riding on the courage of half a bottle of excellent pinot noir and Mad Max's admiring gaze, Nadine did her best to imitate a model and swayed across the room. "Vera received our message," she said in triumph.

"Or she checked your old Dropbox just in case," Magnus said, but his tone didn't sound argumentative. He wasn't saying she was nuts, and that's what mattered. "I forwarded the address in her message to Conan," he added.

Nadine rolled her eyes. So much for seduction. "That was stupid. I told you, she scares easily."

She hurried over to her laptop to send a message to the Dropbox to warn Vera of the approach of strangers.

"Tell Conan to use the code words *Maximus Grandus*, and she'll know he's safe," she ordered as she typed.

"Way to kill a mood," Magnus grumbled, grabbing his phone.

She was standing there bare-assed naked, and they were both typing on keyboards. This was so not what she'd intended.

"You're the one who shot off her address without warning me." This was probably why she'd never have sex. She didn't know how to shut up. Still, she had to learn to stand her ground or be walked over by obsessive military take-charge types for the rest of her life. Wine nicely removed her inhibitions. "Two-way street, buddy. If you want to go your own way, leave me out of it, and I'll go mine." She turned to face him.

His chest and shoulders filled her field of vision. Nadine whacked him on a shirt button. "You're not Tarzan and I'm not Jane."

He grabbed her waist as he had earlier, lifting her until they were face to face. Only this time his rough hands dug into flesh, and her bare breasts rubbed his soft polo shirt. He smelled of raw male with a hint of salt air and sent her senses reeling.

She propped her hands on his gorgeous shoulders, meaning to blast him again, but he wrapped his arms completely around her and crushed her against him. Before she completely understood the turn around, Magnus kissed her. One big hand slid through her hair and pressed her closer.

Forget argument. She nearly strangled on the rush of desire. Falling into those firm pecs, she wrapped her arms around his neck, and returned the kiss with all the fervor that had been pent-up inside since he'd stomped into her life.

His tongue touched hers, and in an excess of energy, she wrapped her legs around his waist and thought she might never let go. He took her weight without flinching.

Bliss and excitement and raging need spun her head far more than wine.

He explored her mouth while she explored his. He still tasted of coffee. His jeans abraded her thighs as he carried her toward the bed, as if she cared about abrasion when she had his tongue claiming her mouth. She wanted his shirt off but couldn't work out how to do it while she was clinging to him for dear life, feeding on the heady elixir of his desire.

Magnus set one knee on the bed and lowered her, still covering her with soul-searing kisses. His bristled jaw scratched her cheek, but his big hands were gentle as he settled her against the silken sheets. He stroked and squeezed her buttocks until she tugged inexpertly at his shirt, and he had to let her go to help her pull it from his jeans.

Big silent Max didn't say a word when she ran her hands under his shirt and explored the powerful muscles he concealed there. He was solid as rock but warm and smooth, and she didn't think she could ever let go. She found his nipples and tweaked, and he finally growled and climbed over her.

"You're not going to tell me tomorrow that you were drunk and didn't mean this?" he asked, tearing his lovely lips away from their plundering.

"I'm not any more drunk than you are, and I'll regret it more if we *don't* do this," she said honestly. Even her awkward timidity didn't stand a chance against the burning desire to *feel*. For once in her life, she wanted to surrender all thought and just enjoy the moment. "No strings, I promise. Just please, let's have this one night."

He hesitated, but Nadine caught his hand and tugged it toward her breast and there was no turning back. She cried out with the sensual wonder he created with just the brush of his rough hand against sensitive skin. Need coursed through her like liquid flame.

He bent and licked the nipple he'd just set on fire, and she grabbed his hair, murmuring senseless encouragement as her body came truly alive for the first time in her damned sheltered life.

At some point, she became nothing more than sensation. The surf pounded against the rocks in time to the beat of her heart. The night smelled of salt and male sweat and sex, and hunger consumed her. She cried out at the chilly air when Magnus rose to remove his jeans. She shuddered happily from a different sensation when his naked heat covered her again.

She reveled in the brush of his hairy masculine legs against hers as much as in the soft caress of his kisses along her belly. He pried her thighs apart, leaving her vulnerable and aching. When he applied his tongue there, she nearly shot off the bed.

She needed only that slight spark to ignite a river of desire. Twisting, rocking, more out of control than in one of her psychic seizures, she wept with pleasure as he tormented her with his tongue. Tremors rushed through her in waves more forceful than the surf outside.

Finally, when she was limp and wrung out, Magnus rose on his powerful arms, kissed her cheek, and rolled over to don a condom. She tugged him back, needing his heat and strength to hold her together. He resisted until he was ready, then sprawled on top of her again.

"You're amazing," he murmured, spreading his kisses across her cheek and nibbling at her ear. "I may explode if I don't have you now."

"Now, please," she whispered eagerly, opening her legs, needing more than she could possibly explain.

He lowered his hips until his rock-hard penis brushed wet, aroused tissues. Mindlessly, she rose up to meet him.

He was huge.

She obviously wasn't.

He pushed. She cried out and backed away.

He slid gently back and forth to arouse her again, then pushed deeper.

She dug her fingers into his biceps, bit his shoulder, and tried not to fight him.

"Damn, you're tight," he whispered as if it were a good thing.

"Wrap your legs around me." He helped her raise them to show what he wanted.

Dazed, she did as instructed. He sucked her breasts until she whimpered and squirmed with need again. And then he pushed so fast and deep that her head hit the headboard, and he filled her so completely, she no longer existed.

That's when her vision opened and she saw him in entirety, as if she had slipped outside herself.

Nadine watched his large, magnificently male body bucking over hers, filling all the empty places, taking charge—*possessing* her. She saw his taut buttocks pump, his hard tree-trunk thighs conceal her more slender ones, his wide back obliterating all but her inner vision.

And she fell apart, weeping, clinging, hanging on as he overpowered her with sensation, as the tides of pleasure ripped through her, and Magnus shouted his own release.

Exhausted, unable to separate what was real and what was not, Nadine fell asleep in his arms.

Magnus considered himself an uncomplicated man. He'd had his fair share of one-night stands, walking away in the morning without regret. Sex was sex, just as food was food.

Nadine turned that theory on its head and whacked the stuffing out of it in ways that Diane never had.

He woke in the morning with her head on his shoulder, her breasts cuddled against his side, and her hand curled trustingly on his chest. His morning woody was ready to play.

He had the uncomfortable notion that he'd hurt her last night, and she wouldn't be as eager as he was.

Words like *sheltered* formed in his brain. *Naïve. Inexperienced.* He nudged uncomfortably around *virgin*. She was twenty-three years old, dammit. Surely...

How rough had he been? Alarm and regret roiled through him. The black cloud of responsibility formed. It ate at his gut as she stretched and shifted to warm herself against his body heat. They'd left the balcony door open and the air was damned chilly.

He'd *hurt* her. She should have warned him... Damn, but he was the one who should have known.

He didn't have time for inexperienced females and nut cases, Magnus reminded himself. Diane had wiped out all hope that he might learn how to do relationships. Nadine *knew* he wasn't the lovey-dovey kind of guy that women wanted. Besides, she would be off with her sister in a day or so, and there was no sense in getting used to this.

And he was lying through his teeth. He *wanted* the comfort Nadine offered. He wanted to teach her that last night wasn't what real lovemaking was about. He wanted to watch her reaction to each new discovery in the world she scarcely knew. She was even more intriguing than the damned new Camaro engine.

There be dragons. Magnus carefully unwrapped himself from Nadine's embrace, pulled the covers over her luscious curves, and took his hard-on to the shower.

He'd left his clean clothes in another room and had to don yesterday's. She was awake when he emerged. Her big green eyes filled her elfin face.

Magnus wanted her nimbus of hair back. It had made her look stronger and older. Short curls emphasized her vulnerability.

"I'm going to fix some coffee. Conan will bring your sister here if he can. We'll hear from him if anything goes wrong." Magnus felt like a heel as she watched him with a hint of wariness.

"How long will it take to drive across the mountains to here?" She pulled the sheet around her and up to her chin.

"I'll check online. Go back to sleep, if you like. We have time." He walked out with a ten-ton load of guilt on his shoulders.

Francesca was already downstairs, fully dressed, sipping coffee, and reading from her tablet computer. She gave his unshaven jaw a cursory glance, snorted, and returned to reading.

The whole damned family would know what he'd done by sunset.

Thirteen

Disoriented by Max's abrupt departure, Nadine checked the time and hurriedly rolled out of bed. She was sore, damned sore. At the same time, she felt remarkably centered.

She'd done it. She'd finally had sex. And it had been miraculous. And incredibly painful. Exhilarating and...dangerous to the heart. Rather like she'd imagined a roller coaster ride.

It had almost made her mind as sore as her lower parts. She'd never had a vision that had taken her outside her body! Or maybe that had been the wine.

She wasn't certain she wanted to try again, but the craving for the adrenalin rush was strong.

Except, Magnificent Max had made it perfectly clear that she'd merely been a one-night stand. She was good with that. More than good. She didn't think she could take another night like that.

But her stupid heart yearned for hot kisses and tender touches. And adrenalin rushes.

Vera. Vera came first.

Nadine hurriedly showered and dressed. Grabbing her glasses and the laptop, she headed downstairs, following the scent of coffee.

In the kitchen, Maximus was leaning against the counter top, sipping his coffee, while gorgeous Francesca munched daintily on some granola concoction. Nadine grabbed the cup Max handed her and headed out to the patio to avoid interaction. Francesca's mind was an uncomfortable place.

Max followed and flung a blanket from the cabana over her shoulders. The morning was still misty and chilly.

"Conan's team is stationed around the address, making certain no one is watching but them." He leaned over and hit a few keys on her keyboard. "I set up this account for you earlier. That's where they send their reports."

She was placing a lot of trust in the Oswin family, for good reason, she supposed. They'd accomplished miracles over the past year. She wished she could be the one rescuing Vera, but she was smart enough to know that her presence was more danger than help. The general would kill to find her.

Donning her glasses, Nadine impatiently scanned the cryptic notes of the team members, then hit the live video links. Her heart raced as the computer called up the images of the team stationing themselves around a simple bungalow. The camera showed a house on a street of similar tiny houses with patches of sand for yard. Landscaping consisted of a few scraggly palms and extremely large cacti.

Magnus hovering over her with his big hand on the chair back reduced her formidable concentration to nil. Nadine sipped her coffee black, forgetting that she hated black coffee.

"Who's filming this?" she asked as a scrawny dog or coyote raced down the street and a rusty Ford pick-up trundled past on the screen.

"I doubt it's Conan. He's snug in bed with Dorrie. One of his team, I assume. He makes certain they have the latest tech. This looks like a dashboard cam. He's been building the team since the nanny snatched Oz's kid. It practically runs itself these days."

"They find lost kids?" Nadine asked, just so she didn't have to think too hard about Vera and never seeing Magnus again after this.

"Lost and stolen kids mostly. Teens are tougher because they often go off on their own. But Vera wants to be found, apparently, and that's a different angle. Besides, we've pretty much declared war on the general for what he did to Dorrie's family and others like them. Conan would finance the devil to bring him down."

Nadine didn't say anything in response, couldn't. The front door of the bungalow on the screen was opening. Vera walked out carrying a backpack and walking a small fluffy dog.

Nadine closed her eyes and sent up a prayer of gratitude. Eagerly, she returned to the screen and the dashboard view of Vera.

The blond wig looked ridiculous, but Nadine recognized the way her sister held her shoulders and strode with grace and purpose. She wasn't acting terrified. Vera pushed open the gate to a little park next to the bungalow, as if taking her pet out for its morning constitutional.

The gate closed, shutting her off from the camera.

Magnus instantly punched his phone screen. "She's out of sight. Have your guys spotted her?"

Conan spoke sleepily through the speaker phone. "The team is stationed on both sides of the block. There's another gate over there, but my guys don't have a camera on that side. Keep your hat on."

Nadine chewed her thumbnail and stared at the empty street on the screen, as if staring would bring Vera back in sight. Magnus squeezed her shoulder but even his understanding didn't reassure her.

"Jessica is approaching our target through the back gate," Conan reported through the speaker phone. "She's carrying a flyer bearing the code words."

"How does he *know* this?" Nadine whispered, listening raptly. "Sending a woman was brilliant. The general doesn't usually employ women."

"Conan's team will be reporting directly to him. He has about a gazillion monitors and computers tuned in to anything he deems important. He's probably hacked security cameras in the area, and he'll be receiving text messages from the other members of the team. He may sound like he's half asleep but Conan can do this with his eyes closed." Magnus checked her laptop screen over her shoulder. "No one's moving in the street. If she's being watched, they're not looking for her yet. Making contact behind the walls of the park was good strategy. Your sister isn't dumb."

"We've got her," Conan murmured neutrally. "The driver says she's walking with Jess toward the car. They're carrying the dog and acting as if they're discussing pets. We're good. No one in sight."

Nadine reached up and squeezed Max's hand in excitement. "Please, let them be okay."

"They're in the car," Conan reported. "Hang up and I'll have her call."

Magnus handed her the phone. Nadine clutched it with hope and a prayer. She'd been terrified for weeks. Her throat clogged with all the things she needed to say. Please, let Vera be okay.

The video on her laptop went dark but text messages started flying back and forth across the screen, mostly in gibberish she didn't attempt to interpret while she waited anxiously for the phone to ring. Magnus read the text over her shoulder.

Finally, the phone broke into a weird rap song. She punched it on, glancing at Magnus with a quizzically lifted eyebrow at the choice of rings.

"Unknown caller ring," he whispered.

"Nadine?" came a familiar voice, sounding just a little excited and worried.

"Vera!" With relief, Nadine clung to the phone and tried not to weep. "You're okay?"

"I'm fine. These people said they're taking me to you. I hope that doesn't mean they're locking me up with you."

"No, no, you're in excellent hands. I'm in a secure place. We'll discuss what to do next after you get here, but you're safe. Is that your dog?"

"You saw Mr T?" she asked in delight. "I found him. Can I keep him?"

"I guess that depends on what you tell us when you get here. I'm just thrilled to know you're safe. You scared me to death."

"I know, I'm sorry, I didn't have a choice. Jessica says we can't talk long. They're really cautious. Are they spies?"

"Better. You'll meet everyone eventually. I love you, kid. Stay safe."

"Love you, too, Sis. I'm so happy I'll see you again! Too-da-loo." She broke the connection.

"Too-da-loo?" Magnus asked gravely, taking the phone while Nadine wiped moisture from her eyes.

Trying to pull her shattered nerves together, she was grateful for his silly question. It gave her time to breathe instead of plot and plan.

"Mama used to say things like that," she said, remembering a kinder era with fondness. "Drove Jo-jo crazy. He called it nonsense talk, but now I know he was afraid we were speaking a language he didn't understand, and he couldn't control." Still shaky from speaking to the sister she hadn't spoken to in two years, she took the offer of Max's strong hand to stand up. She dropped the blanket on the lounge.

"He thought you were using magic curses?" he asked in amusement.

"Maybe. He's ridiculously superstitious, which is probably another reason he hunts my family. He really believes Po-po was cursed by a Malcolm witch. What he can't control, he'll destroy," she said sadly, understanding so much more than she had as a child.

Inside the kitchen, Francesca was adjusting her shoulder bag and removing her keys. "I take it the lost lamb is found? Maybe she can give us the general's direction." Her look was challenging.

"Don't place any bets," Nadine warned, no longer as intimidated by Francesca's curtness as she had been. But she took off her geek glasses anyway. No point in advertising her lack of elegance. "The general won't be easily found, and I doubt that it's safe to look for him. I thank you for helping find my sister. I don't want to repay your kindness by causing harm."

"Nadine's a wuss," Maximus Irritatus said. "We'll bring her around."

She elbowed him in the solar plexus but he didn't even grunt. Rather than argue, she aimed for the dauntingly large refrigerator. Eggs, she could cook.

"We'll see you at the wedding then. Bringing down the general would be a lovely wedding gift considering what he's done to Dorrie." Francesca swung out, looking model-thin, gorgeous, and supremely self-confident.

"I hate her," Nadine said to no one in particular as she hunted for ingredients to go with the eggs. "She's another militaristic control-freak like you, isn't she?"

"No, that's just your paranoia speaking." Magnus reached over her head to a carton of juice. "Francesca is just a normal, run-of-the-mill, bossy bitch."

Nadine elbowed him again and slipped out from under his arm. "You don't get to call women bitches unless you allow an alternative derogatory term for men."

"There isn't one," he pointed out. "Men got to invent vocabulary for millions of years. About the best term I can summon is randy dog, and that's almost a superlative in comparison."

"Cantankerous grouch works for me." Nadine buttered a skillet and whacked an egg into it. She was too jittery to be reasonable.

"Except that term doesn't relate to sex."

He may have meant that as an insult to her current behavior, but *sex* hung in the air between them. She'd told him she was good with no commitment, just a simple roll in the hay. Why then, did she see SEX written in capital letters over her head?

She steamed silently, unable to find a suitable retort.

"Are we arguing?" he asked with interest, sprinkling green herbs on two of the eggs she'd dropped in the skillet.

"When have we not been?" she countered, poking the yolks of her eggs until they bled out. "We're from different planets."

"You're a space alien?" he asked with that same noncommittal curiosity. "*To-da-loo* really is a foreign language?"

She smacked his hand with the rubber spatula. "You know what I mean. You're a man of the world. I've never been outside Southern California. You have a job and family and a normal life. I'm living under an alias and hiding from so-called family. Different planets," she asserted.

"Put the general behind bars and you can have normalcy." He backed off to drop bread into a toaster.

Unaccountably, she missed his presence looming over her. She had to get away from him quickly before she became a pawn again—this time on the opposite side of the fence.

"I can't do much without access to his systems, and so far, I haven't found any. Once Vera and I are out of the country, we'll help in any other way we can," she agreed. "But I don't think there's much we can do or we would have done it."

"Nope, you probably wouldn't have," he corrected, while hunting through the refrigerator. "Revisit Stockholm Syndrome—hostages are known to develop sympathy for their captors. But now you're out of his clutches, you can clear your head. He'll find more victims if he's not stopped."

"Vera and I are the only crazy stepdaughters he has to torment," she answered dryly. "I don't think he'll take in anymore."

Even as she said it, she realized the flaw in her statement. She had been speaking from her narrow childhood and not reality. Nothing prevented the general from marrying again, from adopting any children he liked, or playing the part of sympathetic generous donor to families in need of help...

And he had that entire Malcolm genealogy website full of psychic possibilities. She should have dismantled that sticky web when she had a chance—except she'd hoped it would lead her to more people like her. Now the general had the names and addresses of every gifted Malcolm child whose family had ever tracked their family name.

Reality sucked.

"How long before Vera and the others will arrive?" she asked as they ate their breakfasts and read their on-line newspapers.

"ETA around noon. We have a few hours. Conan's people aren't cops. They won't hold her for interrogation, but they may stop for food and whatnot." Magnus glanced up. "You want to walk the beach?"

She didn't know what she wanted. She just felt ready to explode with nervous energy. Vera had been found. She didn't have a purpose any longer except to plan an escape route, and she needed Vera's cooperation for that. She was having difficulty wrapping her head around her lack of purpose while sitting across from the most gorgeous specimen of manhood she'd ever met. And she couldn't have him. Didn't want him, she corrected.

SEX still hovered over their heads. Magnus didn't precisely hide his interest. Her awareness of his physical proximity was so high up the scale that she could scarcely function.

She got up, washed her plate and the frying pan, and was practically bouncing in nervousness. "Will they call again?"

"Probably not. They'll want to change phones and lessen the chances of being tracked." Magnus sudsed off his plate with the sponge. "There's enough food here to feed an army. We don't need to hunt groceries."

"As long as they're happy with sandwiches. I can't cook." She wanted the reassurance of Mad Max's hug, but she knew where that led now. Not going there. Thinking about what they'd done last night left her even more jittery. She'd had all that raw male muscle in her arms... "Does this place have music?"

He pointed at a speaker in the ceiling. "Everywhere." He led the way down the hall to a casual room filled with plump sofas, a fireplace, and a view of the terrace and pool. He opened a cabinet. "Looks like it's filed by genre. What would you like?"

"To dance," she decided impulsively. "Let me run upstairs to brush my teeth. Find something that plays fast."

La Loca wanted to dance. He really should quit calling her that but he wasn't as adept at nicknames as Nadine was. Maximus Grandus! Loca, it was.

They could spend the next few hours happily in bed working off their excess energy—and she wanted to dance. Could he hope that one would lead to the other?

Not a smart idea, all things considered, but he wasn't as good at smart as his brothers. He operated in simple terms. He wanted

Nadine again. Last night had been the best thing to happen to him in far longer than he'd like to ponder. He felt as if the covers had been pulled off his head and the sun beamed down.

Except he had this nagging suspicion that sex with Nadine was a little more complicated than just sex, so maybe it was better if they just danced.

He returned to the family room before she did and hunted for a few basic tunes.

An easy salsa blared from the speakers by the time Nadine returned. She was wearing a long, flouncy skirt—as if she'd anticipated his choice of music. If she really was psychic, maybe she had.

If she was really reading his mind, they would be upstairs in bed, not down here pretending everything was cool.

She twirled around in the empty center of the tiled room, swaying with the beat. "What do I do?"

"Stand still," Magnus said dryly. "Press your hand in an L-shape on my shoulder so you create tension. Follow my lead and the tempo. It's pretty basic. Count the beats. The even beats are the ones where your feet move."

"Beats?" she asked in amusement. "I'm supposed to know what that is? How do *you* even know what that is?"

"Behavior modification therapy apparently," he replied, catching her hands and showing her the position he wanted. "I wasn't socially adept. I had no interest in books. After I took my father's Mercedes engine apart, he decided I must be bored, and rather than reward me with more sports, he assigned dance lessons."

He counted the beats for her and walked her through the first few measures. Her waist was supple. She swung her hips naturally to the steps, distracting his counting. Or maybe it was the way her breasts bounced in that flimsy halter top.

"You're wearing heels," he said. "Where did you get those?"

"Someone had an entire closetful, and luckily, they're my size. I'm short and you're tall. I didn't want you looking down my shirt while I tried to learn steps." She offered a blazingly innocent smile that forced him to meet her eyes.

The pain behind the laughing green nearly slayed him.

"I can still look down your shirt," he retorted, avoiding any interaction with emotion by moving her further down the floor and adding his own cha-cha hip motion. "And you're not short. You're average."

"And you're not. I need an advantage and heels are it."

Almost defiantly, she picked up the count and the steps incredibly fast. He had her dancing backwards and sideways in the first half hour. Her quickness forced him to think outside his usual box to keep her moving. They weren't aiming for a dance competition, so he didn't feel compelled to torture her with proper instructions. He liked the way she swayed and followed whatever he did.

Apparently, he didn't need to explain anything. She analyzed his every motion, even to the stiff torso and keeping his legs close together.

"More drama!" she finally demanded. "I watched those TV shows in the break room. The dancers did more than walk back and forth."

"I do patterns," he informed her, "not creativity."

She pulled loose from one of his hands and swiveled on her own, as if she'd been made for dancing, even if she threw her head back and kicked when she shouldn't. She stayed in time with the music. Her flirty skirt teased at slim legs, her smile beamed with the force of a thousand stars and maybe a moon thrown in.

He was making her happy.

A little warm ball of pleasure grew in his gut watching Nadine enjoy herself.

They were just filling time until her sister arrived, right?

Fourteen

Nadine thought she would self-destruct if she took one more beat-step where Magnus drew her into his arms and pressed her close. She wanted to say to heck with dancing, yank his head down, and kiss him until every cell in his body hummed as hers did.

Instead, she threw herself into the music, making him frown by screwing up his confident lead and smooth patterns.

A man who could dance! Her heart skipped a beat just thinking of what it would be like to spin across a floor to pounding music with Maximus Grandus holding her as if she were truly special.

She would never know. So she needed to find a better outlet for her energy. After the big oaf swept her out of one more wild swing, she grabbed his biceps, shoved him back until he freed her waist, and ran off to the CD cabinet. She knew nothing about musicians, but she grabbed a disc from the shelf marked *rock* and slammed it into the player.

A blaring guitar and pounding drum beat vibrated the enormous room from half a dozen speakers. Elated, Nadine beat her hands in the air, swung her hips to the music, and just moved where the rhythm took her.

Magnus stared at her in puzzlement.

The poor man needed *patterns* to express himself.

Maybe she ought to thank him for finding her sister by helping him break out of his frozen life. He'd had all the freedom she'd ever craved, and he crammed it into a little box smaller than the one the general had kept her in.

Nadine danced circles around him. She teased his hair, grabbed his hand and lifted his arm to dance under it, then tauntingly danced backward.

That last move finally snagged his trigger. Tarzan stalked her as she swirled across the floor. Psychology classes hadn't taught her anything about male behavior, but instinct did—men liked to hunt.

She swung around and shimmied her ass at him. Shake that booty! Just before he could grab her, she side-stepped and danced around him again.

His arm whipped out and caught her anyway, sweeping her off

her high heels. With his arm firmly around her waist and her feet off the floor, Magnus rocked her around the room, still sticking to beats more than rhythm.

It didn't matter. From this lofty position, Nadine daringly kissed his taut jaw. He'd taken time to shave, and she missed the bristles. He lowered her just enough so that he could run his hand into her hair.

"You need your wild mane back," he muttered. "This is too tame and shiny."

Before she could smack him, he kissed her. He kept moving to the music but his mouth didn't miss a beat either.

The man knew how to light fires, slow lavish fires with sweeping tongue and hungry mouth.

The song changed to a slower one with a seductive rhythm that her Tarzan adapted to quickly. The pulsating beat rocked their hips together, and his big hand slid upward from her waist to brush her breast. Ecstasy pulsed with the music.

He terrified her. He intrigued her. She'd never been so confused and shaken in her sheltered life.

The doorbell rang. It was too soon for Vera to have reached them.

Nadine hastily shoved away, biting her lip and worriedly glancing around, still slightly dazed but realizing something was wrong.

Magnus cursed, tucked his shirt back in, and stalked for the front door, apparently not afraid of whoever had intruded.

Another lesson learned: normal people weren't afraid of doorbells.

Processing half a dozen reasons why she ought to be afraid—including the fact that no one knew they were here and the security guard used an intercom to notify them of visitors—she cautiously followed Magnus the Magnificent.

She breathed a little—only a little—easier when the door opened on Conan and Dorrie.

"Pippa and Granny are arguing over the feng shui benefits of waterfalls over flowers. We left when they started talking about diverting rivers," Dorrie explained, waving hello, then staring in disbelief at the atrium waterfall.

"Well, hell, we could have just brought them here," Conan said, following her gaze.

Dorrie started to giggle. Nadine wanted to laugh with her, but she wasn't entirely certain that she understood the joke. She'd almost been feeling *normal* with Max, but confronted with relative strangers, she shrank back into her usual nerdish self.

"And you drove down the mountain just to escape wedding planners?" Magnus asked, crossing his arms and staring down at his younger brother.

"Of course not. We want to meet Nadine's sister, see what drove her off, and then put the general behind bars before the wedding so we can enjoy ourselves." Dorrie smiled confidently at Magnus, then peered around him to Nadine. "Is he behaving himself?"

"I'm learning to dance," Nadine said carefully, trying to judge the direction of the social waters.

"Is that what they call it now?" Conan asked enigmatically. "Thought we'd warn you that the police impounded the Camaro. They questioned me and they want to question you. I told them the car had been stolen while you were on a camping trip in the Sierras, and I'd have you call when you checked in. But they've got nothing. It's our car, so if it holds our prints, it's no biggie. My guy wiped everything, but if they find Nadine's prints, big shrug. They have nothing to track her so-called kidnapper. For all they know, she drove it herself."

"I want my car back in one piece," Magnus growled. "That's a big deal. Did you find anything in the general's archives that we sent you?"

"Ran them through everything I've got," Conan said. "They're old. Most of the addresses have been abandoned. Haven't found a pattern yet. I've got more people looking."

"Shit. He may have scientists buried like he almost had me and Bo," Magnus reminded him. "I want the bastard stopped."

Conan made an inelegant noise that Nadine loosely translated as *So what else is new*. His phone buzzed before he said more, and he answered it while aiming unerringly for the kitchen.

"He's trying to wrap up segments of two important projects before the wedding," Dorrie explained, falling into step with Nadine when Magnus followed on his brother's heels. "We were hoping to get away afterward, just the two of us with no phones or computers."

Which wouldn't happen if they feared the general, Nadine

realized. And the general would be breathing down their necks if he knew the Oswins had anything to do with her disappearance—which he did if the police were impounding their getaway car.

"Way to lay a guilt trip," Nadine muttered. "Vera and I owe you big time, but do we owe you our lives?"

Dorrie looked startled. "Not shy, are we?"

Nadine thought about it. "No. I just don't know social boundaries. I never really had a reason to care before. Computers are my boon companions."

"And how's Magnus taking that?" Dorrie asked in amusement. They lingered in the kitchen door while the men grabbed beer and inspected the refrigerator. "He's not really a computer type."

"Magnus has his own hang-ups. If I can hack one of the general's servers, I'll gladly take out his entire network. So far, I haven't found a way into his new set-ups. Beyond that, what do you think Vera and I can do to help you find the general? I'm warning you now, I don't think he *can* be found, not physically, unless you're a government official with unlimited authority."

Dorrie watched her surfer-dude fiancé with affection as he piled sandwich makings on the table. "Do not underestimate Conan. What officialdom he can't tap legally, he can hack. Your fear prevents you from seeing your stepfather as human, but he is. We've foiled him before. *You've* helped us."

"Conan hasn't been able to hack Jo-jo," Nadine reminded her. She had difficulty believing the beer-swigging Conan, leaning against the counter and belching, could hack his own e-mail account. He winked at Dorrie, clinked beer bottles with Magnus, and wrapped a piece of bread around a hunk of meat rather than prepare a proper sandwich.

But Nadine had a good idea of all he'd accomplished and took Dorrie's word for the rest. "Appearances are deceiving, I suppose," she said with a sigh, riffling the short hair at her nape and trying to understand why she was resisting.

"Exactly," Dorrie said with approval. "I like your hair cut. Now we can see your face better."

Nadine was about to ask why anyone would *want* to see her face, then decided that was one of those non-social questions she shouldn't ask. She glanced to Magnus for help, but he was being his usual non-communicative self.

"I'm not good at small talk," she finally admitted. "Computers don't talk back—or if they do, I can shut them down without offending them."

"Then you and Magnus must be having a fine old time, out-silencing each other," Dorrie replied with a grin. "Frankie didn't mention any problem conversing with you."

"Francesca? That's because we had a job to do. That's not small talk. That's problem solving." And getting drunk, but she probably wouldn't try that as a curative for her lack of social skills.

Dorrie tilted her head and regarded her with interest. "Your chi roils with energy. You're strong, maybe stronger than Magnus right now. I think losing his fiancée ate at his soul."

Nadine glowered. "I think his fiancée was an emotional vampire who *ate* his soul before killing herself in hopes of killing him."

Dorrie's eyebrows skyrocketed. "Are you sure you can't read chi?"

"I read people enough to avoid the negative ones." Nadine couldn't fight her curiosity any more. "Are you saying you can *read* a person's chi?"

"That's what I'm saying, yes," Dorrie said almost defiantly. "My grandmother has the same ability, along with some of Frankie's psychic talent."

"And what kind of chi is Magnus giving off right now?"

Dorrie laughed. "I don't need to read him to know he's hot and bothered and trying not to look this way. Your lack of small talk must turn him on."

"We were dancing. Or trying to." Nadine finally entered the kitchen to appropriate the bread and sandwich fixings the men had ignored after taking what they wanted. She didn't need to read chi to know Magnus was as physically aware of her as she was of him.

"Maximus Grandus wants to attend your wedding. I'm not sure it's safe." Nadine said.

"Your concern has always been for others. I can see that." Dorrie helped herself and began assembling a line of sandwiches. "The problem lies in interpretation."

"Interpretation?" Nadine sliced tomatoes and cheese for assembling.

"You think protecting people means removing the danger or luring it away. I prefer direct confrontation and elimination of the problem."

Nadine tried to imagine that. The bride-to-be wasn't any larger than she was, probably smaller. Yet Dorrie had been the one to force the Oswins and her entire family to hunt for Magnus and Bo. Dorrie had been shot for her efforts, and still, she hadn't given up. Behind the pleasant demeanor lingered one strong woman.

"Nadine is more a spider who lurks in dark corners and sets traps," Magnus offered solemnly, sipping his beer.

"I like that in a woman," Conan said, lifting his beer in salute. "Silent and unseen."

Dorrie smacked the bottom of his bottle so it splashed beer in his face. "They were *dancing*. Do you know how to dance?"

"You can't win no matter how you answer that, bro," Magnus said with a grin. "The dance floor is all yours. Practice up."

Dorrie beamed in delight.

Nadine thought she'd curl into a warm puddle of goo just watching the arrogant computer genius melt into a grinning fool as his fiancée dragged him into the other room. Warm feelings were not programmed into her knowledge base.

She finished slicing tomatoes and fixing sandwiches for the crew she hoped was bringing Vera to her.

"We could finish our lessons," Magnus suggested.

"No, we can't, not with others watching, not the way we were dancing." She tilted her head in the direction of the music. "You will note they are playing a slow dance and that they hoped to *get away* after the wedding. One assumes that's because they don't get much privacy."

"I'm starting to understand that problem," Magnus retorted with feeling, before swigging from his bottle.

"I doubt it," she retorted. "You're just wanting action. You haven't even begun to *think* about anything else. And privacy has more to do with romance and wanting to be with each other than sex."

"How would you know?" he asked in a challenging tone, helping himself to one of the newly prepared sandwiches.

"I'm reading their minds," she said airily. "Or maybe I read chi, too."

He studied her for a minute, then took another bite of sandwich, chewed on his thought while he chewed the bread, then concluded, "You're messing with my mind. Oz does that. If you could really read minds, you could tell me how close your sister is and if we have time to go upstairs."

Nadine laughed. She couldn't help it. She just cracked up. He contentedly ate his sandwich and waited.

"One track mind," she sputtered. "I've read about that but never completely understood until now. Jo-jo is obsessive, but his means of achieving his goals are multitudinous, so I never quite observed the simplicity of the normal male mind. I'm a turmoil of conflicting needs and fears and planning. You just stand there, feed your face, and want sex."

"Life is simpler taking it one minute at a time," he said with a shrug of his big shoulders. "We can't make your sister arrive faster. We can't plan until we learn what set her running. Fear is a total waste of time. Give me a problem and I'll look for a solution. Right now, we have no problem."

"Yeah, we do, but it's too big for your limited scope to comprehend," she scoffed. "Open your eyes, widen your mind, let the world come in. A socket wrench won't fix what's wrong."

"Another egghead," he said with disgust. "Why do I keep hooking up with women who have to intellectualize everything?"

"Because you're smart and you want an equal. You just won't admit it. Good luck finding a mindless dolly who won't bore you to death in a day." Nadine grabbed a sandwich and some iced tea and headed for the sunny terrace.

The intercom from the guardhouse on the street announced a visitor. Nadine froze. The music in the other room cut off in mid-beat. Magnus flipped a switch and grunted a greeting.

"Mr. Dick Tracy and guest," the inhuman buzz broadcast.

Fifteen

Magnus rolled his eyes at the *Dick Tracy* intro and said into the intercom, "Yeah, and if he's got Lois Lane with him, let them both in."

He grinned as the security guard actually asked if the second visitor was Lois Lane. Nadine smacked him on the back, but Magnus shrugged off her mosquito bites.

He was less impervious to her comment about finding companionship with mindless dollies, but her laughter had soothed his earlier irritation. She hadn't said sex wasn't happening.

Apparently understanding that Vera's driver was using an alias, Nadine rushed to the wall of windows to watch for the car. She bounced on the balls of her feet, almost ready to boil up right out of her skin. Magnus gripped her shoulder both to reassure her and keep her from floating to the ceiling.

She threw him a grateful look. He wasn't sure why, but his hand felt right on her shoulder, so he kept it there, absorbing her nervous energy and balancing it with his steadiness. He could do psycho psychic too.

Conan and Dorrie had joined them by the time a nondescript Toyota rolled into the drive. Magnus identified the Chinese-American driver by the blue-streak in his hair— Jack Ling Simon, one of Dorrie's many cousins. This one was a bodyguard and security consultant who claimed the curious ability to pick up emotional traces of people on objects. In his late twenties, he was built like a sturdy Chinese pug.

Carrying a furry-faced terrier, the woman who climbed out when Jack opened the door was about Jack's height, willowy, wearing the kind of flowy sundress Magnus had tried to persuade Nadine to wear. The newcomer had removed the blond wig to reveal seal-dark hair she'd had cropped at the nape much like Nadine's, only not as neat. Her eyes widened as she scanned the size of the house. The dog yipped and wiggled to be set down.

Beneath his hand, Nadine vibrated. She reached up to squeeze his fingers. Releasing them again, she flung open the front door and dashed down the steps to grab her sister.

Magnus simply watched the tableau from the window, not wanting to interfere in the reunion.

Jack stoically took the dog as the two women hugged and wept. Jack said something that forced the women to hurry up the steps and out of sight of the neighbors. Jack remained behind, letting the dog water the lawn.

Nadine might call herself an autistic, clueless nerd, but she wept just like any woman Magnus had ever known. He backed off warily as they entered.

"Your hair, what have you done to your beautiful hair?" Vera was. "You don't look like you anymore!"

Magnus kind of agreed with that but it wasn't his place to say so.

Nadine rubbed at her tears and nodded in response to her sister's excited description of her rescue. He appreciated Nadine's lack of hysterics over a situation that had been fraught with danger.

"You need to meet our friends," Nadine finally said, giving her eyes a final swipe and releasing Vera.

The young woman turned her attention from her sister to realize they were surrounded. "Oh, sorry, it's just been so long, and I've been soooo worried." Vera glanced with curiosity at their audience. "I'm Vera Malcolm, and if you rescued my sister, I owe you everything, thank you."

Jack arrived with the dog and dropped the wriggling creature into Vera's arms. She cuddled it for a second, then let the animal down again. It aimed straight for Magnus's toe. Magnus let it sniff while Nadine provided brief introductions.

Nadine introduced him as "the stubborn problem-solver who figured out my code." He hadn't expected to be called *lover* or *friend,* but he was stupidly resentful anyway. He wanted to wrap a possessive arm around her shoulders, keep her from nervously vibrating and bouncing, but he apparently didn't have that right. So he picked up the damned dog instead. He growled at it to keep it from licking his face.

He wanted explanations.

The women made noises about food and gravitated toward the kitchen.

Frustrated, ready to leap into his car and take out a general, Magnus had no choice but to bite his tongue and follow—and hope he'd hear the story if he listened close enough.

"You made good time getting here," Magnus said, falling in step with Jack. Dorrie's cousin was heavily muscled but short. Entering the kitchen with the women, Magnus dropped the wriggly creature back into his arms.

"Once we let Jessica off, we made good time. The general is playing havoc with the media, so we tried to avoid cops," Jack said, accepting the burden, only to put the dog down again. "I wanted to make certain no one was following and took a few shortcuts."

"At what point do we inform officialdom that neither of the women lived or worked with their stepfather?" Magnus followed Nadine with his eyes as she settled her sister in with food and drink. They weren't talking important things—yet.

"We can't reveal where they're hiding until we take out the general, but the cops have been given a few anonymous reports about their circumstances to check out. Might take them a while. Beer?" Jack set the dog free again and indicated the refrigerator.

"Help yourself." Magnus leaned against the counter behind Nadine while the furry brown dog sniffed toes under the table. Nadine obviously didn't want him interrogating Vera the instant she arrived, but they didn't have time to waste.

"I knew you didn't think we should communicate," Vera was saying, "but when I sent code to all your usual places and you didn't answer, I was frantic. I had no idea that he'd locked you up!"

"I was just waiting until you graduated before I took off," Nadine replied with confidence. "It wasn't any different from working in his office."

Magnus figured she was lying through her pretty white teeth just to reassure her sister. Interesting. Maybe *he* was learning to read minds.

"I'm sorry. I know you wanted me to have a degree, but I just couldn't let the poor parents of those students keep on thinking the general was helping them! When I couldn't reach you, I had to do *something*."

"What students?" Magnus asked. He settled in to hear the rest of the story.

"Do we need to record this?" Conan asked, interrupting the damned story.

Magnus wanted to smack him, but grudgingly, he could see the point.

"Let the poor kid eat her lunch," Jack insisted. "We flew down here without stopping, and she needs to catch her breath."

Interesting that Jack took the girl's side instead of insisting that she be debriefed.

Nadine looked to Magnus, apparently catching this anomaly as well.

He shrugged. He didn't know Jack well. He looked like a mean pit bull. But Jack was feeding the dog before himself—probably on caviar, given the refrigerator's contents.

"Let's take our lunch and sit out in the sunroom and enjoy the day a bit," Dorrie suggested, picking up the platter of sandwiches.

Vera helpfully carried the tea pitcher, Jack lugged the dog, and Nadine fell back beside Magnus.

"Is recording Vera's story a good idea?" she asked. "Worrying about a recording falling into the wrong hands... makes it difficult to be open and honest."

"If we need evidence for lawyers, a recording might be good," he said, but he understood her concern. Score one for him. "But I guess lawyers wouldn't much like where you start talking about the weird bits."

"Exactly." She looked relieved. "Should it ever come to testifying, we'll do our part, but let's not go that far yet."

Magnus held out a chair for her near her sister, then strolled over to talk with Conan who was examining the music cabinet. "No recording," he announced without preliminary.

Conan didn't look concerned. "That's what Dorrie said. That means they want to talk weird."

"How do you deal with that?" Magnus asked, watching the women chatter excitedly. Jack had filled a plate and wandered off with the furry creature under his arm, apparently to find a TV if the sound of a game coming on in the other room meant anything.

"They do things that aren't scientifically explainable. That doesn't mean they aren't doing them," Conan replied. "I've never figured out how moving my desk and files around can help me, but funds have been rolling in ever since Dorrie did her feng shui shtick."

"That's because you're good at what you do," Magnus argued. "But that thing with Francesca and Nadine where they sat there sending numbers into space, that was just freaky."

"Let me know when she starts reading your mind and I'll stay away," Conan suggested.

"Big help, bro," Magnus said, punching his brother's shoulder.

Magnus drew a chair up near Nadine and waited. He was good at waiting. And listening—until he got what he wanted.

It didn't take long for Vera's story to start spilling out. Nadine might call herself an introverted nerd, but she wasn't shy, just painfully blunt.

Once she was out from behind her computer, she was a little *too* perspicacious. That gave Magnus food for thought about the painful reality of mind-reading and how it equated with the need to bury her head in the sand—or computer.

But she had a deft way of steering her sister in the right direction, and he preferred to concentrate on the now.

"I was student teaching in Irvine," Vera said to Nadine's inquiry. "One of our best, more intuitive students suddenly transferred to some obscure private school in the valley. We were all concerned because Raul was extremely sensitive and had just started coming out of his shell."

"Sensitive?" Nadine asked. "When you use *sensitive* and *intuitive,* are you saying he was alternatively gifted?"

Magnus wanted to snort at that euphemism for *just plain weird,* but he had to admit there weren't too many words for what the women did.

"I think so," Vera said uncertainly, "but it wasn't as if I could test him or explain to the other teachers. So I just went along with everyone else, learned what I could about his transfer, then started exploring independently."

"Good girl," Nadine said with approval. "What did you find out?"

"I found he'd been entered in the Joseph Academy for the Extraordinarily Gifted."

All other chatter stopped and all eyes focused on Vera—everyone in this room could be classified as *extraordinarily gifted* in some manner. In this past year, they'd learned that meant they were targets of the general. Tension escalated. Even Magnus, as dense as he knew himself to be, squirmed for the kid. But Nadine took her sister's hand and seemed to hypnotize her into not noticing their audience.

"Jo-jo?" Nadine asked encouragingly.

"I'm pretty sure," Vera agreed. "I'm not as good at research as you are, but the Academy filed the appropriate documents with the state, and I dug those out. Feng Po-po was listed as an administrator. So are all four of her sons."

"Feng Po-po is dead," Dorrie cried. "And so is her first son Feng Won. And second son Li should be back in jail!"

Nadine lifted a cautionary finger to silence her, then returned to stroking Vera's hand. "Only Jo-jo would know their names and their social security numbers and be able to forge the papers. I doubt the state checks death certificates or prison populations. So we know Jo-jo founded a school. The one where you sent the supplies?" she asked in sudden alarm.

"No, that was just a poor charter school I was working with. That came after I traced Raul to the Academy and moved into the Valley to investigate. I volunteered at the charter to see if I could make connections."

"Is that when you sent me an image of a classroom packed with students?"

Vera nodded. "I was shocked by how little they had. I didn't do it deliberately. I was running on scared by then, thinking about Raul and what could be happening to him, and I just kind of focused like you tried to teach me and ...blanked out."

"You did it just right. I got the message and knew you were alive. Until then, I'd been really worried. I was afraid the general had found you."

Vera shook her head. "As far as I know, he has no idea where I am or what I'm doing. But once I found out about the Academy, I had to look into it. I'm sorry, Nadine, I had to." She looked grave and focused on her sister. "After what we've seen... I'm afraid of what the general might be doing to those students."

Nadine held up her palm to slow her down. "Give us the facts first. We all understand the fear."

Vera nodded, then visibly sorted back to where she'd left off. "I used a little of our credit to buy the charter school some basic supplies," she said apologetically. "And then I realized I shouldn't be using the card if I was hiding. So I gave it to a friend to charge something far away in hopes that would muddy the trail."

"You did everything right," Nadine said soothingly. "The purchases let us hope you were alive and well and led us to you. Jo-jo doesn't know about the card, so he couldn't have tracked you easily. What else did you find out?"

"After I found the papers with the Feng names on them, I got a little panicky and tried reaching you. That was before I left school. I knew the papers had to have been filed by Jo-jo, but I had no way of knowing what he was doing with that school."

Magnus finally noticed that the girl had dark circles under her eyes and looked frail and stressed. He really was dense about people, but somehow, he was seeing Vera through Nadine's eyes, feeling her compassion for the sister who'd risked herself for her students. No woo-woo was involved in this connection, he assured himself. There was no one in his brain except himself. But he was starting to understand Nadine, read her body language, and she was worried. Which meant, so was he.

"When I couldn't reach you..." Vera closed her eyes and steadied herself while Nadine kept patting her hand. "I was terrified I really was on my own. And I remembered what he did to Mama and how he'd turned you into little more than a slave to his obsession, and I knew I had to do something. I simply couldn't keep playing safe."

Magnus ignored the questions in Conan and Dorrie's eyes, shook his head, and kept his attention on the sisters. He'd interrogated men before and hadn't cared one way or another if he'd caused them pain. This was different. This was very personal. And he hurt just listening. For the sisters, it had to be excruciating.

"I persuaded a friend to take me to Topaz for a weekend so I could just ask around a bit," Vera continued. "That's where the Academy is, way out in the Valley."

Topaz. Magnus made a mental note to look it up, but he assumed it was just another little desert town, population 500.

"And?" Nadine asked with a hint of impatience.

The unresponsive robot the general had created was starting to crack, Magnus realized with interest.

"And nothing," Vera said with a shrug. "The Academy is off the beaten track. The townspeople know nothing except that it occupies an old ranch. There's a bit of resentment that they apparently buy supplies elsewhere, but it's not as if the Topaz grocery keeps anything except dusty tin cans."

"So you decided to quit school, run off to a nowhere town, and *what?*" Nadine asked, definitely losing some of her cool.

Magnus started stroking Nadine's hand the way she'd stroked Vera's. "And scare Nadine out of hiding, right?" he asked the kid.

Vera shrugged her skinny shoulders. "I thought if Nadine was still alive, my leaving school would catch her attention, but mostly, I wanted to find some way of talking to those kids. I couldn't do it from the city. I tried. I went out there a few times on weekends, but I couldn't get close, and I was afraid someone in Topaz might notice me."

Magnus could practically feel Nadine forcing herself to relax. The woman practically vibrated with emotions.

How the devil had she kept all that steam pent up for so long?

"I need a map," Nadine announced. "How far were you staying from the Academy?"

"Victorville is about half an hour down the road." Vera tucked a stray strand of hair behind her ear and nibbled her sandwich worriedly. "When I was visiting Topaz on the weekends, I started feeling like someone was watching me. And then I was sure someone followed me from Topaz back to Irvine. I got nervous. I didn't have much money, but a friend had an empty house in Victorville. As long as I had to run anyway, it might as well be to do something useful."

Magnus squeezed Nadine's fingers and stepped in very carefully. "How did you hide in Victorville?"

"I was afraid to use my student name if someone really was tracking me. I made up a new name, only I couldn't get a job without ID. That's when I volunteered at the charter. I couldn't let Jo-jo torture sensitive little kids," she said anxiously, pleading for understanding with her eyes. "So I kept biking the trails around Topaz, hoping I'd learn something."

"And?" Nadine asked.

Vera rubbed her knuckles across her brow, then lifted her gaze to Nadine and Magnus. "I found a new grave in a creek bed near the Academy. It wasn't adult size."

Sixteen

Nadine couldn't believe teachers would kill kids, but she winced as the room exploded in outrage, both silent and vocal. She hadn't realized how *sensitive* she was to emotional assaults. She'd been insulated against them most of her life.

She'd been a *sensitive* kid. She'd blocked a lot of it—because her mother had shielded her from psychic trauma. Not until her mother was gone had she needed to hide behind computers. So many things would have made more sense had her mother lived!

Nadine squeezed her eyes shut and realized she was also squeezing Magnus's hand. In some manner, he shielded her, too. She wanted to lean into his big shoulder and make the world go away.

Her conscience wouldn't let her ignore children in trouble if she had the ability to save them. The world wasn't going away anytime soon.

"You reported the grave?" Magnus asked in that deep voice that resounded through Nadine's insides.

"To the police, anonymously," Vera said, voice wavering. "I've been living in terror ever since, not certain what to do. I've been afraid to go back to classes. I've not seen a word in the media about anyone discovering a grave. It was awfully near the school."

"He'll have tapped the local sheriff's office," Nadine said into the silence. "That's what Jo-jo does—surrounds his facilities with a network of phone tapping and computer hacking. If one of the teachers tweets a concern, he'll know about it—if his new IT person is as good as I am, anyway."

"Having that kind of information builds a stronger wall around the school than a fence," Conan said with a frown. "Of course, if the teachers discovered the surveillance, they could just drive away."

"He'll have security cameras near the school to see that happening," Nadine pointed out. "And if anyone knocks out the camera, he'll instantly have people blocking the road. The location was not chosen lightly."

"Yeah, once when Dorrie and I tried getting into Adams Engineering, security was all over us in seconds," Conan said with a degree of rue.

Nadine winced at the thought of either Dorrie or Conan being trapped in the general's sticky web. She hadn't meant for anyone else to get involved.

But she couldn't abandon these people who had helped her so much. They had no idea of the danger they were facing. Worse, she was starting to realize that—even though she couldn't shut down the general's network as she'd hoped— she might actually have insights that could help. And that she couldn't run forever.

She hated the idea. Just as she was starting to enjoy a taste of freedom, she felt trapped again. When would she ever escape to have her own life?

She shoved Mad Max's hand aside and stood up to pace the room.

Magnus rose with her. He opened the sunroom door, and she gravitated outside into the chilly sun. He threw the blanket still lying on the lounge chair over her shoulders.

"Stop hovering," she said crossly.

He leaned against the cabana and crossed his arms.

"The others won't follow me out here if you're here," she said aloud, grasping his purpose in hovering.

"No guarantees," he agreed. "But if I tell them to back off, they will. You've got to understand Dorrie's position. As far as she's concerned, the general and his sons have hunted her family, killed her mother, and nearly killed her. She wants the general strung up on a hot wire. And what Dorrie wants, Conan will provide. Adding that bit about the kid just gave them more reason to escalate the search."

"We don't know *anything*," Nadine asserted, just because she could.

"Totally agree," he said with annoying pragmatism. And then he waited.

Nadine wanted to bash him over the head with a lawn chair. "You're waiting for me to tell you what we need to do, aren't you?"

"Reading my mind," he said laconically.

She flung a pool noodle at him.

"There are probably balls and floats in the cabana. Want me to blow them up for you?" He flung the noodle into the heated pool.

She paced the fenced-in area, dodging chairs and umbrellas,

staying on the opposite side from Mad Max. The man made her crazy. Crazier. If he wasn't around, she'd grab Vera and run, she knew she would.

But like a mammoth boulder, he was there, and he wasn't going anywhere. And he was telling her he would stay by her side and support her in whatever she wanted to do.

He was putting her in charge, not telling her what to do.

That much freedom was damned scary. Oh crap. How did people do this?

She hugged her elbows, but the universe wasn't providing answers. Vera was frightened. Nadine knew that much. She had to protect Vera.

But her sister was a nurturer who needed a real life, one that involved finishing school, getting married, having pets and children, being happy. Could she do that in Costa Rica under an assumed identity? Provided Jo-jo hadn't learned the name they'd forged, because inventing a new passport wouldn't be easy without his network.

Damn, damn, and double damn.

"With your genius and Conan's team, you have the general trumped," Magnus reminded her.

"That depends on the quality of my replacement. Vera first," Nadine insisted. "We don't know if he's discovered her new identity or if she's just scared for nothing."

"All right, we'll start there. Dorrie's cousins are security experts. Conan has a detective team. If you have any suggestions of how to infiltrate the general's security, we can search his databases as well as doing whatever it is they need to do to check from Vera's end."

That's what he really wanted—access to the general. But now that she had Vera safe, Nadine no longer cared what they did to the menace. Her childhood hero had died long ago in her head. She was still wrestling with the shadow of the respectable military man left behind, but she was getting stronger. Ideas that her brain had suppressed had started surfacing.

She was afraid, but that didn't mean she should run and hide any longer, she realized, drawing a deep breath. Backbone—she needed to straighten her backbone and face reality.

"I've given Conan all the ISPs and passwords I can remember," she said, thinking her way through this new task, "If nothing has come of them, I doubt anything else I recall will help. Even the networks I accessed at Woodstar will have been changed by now. It's SOP. I hadn't counted on Jo-jo finding someone as good as I am."

They both digested that thought. Jo-jo had the names of every *extraordinarily gifted* person related to Nadine and every other California Malcolm. One of the names on that list could easily have her talents.

"One step at a time," Magnus reminded her. "We're safe here for a while. Let the others go to work. You and Vera catch up. You no longer have to do it all."

Nadine sagged. The burden she'd carried had been heavy, but without it, she had no purpose. Magnus crossed the tiles to wrap an arm around her waist, and she finally leaned into him.

"I'm afraid I'll become an empty, purposeless shell," she whispered.

He made an inelegant noise. "That's not possible. Your battery simply needs recharging. Let's fix margaritas and throw a remember-this-ISP party. I bet Vera can help."

The tension in the room was nearly visible when they returned. Even the dog leaped into Vera's arms to wait expectantly.

Nadine didn't have the necessary words to say she'd stay and help.

Magnus crossed the room, pulled down a large bottle of alcohol from a shelf behind a bar, and said, "Margaritaville."

For reasons beyond Nadine's comprehension, that broke the tension.

Magnus mixed drinks and watched as pens flew across paper and fingers across keyboards while Vera and Nadine attempted to summon all the names, databases, and server locations that they remembered in connection with Adams. Magnus figured he was no help in this. That was okay. He had been a bartender in college. Once they came up with places to look, he could knock down doors. Until then, he could mix drinks.

"Mr T needs to go outside. I'll be back in a minute." Vera stood and the dog leapt into her arms. She carried her pet toward the kitchen. Jack fell in step with her.

"Did you have pets when you were kids?" Magnus asked

Nadine, watching the pair depart.

"No, the general was allergic. We found a kitten once and hid it in the back yard, but it grew up and ran away." Looking for all the world like a stereotypical geek in her black-framed glasses, Nadine didn't look up from the flashing screens on her computer.

"Then maybe she's had a dog at college," Magnus decided, watching Vera through the window as she talked to the dog and set it free on a patch of lawn.

Dorrie looked at him oddly, then watched the window, too. "Didn't she say it was a stray she found in town? She certainly has a way with animals if she can make it obey after just a few days in her care. Yorkies are usually kind of hyper."

"Yeah, that's what I'm thinking, but I don't know much about dogs." Magnus chopped another lime and dropped the slices into the pitcher.

The Yorkie was gleefully leaping over Vera's outstretched arms, while normally dour Jack actually grinned at the performance.

Finally realizing the conversation had taken a strange turn, Nadine glanced up to see what they were talking about. She shrugged. "She told me earlier that her dog doesn't like fish but misses her fluffy toy. I guess she's just entertaining it like one would a kid."

Dorrie frowned.

Magnus opened the door and whistled. The dog didn't even glance his way. Jack did.

"Ask Vera what other tricks the dog knows," Magnus called.

Conan came to stand beside him while Vera lifted the fluffy animal and talked to it, nose-to-nose. "The dog had a tracer in its collar," Conan said quietly. "I didn't want to scare Nadine into running. Jack didn't have time to dispose of the collar properly, so he left it under some bushes. If we're lucky, some poor jerk will pick it up and put it on their animal."

Outside, Vera set the dog down, twirled her hand, and the Yorkie tumbled over, played dead, then leaped up to dance on its hind legs.

Magnus swore under his breath. "Remember what I told you about the chips the fucker planted in their heads?"

Conan cursed. He reached for the glass door, but Magnus steadied him, throwing a glance back to Nadine who was dividing her time between watching them and dumping data into the computer.

"Nadine's a hair's breadth from a meltdown. We can't drown the dog." Magnus turned to Dorrie. "How much do you know about dogs? Can they really do tricks like that for a new owner?"

"I have friends with Yorkies. They're high-strung. I've never seen them do anything they didn't want to do. That's about all I can tell you. Why? What's wrong?"

"I think she's talking to the dog," Magnus said, keeping his voice composed.

"Vera talks to chairs when she hasn't anything better to do." Nadine finally got up to see what they were watching. "Smart animal. I don't think we can get it through customs if we have to leave," she said with regret.

"No leaving," Magnus ordered, ruffling her hair but not holding her back. He was finally realizing he had to tread carefully with someone who had been held prisoner most of her life. "Jack," he shouted out the door, "we need to talk. Bring the circus back inside."

The Yorkie leaped on Jack at some command of Vera's. He caught the animal and tried to dodge licks as they returned to the house.

Conan took Mr T the instant they crossed the threshold. He checked behind the Yorkie's ears and sighed. "Microchip. Get Mr T to a vet. Have it scanned. Doubt it records the previous owner though."

"Microchip?" Nadine asked.

Magnus could almost feel her hysteria escalate.

Seventeen

"Microchip?" Nadine asked again, her voice an octave higher.

Magnus pressed his hand against her shoulder. That always seemed to steady her.

Jack cursed and slammed the heel of his hand against his head. "I should have looked, but I thought the collar was our tracer. Two on one animal? Overkill, much?"

"A microchip?" Vera asked timidly. "I didn't even think about those. I should have taken Mr T to a vet to find his owner?"

"There was a tracer in the collar," Magnus said as carefully as he could, hoping Vera wouldn't shut down, too. "We have no reason to think the general planted them. But if he did, it just means we can't use this place much longer. We'll have the microchip checked, and if it's a tracer, we'll plant it on a moving train, and proceed onward."

"I thought he was just a stray." Vera hugged the dog and started to sob into its coat.

Jack was about to launch into a diatribe, but Magnus held up his hand to stop him. Holding both Nadine's shoulders now so she didn't fly off the floor, he asked, "Why did you think Mr T was a stray?"

Vera looked a little embarrassed. "That's how he *felt,* lost and scared and lonely."

Magnus had to cover Nadine's mouth before she interrupted. She licked his palm but shut up. She seemed to be coming back down to earth if she had the poise to retaliate. He almost grinned, except these new developments had his brain spinning inside his skull.

"You were talking to Mr T out there, weren't you?" he asked. "Telling him what to do? Wouldn't that take a well-trained dog?"

Vera shrugged. "He's smart. I just told him what I wanted, and he did it."

Dorrie uttered a muffled cry and fell back on a plump leather sofa. "*She talks to animals.* Grandmother said she knew some of us could, but they were entertainers and beneath her notice."

Vera's eyes widened. Magnus released Nadine, figuring she now had a new discovery to distract her from the more dangerous one.

He didn't expect complete calm, but he hoped he'd averted hysterics.

"Fine. We'll look for zoos in Australia where you can work," were the first words to pass Nadine's lips.

Well, so much for averting hysterics. Interestingly, Vera's mouth developed a stubborn slant. And Jack finally intervened, taking the dog away.

"I'll get him to the vet. Once the chip is removed, you can have him back again. But we all need to get moving."

"It will take time for an intruder to find a way around the security here," Conan said, "but yeah, if anyone is following that microchip, we can't count on this as home base any longer. Vera, how do you feel about returning to school?"

Magnus retreated to the role of observer, waiting for the call to action. Nadine stiffened beneath his hand, but Vera wrinkled up her forehead in thought.

"I'd rather not leave Nadine," she said. "But I'd like to finish school."

Nadine practically deflated. Magnus rubbed the back of her neck. "We can do this," he told her. "Just think like the general and his minions. Make it work for us."

Nadine shook her head and wiped her eyes. "I want to believe you can keep her safe. I just can't. I can't lose her again."

"Even if the general's minions were suspicious of a teacher hanging out in Topaz, even if they followed her back to Irvine, they still don't know who she is or where she came from," Jack said.

Vera looked happier at that thought. "No one at school knows my real name," she pointed out.

Looking as if he had a plan, Conan joined in. "Even if the general's security got suspicious and planted a tracking device on the dog, that doesn't mean they know it's Vera who's been snooping around. That's just normal paranoia. Once we separate her from the dog, they'll relax and go away."

"I'll ask the vet to implant the chip in another stray," Jack suggested. "Then I'll take Vera back to campus. I know people there. We can find a new place, just in case she might have been followed to the old one.

Nadine kept shaking her head.

"I'll be fine, Nad." Vera squeezed the dog and pleaded with her big eyes as well as her words. "I'm a big girl now, and you don't have to watch over me. Find the old goat, get him locked up, and make certain those kids are okay, so I can finish school, and you can have a real life."

"Bait," Magnus suggested, needing to be useful.

Nadine scowled up at him. "I will not let Vera be bait."

"Nope, us."

"Not easy, bro," Conan objected. "Not too many places as secure as this."

Nadine rallied. "*We'll* be bait to draw attention away from Vera? That's easy. Jo-jo is obsessed with Malcolm abilities. All we have to do is pretend we're the proud Malcolm parents of a gifted child. He'll be all over us like bees on honeysuckle." She glared at Jack. "But you damned well better keep Vera under watch every second."

"I'll hide in plain sight, in class, under my assumed name," Vera insisted. "Even if Jo-jo cares about finding non-gifted me, which I bet he doesn't, my presence will divert some of his resources from you, right?"

"If he knows you—in any disguise—talk to animals, he'd have you training dogs to carry missiles into battle," Nadine argued. "You'd better find a new home for Mr T."

"She's probably right about that, babe," Jack said with regret. "I'll leave the dog with one of my nieces until this is over."

Nadine blinked at Jack's familiar tone, wanting to smack the man for talking to her baby sister like that. But Vera lit up like an approving woman, not a child, and Nadine sighed. Her baby sister wasn't a baby any longer. "Life is hell," she muttered.

"Yeah, tell me about it." Magnus massaged her neck again.

He was getting too damned good at pushing her buttons. She slanted him an angry look. "I thought you didn't know anything about people, that all you want is a direction so you can pound someone like a post?"

"Doesn't mean I can't think life is hell. Conan, you better get your bride back to Oz's fortress. We don't want anyone following you. You should have enough info to keep you busy for a while, right?"

"Not that I'll get anything done inside the fortress while the women run around with flowers and lace," Conan grumbled. "I was really hoping we could stay here."

"Then stay here and confuse anyone who comes looking," Magnus suggested.

"No way," Dorrie countered. "I'm needed back at the house until the wedding is over. Get rid of the general and let us have the place afterward."

"Nadine and I will head out..." Magnus quit massaging her neck and gave her a look that said his inventive brain had just kicked into gear. "Proud Malcolm parents? How do we do that?"

"We start with the Malcolm genealogy website, of course," she said, stepping away from his proprietary hold. She was shaken and confused, and right now, he wasn't helping. "That website stays in place, even if they've changed servers, and I can no longer hack the back door. I don't need to hack it. All we have to do is go in the front door like any clueless parent and enter our names as related to the Malcolm family. It's pretty straight forward. We start chatting about our gifted child on the site's sticky chat room, and the general's minion will have bugs in our computers and our address monitored before nightfall. It's how we found all of you, even if indirectly."

Fighting fear and a need to weep or rage, Nadine dropped back to her seat, put her glasses on, and began punching her keyboard.

The men all hit their phones, arranging safe transportation and new accommodations. Vera subsided quietly into a corner with her dog.

Vera talked to animals? Her sister had a Malcolm talent, just as the general had hoped. He just hadn't offered Vera the opportunity to explore the world and discover it. There was a lesson in that, should Nadine live to think about it.

"The chi in here is very positive," Dorrie whispered as she picked up glasses on the table beside Nadine. "If you can, send me a diagram of the next place you stay. I will tell you the wards you need for protection."

Feng shui sounded like supernatural silliness like astrology to Nadine, but she'd freaked out the general enough times to know that what others considered impossible was possible.

"You said you could read the general's mind?" Magnus asked a little later. He was frowning and studying the security on the family room window.

Nadine shrugged. "Mostly, I just knew what he wanted before he said it. We worked together pretty closely."

"Like Radar on *MASH* knowing what the officers needed before they did?" he asked. At her quizzically raised eyebrow, he sighed. "I'll buy you the DVD for Christmas, call it cultural history. But you can't really know what he's thinking right now?"

"Not easily. It would help if I knew where he was so I could focus in that direction. It helps even more if he's in the same room. He radiates intense brain waves. If I can see what he's doing—even if I'm just following his car on a GPS, I'd come closer to getting inside his head."

"We need to work on that, then. I was thinking... if he's tracked the dog here, we may lure him out better if we stay." Magnus continued his inspection of the windows and doors while everyone else in the room stared at him.

"Here?" Nadine inquired when no one else did.

"If we're to be bait, what better place?" Magnus headed for the next room. "Security is damned tight. Who owns this place, a drug mogul?"

"Film star," Conan answered, following him. "Same difference. You aren't really thinking of setting yourselves up as a target, are you?"

Nadine and Dorrie trailed in their wake. Vera and Jack kept at their on-line search for student housing.

"Think about it—Nadine and I could stay here and pretend to be wealthy parents with an exceptional child. We register the fictional kid on the general's genealogy site, looking for more gifted family members. We chat and ask about the Academy. The bug from the website will see us researching the school."

"That's how he found Oz's kid," Nadine pointed out. "Jo-jo's obsession with the Malcolms is his Achilles heel. He has someone check out every new entry on the family tree. He has researchers trace their ancestry when a new person enters their name. He has people who do nothing but study your families and calculate what extraordinary abilities they might have. They follow the discussions in the website chat rooms, looking for people who talk about their gifted children."

Magnus nodded approvingly. "We make up a fictional Malcolm identity, chat about how our kid bends spoons or whatever, and his people will pounce. If the general sends scouts to check us out, what's he going to find? He can't get past neighborhood security. He'll have to either try to lure us out or make an appointment to meet us in person. People who live in places like this won't accept talking with anyone except the owner of the Academy."

"Jo-jo usually doesn't deal directly with his victims, but he spies on them when he has the chance," Nadine said, puzzling out details. "If we make the fictional kid look really good and make Jo-jo feel secure, he might take the bait. He'll like this place."

"What will you do if the general shows up at the guardhouse?" Dorrie asked.

"He'd have to make an appointment, and we'd be waiting for him," Magnus said with assurance.

Nadine could drive a space shuttle through that logic, but she bit her tongue. She was starting to grasp the advantage of staying in one place and having Jo-jo make the first move.

"He'll trace the dog here," Conan argued. "Won't that look suspicious?"

Magnus shrugged. "Just means we performed due diligence by checking out the school first. If we picked up a stray in the process, it means nothing."

Vera looked up eagerly. "Then Nadine could keep Mr T with her?"

Nadine could think of a dozen reasons why this was all wrong, but if the goal was to lure the general away from Vera... It might work, if she just didn't think being blown up was a bad thing.

"Wealthy people would take a stray to the vet," Magnus said. "The vet would check out the microchip. Let's start there. I don't want to be watching our backs and a dog, too."

Well, at least the dog would be safe.

Eighteen

"I think we ought to find some way of making certain those kids are unharmed," Nadine insisted out of the clear blue sky.

Itching to be on the road, knowing he was stuck here baiting the damned trap, Magnus nearly dropped the glass he held when Nadine spoke his thoughts aloud.

"Yeah, and we need to dig scientists out of underground bunkers, too," Magnus retorted, irritated that everyone else was leaving while he had to sit on his hands. "World peace after that."

She was across the kitchen loading glassware into the dishwasher and could do no more than glare at him. "They're helpless children!"

"Nadine and I survived," Vera said pragmatically, accepting the dog's farewell lick before handing it over to Conan to take to a vet. "We have no way of knowing what was in that grave. I was behind trees when I saw it, but we'd have to go into the open area near the school for a closer look. If we go in like storm troopers, people might get hurt. Jo-jo's teachers were hard-nosed, but I can't believe any teacher would torture a kid."

"What if I can find out what kind of security they have at the school?" Nadine insisted. "If I can take it down, can we go in?"

"On what basis?" Magnus asked, unable to believe he was actually interested. He was all for storming the school and bunkers, getting everyone out, and smashing the general into tarpaper, but even he knew the down side of that. "We have no legal right to do anything. We have no evidence of wrongdoing."

Nadine twirled a curl around her finger—a certain sign that she was ready to go ballistic. Magnus crossed the room, crushed her hand in his, and dragged her toward the pool. If he could do nothing else, he could keep La Loca out of trouble. "Say good-bye. We're going for a swim."

"I am *not* going for a swim. I need to get back to the computers." She tried to shake him off.

"Send those items I requested," Magnus told Conan, pretending Nadine hadn't said anything. Keeping her safe meant plugging his ears and going la-la-la so he didn't fall into her tempting traps. "I'll enhance the house's security in payment for our use of the place."

"Will do." Conan saluted while eyeing them with interest. "Need chains and handcuffs?"

Dorrie pinched her computer genius fiancé's arm and turned toward Magnus. "We'll use your fake ID and this address at the vet's. I assume if the general picks up on the microchip, he'll have people down here soon enough. Enjoy yourselves while you can."

"I'll be fine, Nadine," Vera said more softly, reacting to Nadine's furious struggles to escape Magnus's hold. "Really. Luring the general is what we need most, and you know his triggers better than anyone. Once he's out of the way, the experts can handle the school situation. By next week, maybe, this will all be over and you can come visit me."

Magnus let Nadine go long enough to hug her sister, but he didn't let her out of his sight. He'd been around her long enough to know that by now, she was a walking IED.

The instant the door closed on their guests, Nadine made a break for her computer.

Magnus blocked her way. "Let's try the Jacuzzi before all hell breaks loose. There isn't anything else you can do that we haven't already tried."

"There has to be *something*," she insisted, practically jumping up and down. "We can't just sit here like bumps on a log."

"Want me to drive over and spray the school with automatic fire?" he asked with just an edge of frustration. "You can't be everywhere at once. We have to prioritize, and catching the general is our first task. Just because it doesn't involve your computer, doesn't mean what we're doing isn't important. Just be happy that you're free now to do it. Enjoy this brief space where no one is pressuring us."

"You're a fine one to talk." She spun around and headed for the door to the pool, then halted. "I don't own a bathing suit."

"And? That matters how?" Magnus quirked an eyebrow.

Her eyes widened. Magnus appreciated the mercurial swiftness of her mood change as she realized what he meant. Accepting the challenge, she raced out to the heated pools. They steamed in the chilly air. She eyed the smaller one, found the buttons for turning on the jets, and smiled in delight.

Without an ounce of hesitation, she stripped down to her

underwear, tested the water, and slid in. "Ohhh, I want one of these!"

Magnus eyed her breasts bobbing on top of the water, visible through the sheer fabric, and agreed wholeheartedly. If he ever had a house, it needed a Jacuzzi. Following her example, he stripped to his knit boxers and eased in slowly so as not to splash her. "It pays to take an occasional time out."

"To think things through?" she suggested.

"Was that a jab?" he asked without anger. "I do what needs doing when the opportunity arises. Until then, I wait."

She ran her toes up his leg—not far enough. "So, you're not thinking things through? You're just sitting there, steaming yourself?"

"Pretty much," he agreed, reaching for the clasp of her bra. "Steaming, definitely."

"You see yourself as a mechanic, a man of action, not competing with your brainy brother," she concluded as her bra drifted away. "Using your hands does not preclude thought."

"Action works for me," Magnus agreed, unruffled by the comparison. "Did you decide to be a nerd because your sister is more outgoing?"

She splashed her foot but the jets caused more commotion than her small toes. "I'm an introvert. Look up the psychology sometime. I like computers that don't require small talk. I'm energized by being alone. Everyone gravitates toward things they're good at."

"And avoids what they're bad at. Case closed." Magnus ran his foot up her thigh, coming much closer to his target than she had.

"Mind closed," she accused. "That's what happened to Jo-jo, I'm betting. Po-po died tragically. He closed down his grief and focused all his energy on her work, without considering consequences. Obsessive, like you."

"If we're doing petty psychology—you're trying to insult me and push me away because you're afraid to get close to anyone." His toe brushed the slip of silky fabric between her thighs.

She retaliated by wrapping both her legs around his and casually stroking his thigh with her foot. The erotic jolt nearly brought him out of the water.

"If we can't find Jo-jo and stop him, I have to leave the country," she said while his mind evaporated. "What's the point in getting close? Besides you just want sex."

She damned well had that right. "If the sex is good, why not?" He slid deeper so her toe could reach his burgeoning erection. Even hot water couldn't steam the starch out, but he wanted her enough to take his time. "Did I hurt you last night?"

"Yeah, a little," she agreed, apparently incapable of dishonesty. "Sex is probably another of those things I'm not good at."

Max blew a sigh of exasperation. "You know prodigies who are good at everything the first time?" Oops, he probably shouldn't have revealed his conclusions since she hadn't mentioned her inexperience. He waited for fireworks of denial.

Nadine didn't even blink. "Sex takes practice?" she asked in disbelief.

Max dug his fingers into the side of the pool to prevent reaching for her. Wet, her dyed hair clung to her fragile skull, accenting softly rounded cheekbones and high forehead. He tried to focus there and not on all the pale, lush curves beneath the water.

"Even animals require practice," he told her, applying more pressure with his foot until she squirmed. "What we had last night was a thousand times better than most couples ever achieve. We're good together."

Her big green eyes widened in the fading light. "Really? I mean, it was worth the pain and all, but I just don't see the need to repeat it."

He nearly expired of the pain knowing he'd hurt her... and fearing he'd never have her again. Then he worried that he was in over his head if he wanted her this much. This was why he was lousy at relationships. He was clueless.

"Go easy, and there's no pain," he promised, remembering why doing was better than thinking. "All you have to do is tell me to stop, and I'll adjust my position. Or you can adjust yours. Practice. Like learning to fly a plane."

He thought he might internally combust just talking and not doing, especially when she was looking at him as if he'd just offered her the world's biggest chocolate cake. With raspberry ice cream on top.

"It's just mechanics?" she asked, climbing to her knees, her breasts rising above the water like ripe grapefruit.

She'd said she was good with mechanics. "Mechanics, yeah."

Magnus couldn't resist cupping a dripping breast.

She purred and crawled up his leg, letting him caress both breasts. "Teach me."

"Oh, yeah." Cupping and caressing, he encouraged her to lean forward so he could kiss her. She tasted of honey and sunshine and something deep, urgent, and sensually sinful.

He was in danger of needing her too much.

She caught on to the eroticism of tongue play quickly. She almost undid his formidable restraint with a slow, exploratory probe. He encouraged her with his hands, cupping her butt, lifting her closer, and claiming her mouth until they were both mindless.

"Can you teach me in here?" she murmured, running her hands over his chest, locating his over-sensitized nipples.

Magnus ripped off her panties in reply.

Just in time, he remembered condoms. He reached for his jeans, soaked them fumbling with the pockets, while she continued kissing and teasing. She nipped his shoulder, and he finally located the foil packet.

"Boy Scout," she murmured approvingly, leaning down to kiss his chest while he yanked off his briefs and threw them out of the pool. "Be prepared. Take care of others."

"Obsessive," he growled, donning the latex with difficulty while ripe bare flesh squirmed above him.

She laughed low in her throat and continued exploring with her mouth.

He stroked between her thighs, and she cried out loudly enough to set coyotes howling. He didn't stop stroking.

"Oh, yes, I like that. How do I do that to you?" And she proceeded to explore where he needed her touch.

Magnus thought he might expire of relief and need at the same time. "You are the most amazing woman I've ever known." He meant it. He wasn't given to charming compliments. He took her hand and showed her how to stroke him. Her touch alone had him hard and ready. Her cupping and squeezing nearly brought him out of the pool.

He suckled her breasts in return. That was all the incentive she seemed to need to dare lowering herself over him.

"We just don't fit," she murmured in disappointment, rocking back and forth against his tip.

"Mechanics." He licked her ear, caressed her erect nipple, and adjusted his position slightly, so he was just inside her. She was as slick and wet inside as out. "Keep moving. It's okay. I can't break."

"Oh..." She squirmed until he was a little deeper. "...my..." She shifted until she'd taken more of him. "...ohhhh!" She sank onto him fully with a sigh of awe.

He needed no more encouragement than that. Satisfying her breasts until she rocked demandingly against him, Magnus grabbed her bottom, pushed, and she responded by taking him all the way. He pulled back, thrust again, and she eagerly met him.

Barely holding back, he let her lead, let her find her own release. With a cry of enlightenment, she contracted around him, rocking with the intensity of her orgasm. Taking advantage of her abandonment, he thrust high and hard, guiding her to another level of release before he finally and at long last surrendered his restraint. He exploded inside her so hard and fast that it left him lightheaded.

She collapsed against his chest, half-sobbing, and let him hold her.

"That took thought," she whispered below his ear. "Don't tell me otherwise."

"Action, baby," he muttered. "I'm all about the action."

She poked his side as he lifted her from the pool. "You're just too stupid to know what thought is."

Magnus laughed.

Nineteen

Moonlight poured across the bed from the French doors of the balcony. Restlessly, Nadine curled her arm across Max's muscled chest and crossed her leg over his big thigh. He snored lightly and cuddled her closer.

She took every opportunity he offered to savor the fascination of flesh against flesh. She hadn't been this close to another human since infancy, and she needed to explore the experience.

He was rough and hard all over, with bristles on his jaw and crisp curls on his chest, and scars in mysterious places. She might never have another chance to know a man like this, and that saddened her, but she was thrilled to find one who *understood* her as Magnus did. Maybe she was a machine after all, and that's why he got her.

They'd had beautiful, miraculous sex again when they'd finally made it to bed.

Despite losing her mind several times, sex wasn't enough to quiet her brain—or her roiling emotions.

She wanted to smack Magnificus Magnus for opening her up to sensations she'd never experienced—and might never experience again. She wanted to kiss him all over in gratitude. She'd never suffered such internal turmoil and didn't know how to handle it.

Thinking was simpler than *feeling*. Lucky man if he didn't have to think or feel.

She unraveled from the cocoon of blankets, arms, and legs, and inched to the far side of the bed. She'd never shared a bed before. Maybe that wasn't helping. Magnus rolled over on his side and returned to snoring.

The air was chilly as she tumbled out. She pulled on one of his big shirts and her hoodie and jeans. Locating her laptop in the dark, she carried it downstairs to the room with the gas fireplace. She turned on the logs and settled on pillows in front of the fire.

She checked the news sites to see how hard the police were searching for her.

Interesting. Apparently someone—possibly Oz with his media connections—had tipped off journalists. While the police reported they'd been unsuccessful in locating the two missing young women, reporters informed their readers that the stepfather of the missing women was unavailable for comment.

Looked like news conferences with the police had become a question and non-answer session about the secretive general. Apparently Jo-jo had used his Palm Springs address to report the crime, and journalists had staked out the estate—without success.

Surprise, surprise, their neighbors told the reporters they hadn't realized anyone even lived in the house. They'd thought it was someone's holiday residence. Perfectly logical since even the few days he was there, he spent underground.

Her stepbrothers—who were old enough to be her middle-aged uncles—remained taciturn when caught and faced with questions. Feng Chang stuck to the party line and said Nadine was a loyal worker and happy family member who would never run away. Feng Jin hinted that she was a dangerous lunatic who needed to be found before she harmed herself or someone else. Neither said much about Vera. They barely knew Vera existed since she had no gift and had never worked with them.

The news reports were starting to cast doubts on the existence of the general's daughters. But the cops were still looking for them, which was what mattered.

Nadine dug a little deeper, hacked a few news bureaus just to see how far they might go in trying to locate Jo-jo to get a story out of him. Would he hurt reporters? Stupid question. He didn't differentiate between intruders.

One industrious journalist had matched a license plate number to the general's Escalade from the time he'd been at the police station. Someone had spotted the SUV at the Palm Springs estate just yesterday. The reporters hadn't verified the general was in it, but Nadine knew the possibility was good. He liked his chauffeured limo. He was arrogant enough not to feel particularly threatened yet. He'd want to keep in touch with the police if he hoped to find her.

Excellent! She could work with that.

She called up the Palm Springs address on Google Earth so she could focus on the image of the house that paranoia had built. Jo-jo had places all around the country, but Palm Springs was his favorite because of the underground passages. She hadn't let Magnus know that. He'd get himself blown up trying to get in.

Even with telescopic lenses, reporters couldn't see beyond the security walls or trees to catch a good photo. Neither could Google. But satellite photos gave her rooflines.

Sitting cross-legged in front of the computer screen showing images of the house, Nadine opened her mind to the universe. The news quotes she'd just read filtered through the space she emptied inside her head. Her gaze rested on the computer image of the roof, but her inner eyes sought beneath the tiles.

Was Jo-jo there? She called up a mental vision of the tall, iron-gray-haired man who had dominated her life. He seemed diminished somehow, compared to the vibrant strength of Magnus. Her fear of him had lessened over the years. So had her admiration. Now, with distance, she could better see beyond his military strictness to the confused man inside—the vulnerable man he hid with his shouts and blusters.

The man whose mind she could read.

She pushed past the frightening image Francesca had given her of the uniformed general in full rage. She ignored the long-ago ones of a father taking his children for ice cream. She concentrated on the obsessive workhorse she'd seen in the office—signing papers, on the phone, ordering men about. That man with the closed heart distrusted everyone. That was the center of his paranoia.

She no longer saw the computer screen but the basement library where Jo-jo locked himself. He was an insomniac. Even at this hour, he worked through reports, making notes, the kind of notes she had to transcribe the next morning.

She could see his hand tremble as he scrawled it across the page. *He was there*! She was inside his head!

Don't think. Don't blink. Just listen.

Fury washed over her. Frustration. Weariness and a hint of the grief that always clung to him. And under it, deep down, the confusion and fear, the muddled senses that she'd never understood but could always read.

He was lost without anyone to trust, without Po-po, and now, without Nadine. She'd been his right hand since her mother's death, the filter between him and the modern world. Here was the pathetic soul of the real man buried beneath the façade of authority.

As she'd tried before, Nadine attempted to steer his inner vision to Chang, the son who craved his respect. Fearing competition and loss of power, the general resisted. He turned away from the photo of Chang standing proudly in his Marine uniform to scribble notes on paper. Paper, when he had a keyboard right beside him.

Could she see what he was writing? Would it be worth the effort?

She narrowed her focus more, following his hand. She might be the only person alive who could read his execrable shorthand. The link between his hand and mind strengthened, drawing her in deeper.

Fury drove his hand but it was fear driving the fury.

Tap vet. Survey house—stlt? Need inside. Find Oswin.

A phone rang. The pen dropped. Authority replaced fear.

Nadine woke with a pounding headache. The fire still artificially flickered. A screensaver played over the laptop. She wanted paper to write on. Wait...

She picked up the computer and hastily typed everything she recalled from her "dream." When she typed *Find Oswin*, she gulped. Which one?

Troubled, she padded into the kitchen and located a cocoa mix.

Wearing shorts, Magnus sleepily joined her as she poured the mix into a mug of boiling water.

"Want some?" she asked, holding up the box.

He grimaced. And waited. Unlike Jo-jo's blustery menace, Maximus Grandus was very good at intimidating with silence.

"I couldn't sleep," she said defensively. "I can't just do nothing and live in limbo."

He snorted. "You've been living in limbo your entire life. Now you have some control and you want to wield it."

"Quit psychoanalyzing me. You're bad at it." She set the steaming mug on the table and sat down. "Go back to bed."

He opened the refrigerator, found a milk carton, lifted it to his mouth, then caught himself and hunted for a glass. "So, how did you decide to solve your restlessness?"

"Better question." She rubbed her forehead. "By giving myself a headache, mostly."

He sat down across from her. And waited.

"I've been bullied by the best, Oswin," she told him, glaring. "You can't do it with silence."

"That's the first time you've used my last name, so you

remember it. Were you looking us up?"

He looked deliciously rumpled with a pillow crease through the dark bristles of his unshaven jaw. He had just the hint of a curl on his forehead where the barber hadn't trimmed off everything. He must usually get it cut every week to keep it straight, and he hadn't had time lately.

"I know your name," she told him. "I looked you up long ago. The general has entire files on you because of the experimental helicopter. Your brothers, not so much. When he writes *Find Oswin*, I'm betting he means you. I know how his mind works."

"And he wrote this when?" he asked, quirking an eyebrow but offering no judgmental tone.

"Tonight. He doesn't sleep much. I found him the untraditional way." Nadine blew on her cocoa and closed her eyes, trying to shovel all of Jo-jo's paranoia and rage out of her head.

Max's silence was a bit more explosive this time. Interesting. She couldn't get inside his head, but maybe she had some of Dorrie's energy perceptiveness. Her mother hadn't taught her about chi energies as Dorrie's mother had.

"If I were the kind of person to push buttons, I'd start pushing yours now just to break the silence and see if you chime," she said, sipping her hot drink. "Talking would be easier."

She could almost hear him rearranging words inside his head. Act and not react, nice.

"You saw your stepfather tonight?" he asked with that beautifully deceptive calm.

"I got inside his head, yup. Wanta make something of it?"

"I don't think I even know how. What else did you think you saw?"

"Nice, Max. *Think I saw*. Way to work around it."

He rubbed his weary eyes, and Nadine took pity on him. She was, for all he knew, a nut case.

"I *saw* him writing notes to himself. I wrote them down on my computer." She pushed the laptop toward him. "In the morning, he'll tell his new assistant to follow through. I hope his assistant is as good at translating as I am. STLT probably means satellite surveillance."

She waited as Magnus scrolled through her very brief notes, including the ominous *Find Oswin* memo.

"We expected him to follow the microchip to the vet," he said. "That memo could have come from your subconscious. I'm on your mind, so my name showed up."

Nadine shrugged. "Anything is possible. It's not as if we can prove God or the Universe exists or that we're not a microcosm on a piece of dandelion fluff. You just take what you see and go for it. I saw Jo-jo write those notes."

"He didn't mention sending drones to check us out," Max said, pushing the laptop back at her.

"Humor, har har." Nadine shut the screen. "Don't laugh. He has satellite access. If he sees what looks like me or you or a telescope or anything else of interest in the back yard, he can send in drones. Do not underestimate his insanity."

"It's not as if he'll see suspicious activity. There's no blazing sign on the roof saying *trap*. He gets our fake names and address from the website. His minions can't match name to address, so he has to send someone to check us out, but they can't get in, so they spy from a distance. They see us go in and out. Maybe we wear hats so they can't catch our faces. If we're to pretend we have a kid, we may have to stay inside so he doesn't know we're here—because I'm not dragging a kid into this."

She nodded agreement to all his assumptions. Military men thought in logical orders, she got that.

Encouraged, he continued, "Since as far as the general knows, Magnus Oswin is out in the Sierras or under the sea, how will he expect his assistant to find me?"

"He'll start with the usual: credit cards, phone calls. He'll check your regular contacts. Then they'll start following everyone you know. I'm sure he's done a lot of that already and the note is just frustration. He's not happy. If you really think we're safe, shall we start creating a kid?"

When Magnus jerked back, disconcerted, Nadine grinned. "Gotcha. I mean inventing our fictional kid to post as bait on the website. If you want Jo-jo and not his minions, we have to invent a target juicy enough to draw him out personally. He's not likely to bother looking for *you* himself."

"Where is he?" Mean Max asked in a growly voice, ignoring her snub to his importance.

"What difference does it make?" She shrugged and sipped her

cocoa. "By tomorrow, he could be hundreds of miles away. Even if he stays where he is, you can't go in without blowing up half the neighborhood and yourself. As you told me, our only hope of getting our hands on him is to draw him out, preferably, draw him here. Think in terms of the leader of a third world country, and you're coming close to the level of difficulty of reaching the general. And third world countries don't have the money and technology that Jo-jo does."

Magnus rubbed his bristly jaw. "If I knew where he was, I could have Bo take out the helicopter..."

"No," Nadine said firmly, looking him square in the eyes. "No, no, and no. You do not go after him on his own ground. Bad tactics and dangerous to too many people."

"And you really think he's stupid enough to fall for bait like a kid that doesn't exist?" Magnus asked with anger flaring.

"Not stupid, obsessed. He's looking for the impossible. We just need to give it to him."

Twenty

Magnus closed his eyes against the relentless ball of energy who held his goal in her hands, hands that had tormented him with pleasure just hours ago. Nadine's hair had dried in a halo of brown curls. She was still wearing her geek glasses and ridiculous clothes, but he saw the brilliant flame of the woman beneath. The Librarian—unplugged.

He wasn't certain that she saw herself as he did—an intelligent woman with immense potential to save the world. She still clung to the fantasy of the father she'd never known—not the deadly danger the general represented, the danger Magnus intended to apprehend.

Normally, he'd admire her fierce loyalty.

Normally, he wouldn't roll across a mattress with the object of his interrogation. She was seriously messing with his head.

"All right, let's create a child," he growled, still wobbly from her little joke. Creating children was pretty much the last thing he wanted to do, but there for a moment... He shut out that weakness. "A nine-year old whose mother is too controlling."

She laughed, and he opened his eyes again. Cocoa froth coated her upper lip. Magnus resisted the urge to lick it. Fortunately or not, she did it herself, and he had new fantasies about that talented tongue.

"A little girl with orange curls and a penchant for finding lost objects," she added. "Jo-jo has been hunting for a finder for years."

"Yeah, every cop under the sun would like one of those. Does she find people, too?" *Orange curls*—he was already imagining an impish kid with curls and green eyes.

He could never be a family man. He didn't have what it took.

"Sure, why not?" she said with a verbal shrug, typing their description into the laptop. "I haven't seen my mother's or Po-po's journals, but I'm betting there was some reference to an ancestor who could find valuable objects, at least. People are valuable, so why not find people? I think the kid's bad at math, though. Maybe she likes looking more than studying."

"Do you know if the general still has those journals?" Magnus asked, hoping to distract himself with ulterior motives.

"He'll have Po-po's. They were filled with her scientific findings and experiments. I'm pretty sure he kept my mother's recent ones and may have even hid the ones from before the house burned. I have no proof though." She sipped her cocoa with her forehead screwed up in thought.

"If we can get inside the general's homes, we could look for the journals," he suggested. "Does he have cleaning services?"

"Cut it out, Oswin," she retorted. "We're drawing him out, not going in, or I'll just head for Australia now and let you blow yourself up. That won't help those kids any."

"And I'm supposed to believe that this megalomaniac will personally show up to interview a nine-year-old kid? Why can't we try this both ways?"

"One, because I have no good reason to trust your men. Two, because the instant I give you any info, you'll lock me up for safety and take off on your own, and I'll have to kill you. Three, because I don't want anyone to get hurt. We either do it my way or not at all."

"Diminutive dictator."

"Trained by the best," she agreed without rancor.

Magnus ran his hand over his head. She was probably right on all three counts. That didn't mean it shouldn't be done his way. He simply wasn't accustomed to someone who stayed three steps ahead of him. "So we're supposed to just sit here, making up tall tales, while kids could be in danger?"

"Yup," she replied complacently. "I've seen your brothers in action. You can't guilt me. Where is our kid going to school?"

She was perfectly right. Since Oz's kid had been stolen, Conan had become all about saving kids. His team was already surrounding the Academy, looking for ways to infiltrate. The kids were about as safe as they could be. Frustrated, Magnus dragged the computer over to his side of the table. "She'll need a birth date and social security number."

"She's attending a private boarding school because we travel a lot," she added with relish.

"You're a rotten mother, not a controlling one, then. A poor kid with finding gifts needs understanding." He sent Conan the specs for setting up a new ID.

She smiled in delight. "Spoken like a good father. That's why you're asking about special schools, and all I'm doing is checking our genealogy. Jo-jo may relate better to another man. How did we find out about his school?"

"Cousin," he replied. "More potential victims."

They settled into peaceful give-and-take until Nadine started yawning. Magnus escorted her upstairs, offered to let her sleep alone so she might sleep better, and appropriated the computer without her noticing.

Back in his own room, he inspected the history of her searches and found the news sites. Damn, but she was good—and he wasn't. He sent the information to Conan and returned her laptop to her room.

Using his own computer, he drew up a few preliminary sketches for the additional security he planned for their safe house, and hit the bed. He hoped this time he might sleep instead of dreaming of a vivacious female who craved his body and nothing more.

In the morning, they both dragged down to breakfast late. Magnus blearily prepared coffee. Nadine poured orange juice and went outside to dance in the sun. Dance.

Magnus blinked and studied her crazed moves with interest. She wore shorts, a tank top, and some see-through shirt that revealed her every curve—and an earplug. Absolutely nothing was sacred to that woman. He was going to owe their landlord a fortune.

It was worth every penny to see her pagan sun ritual or whatever it was.

He tried to muse on freedom and how the lack of it had affected her, but he preferred enjoying his coffee and the show. Nadine's fluid movements marked her as a natural dancer.

"I had a message from Vera," she said with joy when she returned to the kitchen. "She's surrounded by Jack's friends and relatives and being escorted everywhere around campus. One of them is driving over to the vet's today to pick up the dog. They removed the microchip and threw it out. I love communication!"

Magnus loved watching the Librarian unfurl like a new rose. He suspected more than lust was driving him when he pictured taking her to Conan's wedding and dancing until dawn.

He knew he was in serious trouble after breakfast when he agreed to teach Nadine how to drive around the private streets of the gated community. She jumped up from the computer and excitedly planted a kiss on his cheek. "You are a man among men!"

She ran off to find shoes while he sat there, wondering what had just happened.

Standing beside the ratty rental car, Nadine impatiently held her hand out for the keys.

"I knew how to take a car apart and put it back together before I was old enough for a driver's permit," Magnus told her, not giving her what she wanted.

He stood there in his bad-boy black t-shirt pulled taut over spectacular pecs, looking all military gruff and authoritative. Only the palm leaf dancing above his head kept her from kicking him.

How could he make beautiful love to her at night and turn into King Kong during the day?

"You expect me to take a rental car engine apart?" she asked in incredulity. "I can't even open the car door without keys!" She rattled the locked handle.

"You could if you knew the mechanics. It's useful information should you lose your keys." Relenting, he pushed the electronic lock button so she could slide into the driver's seat.

Nadine smiled in satisfaction at the array of dials and waited for him to climb into the passenger seat. "I once tried to persuade the chauffeur to teach me. Jo-jo instantly had extra security installed on the garage so I couldn't even get near the cars. Don't hold me captive, Maximator."

With an exaggerated sigh, Magnus handed her the keys. "Guilt works. So he doesn't actually live underground?"

Nadine snatched the keys and inserted them into the ignition. "A normal person would have asked how it felt to be trapped in an office all day with no other entertainment. Most of the time, I worked in damned basements and couldn't even see out. That's underground enough for me. And no, I'm not telling you where."

The dials lit up when she turned the key. "Freedom," she murmured in relief. "Thank you."

"So, essentially you've been locked up in a loony bin most of your life, with no chance of being normal."

Nadine shot him a look of irritation. "The car isn't big enough for both of us if you're going to be overbearing and tedious."

The car wasn't big enough for Magnus any way she looked at it.

His head brushed the roof and his shoulders crowded her view, and she was entirely too aware of his proximity.

"Tedious is what I am. Impulsive and unpredictable are who you are. I don't think that changes. We just have to deal," he told her. "Learn the controls first. They need to become habit, so they don't require your attention when you're on the road."

His calm reaction to her hyper insult eased her tension. "I really don't like confinement," she admitted rather than apologize. "If I ever have a chance, I'll own a convertible." She pulled levers to see what they would do.

"Find a sedan with a bench seat in back and I'll show you the value of privacy," he said without a hint of a smirk.

But she knew he was smirking inside. She shoved his big shoulder and tried not to blush. "Outdoors, under the stars, to heck with privacy," she told him. "I've had all the privacy I can tolerate."

"I can handle that." He eyed her hungrily, and the tension dissipated. The man had *heated glower* down to a science. Her gonads melted.

Magnus showed her how to turn levers for different actions and pull back and forth or up and down on others. Nadine grasped the mechanics swiftly, but the Magnificent Hulk was too close, too much in her space, and her mind kept drifting. She could picture running her fingers over his biceps, and she didn't want to smack him away.

"OK, I've got all the important stuff," she insisted when he put her through a list of commands. "I'll worry about cleaning the windshields should I ever really drive." She turned on the engine and admired its purr.

"What we'll be doing today is basic mechanics, not driving. A car is a two-ton bomb, a weapon of destruction. You have to learn to treat it with respect and know how to avert danger."

"You mean I can't make it dance?" she teased. "Lighten up, Oswin."

"I can't. I'm handing you the keys to escape and disaster," he said gloomily. "I'm not the general. I can't hold you prisoner, but I understand the temptation. Your head is full of dangerous information, and you're an incendiary device rigged to explode."

"Nice analogy." She attempted to back the car down the drive but had no idea where the rear bumper was. "Why don't all cars have back up cameras?" she asked in frustration after several attempts ended up in the landscape gravel.

"An experienced driver develops a sense of where their vehicle begins and ends. That's what I'm trying to warn you about. You can't just jump in the car and go."

"Damn." She put the gear in forward, pulled back onto the pavers, then reversed and attempted again. "I'm a prisoner of my own ignorance!"

"Some people are a prisoner of poverty. We all have our burdens to bear. Yours can be overcome with education. And even without that, all you have to do is produce your credit card and call a limo. Others aren't so fortunate."

She gaped at him. "There *is* a brain behind that brawn, I knew it!"

He sent her a look that sizzled all her nerve endings.

"I could drive off and just leave you here," he reminded her.

"Me and my credit card," she said cheerfully, finally maneuvering the car down the pavers to the street. "And you can't do anything without me! I think I'll let power go to my head."

He sat silently for a minute, watching her steer along the empty street. "What happens if you have a vision while driving?" he finally asked.

Nadine cursed, hit the brakes at an intersection, and glared out the windshield. "Maybe they'll go away once Vera and I are safe."

"How often do you have them?"

"Only when there are naked thoughts flying around, and I happen to run into them, or someone directs them my way. It's like when someone leaves open an unencrypted network. If I get close enough and I turn the computer on, I connect." She turned at the side street and poked back to the house, shaken by his question. She couldn't drive a freeway at ninety miles an hour and suddenly have someone inside her mind. She had freedom in her hands, but she was imprisoned by her own damned head. "I have good reason to stay isolated."

"Learning to drive is still necessary," Magnus insisted. "Emergencies require taking risks. You need as much knowledge as you can acquire so you can adapt to whatever happens. Try to have someone with you prepared to grab the wheel, maybe. It's a pity you have no one to teach you to block out broadcasts."

"What does Francesca do? She's a pilot!"

"Helicopter, not plane, and she always has a co-pilot with her. Still, she might know tricks. Education is important. We need to end this standoff with the general so you have an opportunity to learn."

Bleakly, Nadine let that truism sit there, unacknowledged.

By the time they returned to their computers, Conan had conjured the ID of a nine-year-old girl named Lydia MacArthur.

"Can her parents be traced?" Nadine asked anxiously when Magnus showed her the screen.

"No. Conan will have found someone who died decades ago on the other side of the country. He's building an on-line identity for her parents now. He'll erase them when this is over."

Nadine studied the information. "I'll fill in only the bare minimum on the genealogy site, just enough to catch someone's notice, if they're watching. We don't need to give them everything at once," Nadine said. "Most people are hesitant to reveal too much. When I monitored the site, I used to keep an eye out for new people and do my own investigating. I don't know what anyone's doing now."

"Can you find out?"

She shrugged and tapped out access keys to the sticky Malcolm website she'd created and knew inside and out. "Nothing was happening last time I checked. I don't dare take a look in the back door for fear someone is expecting me to do just that."

"It's okay if they trace Lydia to this address and computer, but it's best not to let them know it's you hacking in their back door," he agreed. Mad Max returned to fiddling with a mysterious circuit box that had arrived by UPS earlier.

"In case you haven't noticed, I'm not good at pretending," she admonished.

"This is the method *you* chose to reach the general. Learn," he said without sympathy. "Once we have him, you're free to be you." His eyes crinkled at the corners when he glanced up at her. "I just hope the world is prepared."

His grin eased a tightly wound wire inside her, and Nadine turned back to her own website with less concern. "Positivity instead of negativity. I like that."

"Same as doing instead of thinking." He returned to tinkering.

"You have a strange idea of thinking then, if you equate it with negativity. I'm putting in your occupation as master dancer and choreographer when I'm ready to fill out the form."

He snorted but didn't object. She liked that about him.

She liked him too damned much. She needed to get the hell out before she ended up as another man's appendage.

Twenty-one

Monday evening, Magnus finished installing his version of a spyware detector on the back of the house and began running wires for his next level of security.

He fretted over Nadine's implication that she felt trapped—with *him*—as she had with the general. Knowing how she felt—was damned uncomfortable.

Thinking about that was negativity any way he looked at it. He'd rather put her in a car and set her free and be done. Since that wasn't possible... He pondered some other action that might let her enjoy her new-found freedom.

"Someone downloaded the latest info from the Malcolm website on Friday," Nadine reported as he finished the wiring. "Lately, they've only been checking it on Fridays."

"Crap. You're saying they might not find our bait for nearly a week?" So not what he wanted to hear.

"Can't say yet. Anything is possible. If Jo-jo chose my replacement from that Malcolm family tree, we could be up against anything."

"Employee archives are inaccessible?" He set up his laptop and connected the wireless to his new network.

"Not totally. I set up a layered system of passwords, and someone has changed all of them in the servers I can locate. I'm running software on them now, but I suspect the vital servers have been moved. It will take a while to locate them. What are you doing?"

He pushed a button and grunted at the screen. "Detecting. I'm playing with a new security system. It's located a night vision scope on the bluff." He swung the screen around to show her. "I'll install the program and leave instructions for the guy who owns this place so he'll know if photographers are up there."

She leaned over his shoulder, and his brain immediately clouded with the brush of her breasts. Damn, but he had it bad.

"You think that's paparazzi out there?" she asked in disbelief.

"Nope, I think the general had someone trace your sister's dog to this address, and he's spying on the person he thinks was spying on him. The fact that the dog was taken to the vet and is no longer present hasn't deterred him. The general is really and truly paranoid."

"Nothing new. Wow. You just put this together? Impressive." She studied the red beam on the grid. "What do we do now?"

"We can send security to take him down, but chances are he's just hired help and won't know anything. We can leave him up there and not give him anything to report—my recommendation. Once the minions discover we've entered this address on the website, we should get some action."

Magnus knew the action he wanted, but now he felt like he was taking advantage of a prisoner. He'd not exactly left Nadine many choices.

"So we're stuck in here until someone looks at the website again?" she asked with distinct dismay.

"I think there are enough bushes and trees and umbrellas around the pool to conceal us, so we can go outside in that area. We have good security, but the balconies will be off limits, and if we drive out, we may have a tail."

She returned to the sofa she'd curled up on, and Magnus could see her shoulders slump. She wouldn't nag or complain, but he didn't need to be a mind reader to know she wasn't happy.

He tried not to compare her moods to Diane's. Nadine had a right to be bummed about the situation.

"We still have credit cards on our fake IDs," he reminded her.

She squinted at him questioningly.

"Limo. We sneak out the pool area so he can't see us. If we stick to the walls and shrubbery and make our way to the neighbors, we can make it look as if we're emerging from a house down the road. Our spy can't watch everyone."

Her eyes widened again. "We can pretend we're the rich people down the road and order a limo? Majorly cool. Where would we go? Can we visit Vera? Or what about the Academy?" Her expression grew more excited. "Could we check out the Academy?"

"I thought you'd want to go to Santa Monica or something." He ought to just shoot himself in the head for thinking he'd guessed what she wanted. "We can't let ourselves be seen near the school until we go through all the crap of applying and get permission to go in there."

"But *we* can't go in," she said in dismay. "Jo-jo would recognize us."

"No, we can't go in. Conan will send his operatives with our cooked-up credentials. Your dancing master can really be one, if you like."

She ran her hands through her hair, spiking it. "Crap. I want this done and I want it done *now*. I hate doing nothing."

Magnus sympathized, but he refrained from saying *just give me Jo-jo's address*. She'd made her point clear there. Conan was following up on the Palm Springs reports but hadn't verified that the general was in residence. Distracting Nadine seemed reasonable, even if it required limos.

"There's a nightclub in Santa Monica with a good local band. If you're confident that your connection with Vera is secure, you could see if she's available to meet us there. But she's behind a week on her studies. Don't be surprised if she can't," he warned. "By the time we get there, it will be pushing ten, even if we hurry."

"We can't get a limo that fast," she protested.

Magnus raised an eyebrow. "You don't know Oz very well, then."

Finally, hope appeared in her eyes. "You think we can really go to a nightclub and be safe?"

"Would I suggest it if I thought otherwise?" Well, yeah, probably, because he was a desperate man, but he didn't think his expectations were unreasonable.

"Then, yes, please! See if we can find a limo. Anything is better than sitting here, waiting." She leapt up, kissed his cheek, and raced for the stairs before he could grab her.

Damn, Conan was going to kill him.

Nadine hurriedly pulled on the one dress she'd bought in her shopping spree. It didn't have spaghetti straps or flounces, but it had a halter neckline and a full skirt in a simple blue. She glared at her curly hair, grabbed some gel, made it stand up. Then she took the scissors and began whacking off curls in a disorderly pattern so it didn't lie flat or curl but looked as if it had been blown askew by an airplane propeller. That worked.

She hadn't bought make-up but whoever lived here had a closet full of it. She just borrowed an unopened tube of lipstick. And some shoes. She couldn't dance in sandals.

She knew it would be impossible to summon a limo in the half hour she'd taken to get ready, but she danced down the stairs anyway, eager to be out of the house.

That startled her. She hadn't minded sitting in front of a computer day and night when she was a teenager. She'd loved that she was safe in her basement from the pain of unguarded thoughts, safe from any kids who laughed at her. She'd loved the freedom of cruising the internet.

She'd only learned to be wary of computers after she'd started doubting the wisdom of what the general was doing with his psychic experiments.

Gazing on the magnificence that was Magnus waiting in the atrium, Nadine thought maybe he was a large part of her need to get away from the monitor.

He'd changed into a crisp white shirt that he'd rolled up to the elbow. He wore it with the collar open, exposing his bronzed chest, and the tails tucked into form-fitting jeans. She salivated and almost told him to forget the limo.

"We have maybe ten minutes to perform our disappearing act. The limo will meet us at the end of the street."

"Did my jaw just drop?" she asked. "You're a magician, right?"

He caught her arm and steered her through the darkened family room. "Oz is the magician. I'm the mechanic, remember? He called a friend in the neighborhood with a chauffeur. I'm installing the same night vision detector software in the guy's house in exchange for the use of car and driver. It all works out."

"And I suppose you've invented an invisibility cloak while you were waiting?" She watched him set a timer that hadn't been there earlier and didn't even bother to ask.

"Still working on invisibility," he said without a hint of humor. "Until then, we stick to shadows." He donned a black blazer over his white shirt, turned his gaze to her blue dress—and stopped talking.

Nadine poked his chin up. "I am not the only female in the world with mammary glands. Do I need to wear something darker?"

"No, ma'am, I like what I see just fine. But if you fall out of that dress while we're dancing, I won't be responsible for the consequences." Over her shoulders, he dropped a dark raincoat.

Nadine shrugged it on rather than try to hang on to it. "Okay, lead on, Sherlock."

They slipped out the sliding doors. Magnus performed some magic feat with the security alarm, then guided her along the dark cabana to the towering hibiscus hedge on the far side of the pool.

He located a narrow wooden gate in the wall behind the hedge and opened it. She bit back a gasp of surprise when the house suddenly lit up like a Christmas tree, and a blast of music blared from outdoor speakers.

"How did you...?"

He covered her mouth with a finger and peered around the gateway. He dragged her through the opening to a narrow alley running along behind the property. A security light overhead that should have come on, didn't.

"I pulled the breaker on the light," he whispered.

He halted, gauged the distance to the next security light, and dragged her along the wall. "Cross to the other side. There's no light there."

They dashed across the dark alley to open brush.

In minutes, they'd found the street intersecting with the alley and sauntered down it, hand in hand, just another couple out for an evening stroll.

They waved at a father and his kids walking up from the beach, just as if they belonged there.

Heart racing, Nadine clung to Mad Max's big hand as they reached the main road and saw a low-slung sports car waiting for them. "That's not a limo," she murmured worriedly.

"No, that's Oz's love of classic cars. Late model XK-E coupe with twelve cylinders would be my guess. He doesn't know people with mere Bentleys or Cadillacs. My back aches just looking at it." He leaned in the open passenger window. "Looking for passengers?" he asked.

"I'm yours for the evening," the driver said.

"Santa Monica, then, and keep an eye out for anyone tailing us." Magnus held the door so Nadine could climb into the leather interior.

"Oh, wow," she whispered. The seat practically enveloped her like a glove. The car's engine woke with a quiet roar. Magnus squeezed in beside her. "I feel like Cinderella."

"We don't have to worry about midnight and pumpkins, and glass shoes had to hurt."

"Not to mention you're a prince with no castle, got it. I IM'd Vera. She can't make it, but she says she's good. Do you think Dorrie's cousin is still hanging around her?"

"Jack has a job, but I'm betting his spare time is spent in Vera's vicinity, yes. That okay?"

"He's a bit older than she is," Nadine said worriedly.

"I'm older than you. Do I need to back off?"

"Probably, for your sake, if not mine. If what we're doing blows up, I'm leaving the country by any means possible. I'm not risking ending up in a loony bin again. I'd rather be dead."

Only then did Nadine remember that Magnus Magnificus's fiancée had killed herself. She bit her tongue—hard.

Twenty-two

"New rule," Magnus declared. "You do not mention loony bins and death in my presence if you do not want to detonate Mad Max. Got it?"

"You're practically vibrating," Nadine replied in awe. She really hadn't meant to hurt him. The sports car's back seat was scarcely big enough for his wide shoulders. She could actually *feel* his intensity. "I felt your vibrations when you arrived at Woodstar. I'm amazed you're not causing earthquakes."

"That's not the *point*," he said grimly, reaching over to crush her hand against the leather seat. "The point is that I have limits and you're pushing them."

Nadine processed the data—he was squeezing her hand as if he couldn't let go. He'd lost someone he'd loved to violence. He feared she would do the same. Got it.

The thought of Mad Max caring that much about her... She swallowed hard.

"I will not kill myself," she told him, wrapping her fingers around his. "I will go after Jo-jo with a machete, which may be the same thing, but I will not leave you in such a wimpy manner as slitting my wrists, got that?"

His grip relaxed somewhat. "Thank you. I'll keep machetes out of sight."

Nadine giggled. It had been a long time since she'd felt quite this giddy, and Mad Max had been the one to set her off. He made her feel as if she *mattered.* She bubbled inside, and needed some outlet to express the sensation. She couldn't think of an appropriate one.

Instead, she snuggled against him—not difficult to do in this tiny backseat. He obligingly put his arm around her and let her closer.

"I've been taking care of myself for quite a few years," she reminded him. "I'm not your responsibility."

"That's about the stupidest thing you've ever said," he said, evidently still not over his snit. "You've lived a sheltered life that blew up on you. I'm trained in military combat. You saved my life. I owe you one. You're my responsibility."

Had he been the general, she'd have been cringing in fear. Instead, she laughed, and leaning into him, blew on his neck. "Run that last part again... I *saved* your life. I am not a helpless infant. I'm just wired weird. And for what it's worth, Jo-jo wouldn't have killed a valuable scientist like you. He would have just made you miserable."

"One of us would have died," he retorted. "Maybe you should have left me down in that hole."

She pinched his biceps. "No killing. You're not in the military any longer. Join the police force if you want to shoot baddies. Let's practice dancing for Conan's wedding, and forget about the rest for a few hours, okay?"

"I'll try," he agreed reluctantly.

With a driver not more than a few feet from their whispered conversation, Magnus figured arguing further wasn't worth the effort. Besides, Nadine's hot body pressed against his side had sent his brain south. Dancing would work off a little of that energy while he tried to process the level of her desperation—and his.

But he was pretty damned certain he couldn't survive weeks of inactivity waiting for her bait-and-switch routine to work.

At Magnus's direction, the driver dropped them off in an alley behind the club. It was just a Monday, so most of the pier attractions had closed early, but the night club was revving up. The DJ's blaring speakers shook the walls as he steered Nadine through the shadowy alley and into a side entrance.

He kept her hand firmly in his grip as they entered the room of swirling dancers, flashing spotlights, and pounding salsa. She clung to him and stared at the crowd. Her eyes were as big as emerald lakes, and her grip on his hand was fierce.

"How's your head?" he asked, worried that this might be too much stimulation.

"It's better than I imagined," she shouted in what sounded like relief.

"Your head or the music?" he asked, finally relaxing a little.

If nothing else, Nadine was never boring. In her borrowed heels, she came past his shoulder. He was tempted to press a kiss to her cheek but resisted a sign of affection.

"Both," she concluded. "How can anyone think like this? It's your kind of place—everyone is dancing instead of thinking."

"Works for me." Relieved that she wouldn't be having any seizures, Magnus grabbed a table as a couple departed. "If you're okay, hold the table while I get drinks."

He didn't bother asking what she wanted. He already knew she didn't have a clue. At the bar, he ordered a margarita, easy on the tequila, and a beer for himself. Dancing made him thirsty, and even with a chauffeur, he preferred to limit his alcohol consumption.

Setting the drink in front of Nadine, he let her taste it, and make an approving nod, before indicating the dance floor. "This is an easy one. Do you want to try?"

She jumped up eagerly, taking his hand as if they really were a couple, and she hadn't practically accused him of holding her prisoner. Maybe he should think of her as a prisoner, but that was anathema to his ethics, especially when she came into his arms like she belonged there. She was all curvy and soft and breathless. He wanted to take her home right then. Which was why he needed to work off the energy.

"They make it look so easy," she said with admiration, watching another couple clear the floor with their moves as Magnus swung her into the dance.

"They've been practicing for years. You'll learn faster than they did. You move beautifully," he assured her, feeling her hip sway beneath his hand as he led her backwards, remembering what her curves had felt like naked.

She beamed up at him and added extra sway.

The crowd parted to give another talented couple room. Recognizing the spotlight-hugging pair, Magnus cursed. Nadine peered over his shoulder to see what had set him off.

"Oz and Pippa," Magnus told her. "They hired the driver and knew where we were going. Want to leave?"

She turned in his arms to watch his brother show off. In this position, while wearing stolen high heels, she danced with her ass nearly at his groin. "Why leave?" she asked.

"For their own damned safety, for starters," he grumbled. He'd have to buy her a pair of heels and replicate this experiment sometime when they had a life of their own. "There's a reason they live in the mountains behind fortress walls."

"Oh?" she inquired. "Is Pippa a prisoner? Or Oz?"

Magnus didn't explain. That was Pippa's story to tell. "Pippa has issues. If she's agreed to take this risk, her curiosity must be stronger than her fear."

"Her mother is a Malcolm, that much I know. Having psychic gifts is not the same as being Frankenstein's monster."

"It can be," he argued, knowing Pippa's story.

"She's beautiful and a really good dancer." Nadine tugged him to a halt to watch. "Oz isn't bad, but he's not in your league. Go tap your brother on the shoulder and see what happens."

Magnus gave her glossy brown spikes a look of incredulity. "You want to get me killed?"

"Jealousy is a product of insecurity. Your brother does not strike me as an insecure man," she said with confidence.

"You're loco," he informed her, but the devil was in him now. He entered the circle and tapped Oz on his outrageous Hawaiian shirt. "You asked for it," Magnus told him, grabbing Pippa's hand and swirling her away when Oz stepped back in surprise.

Nadine grinned as the Maximator and Pippa practically shut down the dance floor with their moves.

It didn't take Oz long to locate her. The man had a sophisticated movie star/surfer dude thing happening that had feminine heads turning.

"Wanta dance?" he asked grumpily, looming over her.

Once upon a time, she'd dreamed of a handsome man sweeping her onto the dance floor. Tonight, she shook her head no. "I do, but not with you. I'm inexperienced. Max is a patient teacher."

"Max?" He eyed her skeptically.

He probably wasn't used to rejection and had reason to believe her nuts. Nadine brushed off his skepticism and nodded at the dance floor. "He wasn't happy with you following us here. He needs to blow off steam. Your wife's a better dancer than I am."

She didn't mind the looks Oz attracted, not in the same way it annoyed her when women eyed Magnus. The Maximator could have any woman he wanted, and he didn't even notice.

It seemed strange that he'd want chubby, nerdy her.

"Magnus needs an engine to tear apart, not a dance floor," Oz corrected. "He hasn't built any assault weapons yet, has he?"

Nadine sent him a look of amusement. "He simply needs an outlet for all that energy. You *are* seeing the same man I'm seeing out there, aren't you?"

As far as she could tell, Magnus applied the same intensity to his dancing as he did his lovemaking. He was magnificent, all smooth moves and grace and fluid steps, one with the music and sexy as hell. Maybe she'd leave the music on when they went to bed next. She sure hoped there was a *next*.

"I see my brother making a spectacle with my wife, who seems to be enjoying the show they're putting on. Pippa doesn't get out much, so I guess I won't beat him to a pulp. Yet." Oz crossed his bronzed arms and scanned the crowd. "Keep an eye out for paparazzi. We don't need our faces on YouTube."

"Did you come here just to harass Magnus or for another reason?" she asked as the DJ finished with a flourish and called a recess.

She watched as Magnus blocked his tall, but rail-thin, sister-in-law from the press of people as they made their way through the crowd. He had his hand at Pippa's back, but his gaze was completely focused on Nadine. A pool of molten lava settled in her lower belly at the heat in his eyes.

"Pippa wanted to meet you," Oz said. "As far as she's concerned, you're family. She doesn't have much family, and she's convinced all of you need to stick together." Oz nodded at Magnus and Pippa as they arrived. "And Pippa thinks Oswins are bullies, right?"

"You are," the tall redhead said without inflection. "It's part of your charm. Glad to finally meet you, Nadine." She held out her hand. "And thank you for loaning me your date. Magnus is a superb dancer."

"And I'm not?" Oz growled, appropriating his wife with a hand at her back, elbowing Magnus away.

Elegantly slim in her off-the-shoulder silk gown, Pippa leaned in and nibbled her husband's ear before replying. "You're a good dancer but you have more interest in the people around you than in the music. Magnus is on a mission when he's on the floor, a tonal difference you won't understand." She patted his broad shoulder sympathetically.

"I like your family," Nadine decided, taking Mad Max's arm as they returned to their table. "I like the way you look out for each other."

"Genetic flaw," he muttered. He swigged his beer and eyed his brother with disfavor. "I don't owe you for the car and driver if you used him to find us," he told Oz.

"As I heard it, you've already agreed to pay with some new invention," Oz said without inflection, signaling a waitress. "Would you deny Pippa her fun?"

"At my expense? Yep."

Nadine elbowed him. "What about for my sake? Isn't that how this started? It's not as if you had any interest in dancing."

"I did," Magnus said solemnly. "I've been told I'm very good at it."

Shouldering a dazzling purse that probably cost a small Lexus, Pippa took Nadine's arm. "C'mon, let's find the little girl's room while the oafs take a few verbal slugs at each other." She steered her toward a side corridor.

"Serious case of testosterone poisoning in adolescence?" Nadine inquired innocently.

"I think they brush their teeth with it. If you haven't killed Magnus yet, you have the patience of a saint. Although he's not as bad as Conan. I have to push Conan in the pool every time he comes over. He may get married in a wet tux."

Nadine laughed at the idea of this polished woman shoving anyone in a pool. Over the chattering crowd, she heard a shout but thought nothing of it until Pippa tensed.

She turned to make certain they weren't being followed. A flash nearly blinded her.

Without warning, Pippa grabbed Nadine's arm and shoved past the line waiting for the restroom.

"The general didn't send photographers after me," Nadine protested.

"Not the general. They're after me." Ignoring cries of objection from the women waiting in line, Pippa pushed through the door of the ladies lounge and looked frantically around. "Trapped," she concluded. "Go back out and pull a fire alarm."

Her elegant new friend really did have the terrified look of a trapped rabbit. Nadine responded instantly to her panic. "I have no idea what this is about, but there's a painted-over window on that wall. Will that do?"

Pippa eyed the paint warily. "Even if we can pry it open, I can't fit through that."

Women maneuvered around them to reach the sinks and mirrors. More women pressed inside. Nadine heard a cacophony of excited shouts in the room beyond, but no one seemed in any particular danger.

"How important is it to get out?" she asked, eyeing Pippa's fancy silk gown.

"I just told you to pull a fire alarm. That's my level of panic. Maybe I can hide in a stall until you fetch Oz." Pippa seemed prepared to do battle as the next woman shoved past her to grab a stall door before she could.

"Okay, got it. Let's avoid fire trucks and the mass hysteria of trying to smuggle a man in here."

Holding Pippa's arm, Nadine worked her way back to the wall. She studied the window, found the lever, and wacked it with a martial arts chop. The paint cracked. The window probably did, too, but it was hard to tell beneath the paint. All that mattered was that the lever moved.

Pippa gasped at Nadine's brute reaction. Not raised on nicety, Nadine grabbed the pricey shoulder bag from Pippa. Wrapping her hand in the cloth, she slammed her fist against the lever again, this time pushing it outward.

Miraculously, the window swung open.

Nadine scrambled up on a sink, worked her shoulders through the opening, and deciding the drop to the ground was safe, wriggled through until she could throw her leg over the edge. She couldn't see Pippa's expression from the other side of the painted glass, but she wished she had a camera anyway. There had to be gawking going on.

With a painful wriggle that probably ruined her one dress, Nadine was sitting on the window ledge. She leaned back in. "If I can do it, you can, but I advise going legs first."

"This is insane, but I like it," Pippa said from near the window. "I'm coming through. Get down."

Nadine leaped into the dirt dividing the wall from the parking lot. Pippa's long bare legs swung out shortly after. With a far more graceful maneuver, Pippa swung down to the ground using her hands on the window to swing outward. She shimmied her slim gown back into place.

"Oomph, that was fun. *Not.* Oz is going to kill me." Pippa glanced around. "Do you have a phone on you?"

"Nope. Magnus hogs the phone. You don't carry one?"

Pippa took back her shoulder bag to rummage through it. "I never go anywhere to need one and keep leaving it on my desk. They're going to kill us both. Want to run away?"

She said that while lowering herself to a low concrete wall and pulling off her shoes to inspect the heels.

"Tried that. That's how I wound up with Magnus." Nadine followed her example and sat down on the wall to watch the front entrance expectantly. "I have every confidence that he'll figure it out pretty quick."

Pippa eyed her with respect. "You've learned that much about him in a week? You really must read minds."

"If I did, I'd know what that was all about. Want to explain?"

"Someone thought they saw Syrene," Pippa said with a shrug. "It's like yelling Elvis entered the building."

"Elvis is dead," Nadine said, trying to puzzle out what a Syrene was.

"Yeah, so is Syrene, but tell that to the paparazzi. If Oz says 'I told you so,' can you take him down with that nifty karate chop?"

"Did I just step through some kind of mirror?" Nadine asked. "Is a Red Queen going to chop off my head?"

Twenty-three

The flashing cameras and excited screams wouldn't have stirred Magnus into action, if his big brother hadn't jumped up, cursing creatively. Magnus wasn't used to paparazzi. Oz was. His brain instantly switched to protective mode.

Oz brutally shouldered his way toward the restrooms and the line of irritated women, doing his best to block the flashing cameras and phones aimed at Pippa's escape hatch.

Leaving his brother to act as obstacle, Magnus morphed into a heat-seeking missile in pursuit of Nadine. His job was to keep her face off the Internet and this was not the way to do it—damn Pippa's recognizable phiz and addled-fan mystique.

He plowed his way through the crowd by crushing anything flashing in his face with his bare hands.

"No cameras allowed," he told one freak who was apparently taking cell-phone photos of everything in sight in hopes of accidentally capturing anything interesting. Magnus knocked the phone to the floor, stomped on it, and made his way toward the ladies' room. He couldn't leave Nadine trapped or let her walk out into this melee.

Oz followed in his path. "Syrene has been off the market for years. What's with these morons anyway?"

A professional photographer with a real camera around his neck shoved through the crowd on their heels. Magnus turned abruptly, and the jerk crashed into him. Which gave him a fine excuse to chest bump the pricey piece of equipment, knocking its lens askew. "Oops. Let me fix that for you." He broke the strap holding the camera and twisted off the scope. "Here ya go."

The photographer screamed bloody murder and swung at him. Grinning, Magnus swung back, propelling the photographer into the mob behind him.

"Oh goody," Oz muttered. "I haven't done this in ages." He kneed the next guy trying to get past him and put up his fists. "Bar fight!" he yelled.

Shouts of "We want Syrene" echoed off the high metal beams of the ceiling. Magnus knew a lost cause when he saw one. Nadine was more important than convincing a crowd that Syrene didn't exist.

The women waiting in line looked as if they'd like to bar him from their watering hole, but Magnus produced a scowl fierce enough to frighten Maori warriors. When they retreated, he barged into the ladies' room, scattering screaming women. "Nadine!" he shouted.

No chirpy Librarian replied. The open window at the rear of the room spoke for itself. Counting to ten, Magnus swung around and dodged back to the hall. He grabbed Oz's collar and dragged him toward the back door while the brawl continued uninterrupted on the other end.

"If she's gone, I get to murder you, right?" he asked as big brother staggered, jerked free, and punched his ribs in retaliation.

"You need more confidence in your woman," Oz scoffed as security bore down on them, looking grim.

"My woman?" Magnus pondered that as they retreated. *His woman.* La Loca?

He knew he was in trouble when the idea warmed him with pleasure. With enthusiasm, he punched out a security guard keeping him from reaching *his woman.*

"So, okay, Syrene is dead to the world, and like a phoenix, Pippa the Philanthropist has risen in her place," Nadine summarized, chewing on popcorn they'd bought from a vendor while waiting.

"Not much of a philanthropist," Pippa said dismissively. "I just encourage people to do what they need to do."

"With your voice," Nadine said. "You persuade and charm and cajole with your Malcolm talent, and people do what you ask. I like that. That's a really useful talent. I want one like that."

"No, you don't. I've driven men to their death with that gift. I don't even know it's happening half the time. Oz is the one who showed me what I was doing. We're freaks of nature."

"And now you hide from the world because chaos erupts when people see you and recognize the famous rock star Syrene." Nadine pondered that for a moment and saw the downside. "I know what hiding is like and it's tough. It would be a lot more useful if I could project thoughts instead of reading them. I could shut up the mob before it got started, divert them to something more interesting."

Pippa laughed. "Then you'd have to be my bodyguard. If you like, I could sing and make them all cry, but then they'd *know* Syrene still exists, instead of just hoping I'm hanging around. Not a wise idea."

"Pity that. You might want to try it on the two simmering hulks approaching." Nadine nodded toward the big men storming down the alley.

"They're just worried about us," Pippa said with a shrug. "They'll calm down now."

"Mad Max is vibrating again. I don't think that's calm." Nadine watched in admiration as the two Oswin brothers scanned the parking lot and immediately located them sitting in the shadows. "Got any songs for this situation?"

Pippa began singing a silly song about monkeys walking down the street. It sounded cheerful. The men didn't appear to be cheered.

"Oswins don't respond well to my voice," Pippa explained. "You're not sounding very cheerful either, so I assume I can't persuade you into running into Mad Max's arms and placating his vibrations."

Nadine snickered as the elegant, sophisticated producer's wife resorted to her nickname for Magnus. "I adore his vibrations, even if it means he's going into obsessive protective mode."

"Conan says Magnus has a Zorro complex. Oz just steps back and lets him go, then cleans up the result afterward. Personally, I think he's more the Lone Ranger type, riding in to save the day and disappearing into the sunset. No flashy Z's carved into the furniture."

Having spent her childhood with computers and not old movies, Nadine had only a small understanding of what Pippa was talking about. Besides, she was more interested in watching Magnus approach with that male swagger he adopted when suppressing explosive emotion. Really, it was a wonder the ground didn't shake.

"Want to find another dancing spot?" was all he asked when he arrived.

The rumble of his deep voice and his heated look and his acceptance that she hadn't been at fault ignited a core she'd thought long gone cold. "I think I've had enough excitement for the evening. How about you?"

His lips curved upward a fraction. "You're excitement enough for me. Did Pippa threaten to throw the fire alarm again?" he asked, glaring at his sister-in-law.

"I had alternatives prepared," Pippa responded serenely. "I just didn't think you'd like them."

Oz helped his wife from the curb and grabbed a handful of her popcorn. "Find a song for causing mass memory blackouts of Syrene, and we're good."

"They've been fighting," Nadine concluded, standing up without aid since she'd removed her heels and was barefoot. "Lesson learned. If we don't want them to yell at us, give them someone else to beat up."

"I don't beat up women," Magnus objected.

"Nah, he beats up cameras," Oz explained. "A few people are going to have a hard time explaining crushed phones come morning. If only we could paint him green, we'd have a hit."

Pippa giggled. Nadine actually caught this pop culture reference and could appreciate the image of the giant green Hulk busting through his shirt. She held Magnus's arm and tugged her shoes back on. "Someone needs to send me the videos of all these shows everyone talks about. I have a lot of catching up to do. Start with Zorro, please."

"I am not Zorro. We're riding off in a Jag XKE, not on a horse. And next time you're bored, Pippa, just invite us to visit. It's easier on the knuckles." Holding Nadine's hand to his arm, Magnus pulled out his phone to call the driver.

"It's been fun and informative," Nadine said in farewell. "Call me anytime you want to start another riot."

"Will do," Pippa agreed cheerfully, striding away ahead of Oz, forcing him to catch up.

"I want to be her when I grow up," Nadine told Magnus when he clicked off the phone.

"Pippa's one of a kind. So are you. Leave it at that." He dragged her toward the street as the music began pounding again inside the club. "Sure you don't want to dance some more?"

"I doubt they'll let you live if you go back inside. We can dance at home. You really think I'm one of a kind?" Nadine asked, uncertain if that was a good or bad thing—or why she cared what he thought.

"Unique," he agreed. "We ought to label you and put you in a museum."

She snorted. "Yeah, that's what Jo-jo tried to do. Thanks."

"You're rare," he asserted, dragging her toward the alley where the car waited. "It's instinctive to want to protect what's precious."

"Precious? Hardly." Although she thrilled a little that Magnus thought her so. Stupid female reaction. "I'm nowhere near as talented as Pippa. Mind reading is pretty useless when it means I have to wait for other people to tell me their thoughts. And even then, I can't do anything about them. Speech is more effective."

"You got inside the general's mind the other night," he reminded her. "You just don't like doing it."

"You believe me?" she asked warily. He'd been pretty ambiguous about her gift.

"I don't think you're a liar, much," he agreed.

Magnus was not a black-and-white sort of thinker, and yeah, she'd probably lied a few times, here and there. She couldn't argue his point.

"I just believe in scientific explanations more," he continued. "But I think you did something special when you reached Vera, so I've got to think you reached the general too."

She wanted to preen a little, to feel good about herself for just a little while. This intelligent, capable, scientific man thought she had something *special*. She let the notion warm her insides just a moment, until she reminded herself of reality. She knew the pitfalls of specialness.

She released his arm and stalked toward the waiting car. "It gives me a headache," she said as she slid into the dark interior.

"Waiting to get my hands on him gives *me* a headache," he retorted, sliding in beside her with the grace of an athlete, despite the narrowness of the seat. "I'm not asking you to spy on anyone's brain. I'm just pointing out that you can do something no one else in the world can do."

"Read Jo-jo's mind, big deal. It would be more interesting to read the mind of a president. I don't need to read Jo-jo's mind to know what he's thinking, which is why I can do it. We connect on familiar levels." She crossed her arms and sank into the leather as far from Magnus as she could get—which wasn't very far. She could feel the heat of him all up and down her side. She might be developing claustrophobia. "I know him. I know how his mind works."

"I get that, and I'm grateful you can't delve into mine. But if you've learned the general well enough to do what you did the other night, you're picking up something from him that others can't. And it's possible you could do it with other people, if necessary."

"Why would I ever want to mess with anyone's mind?" Nadine thought of her juvenile attempts to read her teachers' minds. She'd picked up thoughts and emotions here and there, but she could have imagined them. She had no way of proving that her science teacher was looking at the class as a bunch of monkeys.

"Caretakers need to be empathic so they can know what's wrong with a child or patient who can't tell them what's wrong. You could do something similar. Since you basically see images and not thoughts, you might be able to see where people are if they get lost. You need more experience to know what you can really do. The general prevented that."

Magnus sat in the shadows, face forward, so she couldn't read much of his body language. He sounded like a teacher, not a disapproving tyrant. Nadine was simply accustomed to reacting defensively to Jo-jo's demands. She had to break that habit.

"I need practice, I grant. Maybe Francesca can help me. You want me to try planting images in your head like she did mine?" She knew she sounded grumpy. After the evening's high, she didn't want to be brought down to the current situation.

"Not unless they're images of you naked," he said in the same tone as earlier.

A grin tugged the corner of her mouth, but she couldn't let Magnus Magnificus get the upper hand or he'd run over her. "I'm still angry. You can't sweet talk me into telling you where the general is. If I could only find a back door into his network so I could take it down, that would isolate and handicap him until everyone is safe. That's all I'm willing to concede before I go in after him."

"You are *not* going after him," he said emphatically. "That's disaster waiting to happen."

She punched his rock-hard biceps. "Bullying," she reminded him. "My choice."

He ignored her punch. "We need evidence of wrong-doing, and we need to get him out in the open. I'll willingly press charges and so will Bo and probably the army if we can prove General Adams highjacked us, but we need concrete evidence. I don't even want you charging him with illegal incarceration or whatever because that's not enough to hold him. We need inside that school. First things first."

Nadine crossed her arms and slid deeper in the seat. "There's a reason he's never been charged. No one can pin anything to him. If you're waiting for evidence, I might as well move to Australia now. The general is not dumb. He keeps his hands clean. And if life gets too hot, he drops out of sight until he's forgotten. Now that reporters are hunting him, he's likely to abscond to Alaska."

"Just get us into the school or one of his underground labs, and we'll take it from there. He has you brainwashed into thinking he's God, but he's not," he said angrily. "Bo and I went back out to the desert hangar where he kept us, but he'd arranged for the army to use it as a bombing range. It's gone, along with all our evidence. I want to be one step ahead of him this time."

"And you'd like to strangle him rather than turn him in," Nadine replied, understanding entirely too much after tonight. "He's not worth wasting your life on."

They rode home in simmering silence.

The limo driver dropped them off where he'd picked them up, and they slipped down the back alley again, returning through the pool door. Magnus locked the gate, then held Nadine's elbow to lead her down the path shielded by tropical foliage. She shook off his hold once he'd unlocked the patio door.

Still miffed, Magnus wandered off to check the outdoor security system.

Entering the darkened family room with her mind in turmoil, Nadine caught a flicker at the far end of the room from the corner of her eye.

She froze in place, her pulse escalating after the evening's anxieties. She studied the far corner, unsure if she had simply seen some trick of the moonlight.

A translucent shadow darted behind the draperies.

Her blood froze, and goose bumps rose on her arms. *Shadow*. Not solid.

"Who's there?" she tried to call, but her voice was nearly paralyzed. The question surfaced as a mere whisper.

The shadow quivered. The draperies didn't.

I can't sleep.

Did she hear that spoken aloud? Or inside her head? Either possibility left her icy with fear.

"Who are you?" she asked, a little more strongly, when no one with a gun emerged.

Entering behind her, Magnus must have heard her question. He shut the sliding door cautiously, not moving until he'd studied the situation. Nadine breathed easier having him there, but she was still terrified.

Mikala, the shadow replied with reluctance.

Nadine still couldn't tell if she was actually hearing the answers. She held up her hand to indicate that Magnus stay away. She didn't know how much he could see in the dim glow of the security light.

With a lump in her throat, Nadine managed to ask, "Who sent you?"

Feeling the Maximator's nervous jump, she motioned again for him to stand still.

The general, the small voice replied.

"Where are you?" Nadine asked instinctively, trying not to process too much while dealing with unreality.

At school. The little kids keep crying, the voice said plaintively. *I can't sleep. He said he'd help me if I found you.*

Although she felt frozen, sweat still ran down her forehead. Holding her elbows, she swayed, lightheaded with concentration. She focused on the corner and not the man behind her. "The school in the mountains? Should we come get you?"

I don't know you. I want my mama. The shadow flickered and was gone.

Releasing the image, Nadine crumpled. Max's strong arms caught her as her mind went dark.

Trying not to panic, Magnus scooped up Nadine's unresponsive body and carried her out of the room. He wanted her safe, and the family room didn't feel safe, not if she was talking to things he couldn't see.

He took her upstairs to the bedroom she'd claimed. She'd left her clothes scattered across bed and chairs and not made her bed. He lay her down among the rumpled covers and tested her pulse.

She stirred before he found it.

Heart in throat, he briefly left her while he filled a glass with water. When he returned, he helped her sit up and sip. She grimaced at the tap water but didn't fight his hold.

"What happened?" he demanded. "Do I need to hunt for an intruder?"

"Astral projection," she murmured, in what sounded like wonder. "No wonder Jo-jo has started a school. He's found a kid who can project where he tells her."

"That's ridiculous," Magnus said without thinking. "You're saying a ghost image of some kid was down there?"

"If you couldn't see her, then I was picking up her... spirit? I have no idea how it works. It's just another of those psychic abilities that the general keeps hunting for. That poor kid. He'll be relentless now that he has her." She leaned against the pillows and looked hollow-eyed with exhaustion.

"Her? You know it was a girl?" Magnus had no idea how to interrogate the impossible—not while his main concern was Nadine. His heart was still pounding from watching her in action, and she looked too damned *fragile* to bully.

He would have to play this new phenomenon by ear and trust in Nadine's knowledge of the impossible.

His heart nearly stopped at the thought. Releasing control to La Loca was a pretty long step off a steep cliff for him. His grip tightened on the glass she returned to him.

"She said her name was Mikala." Nadine hesitated, apparently searching her memory banks. "She said the little kids were crying and that the general sent her. I didn't get more than that, except that she seemed terrified."

Nadine sounded as plaintive as the child she must have heard in her head. Magnus mentally cursed but stuck to offering more water. When she sat up, he rubbed his hand in a circle on her back, trying to ground her. "Does your head hurt?"

"Yes. No." She rubbed her temple. "I don't know. It was just weird, like talking to ghostly vibrations through some quantum break in the space-time continuum or whatever string theory is about. Except I think she's alive."

"I'm not a physicist, just a mechanic. I can't explain any of that except in terms of Star Trek," he said in resignation. "It's late. We can't do anything tonight. What will it take to get you to sleep?" He sought the fastening of her dress without being told.

"You," she responded with a sigh. "You balance me."

Magnus had no idea what that meant, but he accepted it with gratitude. Right this minute, he needed to be needed. It was the only thing preventing him from riding into the dawn with weapons drawn.

He must be growing brains because even he realized now that riding after a man as dangerous and demented as the general would be beyond stupid.

Twenty-four

Tuesday morning dawned foggy and gloomy. At the breakfast counter, Nadine scanned her laptop screen and spooned cereal. "The info we added to the genealogy website has been picked up," she commented. "And the IT guy is probably now following everything I do on this laptop. I can't find anyone called Mikala through the search engine. I'd need to hack the back door to see if she's been hidden."

Magnus shoved a bowl of fruit in her direction but didn't respond otherwise.

He had made gentle love to her last night after she'd practically begged him. Today, he was treating her like a piece of porcelain, even though she felt fine. He was probably plotting ways of locking her up again. Men! They were simply too exasperating. She crunched her cereal and ignored his taciturnity.

She would not be shut up again.

"Since the bug in that website probably tracked us, Jo-jo could be sending an astral scout to check on the students before he enrolls them," she suggested. "I wonder if Mikala needs a strong location, like I do, before she can project."

"*Astral* scout." Magnus growled into his coffee, as if she'd offended him.

Okay, so he thought she was nuts. Astral scout sounded whacko even to her. But sometimes, one simply had to accept that the world was not as it seemed.

If he couldn't cooperate... She hadn't wanted to rebel against his protection so soon, but she couldn't let that child suffer alone.

She clenched her teeth and steeled her nerves for whatever Magnus threw at her. This was it, the moment she broke the reins and decided her own fate. "I can't wait for the general to find us. I have to find Mikala. I'm going out there," she announced.

He raised one dark eyebrow and slathered a burned piece of toast with jam and said nothing. She wanted to fling things at him. She'd just declared independence, and he shrugged it off as if she'd said she liked eggs.

"If I can get closer, I might be able to lure Mikala out to me," she said insistently, even though he wasn't arguing. "I *have* to test my ability to reach her. She said the little kids were crying for their mothers!" Nadine squashed all her hopes into a tiny box and reached for the cell phone he'd left on the counter.

Mad Max's large hand covered hers. "Not without me."

She smacked his hand. He didn't remove it. "You're rather noticeable," she pointed out in irritation. "I'm more inconspicuous. I could just be hiking along a country road. I can *do* this."

"Not without me," he repeated. "The general could just be baiting a trap."

Admittedly, that hadn't occurred to her. She yanked her hand away. "I need to go *now,* while I can still feel her... thought waves... or whatever it is. I need to be able to reach out and find her mind inside the school. *Soon.*"

He picked up his phone and hit speed dial. When someone answered, he began snapping orders. "We need an RV, one large enough that thermal imaging won't find us inside. We'll exchange it for our rental a few miles from the general's freak school."

Nadine froze in astonishment. She assumed he was talking to Conan. Magnus generally wasn't rude to anyone but his brothers.

"We'll need a driver so we can hide inside. We have to make the RV look like it has a flat when it's near the school," he continued. "The driver can make a show of riding off with a tow truck, so it looks as if he's abandoned it. And apparently, we need it now. Or by the time we get up there."

When he put the phone down, Nadine was still dazed. Mad Max had listened? He was helping with a *child* instead of insisting they find the general first? Glory, hallelujah! She hadn't realized how much she hadn't wanted to do this alone.

She leaped from her seat and hugged him. "You were already planning! Thank you. I'll fix food."

"I'm not buying ghosts," he muttered, returning to finishing his cereal. "But if the general is sneaking holographs into the house, it's better if we're not here."

"Holographs!" She laughed and started digging through the refrigerator for enough food to last them a few days. "Have it your way, Mr. Mechanic."

"If he has heavy security near that school, this is an insane idea," he warned. "They'll play kick the can with us."

"He may be doing worse to *children*!" she yelled back from inside the enormous refrigerator. "How do we sneak out of this place in broad daylight?"

"We don't. We put on our Goodwill duds—no spike heels, please—wear hats, get in our trashy car, and drive to the grocery store like normal people. You take only what fits into a large purse. If you think we need a change of clothes, wear them on top of each other." He carried his bowl to the sink and rinsed it out. "We'll have another rental waiting for us at the store."

She stared around the stainless steel door at him. "Special Forces training? Or are you just this way all the time?"

"Both." He laid his palm against the SubZero door and shoved it closed, then grabbed her waist and hauled her off her feet. "You're the only woman in the world who can push me this far. Don't get too smart, okay?"

She was too dizzy to reply. He kissed her before she could even begin to think. His words had her spinning as much as the kiss. His arms enveloped her in steady strength and a security that didn't leave her feeling trapped. When he set her down and stalked out, Nadine stood there stupidly with her fingers over her swollen lips.

She was the only woman who could push him? What the dickens did that mean? Any way she took it, it had her inexperienced heart thumping faster than it should.

Hours later, in the fields outside of Topaz, Magnus examined the RV that Conan had provided. He offered a thumbs up to the RV driver waiting for his approval. "This the tin can that Oz was living in when he was stalking Pippa?"

"Oz says he bought it at a DEA auction for a steal," the driver agreed. "It has special insulation. Those druggies have to be seriously paranoid worrying about infra-red. Glad it can be put to use helping kids instead of hurting them."

"People like you and Oz restore my faith in mankind," Nadine said fervently, bouncing on the narrow cushion of a couch like a manic elf. "The possibility that we should even need this thing is the real crime."

"Good versus evil, old story." Magnus turned to the driver. "Conan explained what we need?"

"We're about ten miles from your destination now. I think we've got the rear tire rigged to go flat just before we reach it. This area is too far out to call a tow shop, so I've got a bike on back. We'll drive out, and I'll stop the RV in the safest wide spot along that route, then bike away as if going for help. If our calculations are off, I can drive the rim for a while. Oz doesn't care. There's a box of those mirrors you requested on the table."

Magnus nodded his approval. They'd argued over the distance from the school on the drive over. Nadine had scoffed that a child who could project hundreds of miles would have difficulty finding them half a mile down the road. Or that the distance would deter her mind reading. Magnus couldn't argue since she'd *seen* the general across an entire state.

"That works, thanks." He opened the mirror box while studying the seating in the rolling tin can. "If the general's security is any good at all, we can't move around much once we get there," he warned Nadine. "Choose your position."

As the RV rolled down the deserted road toward the school, and Max installed his mirrors, Nadine fluttered about the doll house interior, exploring every cranny. "This is adorable! I've never been inside one of these. Look, the bench lifts to make a bed!"

"Not big enough," Magnus muttered, even though he knew they wouldn't have a chance to try it out. And that he needed to prepare himself for farewells if the gambit should actually work.

Nadine was counting on finding a kid. Magnus was gambling that they'd draw out the general. Either way, their adventure was almost done.

He didn't like farewells. He liked things loose and easy. Uncomplicated.

No one was more complicated than Nadine. And irrationally, he liked it that way. Working that out required a wrench in his hand. The screwdriver he used on the mirror had to do.

When he was done, he folded the table under, opened the bench beneath, and took the biggest seat in the room.

Nadine produced her laptop and sat down beside him as if she belonged there. He kind of liked her confidence—or her lack of boundaries.

"Don't worry, I've turned off the tracking devices and disconnected the internet," she told him. "I'm just making notes."

Definitely lack of awareness of anything but the project at hand, he concluded.

She smelled like orange blossoms. The fragrance suited her. Magnus wanted to ask if the general had bought her perfumes or why she'd chosen to appropriate this one, but he couldn't let himself get any more involved.

He and the general were heading for a knock-down, drag-out, and he needed to push Nadine far, far away.

"You won't need to move around much once we stop, will you?" he asked at one point, while she was shifting for a better position—and the brush of her leg sent his mind to the bed beneath them.

"No, I'm good. I'm working out the kinks now. Once I hit trance stage, I don't notice anything." She kicked off her shoes and wriggled her bare toes at him.

"My second toe is longer than my big one," she said, holding up one foot and examining it critically.

"I think it's sexy," Magnus said, because he did. Which was probably nuts. He'd never thought about a woman's toes before, but he loved her long, lean ones. "The freckle on the back of your neck is sexy, too. And your eyes are so far beyond sexy that they ought to be banned in respectable places. Is insanity contagious?"

She giggled. Giggled, when they were hurtling down the highway for a confrontation with the impossible.

"The sex is that good, huh?" She leaned against his shoulder as if she belonged there and continued typing.

"Yeah, that must be it," he replied. "It will probably wear off in a few months. Don't get yourself killed before then."

She elbowed his ribs.

The RV started rolling awkwardly, making loud flap, flap noises.

"Almost there!" the driver shouted. "There's a shady spot up ahead. Not many of those hereabouts. That will keep the temp down a bit."

Magnus figured nothing would keep his blood from boiling while Nadine lay curled against him. He rolled over her and took the bench seat on the other side of the aisle, propping his boots where he'd been sitting.

She shot him a quizzical look but busied herself shutting down their communications.

"How soon do you want us to send someone out?" the driver

asked.

"We'll buzz Conan when we're ready."

"It could be night," Nadine said apologetically. "That's when they relax their guard."

Magnus figured she was talking about the kid's mind and not security, but he saw no point in explaining Nadine's mind tricks to the driver, not any more than he'd explain the mechanization of a satellite.

The driver climbed out, removed his bike, and pedaled off, leaving them stranded in the desert with the general's minions half a mile down the road. Or less.

"Can we talk?" Nadine whispered.

"Not too loud. Don't you need silence to connect with the kid?" He was curious. He couldn't help it.

"Yes, but I didn't want to worry about anything I might say aloud while I'm connecting with her. I'm never certain what will happen or what I'm doing when I'm... elsewhere. I'd rather look out the window and direct my thoughts toward the school, but that's probably not a good idea, right?"

"Right. Security will be scoping us out right now, if they're any good at all." Which gave him an itchy feeling between his shoulder blades. "Let's see if we can make this quick."

"All right. Here goes." She sat cross-legged, shut her eyes, and curled her hands palm upward on her thighs.

Twenty-five

Leaning against the RV's wall, with his boots propped across the aisle, Magnus studied Nadine's pointed chin and pert nose and felt an ache in his midsection that he'd prefer to ignore. Even the tiniest bit of thought would tell him that he had to let her fly free, once this was over. The gap in experience between them was unbridgeable. She had an entire life to catch up on.

He was ready to settle down with one woman. That realization floored him. It shouldn't have. He'd actually considered marrying not too long ago, until the ground had been ripped from under him. He thought he'd learned his lesson. Apparently not.

Her eyelids blinked rapidly, and her hands twitched. Magnus set his mouth and studied the mirrors he'd positioned to catch views through the windows. A cluster of crows flew up abruptly, cawing protests. Without moving, he couldn't see far enough to tell what had disturbed them.

Conan had the RV under surveillance, but his men would be too far away to help if anyone broke in. Magnus counted his improvised weapons, primed his muscles for action, and waited.

He was damned tired of waiting. They couldn't use any communication that the general's minions might intercept while they waited like sitting ducks. Once he could use his phone again, he'd ask Conan if he'd succeeded in getting his Camaro out of impound yet. His smart car would be an excellent tool for tracking the general.

He didn't want to focus on Nadine, but his eyes were drawn to her without deliberation. If he were a man who thought in literary terms, he'd compare her to the gleaming temptation of an entire toolbox stocked with everything a man could imagine. But he was a mechanic and she wasn't a tool and he couldn't fit them together in any other context.

She sighed in frustration and straightened, turning to him with open eyes. "We'll need to wait for dark. There's too much activity inside. I can sense her, but I can't reach her."

"Nap, then," he suggested. "You'll need your strength later. I'll keep watch."

She glanced at the clock on the tiny microwave. "It will be dark in about two hours, right? Let's eat our sandwiches, then I'll try to nap a bit. I'm not good at it."

He attempted a suggestive leer and she snickered, but they both knew the RV couldn't be seen moving. Their motions had to be slow and cautious.

He had to find a way to make certain last night wasn't the last time they made love. That was as far as he could plan.

Magnus watched the sun fade into desert darkness. He could see nothing in his mirrors now. Nadine had finished her sandwich, made a pretense of napping, then settled into her meditation position again. If this didn't work, he was driving to Palm Springs. Maybe he'd borrow a tank and just drive over the general's fence and minefields. Getting arrested would be better than this idleness.

Nadine seemed to be murmuring a senseless conversation he couldn't quite follow. But she didn't seem to be in a panic that might require action.

He clenched and unclenched his fists, feeling useless. He should have brought his weights with him. A few arm curls would help.

A small thump hit the side of the RV. Nadine slumped, but she was on a bed. She couldn't hurt herself. He didn't have to panic and disturb her concentration by touching her. He was actually starting to accept her little *spells* as normal.

Magnus gripped the hammer he kept at his side. It looked like the kind of weapon a normal RV driver might have on hand, except he knew how to use it in lethal ways. He dropped his boots to the floor and waited for another sound. He didn't want to reveal their presence if a raccoon had just tested the water reservoir.

A man shouted. A child whimpered. Magnus was on his feet and half way to the door when Nadine roused.

He held up his hand. "You can't go out there. This could be a trap."

"I hate when you do that," she muttered, rubbing her temples.

"You hate when I'm right," he corrected. "You're used to being the only one who is right."

She snickered, and relieved, he cracked open the door. A child cried out in... startlement? Holding his hammer at his side, he stepped down from the RV, closing the door behind him. No headlights flashed down the dark highway.

An owl hooted in the grove of trees down by the dry creek bed. A streak of white darted around the corner of the RV.

"Kid, get your ass back here before I whup it good," a male voice shouted from behind the cactus hedge marking the school's boundary. "The coyotes are going to eat you if you don't get back here."

As if in agreement, a coyote yipped in the distance. The trees rustled with a chilly night breeze. Magnus stuck to the shadowy side of the RV and eased to the corner where he'd seen the glimpse of white.

"Kid? You okay?" he whispered, figuring it was probably one of the most asinine things he'd ever spoken to thin air. But he'd seen the kids in Kabul disappear into crevasses. He hoped this one spoke English.

"The lady said she'd be here," a plaintive whisper replied.

Nadine had done it. She'd brought the kid out. His pulse pounded as he hit fight and protect modes at the same time.

"She's inside," he whispered, still off balance from this impossibility. "She can't come out. Are you Mikala?" He thought he saw a flutter of white on the driver's side of the van.

"You're the man?" she whispered back. "You'll help us?"

"That's why I'm here." He hoped. He had utterly no clue what he was expected to do with a runaway child. He was a law abiding type, not a kidnapper. "Don't go away," he warned. "It really is dangerous out there."

"I want to see the lady," she insisted.

"Let me handle this guy looking for you first." Magnus could see the guard storming toward the RV.

He stepped out of the shadows, into the road to meet the guard half way. "Trouble, mister?" he asked calmly. He loomed a head above the rotund guard. Sometimes, his size worked for him. "I heard shouting."

"You with that thing?" The guard nodded at the RV.

"I'm waiting for my partner to return with a tire. What's the problem?" he asked again.

"Mind if I take a look inside?"

"I most certainly do. Maybe I should rephrase the question—

who the *hell* are you?" Magnus crossed his arms and blocked the guard's view of the van.

"I'm from the school down the road. We've got a runaway. You could be some kind of sick sex maniac." The guard spoke into his radio.

"What kind of kidnapper would sit out here with a flat tire?" Magnus gestured at the vehicle and pulled out his cell phone. "If a kid is missing, the sensible thing to do is call the cops, isn't it?"

The guard hastily signaled for him to put the phone away. "No point in getting ahead of ourselves. If I can just get the kid, there's no problem."

Magnus punched in 911 anyway. He had confidence in Conan's people. Besides detectives, the team contained teachers, social workers, and law enforcement officers who cared what happened to missing children. Conan would have had them monitoring the situation out here ever since Vera had told them about the school.

"Just let me look around," the guard pleaded. "She's just a brat that needs to be in bed. We don't need cops for that."

"Kids usually don't run away for no reason." He couldn't chase this guy off through intimidation. Time for Plan B… "If she's around here… Hey, kid," Magnus called over his shoulder. "If you're there, do you want to go with this guy?"

"No!" came a firm reply. "They'll lock me up and give me bread and water like they did Robby. I want my mama."

Magnus shrugged. "Looks like we got ourselves a runaway after all."

He spoke into the phone to the dispatcher answering. "We have a bit of a problem, ma'am," he said in his best *aw shucks* voice. He gave a description of their location and kept blocking the guard from going around him. He was faster on his feet than the round guy. "We've got a kid saying she and others have been abused, and a guy who just threated to whip her. I'm not letting him have her until some official tells me it's okay."

The security guard screamed urgent orders into his radio.

Magnus leaned his shoulder against the RV's door, opening it just enough so Nadine could overhear. "What's your mama's name, kid?" he asked. "Can I call her?"

"No," the little voice said forlornly. "She's not there. She's never there. I've tried and tried to call."

"That doesn't mean she's not there. We'll work it out. The sheriff is a real nice man. He'll help us, too. You want to come out here where we can see you?" Magnus held his breath and thought he heard Nadine bite back hers.

The kid didn't reply.

Behind him, Nadine hissed. "Say we have Oreos."

"Look, I'll get some Oreos from inside, and you can just sit here on the step behind me until the sheriff comes, okay?" he said, willing to try whatever Nadine suggested.

The situation made him antsy. He couldn't fight off an army of security if they arrived. He couldn't even escape on a flat tire. He hadn't quite thought that part through. He'd counted on Conan's team flying to the rescue, but they were a little slow tonight and the situation was escalating faster than anticipated.

Planning ahead was not his strong point.

A motorcycle roared down the road just as the white figure passed in front of the RV, drawn by the offer of cookies. The headlight caught a stocky child, with thin straight mouse-brown hair, wearing an ankle-length nightgown. She froze in the glare, then darted toward Magnus.

He stepped into the road, blocking the kid from the guard making a grab for her. A little music, and they could cha-cha. "Your dance moves need work," Magnus said, causing the guard to look at him if he was crazed. Obviously, he was. A sane man wouldn't be out here with a broken down RV protecting two mental cases from a seriously paranoid berserko.

The motorcycle halted in the road. The driver took off her helmet and swung a head full of blond hair free. "Problem, boys?"

"Nothing to do with you," the guard growled. "Move along."

A Jeep rumbled up the drive from the school, and the guard relaxed a fraction. Reinforcements had arrived.

The child hid behind Magnus. He noted that a package of Oreos had materialized on the step of the RV. The child settled into the safe enclosure of the steps and munched contentedly.

On the off chance that the motorcycle rider was one of Conan's plants, Magnus shrugged when she glanced his way. "He's hunting a runaway. The runaway is crying abuse. I've called the cops. If that Jeep over there starts shooting, you might want to hightail it out of here and warn someone."

"Is that the runaway behind you?" she asked, ignoring his warning. "Do you have a name, hon?"

Magnus heard Nadine whisper urgently when the girl hesitated. The kid glanced uncertainly up at him, then reassured, she turned to the woman and nodded.

"My name is Mikala. I want my mama."

That seemed to be all the inspiration the motorcyclist needed. She rolled the heavy bike between the van and the Jeep screeching to a halt in the middle of the road. "Well, then, I guess I'll just sit here and make sure Mikala is safe until the sheriff arrives. We girls have to stick together. Hi, I'm Alista Mayhew, a special ed teacher at the local middle school." She stuck her hand out to Magnus.

"Good to meet you, Alista." He shook her hand and heard Nadine snort. He didn't try to interpret the snort but refrained from getting too friendly with the pretty blonde. "Thanks for standing in. I figure my wife would raise a ruckus if I didn't step in to help a kid. I know my nephews can fib at the drop of a hat, but I just can't take that chance, right?"

Oz ought to hire him as one of his actors. Life had been easier when all he'd had to do was shoot the bad guys.

A taller, more menacing guard stepped from the Jeep. This one wore a holster. "She's one of our students. Her parents left her in our care. Step aside, and we'll take her back to the school where she belongs."

"Not until she talks to her parents and the sheriff says it's okay," Magnus said, continuing to block the door where the kid sat. "If the sheriff is satisfied, then I'll just go back to my nap. Do you know your phone number, Mikala?"

The kid looked to be about ten. She nodded and gave him a number. Magnus plugged it in, but the bars on his phone had suspiciously dropped out. "Well, now, looks like we suddenly have a little reception problem. Maybe the sheriff's line will work. Looks like him coming now."

Red and blue lights flashed down the road.

Two more guards from the Jeep got out and approached. Magnus knew he was outnumbered. So did the guards.

"You don't need to get involved," the guy with the holster said with what was supposed to be reassurance. "The sheriff knows the school houses troublemakers. Just go back to your nap and we'll handle it."

"Nope, that's not the way I look at it." Magnus tried to look non-threatening, but he maintained a stance directly in front of the child. He was eager for action, except bullets and children didn't mix.

As expected, two of the guards attempted to grab him while the third reached for Mikala. Fully prepared and happy to mix it up a little, Magnus whacked his elbow into the nose of the guy on his right, swung his hammer into the ribs of the one on his left, and booted the crotch of the one reaching for Mikala.

The sheriff's car pulled up with lights flashing just as the victim of the crotch blow covered his nuts and crumpled.

"Got a little trouble, boys?" the uniformed officer asked, stepping from the car and taking in the situation.

"Want an Oreo?" Mikala whispered behind him.

A grin tugged the corner of Magnus's mouth. That sounded like something Nadine would say. "You putting ideas in her head?" he murmured while the sheriff dusted off the guards.

"No, she's just generous," Nadine whispered back. "Can I come out now?"

"No," he said firmly, before hauling up the guy with the bloody nose. "They attacked me," he asserted loudly. "Miss Mayhew can testify to that. Mikala, you can come out now. The sheriff is one of the good guys." He hoped.

A woman stepped from the passenger side of the sheriff's car carrying a clipboard and looking officious. The sheriff gestured in her direction. "This is Ellen Ramirez. She's with social services."

Magnus shook her hand. Alista and Ellen seemed to know each other and exchanged greetings.

Mikala peered tentatively around his legs. "Can I call my mama to take me home?"

"We can try, Mikala," the social worker said. "Can you tell us your name and where you live?"

The child happily spelled out her street address, her name, her parents' names, and gave them her phone number. Magnus leaned against the RV and kept an eye on the surly guards. Nursing their injuries, they were angrily talking into their radios— blocked cell reception must be frequent out here.

The social worker couldn't make her phone work. The officer used his radio. As they conferred, the RV's driver pulled up with a tow truck and a tire. Conan must have alerted them when the 911 went out.

An RV wasn't exactly the kind of vehicle Magnus had in mind for chasing down the general, but if that was all he had... He hoped Adams had been alerted and was monitoring this situation involving one of the school's most valuable assets.

"Want to sit here?" Mikala asked from her balcony seat. "I can make room."

"Nah, I like standing," Magnus assured her, standing to one side now that the law had arrived. "I'll take one of those cookies now, if you don't mind."

She solemnly handed him a cookie, and they munched while they watched the guards yelling, officials consulting, and the tow truck lifting the backside of the RV. The special ed teacher wandered over and took a cookie too.

"If they can't reach your parents, Mikala, will you be okay going with Mrs. Ramirez? I know her. She's real nice. She'll take you to a home to spend the night, until they reach your parents."

Magnus hid his grimace. The foster system didn't seem like the best choice for a sensitive, possibly abused child. He didn't have to be a mind reader to know what Nadine thought about that. He could practically feel her tension.

"I want to stay with the lady," the child said, as if that was a given.

Damn. Magnus wasn't a creative genius like Oz. He needed a story and didn't have one.

"The lady?" Alista asked in puzzlement.

"Yes, the lady who talks with me in my head and can see me when I'm not there."

Magnus choked on a cookie crumb and caused enough disturbance to cause the girl and Alista both to turn to him. Not that it was likely they could have performed a Heimlich on him if needed.

The officer and the social worker strolled past the angry guards in the direction of the RV, further distracting from Mikala's demands.

Magnus quit choking and waited to hear what came next. The rotund guard rushed up to raise another protest. The officer lifted a hand to hush him.

"The parents have requested that Mikala be taken to friends

over in El Padre," the sheriff's deputy announced.

"What about the little kids?" Mikala demanded before anyone else could react. "They're crying. The lady said she would help them."

Magnus decided it was easier to nail a thug with a hammer than sort through all the talk, but he recognized *El Padre*. Oz and Pippa lived in El Padre. Conan and Dorrie were staying there before the wedding.

He figured there was no chance in hell that Mikala actually came from El Padre, where Pippa knew everyone. Somehow, Conan had interfered with phone communication to get the kid sent to them.

But what the devil did he do about "the lady" and the school? Damn Nadine and her sweeping promises.

"We talked to the boss," the guard shouted, interrupting. "He says we can't let a kid go to strangers. The school is responsible for her and we can get sued."

The social worker, sheriff, and special ed teacher ignored the guard and focused on the kid.

"Why are the little kids crying, Mikala?" the social worker asked. "Are they hurt?"

"Sometimes," she said defensively. "They want their mamas, too."

That wasn't a line that was going to take her far. Magnus prodded the process. "Mikala told me earlier that they went hungry, and I heard the guard threatening to beat her. That's the reason I insisted on calling the police. You might want to check on the other kids." He gave the Jeep of armed guards a narrow-eyed look that the sheriff picked up on pretty fast.

Magnus figured everyone in town was dying to get inside that school. He'd just given them reason to do so. If that didn't bring the general down on his head, the guy must be dead.

Twenty-six

Nadine held her breath, bit her tongue, sat on her hands, did everything she could think of while the fate of a bunch of special children hung in the balance—and she could do nothing.

Now she understood why Magnus preferred action to waiting. She was about to come unplugged. Or explode.

She dearly wanted to hug Mikala, go with her in the sheriff's car, reassure her that all was well... But the general stood in her way. She got that now, too.

If she wanted to help these kids instead of using them for experiments, she had to stop Jo-jo. And the only way to stop Jo-jo was to get him arrested.

She might as well construct a nuclear bomb. She couldn't. But Magnus could. So she had to wait and listen until he told her otherwise.

She pinched her nose as the guards raised holy hell and the sheriff called in reinforcements. This was turning into a long night.

She heard a heavy engine that reminded her of the souped-up Camaro. Escape had arrived?

I know the ladies in El Padre, she told the child in her head.

In all her practice with Vera and others, she'd never really been able to send verbal thoughts. Francesca had been as close as she'd come to mind-speaking, and those had been numbers and images. But Mikala's child-like mind was wonderfully receptive when she left it open, which she was doing now.

Nadine couldn't be certain the child understood the words or how they sounded in her head, but she had no images to project except the one of Pippa and Dorrie. She conjured an image of Mad Max's Camaro and sent that, along with the message, *We'll follow you.*

She could sense the child's sulk, but the argument was too distracting for more.

"You can't take the kid anywhere until our lawyers get here!" one of the guards shouted.

"Then let us in the school to prove her accusations aren't true," the social worker countered.

Nadine pounded her head with her fist and wanted to strangle everyone.

She heard more cars stopping. She wished she could see outside. New lights flashed through the windows, so she assumed another police car had arrived.

Mikala sent her an image of the Camaro—not the same one that Nadine had sent her but a more glamorous one, with black paint and red flames down the side. So, that really had been a muscle car she'd heard.

She could practically hear Mikala's question. But it was Magnus who answered, just outside the door so she could hear.

"Hey, bro, you're a little late. The tire's almost fixed." Mad Max spoke in a lazy baritone, as if all hell wasn't in the process of breaking loose.

"Yeah, well, I figured I'd wait to see if the good sheriff would haul your ass to jail before I bothered wasting my time coming out here. Hey, Alista, Ellen. How's it going?" *Conan.* Conan had arrived in the flashy Camaro.

Nadine hadn't realized she was feeling Max's tension until he relaxed. It was like a balloon deflating. Which probably meant that was *his* car out there and he had a plan and it probably didn't include her.

Crap on that. She'd had enough uselessness for a lifetime.

Nadine eyed the big window she'd decided was an emergency exit. No one would notice if the van bounced up and down with all the commotion happening out there. She eased from the floor and studied the window. It popped out just like a bus exit. Easy.

Go with the good people, she tried to tell Mikala in her head. *I have to leave now, but I'll find you tomorrow. The little ones will be fine now. You did good.*

She thought Mikala's sulk lessened a little.

She carefully placed the exit window on the bed and studied the scattered grove of trees following the creek bed. Vera had said there was a grave by the creek bed, but that was probably on the other side of the road, by the school. She wasn't stupid enough to trespass on the general's territory. Even the sheriff would require a search warrant for that.

It was dark, but headlights and police flashers crisscrossed the road and the land. If anyone lurked out there, she couldn't see them.

She was an experienced window climber now. She knew to throw her legs out first.

"The general will be ordering all cars followed," Magnus told Conan. They eased further from the doorway so Nadine couldn't hear them.

The cops were currently threatening to cuff the school guards, which ought to be keeping Nadine entertained. If not, the women talking Mikala into getting into the sheriff's car should keep her busy until he worked out his strategy.

"If we separate, we're in more danger than if we stand together," Magnus continued. "Let's send the sheriff with the kid, the RV, and everyone to Oz's compound, including you and Nadine."

"And you'll be doing what?" Conan asked, perspicacious as always.

"Taking the Camaro to Palm Springs," Magnus said in satisfaction. "This mess has to stop. Adams knows I'm behind this situation and that I'm the one who can press charges against him. He's probably watching us right now. He knows my car, even if you have gunked it up with that paint job. He probably has a transmitter in it. He'll come after me first, because a single car is easier to pick off than a caravan."

"And then he'll offer to trade you for Nadine," Conan concluded. "Ugly. Better if you just join the caravan."

"No, if he has men follow the caravan, then he'll know exactly where Nadine is, and he'll go after Oz's compound. I don't like giving away Oz's location, but if Pippa is offering to take in Mikala, then it looks like war anyway I see it. We need to stop it immediately by cutting off the general before he figures it out."

Conan uttered a few foul curses and studied the madness around them. "I don't like it, but we couldn't find the kid's parents. They're apparently out gallivanting in the Galapagos or somewhere. Pippa and Dorrie had fits when they heard the kid would have to go to foster care. We didn't have time to do a lot of research, so the team just intervened and acted in place of the parents—illegal as hell if anyone finds out. I assume Nadine had the same reaction?" He glanced up at the RV.

"She's keeping her head down, but yeah, she would have run

over me with the RV if I'd agreed to foster care. These kids don't fit into their own homes much less into strange ones. At least Dorrie and Pippa know what to expect." Magnus didn't attempt to explain how Nadine and the kid were communicating. "The only other safe place would be the house on the beach, and since the general knows the location, it's not much better."

"Oz has a whole town willing to stand between him and the general. We'll call in Dorrie's family, plant them all around. Circle the wagons, just as the Librarian told us earlier. Nadine was right about that. We'll be good." Conan tried to sound unconcerned.

Conan wasn't an idiot. He was as concerned as Magnus.

Magnus took the Camaro keys and left the RV and Nadine to Conan and the RV driver. If he tried to explain, she'd throw a tantrum, and he'd waste time better spent in doing what had to be done. Act now, think later.

He eased toward the rear corner of the RV, sticking to the shadows. As Nadine had said, he was fairly conspicuous, but everyone was caught up in their own drama and had lost interest in him. One of the school guards might be radioing for reinforcements and watching him, but that was just fine. He'd lure away as many bad guys as he could.

Except for the damned silly flames, the black two-door coupe blended nicely into the darkness. The sleek hatchback in this particular model had no rear side windows, providing lots of privacy. He slid into the driver's seat like coming home. He didn't have time to inspect it for tampering. Tampering didn't matter. He *wanted* the general to know where he was.

The engine purred like a kitten. Thunderous roars were for attention getters. Magnus preferred stealth bombers. He eased the car down the road, and no one followed. Not immediately.

He ran all his systems through his checklist. The car's computer identified a tracking device, as expected. He'd decide how to work that information once he was further down the road. He switched on his GPS and directed it toward Palm Springs.

Taking back roads through the parks, heading south, his mp3 playing salsa softly through the stereo speakers, Magnus tried not to think too hard about how furious Nadine would be. She was better off without him, he acknowledged, and she might as well discover that now. He was a natural loner who had to act on his own. He couldn't take responsibility for anyone else. It was the only way he could do what needed to be done, when it needed doing. Like now.

That didn't ease the pain around his heart. He switched the salsa to hip-hop.

A groan from the back seat nearly slammed his aching heart to a stop. The car hit the narrow edge of the road and bounced. He yanked it back and luckily found a pull-off as the moans escalated. The hair stood up on the back of his neck, but he wasn't afraid of ghosts.

Nadine, however, had the power to terrify him.

Pocketing the keys, he stepped out, pushed back the driver's seat, and in the faint illumination from the overhead light easily picked out what he should have noticed earlier—a dark blanket covering his floor board. Of course, earlier, the blanket hadn't been twitching and moaning.

He didn't know how she'd wedged herself into the tiny space left after he'd shoved his seat back. Maybe she'd been on the seat earlier, although the bucket cushions couldn't have been much more comfortable.

Contemplating logistics didn't help. Nadine was having another seizure, and he could do nothing but stand by helplessly until it was over. Helplessness gave him too much room for worry. What could she be seeing now? The possibilities were endless. All the reasons causing her to hide back there could stall his head and wrap it around a lamppost.

The one big take away was that Nadine had known he'd leave without her. The woman knew him too damned well.

She could suffocate under there. Carefully, he crouched down and pulled the blanket back. She was on her knees with her head buried against her arms and shaking violently. Cool mountain air rushed through the open doorway. He hoped that would wake her because her moans had entered every cell of his body and were destroying him from the inside out.

The cold air seemed to work. She shuddered once or twice and quit moaning. An instant later, she collapsed. Relieved, Magnus lifted her up, slid into the back seat, and hauled her onto his lap. She hugged his neck, buried her face in his shoulder, and wept.

That couldn't be good.

"I hate him, hate him, *hate* him," she sobbed wildly, as she'd never done before. “Why? Why does he do this? He ruins everything.”

The cool, calm, collected Librarian was having a meltdown.

Remembering the last woman who had gone to pieces on him and the result, Magnus nearly panicked. Except there was no 911 out here, probably no cell reception at all, and this was beautiful, complicated Nadine. No medic would know how to handle her. It was up to *him,* the useless mechanic.

Amazingly, he didn’t want to run. He wanted to make her feel better. He hugged her closer but he had no reassurances to offer. If nothing else, he’d like to add his tears to hers.

“What did you see?” he asked, hoping she could talk it out, praying he didn’t drive her over the edge by asking. So far, with Nadine, talking had worked—as it hadn’t with Diane.

“I saw him hiding in Woodstar.” Her voice cracked, and she hiccuped and wiped furiously at her eyes. “*Woodstar*! With all those poor confused people.”

Magnus practiced a mental litany of curses while rocking her and keeping his voice low. “Why Woodstar?” She seemed to be receptive to questions. At least her bout of hysteria had eased to hiccupping sobs.

“The computer I was using.” Her reply was muffled against his shoulder. She didn’t immediately continue but clung harder.

Nadine usually hid behind blithe intellectual confidence and an autistic-level focus. Her fear now made him frantic.

“He realized you sent me messages from there,” he concluded on his own.

“Yes,” she whispered sadly. “His new technician is probably tracing them.”

“No big deal,” Magnus said with assurance. “I want him to find me. I *don’t* want him to find you. You’re supposed to be on the way to Oz.”

“I’m not the yellow brick road sort,” she said with a sad half laugh. “Pessimism comes more naturally. He wants both of us, Mikala, and the car, but he’ll take whatever he can get.”

“He can have me and the car. You can’t fight him, Nadine. For all intents and purposes, he’s your father. I’ll have to take you back where it’s safe.”

“There’s no time. And he’ll still come after me. I think he’s cracking. Or maybe senility has set in. I don't know. His mind is this terrible ball of rage. He's not thinking strategically, and that's not like him."

She hesitated, holding her temples and shaking. Magnus waited, letting her process impossible information while he tried to determine how much he wanted to believe.

"If I'm understanding his internal uproar, he has his tech setting up automatic detonators," she murmured in horror. "I'm not sure of the triggers or the placement of the explosives. There's too much fear and fury and nothing remotely... rational... about what I saw. I have to go in and shut him down."

Magnus thought his lungs froze. He couldn't breathe just thinking of letting Nadine return to that snake pit. *He* was the one who had to face the general. He was bigger, tougher, more experienced.

He knew diddley-squat about computer programming.

"You can't be certain you understood what you saw," he objected. "I can't let you go back there."

"No choice. No time." Wiping her eyes on a corner of the blanket, she slid off his lap and out the door. "He's where he belongs, but there's no way to make him stay. Got handcuffs?"

Magnus followed her out of the back seat. The cold air didn't unwind his tangled thoughts. "I can't do this. It just isn't in me to let you go back there."

"Even if he blows up the school and everywhere else he has his gifted victims stored?" she asked. "Can you live with that?"

No.

"Is that what you saw?" he demanded, hand frozen to the door latch.

"Yes." She went around the car to the passenger side. "It's us or them."

Magnus had *listened.* He didn't call her clinically insane, which she very well could be. Or would be soon if she suffered another episode like that one. Being inside the general's head was worse than descending into a schizophrenic hell.

She had to trust in what she'd seen—and felt. Magnus had seen nothing, so he had to extend an extraordinary amount of trust to believe her. Where had people like that been all her life? If more people had trusted her visions instead of fearing she was a psycho hearing voices, she wouldn't have felt so isolated or relied so heavily on Jo-jo.

She could just weep over finding the perfect man when she had to die, but weeping would be a waste of time she didn't have. Giving into emotion had weakened her determination. She'd been tough when she'd been hiding behind computers. Now, she needed to be physically tough—like Magnus.

Nadine finally understood why he preferred to *do* instead of *think*—thinking undermined her resolve. So did feeling. No doubts, no fears. She just had to do it—confront the general on her own.

Magnus turned on the ignition but didn't hit the gas. She had a feeling that once his great brain became fully engaged, he was a ticking time bomb. She clenched her hands in dread.

"The general has no way of knowing that you've located him?" he asked calmly enough, easing back onto the road and continuing in the same direction he'd been taking—which probably wasn't toward Woodstar.

"No, he never knows when I'm inside his head." She looked for a compass on his dash but didn't see one. "Where were you headed?"

"Palm Springs. If he's tracing the transmitter he's planted, and I turn around, he'll realize we know where he really is, and we lose the element of surprise."

"He'll have people waiting for us in Palm Springs," she warned. "All you'll do is get us and the car captured."

"We won't be going there," Magnus said. "We're trading cars."

She tried to puzzle out his logic. "How? And how dangerous would this car be in the general's hands?"

Magnus, the warrior, didn't answer the first question. The mechanic in his head responded to the second. "I haven't enabled all the security systems yet. If I did, the engine would ignite if anyone monkeyed with it."

"How difficult is it to enable the system?" Was he planning on blowing up Jo-jo or the guards?

"Not hard, but an engine fire is pretty tricky. It could set a forest on fire. I don't recommend it as a deterrent. I was just experimenting, looking for a means of keeping my designs out of enemy hands."

She nodded, trying to find his logic. "If you're thinking of trading the car for something Jo-jo has, what other fun toys will fall into his hands?"

She couldn't believe she'd told Magnus the general's direction—*and he wasn't going after him.* She could almost hear the tick-tick of the bomb in his brain. Or maybe that was just her struggle to keep from exploding.

Magnus shrugged. "Nothing particularly dangerous. The car has internet access and blue tooth on everything, which is how you made it talk to me. If I tell you more, I'd have to kill you," he said jokingly, but he didn't laugh.

"The car talked to you?" She loved that idea. "You *heard* me?"

"Not you. It read your text aloud. Hands-free messaging. Most of the things I'm experimenting with are consumer-oriented. I've improved the automated steering they're using in German cars, made it easier to parallel park, and removed the blind spots for safer lane changing. The original engine was one of the most powerful on the road, but not environmentally friendly, which was why it got scaled down in later models. It's a classic car and not expected to pass inspection, so I've souped up the engine rather than downsize it—that part's not consumer friendly."

He was a brilliant man who could make the world a better place. So could those kids in that school if they were brought up right, and maybe even the scientists the general had making war machines could find better uses for their talents. Building bigger and better weapons of destruction improved nothing. One more of the general's misguided notions bit the dust.

"His people will see us coming and have time to prepare," she said in discouragement, trying to plan the unplannable.

"Keep looking for reception on my phone. When we have it, call Conan. We need reinforcements."

"You can't drag anyone else into this!" she said in alarm. "He'll hold your family hostage as well as the school. I can't return their kindness that way. It would be better if you simply let me drive to Woodstar alone," she insisted.

"Not happening, babe," he said with regret. "If you're going down, I'm going down with you."

Not exactly words of love, but under the circumstances, Nadine took what she could get. She hugged her elbows to keep from disintegrating.

Twenty-seven

"Listen, Oz, we've got a problem." Conan stretched out on the bench seat in the RV while the driver steered it toward El Padre—in accompaniment with a sheriff's car, a motorcycle, and the school's Jeep crammed with the general's armed guards.

"Yeah, what else is new?" Oz asked. "I'm about to tie Pippa to a chair to keep her from coming out to meet you and the kid." His usually charming brother sounded as if he was about to bite cigars in two.

"Nadine's gone AWOL. She's slipped out the exit window while I was playing circus master, and while Magnus was running away in his SWATmobile."

"Swatmobile, nice," Oz mocked. "What are the chances that Nadine's with him?"

Conan stared up at the RV's sagging ceiling. "If she reads minds, probably pretty high. People don't broadcast any more clearly than Magnus. The alternative will be that she's raiding the school as we speak, but that's probably too safe for our intrepid vagabonds. Social services has people all over the place. Look, I'm going to have the RV pull off at a gas station. The sheriff with the kid will stay on course, so if you want to keep an eye out for them, go ahead. I'm pulling my team in and going after Magnus."

"Just a minute," was all his big brother said. Obviously, Oz didn't like this idea any better than Conan did and was consulting the experts in madness.

Conan scowled and checked his phone's screen, watching a blip on the map crawling further away.

Oz finally returned. "Okay, Pippa says she can call some friends, get some tractors between the sheriff and the school guards so we can slip him and the kid through the gates without interference. Dorrie's people are arriving. We'll sort everything out on this end. Do you know where they're headed?"

"Judging from what I'm seeing here, he's headed for Palm Springs, but he seems to have stopped. I'm not able to reach his cell. The car was in top condition, so I don't think it's a flat."

"He's found Nadine then, poor bastard. He really doesn't know what's hit him, does he?"

"I think Nadine may be even scarier than Pippa and Dorrie put together. She just doesn't know it yet. So, no, he hasn't got a clue. Gonna be fun watching the mighty oak fall, should he survive the battle ahead."

"Go see that they survive," Oz ordered. "We'll hold the fort here and send what reinforcements we can. And remember, you've got a wedding in two days. Make it fast."

Conan chuckled. "Tell Dorrie I'm properly terrified and we'll be home soon."

Conan clicked off and hoped he hadn't just lied to his bride-to-be.

He watched the sheriff's car speed on past the exit where the RV was rumbling off. The Jeep and motorcycle stayed with the sheriff. Conan didn't know how long it would be before he had unwelcome company. He had to work fast.

"Call me, big brother," he muttered, while he punched into his network.

"Keep trying to reach Conan," Magnus ordered. "He'll have hounds scouring the desert in search of you otherwise."

"Yes, O Great One," Nadine said, finally seeing two bars on the screen. "I hear and I obey."

"I am not the general," he growled. "I just don't want you wandering off until we have all our people lined up."

"So, if I fling your phone out the window, you'll not freak out?" she asked innocently.

For answer, he hit a dial on the steering wheel. A mechanical voice asked who he would like to call.

"Conan." Magnus shot her a sizzling look. "I don't *need* you to obey. I'm just hoping for a little help here."

"Fun! Jo-jo never let me play with the cars." She turned on the interior light and studied the dash.

Conan's voice came through the speaker. "Tell me Nadine's with you."

"I'm here, sweetcakes," she crooned in delight. "I adore this car. If it only came with handcuffs, it would be perfect."

"Black box, under the passenger front seat," Conan responded.

"Tell me Magnus is still alive."

"I'm here," Magnus growled. "I may push the lady out so I can go where I need to go. Got anyone in the vicinity to pick her up?"

"You do that, and I'll personally blow up your sweet car. Or maybe just steal it," she added thoughtfully. "I think that's the best idea. You get out and let me drive this mechanical marvel to the general. And then you can set him on fire. It's an automatic detonator like his, isn't it? The one on your engine?"

"No, I can't explode the car from long distance. It explodes itself. And the detonator isn't turned on." Magnus gave her a swift glare, but the road was too narrow and dark for him to take his eyes off it for long.

"Look, I know you don't like planning, bro," Conan said soothingly, "but you can't go off half-cocked this time. Pull over and let's sort this out. What's this about detonators?"

Ignoring the pertinent question, Magnus complained, "What, and have the general's thugs find us while we're out in the middle of nowhere? I can take on a couple of shitheads at once, but not half the army. I can't even get surprise on my side. I'm pretty sure he's tracking us just like you are."

"You planning on ramming the gates and bulldozing through the front door?" Conan asked with heavy sarcasm.

Nadine chuckled. She was pretty sure that was just exactly what Cro-Magnon man planned to do. "Yeah, but he's heading for the wrong gates, which is what has him steamed. We can't turn around and go the right direction without giving away that we finally know where Jo-jo is."

Conan whistled. "Can I go after him, pretty please? Is he somewhere we can drop helicopters?"

Nadine sighed. "Back to detonators, folks. The man has them. Helicopters or any other surprises are out. We don't know where the explosives are. We need a back door into his computer, or I need to walk right through the place and pull the plug. I vote for the latter."

Silence. Nadine didn't like silence so well.

"I'll get back to you," Conan said. And the speaker clicked off.

"There is no element of surprise if we turn around," Nadine repeated softly, knowing Magnus was sitting there steaming. "He's sitting up there on a mountaintop with no neighbors around him. There's only one road in. If we park on the highway and hike ten miles, he'll still know and have lots of time to prepare."

"I can trade in this car," Magnus suggested.

"By the time you arrange it, he'll be gone. Right this minute, he's fixated on us and the car. If you give him time to get his rationality back, he'll realize we're calling in help. Right now, if I'm guessing correctly, he thinks he has the upper hand because he's separated us from the herd."

"Won't we surprise him by turning around instead of heading for Palm Springs?"

"That would probably make him really happy, although it ought to puzzle him for a while. Unfortunately, Jo-jo is a lot like you. It must be the military mindset. He doesn't waste time on puzzles. He takes advantage of opportunity. He's good at long-term strategic planning, but he can't do that here. So we need to be better at planning than he is."

Magnus used a few words Nadine hadn't heard him use before. For a tough fighter, he was exceedingly polite in everyday situations. She assumed he was reverting to military mode. That scared her a little, but her choices were few. She needed his back-up.

"I can pull plugs," he decided, not giving in yet. "I can smash his computers into microchips."

"You don't think he's prepared for that? The computers will be backed up. They'll have fail safes. And if he's really gone around the bend, they'll be set to trigger nuclear bombs if touched. Jo-jo is good at what he does. You've got to let me go in after him," she said as firmly as she was able while her brain shrieked in terror. "He won't see me as a threat."

The tension inside the car reached explosive proportions. Magnus was very good at holding back.

"Equal but different," she reminded him nervously. "You have no right to control my choices, not any more than I could control your decision to drive off without me. I chose to join you. You can choose to drive your car straight through Woodstar. I get to choose going in the back door. We can't go forward together until we get this straight."

Amazingly, that silly speech released some of his tension. Magnus cast her one of his eyebrow-lifting looks.

"We're going forward together?"

Her foolish heart did a happy dance at his suggestive tone. The rest of her melted in a puddle of lust. "I'd rather not go alone." She could be as ambiguous and cautious as he, even while stating all her hopes and dreams.

"If I say you can't know what you want, you'll jump down my throat, right? Even if I have a little more experience?"

"You don't have *any* experience at being me. So let's just start with right now and you accepting that the general won't blow up anything if he sees me, but he might if he sees you." Nadine held her breath as the car cruised through the desert night, getting further away from their target.

"I can accept that," he agreed. "What I can't accept is sending you in there alone."

"OK, that's a start. How do we debug your car so we can turn around?" Nadine bunched her fingers into fists, wishing for alternatives, knowing there were none.

"Buzz Conan. Get us a new car. We'll need a driver to continue taking this one to Palm Springs, making the general drool thinking his cohorts will have me and the car. I'd prefer a rugged-terrain vehicle for us. I don't want to drive up to Woodstar's door if it can be avoided."

"You're very good at plotting when you get past action-hero mode," Nadine said, punching Conan's contact number.

"Still don't like it," he grumbled. "Plotting requires considering consequences. When it was just me, consequences didn't matter. They're damned painful under current circumstances."

Conan's voice spoke curtly through the speakers before Nadine could make her request. "I can't locate the general's computer. Do you know what server he's using?"

"He moves them constantly and keeps adding new ones. I've been off his grid too long to have any idea. If you weren't able to trace my messages earlier, you don't have a chance now, and we're all out of time."

"New plan," Magnus said. "We're going up there. The car is going to Palm Springs. Bring us new phones while you're at it, just in case he's finally tapped into the one we're using."

While the men discussed logistics, Nadine tried to tap into Jojo's thoughts. It was getting late, but he was an insomniac. She couldn't focus enough to reach him, though. She needed peace and quiet, and she wouldn't be getting them anytime soon. The Oswin men were anything but peaceful and quiet, especially in full war mode.

That was actually rather reassuring. It meant her head was a safer place with all that energy surrounding her, blocking out others.

"If we give you a stun gun, can you use it?" Magnus asked, bringing her back to the moment.

"Jo-jo had us target shooting with hand guns before he even married Mom. I hate them. A stun gun, I might manage. Pepper spray, tranquilizer darts, bring them on."

"Nadine is extremely coordinated," Magnus told his brother. "Load her up. I'd prefer a howitzer, but the general has hostages."

"The patients at Woodstar are particularly good ones," Nadine said. "They have utterly no notion of how to fight back, run, hide, or even get out of your way."

Both men cursed vividly.

Magnus reluctantly surrendered his no-longer-stealthmobile in a small town just off the interstate. The former Marine who accepted his keys whistled in appreciation even before Magnus explained a few of the more useful components.

He saw Nadine grimace at the stripped down Hummer they received in exchange. She hadn't had enough time behind the wheel, but she seemed to have enough mechanical ability to understand the dashboard. They'd be driving back roads. He had to squash his protective instincts and give her more driving practice.

Hiding his wince, Magnus handed her the keys. "Your turn to drive."

That earned him a hug that had his blood pumping.

"I don't suppose Oz has a honeymoon suite in his compound?" she whispered before she pried herself off him and headed for the driver's side.

Magnus took a deep breath to cool down before climbing in. She felt too damned good in his arms, and the mention of honeymoon suites wasn't helping. He wanted to take her to the airport and fly her to Tahiti, safety, and a bed, and let the general blow himself up.

He buckled himself in and taught her the Hummer's instruments. She was an eager student. It didn't take long before she grew impatient with his caution and set the wheels rolling.

Amazingly, she steered through the parking lot gate without coming close to scratching the bars. Excellent spatial perception.

"Oz's house will be full of wedding guests," Magnus reminded her. "If we come out of this alive, I'll take you anywhere you like."

"Really?" Her voice lit up the interior better than the sun. "You'd really take me to Costa Rica or Australia if I asked?"

"Really. I thought women wanted London and Paris." He dug his fingers into the seat as she hit the gas and steered back up the road they'd just traversed. At least he knew there were no dangerous hurdles ahead—not until they reached the general's mountain.

"They're cities," she said as if that was explanation enough.

And it was. Cities had too many people to mess up her mind. He got it.

"I'm not sure understanding you is good for my mental health," he complained. "But I'm good with jungles and deserts."

She laughed nervously and kept her gaze on the road. "Just think of me as a jungle and we're good."

"A screaming-monkey, snake-infested jungle or shady, steamy and exotic?" he asked, releasing his grip on the seat to cross his arms and let his mind travel to jungles, beds, and sex.

"Ummm..." She dared a glance in his direction. "Do I have to answer that?"

"Nope. You just have to keep your eyes on the road and get us to Woodstar in one piece."

"And you want me driving why? I didn't notice any AK47s in our arsenal."

Honesty was the only policy he knew with Nadine. "I want you to have the ability to run like hell if necessary. If equality is what you want, then you need all the knowledge you can get. I can't teach you to survive in the woods right now, so the car it has to be."

"Swell." She gunned the motor and steered the next curve at breakneck speed.

"Snake infested," he decided gloomily. "Can I have the flower-wearing exotic scenario when this is over?"

"Naked Tahitian lady coming up," she said much too cheerfully as she floored the engine toward their doom.

Twenty-eight

At the turn from the highway toward Woodstar, Nadine reluctantly surrendered the keys and got out of the car to exchange positions. With the dark woods all around them, Magnus caught her in front of the engine. In despair and weariness, she leaned into him. His strong arms provided the backbone she needed for these next hours.

His erotic kiss gave her the incentive to survive. The knowledge that he cared enough to teach her how to stay alive provided a warm bubble of happiness to shield her from what was to come.

The general had taught her how to kill. That wasn't the same as teaching her to live. So many things were more clear when she had the freedom to examine them.

"This is not a suicide mission," Magnus reminded her. "You are more important than anyone else in there, got that? I know that sounds cruel, but you are unique, you possess vital information, and we need you alive."

"I can't think like that," she murmured, wrapping her arms around him and kissing his jaw. "You just have to trust that I'll do whatever's best to stop Jo-jo."

He shuddered and nearly squeezed the breath from her. "Can you think of me, just a little? Imagine how I'll feel if anything happens to you, and think twice before doing anything rash?"

She chortled against his shoulder. "You're the one who's likely to go off half-cocked, not me. I'm just a nerd. Promise you'll stop and think, no matter what it sounds like in there?"

That he really cared what happened to her melted her heart, but she'd been fooled before. She simply counted on his formidable brain for now.

"We're talking about breaking and entering," she reminded him. "We could be behind bars for a long time. Sure you want to do this?"

"Code word, Mr T," he said in grim acknowledgment, letting her go. "Don't be afraid to use it."

The dog's name would remind her of Vera as well as Magnus—all she loved in the world. She wouldn't use it in vain.

Magnus drove the vehicle off road half way up the mountain. He found a solid clearing, turned it around, and left the keys in their agreed-upon hiding place.

Nadine resisted the idea of driving off without Magnus, but that's what he was telling her to do if anything happened to him. She had to ensure that nothing happened to him.

They hiked the rest of the way through the woods, their dark jeans and hoodies blending with the cool night. It would be dawn soon. They needed to hurry.

"Check the mic," Magnus whispered into his as the villa's lights came into view. His husky voice in her ear from the clip caused a pleasurable shiver.

She'd let her hair loose to frizz around her face. She'd have to hope no one noticed the phone clip.

She tapped the tiny button attached to her bra. Magnus nodded that he heard it. She felt right at home with the crazy spy equipment that Conan had provided. She didn't feel quite so secure in the woods with lions and tigers and bears. She jumped at every rustle.

"We need to circle the building, locate the exits," Magnus said worriedly.

She looked at the vast wall around the villa, glanced at the sky, and shook her head. "No time. There are only two ways in and out of that fence. Once we're inside the fence, they'll spot us before we're half way around the building. I have to go straight in."

He muttered but didn't stop her. Together, they traversed an unlit clearing outside the wall, to the trash pick-up gate at the rear that Nadine had chosen for her entrance. Magnus easily picked the simple lock.

He grabbed her and kissed her quickly. "For good luck," he murmured.

Throat too constricted for speech, Nadine just nodded and squeezed his hand. They both knew the dangerous insanity of her returning to the loony bin. She was just grateful Magnus didn't lock her up for her own good—as the general had.

Mad Max realized that, too, which was the only reason he was letting her go. Nadine would love him for his understanding, if nothing else. He was a horrendously brave man to trust her instincts after he'd already lost someone he loved to the Big Crazy.

She kissed his bristly cheek and slid through the gate he opened before he could change his mind. It had been so much easier manipulating people with computer commands. Actually doing the job herself...was frightening.

In the months she'd been incarcerated in Woodstar, she'd learned every guard and his post and time schedule. She couldn't count on any of that knowledge remaining the same. *Adapt to live* was her new motto.

Because it was so far out in the middle of nowhere, Woodstar had never needed to apply serious security. The guard at the back door liked to smoke and jaw with anyone else outside doing the same.

At dawn, he'd be patrolling the kitchen just to snatch coffee. Seeing no one outside, Nadine leaned against the wall by the kitchen door and listened to voices.

Two males, instead of just the usual one. The general must have brought some of his own people. How did she want to play this?

If she had a choice—in a darkened room with a computer screen. Unfortunately, this wasn't a video game.

She opened the screen door and tested the door latch to the inner door. It was locked. No alarms screamed, but they might if she tried the keypad. She wasn't ready to surrender her freedom this early in the game by attempting to break the security code.

Locating a hiding place behind the recycle bin, she dug a tin can from inside the container. It didn't take an athlete to chuck a can against the kitchen window and hit it. She ducked down, peered around the corner of the bin, and waited.

Both guards appeared at the door.

"It's just a cat or raccoon," the usual guard protested. "You spook too easy."

The more conscientious guard said nothing but rested his hand on his gun as he stepped out to examine the fenced yard in the dim light of dawn. Gun—bad. Nadine grimaced and flung a stone to the far corner of the yard.

Cigarette Guy pulled out his smokes. "Cat, like I said."

Gun Guard moved stealthily toward the back fence.

She'd like to stone Cigarette Guy for blocking her path, but that wouldn't get him moving. She heaved a bigger rock at the opposite corner of the yard, hitting the big trash Dumpster with a tinny thump.

"Check it out!" Jo-jo's trained security hissed.

The real danger was keeping the mentally ill inside, but still Cigarette Guy strolled out, sipping his coffee and sucking his cigarette. It would be so easy to knock the arrogant ass out...

But that would give her away too quickly to Gun Guy. She may have been deprived of television, but she'd learned to think her way through video game obstacles. She needed to enter the building without using weapons.

Neither guard was as far away as she would like, but they'd left the door unlocked and that was all she needed. Nadine kept to the shadows of the wall and eased open the screen. Cigarette Guy should know better than to leave any door unsecured. In another half hour, he'd have inmates roaming all over the yard—worth thinking about, actually.

She slipped into the dimly lit corridor. At this hour, most of the inmates were starting to wake as their sedation wore off. The day staff hadn't arrived yet.

The cleaning supply room was unoccupied.

Nadine pulled a scrub cap over her hair, donned the blue smock the janitorial staff wore, covered her shoes with paper booties—and located the master room key.

Magnus gritted his teeth and listened at the unlocked back gate—Nadine's only escape route—wishing he'd tied her up and left her in the car.

He'd just let a walking Improvised Explosive Device into a confined location. He didn't expect anything less than explosions. If he'd once again misunderstood a female, what happened next was on his head.

The tin can hitting glass froze him into alert position. What sounded like a rock followed, then the voices of the two guards. His heart climbed up his throat. Maybe he'd take up munching tranquilizers so he could learn to accept doing nothing.

When he heard no shouts or gun shots, he tried to breathe again. Praying Nadine was safely inside or she would have let him know, he worked his way along the outside of the fence. He used his phone to send notes and photos to Conan, marking cameras, landing areas, and roof lines. It would take time for Conan to pull together a team for this operation and transport them up here. Not knowing how long the general would be here, they didn't have time to spare.

He and Nadine were essentially on their own.

The parking lot was inside the security fence, as he'd learned that first morning. Through the wrought iron gates, he could see a silver Escalade in the lot. He assumed it belonged to the general. The rest of the cars were small, older models that the night nurses might drive. Doctors and administration hadn't arrived yet.

There was almost no place to hide inside or outside the fence once the sun rose. It didn't matter. He was responsible for whatever happened, and he had to be closer when all hell broke loose. Climbing that fence and running for the house if Nadine screamed wasn't on his preferred approach list. Besides, he wanted her to have more than one exit route.

No night guard sat in the front entrance booth. The day shift would show up soon.

Here was an action he could take instead of waiting like a shackled dog.

Checking for wires on the guardhouse and finding none, he popped the lock. Keeping his head down, he slipped inside and stayed low while he examined the gate mechanism. A handy pocket screwdriver later, and the gate creaked open.

A truck rumbled up the hill as he dashed inside and shoved the gate closed again.

Lights were flashing all over the west wing of the building.

Nadine hummed under her breath, trying to relieve her tension, as she worked her way down the security wing of the building, mopping and unlocking any door she encountered. The computer room was at the far end. No light gleamed under the door, so she assumed the general had finally found other entertainment and gone to bed. Another good reason she couldn't connect with his mind—men didn't think during sex or while sleeping. That was her theory anyway, and who could argue with it?

She'd spent months traversing these floors in slippers and sloppies, listening to the howls and mumbles behind closed doors. She had no idea what would happen once the patients learned they had access to freedom. She'd never seen more than this main hall and wasn't even certain what awaited down the corridors and inside the rooms she was unlocking. She could hope for more doors, lots of patients, and presumably fire exits. She really hoped there were fire exits.

She parked her mop and bucket outside the computer room and tested the door lock with her master key. Glory hallelujah, it opened without setting off alarms.

No longer humming, she shut and locked the door after she entered. Other people had keys, and a good hatchet would probably take out the lock, but rattling the latch would give her a warning. She hoped to be done before anyone found her.

She powered up the main computer. The new IT guy wasn't any fool—he'd set up new passwords. She plugged in the USB stick Conan had given her for hacking passwords, but it would need time she didn't have. Filthy bad word.

A cackling wail outside the office raised her hackles. One of the inmates had presumably discovered an open door.

Footsteps raced through the tile corridor and a nurse shouted. In response, half a dozen voices raised in panicked cacophony.

That ought to keep the limited staff occupied a while. Maybe they'd even have to drag Nurse Wretched out of the general's bed.

Not whistling anymore, she crouched down and pulled out the desk to get at the box containing the hard drives. She'd planned for this alternative, but she didn't like it. Her fingers shook as she pried off the case. She couldn't let self-doubt stand in her way any longer. She could very well be blowing up the world, but if she didn't try, the general would stay in charge.

The general had been in charge far more than was safe. Her turn.

She popped the back of the box and whispered *freedom.*

A fire alarm screamed.

"I'm fine," she whispered into her mic. "I'm all alone and dismantling the computer."

"Thank you," the Maximator's gravelly voice came through well enough to hear his relief. "I was about to start breaking windows. You're in the west wing?"

Amazingly, his calm assumption that she knew what she was doing gave her the confidence to start unscrewing delicate parts. Considering his question, she worked out the home's layout in her head. "Yeah, west sounds right. I let the inmates loose. One must have set off the alarm. They're a little occupied out there. The general will be down soon. I've got to get the box apart before he arrives." Without blowing up anything, she didn't say.

"Roger, wilco. Where are you in relation to the rest of the rooms?"

"End office. Only small windows high up. Negative on entering." She disabled a few wires while they talked... Nothing exploded. She just had to pray there were no automatic triggers on the explosives. She would have built a fail-safe into the program— but then, she wouldn't have built programs to detonate explosives in the first place. "I feel all military. Think the Marines would take me?"

"No. Get the job done and get out so I can go after Adams." He didn't sound happy.

Nadine knew getting out wasn't happening. She was pretty much trapped in here. The confinement grated her nerves to a fine point. One wrong move, and she might mentally explode.

She tried to hum as she worked but couldn't. She was a software person, not hardware. Her fingers shook as she dismantled a memory board.

The shouts in the corridor grew louder, more panicked.

Someone attempted to turn the knob. Here it was...the moment of truth. With nothing better to do, Nadine determinedly continued unscrewing wires and removing chips, decimating the general's plans one micrometer at a time.

She'd delay calling for Magnus until all hope was lost. She didn't need to read minds to know it would be very messy indeed once the general, Magnus, and guards with guns were in the same room.

Twenty-nine

Magnus studied the narrow windows over his head. Nadine was in there, but he'd have to tear down the wall to get at her. Even though a fire alarm screamed like an irritating banshee, he wasn't ready yet to scale walls. She'd said she was safe. He might have to chew nails, but he had to believe her.

He figured he'd know when all hell exploded. Nadine wouldn't go out with a whimper.

The sun was rising behind the trees on the far side of the building, casting a gray shadow over the adobe walls. If he was careful, he still had a little time to poke around and form a more sophisticated rescue plan than "batter down door and all obstacles."

This entire wing was nearly windowless, except for the high narrow ones near the roof. The other wing had an atrium but this was obviously the security wing for the patients most likely to harm themselves or others. He didn't feel real secure thinking of Nadine in there.

He located the fire exits on the north and south sides of the wing. They were some distance from Nadine's computer office, and the steel doors would require a monster truck ramming into them to open. If he remembered the OSHA rules on mental institutions, they were probably locked from the inside as well. Not a good exit for Nadine unless she had the keys.

It would be simpler for him to enter through the front entrance, although that was even further from the office and presumably better guarded.

He crouched between two air-conditioning units and texted Conan. The reply was almost instantaneous: FRANCESCA AND BO IN HELICOPTER. ETA HALF HOUR. CARS TWO HOURS OUT. SHERIFF WITH.

Sheriff with? Did that mean they'd found something at the school that might actually mean the law would finally step in? That brightened his morning. At the moment, he and Nadine were facing years of incarceration for breaking and entering.

The estimated time of arrival did not make him happy—not with the demented screams of hell breaking loose inside. Dorrie's brother and Francesca couldn't catch the general from a helicopter. With luck, they might help with a hasty exit.

The truck he'd heard earlier stopped outside the guard booth. Magnus watched the uniformed security guard climb out, sipping his coffee. The man had his keys out to unlock the door and didn't appear to notice it was already unlocked. He just jiggled the knob and took his seat inside.

The guard wouldn't discover the gate breach until he attempted to open the gate—which could be momentarily. Two more cars were making the final climb up the road.

"Reinforcements arriving," he whispered into the mic.

"Yeah, they're at the door," she murmured back. "Here's where I find out if I've blown up the world."

After that, Magnus just heard shouts, and his blood pressure escalated two hundred percent. He knew how the angry green Hulk felt.

Nadine checked the various objects on the weapons belt hidden beneath her hoodie. Conan had stocked it well. She already knew there were no scissors in the room, no potential weapons for the mentally confused. Even the coffeemaker was the one-cup kind and used paper cups.

She verified the position of her stun gun while grinding a hard drive with her foot. Jo-jo wouldn't be blowing up anyone from here today. Whoever had been pounding on the door had switched to a stronger tool, probably a fire ax.

She still wore her scrub woman's cap and tunic. Pity she couldn't add aluminum foil to complete her fashionable attire for the party.

She wasn't operating under any illusion that the general would miss her invite.

Nervously, she perched on the edge of the desk and looked for sharp shards of plastic in the mess she'd made. Maybe Jo-jo would have a stroke seeing what she'd done. A girl could hope.

The solid wood door finally splintered enough for her guest to batter it open with his shoulder. One of the institution's uniformed guards spilled through first. Nadine stunned him and let him fall, jerking spastically, to the floor.

She glanced down and recognized the toad who'd laughed at her. Good. He'd got what was coming.

Jo-jo stood in the doorway in...*dishabille*. She'd always liked that word. His normally creased slacks were rumpled and unbelted. His unbuttoned dress shirt revealed a white t-shirt and a few crisp gray curls beneath. His gray crew cut had thinned over the years. His unshaven bristles were gray too. He looked like a shriveled, confused old man, not the roaring, uniformed dragon of her nightmares.

"Hi, Daddy," she said brightly, swinging her leg from her desk perch above the debris of the computer. "If any of your targets are set to go boom if the fail-safe is removed, you might want to warn a few people to get out of the way."

He actually looked alarmed. She hadn't thought he had it in him.

"Richard, where's the backup?" Jo-jo roared at a slim young man in glasses peering around him.

"Hey, Dick, good to meet you." Ignoring the chill running through her at mention of backup, Nadine kept her brave face on and called to the puzzled geek. "You'd better hope you can access your backup if the triggers you set yesterday were automatic. You're probably looking at a lot of dead bodies and life in prison otherwise."

He shook his head slowly. "We just set up some military war exercises. Nothing is blowing up. Are you Nadine?"

This was where self-doubt and the craziness jumped in—had she only dreamed Jo-jo's state of mind? Had she *imagined* he was planning on blowing up real targets and not playing war games?

But the school was real. Locking Magnus and the other scientists up had been real. Planting microchips in her head and storing her in a mental institution had been real. She was older and wiser now—and more confident, thanks to Magnus.

It was poor Dick who was delusional. She had to believe that.

Jo-jo roared at someone down the hall. His fury was real. She swallowed hard and started praying. The general didn't know enough about computers to know if dismantling this one would discharge his fireworks. Details weren't his strong point. She needed to pick the geek's brains.

"Sorry I didn't introduce myself. I'm Nadine," she said. Dick the

Geek looked uncertainly from her to Jo-jo shouting for security. "The general is my stepdad, and he's paranoid. He told me pretty stories about war games and military security, too, but they were lies. He really does have explosives under those targets. I think one of them is a school full of special kids."

The stunned guard on the floor was shaking off the surprise of her attack and climbing to his feet. He was a big man. It would be difficult to keep him down. Nadine kept a hand on her weapons belt.

"You can't know that," the Geek argued. He wasn't running to look for backup as the general had ordered, poor delusional fool.

Turning swiftly, Nadine rammed the stun gun against the guard's nuts and held the trigger. His scream wasn't pretty. Maybe she was a little whacko.

As if she was continuing a pleasant conversation, she continued. "I know this sounds crazy, but I read minds." She smiled sweetly at Jo-jo, who looked horrified. "I read *your* mind, anyway, Daddy. It's not a nice place. Hold your hands out, and I'll prove it."

"Don't be ridiculous," he replied with his usual scorn. "Richard, there's a computer in the office off the lobby. Access the network, ASAP."

"Probably best, Dick. It's going to get ugly in here shortly. You don't want any little kids blowing up while we fight this out." Nadine continued smiling like a sociopath.

"Here's a microchip." She tossed it at the general, who was still athletic enough to catch it. "Put it in one hand behind your back, and then produce both hands. I'll tell you which hand it's in."

"I don't have time for this stupid tomfoolery. Richard!" he roared. "Do as I say!"

Nadine tossed Richard the thumb drive from Conan. The geek wasn't as adept at playing catch. He fumbled and dropped it and got down on the floor to find it. "If you need help saving little kids, that will send the general's war game to a professional gamer. You'd better hope Conan knows how to pull the plug."

"Leave the time table as it is," the general thundered over the cacophony of screams and shouts in the corridor behind him. "Just make certain we're still in control of the program."

Nadine didn't know how much Magnus could hear. Just in case he decided to come roaring to the rescue before she had the situation in control, she got down from the desk and took the semi-automatic away from the twitching guard on the floor. With expertise learned from the furious man in the doorway, she removed the clip from the gun and the spare from the guard's pocket.

Jo-jo glared at the geek, trying to intimidate the tool he needed most, but Dick just looked uncertain and didn't move. Neither man tried to stop her as she rendered the gun useless.

The general still thought her harmless and easily contained. He was glancing over his shoulder, looking for more thugs to arrive and hustle her back to her room. She really hoped Nurse Wretched would show up while she still had juice in the stun gun.

Nadine dumped pistol bits in front of the moaning guard. "You've had a mind reader and an animal-talker under your nose for years, Jo-jo. But confining us to your narrow world destroyed our ability to use our gifts. Test me, Jo-jo. Hold out your hands."

"Prove her wrong, General," Dick said worriedly. "Otherwise, I'll have to do as she says and dismantle the program. I can't blow up little kids."

"For chrissake, she's a lunatic! You really think she reads minds?" Jo-jo stuck both rolled-up fists in front of him. "Fine. She has a 50-50 chance of getting it right. What does that prove?"

It proved he was so obsessed that he fell for her stupid delaying trick. He really did want her to be a mind reader.

Nadine removed her hand from under her hoodie, produced the handcuffs she'd taken from the Hummer, and snapped them on Jo-jo's wrists. "You have nothing in either hand," she said cheerfully. "You dropped the chip in your pocket. And I didn't even have to invade your mind to figure that one out. I'm just not dumb."

Jo-jo roared loud enough to bring down the roof. His face turned purple. And booted feet raced down the corridor in their direction.

"Better find that computer, Mr T," she told the geek. "Ugly has arrived."

The geek looked startled at the odd sobriquet, but he did as told and ran for the main office.

The guard and nurse arriving in the doorway carried automatics.

Thirty

In his ear clip, Magnus could hear the general's roars but not his words. Nadine still seemed calm. He wondered if he could nail his boots to the ground to keep from running up to the entrance and bullying his way inside. She'd told him to stay back. He trusted her knowledge of Adams, but he was struggling with his Zorro complex.

A black BMW and a battered Chevy pulled up to the broken gate. When the gate didn't open, a neatly-suited tall Asian gentleman stepped out of the BMW. There was an exchange of words with the gate guard. A couple of uniformed security men stepped out of the Chevy. The exchange became heated.

The Oriental gentleman shook the gate, found the manual mechanism, and shoved it open. Magnus recognized his profile from his research—the general's one almost normal son, the former marine. Here was a man he might relate to and chalk into Plan A and B.

Sirens screamed further down the road. All the newcomers looked startled, then rushed for their vehicles as the gate swung open.

In his ear clip, Magnus heard Nadine addressing the Dick-guy with their emergency code word of Mr. T, with no urgency at all. She was going to be the death of him. What in hell was happening in there?

"Going in," was all he said to his mic. It was almost a relief to finally be in action. He hit send to Conan with the prepared text. He almost had Plan A ready—but it was damned hard planning without knowledge.

Straightening from his crouch, he sauntered around the corner of the building as if he belonged there. The day-shift guards went for their radios. Magnus ignored them and turned to the suit opening the door.

"Feng Chang Adams, I presume?" Magnus asked. At the former marine's wary nod, he added, "I believe we have a situation."

Fire trucks and police cars roared up the highway.

"A mild understatement from the report I received," Chang said gravely. "And you are?"

"Excellent question. I'll get back to you on that later."

The rattle of automatic fire inside propelled Magnus through the open doorway at a full run, terror speeding his action. Chang and the guards followed on his heels.

He raced at quarterback speed smack into a lobby milling with night-shirted patients, nearly bowling over a frail elderly woman tugging at her thinning hair. How the devil was he supposed to *plan* madness?

Adjusting his speed and trajectory, Magnus dodged a gaunt man in a hospital gown ambling into his path. He leapt over magazines flung by a young female cowering in a corner. Bearing toward the west wing, Magnus nearly knocked over a very large woman in a sweat suit carrying a rolling pin and bedpan. For all he knew, she was the cook. She swung. He ducked and ran on. From a cry behind him, one of the guards didn't duck fast enough.

The fire alarm continued screaming but no water sprinklers were in operation. Yet.

Reaching Nadine at the end of the corridor was at the top of Plan A—not easily accomplished in a hall packed with half-dressed, terrified mental patients. The shouting and gunfire on the far end had produced panic in the staff as well. The ones not having hysterics tried to round up the frightened patients and shoo them down side halls. It was difficult telling the difference between inmates and staff.

Considering his mental state at the moment, Magnus figured he fit right in. Where the devil was Nadine?

He skirted around a young boy curled in a ball and a wiry middle-aged woman shoving anyone who approached her. A uniformed nurse sent him a glare, but she had her hands full trying to persuade an elderly man not to punch another patient who simply stood there alternately wailing and cackling. Magnus sympathized with the old man. He wanted to cold cock the screamer too.

He was in an indefensible situation, surrounded by innocents. Plan A called for his canister of tear gas. If he could come in close, he could hold his breath long enough to grab Nadine and run.

The mob scene at the end of the corridor prevented that scenario. *Fuck.*

Magnus halted abruptly and held out his arm to stop the men racing behind him. Chang resisted but Magnus didn't budge.

"Nadine's in there with your father. I don't know who has the guns. It could be the crazies."

That warning forced the guards to a halt along with Chang.

"Situation?" Magnus asked into the mic.

"Nurse Wretched and her minion have the guns," Nadine reported cheerfully, obviously working on her lunatic persona. "They're not very adept. I think they've shot Jo-jo's foot attempting to remove his handcuffs. The crazies aren't as obvious as they appear."

Despite his pounding pulse, Magnus rolled his eyes at her mocking repetition of his term *crazies*. She'd been listening to at least part of what he'd said. *Handcuffs*? He remembered that she'd asked for them. The woman had plotting down to a science.

She'd trapped and frustrated her stepfather, literally binding his hands and rendering him helpless—as he'd done to her for years. Magnus would cheer if he didn't have to be terrified enough for both of them.

"Plan B, then," he told her. "*You* gas 'em."

"Protect Dick first. He's in the main office, dismantling the war games, I hope. Oops, sorry," she continued with forced jollity. "I just reminded the crazies about the computers. They're heading your way."

"Guard the main office," Magnus ordered Chang. "Don't let them mess with the guy at the computer. I'm going in down there." Nodding at the end of the corridor, he didn't wait for argument.

He went for Plan C, D, and E. He drew the can of Mace from his belt—a woman's weapon but the safest one in his arsenal under current circumstances.

A hatchet-faced female rushed at him carrying a long-barreled automatic at her side as if it were a baseball bat. Nurse Wretched, he surmised. Magnus raised his arm and gassed her. She screamed, grabbed her eyes, and brought up the assault weapon one-handed.

The crazies weren't obvious, indeed. She could spray bullets through half the hospital's inhabitants.

Magnus kicked the gun from her grip while Macing the two non-uniformed suits rushing up to her side. Too blind to see his kick coming, the woman let the weapon fly.

It hit the wall and went off, tearing a hole in the acoustic ceiling tile.

Magnus grabbed one startled goon by the throat and held him in a headlock, forcing him to drop his hand-held semi-automatic. The other guard staggered from the effect of the gas. Magnus kneed him and grabbed his similar weapon. These guys were armed for war, not mental patients.

Behind him, Chang had already ripped the nurse's abandoned weapon from a wily patient. The general's son barked curt orders at the rightfully confused day-shift security that had come in with him.

Magnus didn't have time to mind his back. He'd have to trust the ex-marine to restore what order he could.

Dropping the guard he held, leaving him to wipe his eyes and curse, Magnus shoved one automatic into his belt and broke down the other as he ran. Using his shoulders and elbows, he bullied his way past the milling staff and patients at the end of the corridor, and burst into the office.

He skidded to halt and his heart plunged to his feet.

The general held a knife at Nadine's throat. The grizzled, half-dressed old guy didn't seem fazed by his entrance. Apparently the earlier gunfire had succeeded in severing the handcuffs. The chain was broken but the shackles still hung from his wrists.

"Hi, hon," Nadine said brightly, smiling at the dismantled semi that Magnus still held. "I take it Nurse Wretched has been disarmed?"

Swallowing hard, he froze. No amount of planning could fix this. Neither could action. But Nadine was wearing her crazy face and was capable of detonation at any instant. Well, so was the general.

How the hell did he handle an entire building full of unbalanced minds?

"Just stand back and let me get to the computers," the general warned, shoving Nadine toward the door. "This is a family affair. We can resolve it peacefully."

Mad as a hatter, Nadine mouthed, rolling her eyes to get her point across.

Magnus got it. He didn't like it.

The general was taller than Nadine. Magnus had a working weapon and good aim. Trained for action, his finger found the trigger. He could blow off the bastard's head and end this right now.

Except the brain that Nadine had called formidable kicked in, and he didn't raise the gun.

That was Nadine's dad, a man she had admired, a man who may once have been a valuable military mind. Even though Magnus had spent these past weeks bent on taking out the general, he had to resist the urge to act first and think later. He couldn't cold-bloodedly spill her father's life onto Nadine's shoulders. He wrapped both hands around the semi and held his fire.

"Don't listen to Daddy, hon," Nadine said in that unnatural voice she'd used when he'd entered. "I'm prepared to die. Just do what you must to save those little kids."

Horror swept through him at the image of Nadine valiantly and insanely dying in front of him. No way. Not again. He wasn't losing another woman through his own incompetence. Instinctively, he raised his gun— and then his head kicked in again.

Little kids?

This was Nadine. She was crazy like a fox. She'd promised she wouldn't die in front of him, not even for little kids.

Think first. What was she telling him? Was she trying to sound harmless? Was the general ass enough to believe that? Even after she'd *handcuffed* him?

Warily, Magnus backed out of the room. He raised the working gun to the ceiling as if in surrender and placed his back to the wall, clearing a path for the general and Nadine to pass by.

"Drop the weapon," the general barked. So he wasn't totally crazed.

Magnus obediently removed the clip and stuck it in his pocket to prevent anyone else from using it. He lowered the gun to the floor and slid it into the office. He crossed his arms over the hoodie concealing his canister of Mace and itched to use it. Unfortunately, he feared the general would be trained to take his prisoner down with him if attacked.

On the other end of the hall the day-shift guards stood over the still-wailing nurse. With no weapons to wield, the general's personal security goons stayed down, ineffectively wiping their eyes and cursing.

Chang waited outside the office door, arms crossed, weapon in hand, looking more like a thug than the ones on the floor.

"Oh, look, Chang's here to help you, Daddy Dearest," Nadine crooned in her best lunatic mode as the general pushed her past.

Her comment distracted the general from Magnus to the activity at the end of the hall.

"Chang, stop that fool at the computer from sending our coordinates to the enemy!" the old man shouted.

"The enemy, as in those crazy Oswins?" Nadine asked cheerfully. "Or Po-po's favorite family?"

Why the devil was she baiting a madman? Magnus bunched his fingers into fists, bit his tongue, and applied his brain to the problem. She was distracting the old guy, and it was working.

Plan Z, then. As Adams dragged Nadine past him and down the corridor, Magnus slid down the wall, sat on the floor, and yanked off his boots.

"They're unnatural demons, a danger to the fabric of society," the general shouted.

Who was an unnatural demon? Him? His family? Fascinating insight into dementia but not helpful. Climbing to his stocking feet, Magnus fingered the truncheon on his belt. For Nadine's safety, he really needed to remove the knife from the general's hand before taking him down.

With the general focused on the confrontation at the end of the hall, Magnus silently stalked behind him, watching for his opportunity.

The general had slow-going down the crowded hall. The dementos didn't understand their danger and kept blocking the way with muttered pleas and grasping hands.

"The menaces must be stopped," Adams shouted at his son over the head of the wailing banshee. "They killed a good woman. I should have learned my lesson then instead of playing with fire." He pushed Nadine through the mob of weeping, dancing, yelling inmates. "Her mother's family is too dangerous to live."

Magnus began to sweat. Nadine's mother was a Malcolm, as were Pippa and Dorrie, their families, and all the people on the general's genealogy website. The general meant to eliminate *all* Malcolms? That's what the detonators were for?

Rubber-suited firemen arrived at the far end of the corridor, axes and hose in hand, looking for a fire. Chang held up a hand and gestured for them to halt. The growing crowd in the lobby might prevent the general from leaving the corridor, but the computer office was on the general's side of the blockage.

"The Oswins are demons? Or people like me?" Nadine asked, sounding almost sorrowful.

Magnus began to see her purpose, but it wasn't helping any. She wanted others to realize that her stepfather had lost it, force them to stop him—even if she died in the process. Nope, not happening on his watch.

"All of you are anarchists!" the madman ranted at her. "I have to restore the natural order that you and your kind have disturbed, that in my arrogance, I allowed you to disturb. It's all my fault for thinking I could control demons. But once the radicals like you are gone, obedience and respect for authority will be restored, and we can have a country to be proud of again."

Magnus winced. Adams might as well have pulled Nadine's trigger.

"You're planning on eliminating everyone who doesn't think like you?" Nadine asked in the same pleasantly dangerous tone.

Uh oh. The bomb was ticking.

"Just the unnatural ones," the general repeated, sufficiently caught up in his own world not to comprehend his danger. "You and your kind are monitoring their minds. With you gone, the rest of the country will see that we're right."

"Chang, are you hearing this?" Nadine called. "Do you understand what I've been telling you now?

At the end of the hall, Chang narrowed his eyes and didn't move. Like Magnus, he waited.

The general jerked Nadine's head up with the knife. "Don't turn my own son against me. My boys know what's right. They know how to obey. They and my grandsons will follow in my footsteps."

"Jo-jo, you've already killed one son and grandson with your obsession," Nadine argued, not showing a hint of fear. "Another is in prison. A third is heading that way. I don't think you want Chang following your murky path."

Disagreeing with a madman wouldn't end this farce, but Nadine was providing a nice distraction. The general grew red-faced with fury.

Nadine's calm control gave Magnus permission to do what he had to do. She was letting him be the bomb.

Magnus opened one of the doors to the secure ward and pushed the wailing banshee inside, then lifted the young woman curled in a ball inside with her. When the wiry middle-aged woman came after him, he shoved her past the door, too. A fast-thinking staff member on the other side grabbed her arm and slammed the door. Half the obstacles had been removed from his path.

Detaching the cord from the weapons belt Conan had provided, Magnus grabbed two more confused patients, tied them together, and gestured for the nurse at the next security door to take them.

The general glanced suspiciously over his shoulder at the commotion, but Magnus stuck to the alcove with the patients and nurse, doing his best to look harmless. The general's madness blinded him as badly as those of the inmates.

"Richard, do you have those computers up and running?" the general shouted, fixated on his targets and not the real world.

Obsessions narrowed the mind, Magnus concluded. Survival required eyes wide open.

"Fall left," Magnus said into his mic, not caring if Adams heard. He was already close enough to reach the elbow of the general's knife-wielding arm.

Bless Nadine's intelligence, she actually followed orders, even if it sounded like certain decapitation. Nadine stumbled to the left. Simultaneously, Magnus gripped the general's knife-wielding right arm at the elbow. He pressed front and back, applying pressure to the tendon and nerves, paralyzing the arm. The knife clattered to the floor.

"Handcuffs, anyone?" Magnus shouted at their frozen audience as the enraged general fought him with the strength of two men.

Nadine hastily scooted backward against the wall to safety, blessedly taking the knife with her. Damn, but he loved a woman who could think for herself.

No one immediately came to his assistance. Magnus had to paralyze the old man's arm again to wrestle him to his knees on the floor. Subdued, the once mighty military man merely looked pathetic, like a homeless, drunken derelict instead of the proud officer he'd been.

A cop emerged from behind the fire brigade, cuffs out. Finally, the knife-wielding episode had convinced the law that the general was dangerous. After a brief struggle, the policeman shackled the old man's arms behind his back.

Magnus swung to Nadine, hauling her into his arms and

squeezing her tight against him until he was certain both their hearts beat in tandem again. "Ten years off my life, woman," he muttered.

And with a wrench of pain, he knew, once they were done here, he'd have to let her go. The general was no longer a boogey man to haunt her life. She was free now, to be whoever she needed to be. She didn't need him.

She curled into him, sobbing. For now, he stroked her back, treasuring these last few moments. But this was no time for either of them to melt down if the general really had planted explosives.

"Computers?" he asked.

"Damn!" She shoved away and wiping her eyes, rushed off to the office.

Magnus wanted to breathe easier, but now he had to turn his brain to protecting the school and his family. Physical strength had limitations.

"We'll need you and the lady to press charges," the cop was saying as Magnus tried—unsuccessfully— to figure out how to save the world as he knew it.

"Start with assault and kidnapping, terroristic threatening. We have some bombs to find and then we can make statements." Magnus left Chang to look after his cursing, struggling father. A nurse arrived with a needle. That might do the trick.

In the office, Nadine was already frantically talking into a phone and pointing at the map on one of the monitors.

"Conan's downloading the files," she told Magnus as he walked in. "I'm talking to Oz. We have to clear out the town, the school, and half Dorrie's family in San Francisco. Jo-jo knows where they all are."

Thirty-one

"No one could plant explosives in all those places," Dick, the IT guy protested as Nadine shoved him aside to take the keyboard. "It's just a war game. The general is developing new software for the army."

"That's the kind of misinformation he fed me," Nadine told him. "And then he captured an army helicopter with Magnus in it, and we found the scientists he's hiding in underground labs. Take my word, the general is dangerous. You can't trust anything he says."

It hurt to say that. It hurt to realize how badly she'd been betrayed by a man she'd once hoped had cared for her just a little. But the time for castigation wasn't now. Magnus waited, steadfast as a rock, hoping she could point him in the right direction. She was afraid that after all his valiant efforts, they might be too late.

"Can you find out what's happening at the school?" she asked Magnus.

He'd brought Jo-jo down without hurting him. He hadn't barged in like the Hulk and ripped off his enemy's head but had paid attention to *her*, even when she was babbling insanity. No man had ever trusted her so implicitly.

And now she could feel him pulling away.

His job here was basically done—he'd caught the general, which is all he'd wanted. She and Vera were safe. She really couldn't expect more from him.

At her request, Magnus called Conan and didn't attempt to include her in the conversation.

"Anyone at the school yet?" she heard him say into the phone.

She couldn't hear Conan's reply. She could only set aside her own selfish concerns and pray they would get the kids out. For now, she had to figure out just what the general had done.

Using the program Dick had opened for her, Nadine located the target nearest the school and zeroed in. "Give me the phone and I'll give Conan the coordinates."

Magnus handed over the phone. "Conan can't be in three places at once. I need to head back to the school while he deals with whatever's planted in El Padre."

"Go with him, kid," Conan said to Nadine, evidently hearing. "I have the program downloaded and can figure out what's what and can call you if I need anything. You need to convince Zorro on your end that he needs to cooperate, or he's likely to go off half-cocked again. I'll start sending coordinates to the cops in each of these towns."

"How's Mikala?" Nadine asked while she tried to decide if she wanted to deal with Magnus in Terminator mode. He filled the tiny office with his presence and his unfocused need to act.

"The kid's a little spooked and wary, but she's doing okay for now. You want to come here instead of dealing with bonehead?" Conan asked.

"No, I'll stay with bonehead," she said. She had to smile at Conan's accurate assessment of his brother. If Magnus was just being stubborn... She threw a glance over her shoulder and caught the Maximator's scowl. That cinched it. She was going to do what she wanted to do. Let him suck it up. "Tell Mikala I'll be there as soon as I can."

"Sounds like you're able to tell her yourself," Conan said with his perpetual curiosity.

"Not unless I can picture where you and Mikala are. I've never been to El Padre. It's incredibly hard to focus over a distance without grounding the target. Send a drone image to my phone."

Conan laughed and she hung up and handed the phone back to Magnus, not leaving him room to argue. "I need to talk to Vera. Can we get someone to drop us off at the Hummer or do we need to hike down?"

He looked as if he wanted to say no.

She wasn't waiting for permission anymore. And she wouldn't be shoved aside.

Nadine got up and let Dick back into the desk chair. She leaned over his shoulder to point out the school on the screen. "Those are the little kids the general wanted to turn into weapons. I've been there. I've seen them. Believe me. I've been one of them for years. Adams Engineering is going to need you once the dust settles, and right now, Chang and I are the company. I'm relying on you to dismantle any detonating switches in this program. Got it?"

Actually, she was relying on Conan, but it didn't hurt to have two drivers at the wheel.

Without waiting for Magnus, Nadine strode out of the office and headed toward the lobby. Neither of them were known for their social graces, so they'd have to learn to communicate in other ways. Or she'd have to learn to read his obtuse mind.

The police were taking statements from the sane witnesses, but there was no sign of Jo-jo. Nadine almost sighed in relief. She didn't think she could take any more emotional meltdowns right now, when there was too much riding on these next hours.

Even Nurse Wretched was gone. There probably wasn't enough evidence to accuse her of anything, but with any luck, the battleax wouldn't be put in charge of any more helpless patients.

It had been pure pleasure seeing her tormentor Maced and knowing her life was back in her own hands again.

Now, she had to make that life useful. "We need a ride down to our car," she told the lobby at large before Magnus could take the upper hand.

The cops looked to Magnus. He crossed his arms and lifted his eyebrow. Nadine didn't know whether to smack him or hug him.

One of the deputies shrugged. "I can take you down. We still need you to make statements."

"We need to save a few kids first," Nadine corrected, hurrying for the door. "It's hard to make a statement until we know what we're dealing with."

The ride down the mountain was faster than their hike up. Nadine used the time to call Vera and let her know that the general had been stopped but that they still had some problems. She ordered Vera to move Jack and all her new paranormal friends to a safe place.

In minutes, they were back at the Hummer. Nadine grabbed the key first and appropriated the driver's side. She thought she detected a glimmer of appreciation beneath the Maximator's square-jawed sternness, but he had it under control when he took the passenger seat.

Just the hope that he understood buoyed her spirits to ridiculous proportions. She squashed them. "I don't have a driver's license. If we get stopped, do I go to jail?"

"You will. I won't. How am I supposed to know you had no license?"

She punched his big biceps. "Just for that, I'm going to speed. If

I'm going to jail, it will be for a good reason."

Magnus tolerated Nadine's reckless drive down the mountain until they reached rush hour traffic on the highway. Even though this mountain highway wasn't the multi-lane I-5, it was fast and busy enough to test Nadine's skills. Remembering her terror when he'd first taken her out in speeding traffic, he ordered her off at a gas station exit.

He was supposed to be letting her fly free, and he was back in caretaker mode again. He ought to smack himself.

"Coffee," he ordered, handing her his cash. "Anything resembling breakfast would be good."

She looked at him as if she wanted to say something, but she chose wisely and took the cash instead. Only as she stalked off, her short curls bouncing and her rear swaying beneath that ridiculous hoodie, did he realize he was ordering her around—as the general had. Last time he'd done that, she'd run away. Would he ever learn?

He was in the driver's seat, stewing, when she returned with breakfast sandwiches and coffee. Wordlessly, she climbed in the passenger side and began eating. His relief was boundless.

Not knowing where he stood in her estimation, Magnus tore into his food, finished it in a few bites, and drove off.

He didn't want to ruin her life, he told himself. He was backing off, letting her be herself, doing his damndest not to take over.

But he hated this silence between them. He'd enjoyed the camaraderie they'd shared these past days. Okay, so he'd more than enjoyed the sex.

"Any way you can read the general's mind if we find out where he's been taken?" he asked.

"Possibly," she reluctantly agreed. "Really don't want to go there again."

"Fair enough. Just checking in case we needed it. Can't say I know a lot about what you do, so I have to ask."

Her shoulders slumped slightly. "I suppose I ought to learn more about my weird talent, but I really just want to have a normal life. Is that too much to ask?"

"Normal isn't all that interesting," he said, doing his best to ponder her plaint. "But no, it's not too much to ask. I'm betting that the reason more people don't have your abilities is because they're too freaky to understand, and they let them degenerate. Or they're called schizoid and they get medicated. Pippa's theory is that parents need to teach their children how to use their abilities in a safe environment."

"Yeah, I could see that." She sounded a little less miserable. "Instead of teaching the kids to be weapons, we should be teaching them how to help people with their gifts. Or just how to survive without looking like freaks. But we have no instruction books."

"Write them," he said. "Talk to Francesca. Will you really end up controlling the general's businesses? That's gonna suck time and probably not be your idea of normal."

"I just said that to frighten Dick into behaving. I have no idea how control of a military industry is passed on. Feng Jin is a lazy druggie who just wants any money he can lay his hands on. Chang will end up in charge. He knows more than anyone else. But if Jo-jo is insane, it might be difficult to obtain the paperwork to give him ownership."

"So, what do you consider normal?" Magnus asked, trying not to place too much hope on her answer.

She sipped her coffee and stared at the road ahead. "I have no idea. A job. A house. A car. Friends. Travel. No more secrets."

Magnus noticed she didn't add *lover* or *boyfriend* to that list. Maybe she was shy of saying it in front of him, although *shy* wasn't a word he'd apply to Nadine. Oz would come right out and ask. Conan would probably tap her computer and send her virtual bouquets. Magnus had no clue if he even had a right to ask her for a date.

Hell, she didn't even have a home to go to. Of course, neither did he. Did homeless people date?

His phone rang and he handed it to Nadine. He missed his Camaro.

"Conan," she read from the screen before answering.

She listened attentively, sighed with relief, muttered a *Thank, God*, and turned to Magnus. "They took the kids at the school to safety last night. The bomb squad found the explosives at the school—in the 'grave' that Vera saw. They're dismantling it now. Another crew is on its way to El Padre. They think Dick and Conan have disarmed the software triggers but even if they haven't, there's time. Jo-jo had them set to detonate over several days."

"In hopes we'd all gather together after each explosion, and he could ultimately get all of us. Charming."

Feeling as if the weight of the world had fallen off his shoulders, Magnus recalculated his route. "They don't need us at the school now. Tomorrow's the wedding. You want to see Mikala and meet the family?"

Nadine sent him a brilliant but weary smile.

Frazzled, Nadine fell asleep on the drive to El Padre. She woke when the Hummer hit a sizable pot hole a few feet from the town welcome sign.

"They put that hole there so people will notice the sign?" she asked sleepily.

"Or to wake them up so they won't fly off the side of the mountain. Sorry I woke you."

"Sorry I conked out on you." She ran her hand through her curls, discovered she was still wearing the ear clip, and removed it. "I look a fright. Should we stop somewhere and clean up?"

"That's what Oz's place is for. We'll shower, get some sleep, and be ready for the rehearsal dinner tonight."

She glared at him. "You can walk in looking all studly military and cool. I'll go in looking like a scarecrow in a fright wig. Uncool first impression."

He shot her a look so full of incredulity that even she registered it.

"You just saved a school and no telling how many families, including ours," he said. "Do you really think anyone will see you as anything but an angel with a halo? Besides, you look gorgeous."

That was glib foolishness, except Magnus wasn't prone to flattery. Satisfied that he thought she didn't look too awful, even though she knew better, Nadine tried to dismiss her anxieties. Hoping for more pleasant thoughts, she opened her mind.

The shock of joy and recognition that she received was worth every bit of exhaustion. "Mikala's watching for us. Be prepared."

"That's all you needed to read her?" he asked. "The town sign?"

She shrugged. "I don't know. Maybe the short distance. And Mikala's open mind. I have a lot to learn."

He whistled. "I'll say. The general was an idiot."

"He is a military strategist, not a scientist. Po-po would probably have figured out our abilities, but Jo-jo was just looking for weapons."

"Imagination and creativity need to work together with analytics and strategy, got it. Not easily accomplished," he said with regret. He pulled up to a high arched wrought iron gate that revealed only a shrubbery-lined drive. A stucco wall concealed any view of the house.

"From what I've seen, your brothers and their wives have that combination. I don't know how they make it work though." Nadine steered her thoughts from the magical marriage blend of creativity and science. They'd only known each other for a week. Magnus wasn't giving her those kind of signals.

Instead, she gasped in shock at the sprawling mansion exposed as they drove down the drive. "Your *brother* lives here?"

"Oz and Pippa made their fortunes in La-la Land. The cost is their privacy—hence the mountaintop retreat and high walls." He eased the Hummer down the drive to the parking area in front of a garage.

Mikala burst through the shrubbery, running as fast as her stout little legs would carry her. Thrilled at the waves of happiness emanating from the child's mind, Nadine jumped down from the Humvee, crouched down, and opened her arms in welcome. Mikala flew into them.

The little girl felt heartwarmingly solid and real. And wet. "You've been in the pool!" Nadine laughed as the child wiggled her towel around her waist.

"I've been swimming! And there are other kids and we're having fun! Come see!"

Overwhelmed with enthusiasm, Nadine slowed her down. "First, you should say hello to Mr. Oswin. He's been helping us." Nadine stood to introduce Magnus.

He solemnly held out his hand. "Pleasure to make your acquaintance, Miss Mikala. Is everyone at the pool?"

"Yes!" the child shouted, offering a confused expression with her damp handshake. Apparently the adults in her life didn't shake her hand. Undaunted, she continued, "The bomb men were in the trees by the wall, and Miss Pippa said we should stay out of their way. So we've been hiking and finding berries and now we're getting clean."

Nadine intercepted Magnus's inquiring look at Pippa's unusual reaction to a terrifying situation. She translated. "Imagination versus practicality. Why scare the kids? Take them for a hike instead of running away or hiding in fear. Admirable."

"I will assume Oz's wall prevented the general's henchmen from planting explosives on the grounds," Magnus murmured as Mikala ran ahead of them. "So they buried them in the grove on the far side of the wall."

"Didn't see any holes in the road as we drove in," she agreed.

"Maybe the general's first order of business was to remove the barricade for later invasion? Even with trees in the way, I don't know how he got around Oz's security."

"Hacked it," Nadine said. "That's where his military intel worked best. It's really scary what can be accessed with a little time and effort. Can I just not think about it for a while?" She plucked wistfully at a flowering shrub lining the path behind the house.

"I'll not tell you my next project for now," he agreed obliquely. "The pool is just around the bend. Are you ready?"

She took his hand and nodded. Magnus bent and gave her a hasty kiss. She wanted more, but she understood this wasn't the time or place.

She hoped there would be a time or place in the near future.

Mikala had already shouted the news of their arrival to the party gathered at the pool. Wearing a thin yellow cover-up that fell to her feet, Pippa strolled over to greet them.

Dorrie waved from the far side of the pool. The bride-to-be was wearing a short, brightly colored caftan, with her wild black hair loose about her shoulders. Beside her, Conan lifted his sunglasses and lazily saluted them.

Nadine tried to remember the names and faces of the other guests, but there were too many.

"The two of you must be exhausted," Pippa said sympathetically. "You'll need to get some rest before tonight's festivities. If it's okay with both of you, I've set you up in the studio so you won't be disturbed. There's food and your wardrobes have been sent down there."

"You deserve a break today," Oz said wryly, coming up behind his wife to shake their hands in appreciation. "Hero worship will otherwise ensue. Your timing is excellent. Dorrie's grandmother has retired for her nap, so you won't be subject to a genealogical inquisition yet."

"I can handle that easier than a pool party," Nadine admitted. "Food and rest would be better. I got a nap in but Max didn't, and he could probably eat an entire roast pig by now."

"I'm cutting back. Pigeons will do," Magnus said gravely. "Is the studio unlocked?"

Nadine took a deep breath of relief realizing he wasn't abandoning her just yet.

They had a wedding to survive before she went about picking up the pieces of her life to see what was left.

Thirty-two

Assured that Mikala was safe and nothing would go boom anytime soon, Nadine followed Magnus down the desert path to Pippa's studio. It rose like a giant white mushroom out of the sand and cactus on the hill below the guest cottage.

"It's a privilege and an honor to be allowed inside Pippa's safe place," Magnus informed her as he punched in the key code. "This is where she comes when she wants to scream. Either Oz is feeding her tranquilizers, or he's good for her."

"I'm thinking the latter," Nadine said absently, entering the windowless high space. All sound from outside disappeared when he shut the door. "Sound studio?"

"Recording studio, not that she records for the public anymore." He unerringly located the refrigerator amidst all the high-tech equipment lining the walls.

Nadine grabbed an apple from a table and hunted for anything resembling a shower. She found a rack of clothes first. "Costumes?" She fingered the colorful, light fabrics in wonder.

Unwrapping a cheese sandwich, Magnus came over to examine the array. "Pippa said wardrobes. That's my tux." He separated out a black coat. "Dinner suit." He pulled aside a blue coat, a few shirts and ties, then studied the vibrant selection remaining. "The rest is for you. Pippa had fun."

"Where?" Nadine asked in wonder, pulling out a floor-length, apricot-colored sheath wrapped in wisps of shimmering overskirt. "Cirque de Soleil?"

"Oz is a producer. Fashion designers jump when he snaps his fingers. She'll send back anything you don't like. The one you're holding is pretty."

"It's the most beautiful, extravagant gown I've ever seen," Nadine corrected. "And I'll look like a sausage in it."

"Go shower. You can try it on later," he advised. "I don't think Pippa will ruin her production by costuming her players in anything unflattering."

"Maybe." Nadine wrinkled her nose. "But I'm not in the wedding party, so she has no reason to dress me."

"You'll understand when you get to know her better. Trust me."

"Will I ever have your certainty about people?" she asked wistfully, hanging up the gown again. "Computers never had ulterior motives. People do."

"So, read their minds. I want that shower when you're done. Hurry it up." He returned to the refrigerator to frown at the drink selection. So much for hearts and flowers.

She didn't hit him for his cluelessness. He was keeping his hands off her, doing nothing to encourage her to leap back in his arms again. That didn't feel right, but she'd be damned if she tried to read his mind.

She grabbed her bag with her meager belongings and retired to the luxurious shower.

After drying her curls and donning the long nightshirt retrieved from her bags, Nadine emerged from the shower room feeling as if she might survive.

Magnus was punching buttons on Pippa's sophisticated equipment, playing and rejecting various recordings. Wordlessly, he grabbed his bag and entered the room she'd just left, shutting the door behind him.

Confused by his cool behavior and trying not to show it, Nadine stared at the refrigerator's contents without seeing them. Finally grabbing the milk and a bag of prepared salad mix, she sat down at the bistro table and studied the Murphy bed on the far wall. Someone had pulled it out and made it up with an avalanche of inviting pillows.

She tried to imagine having sex with anyone except Magnus on that bed and couldn't. She might be a nerd with her head buried in computers, but she was female. She noticed men. Magnus had been the only man to crank her hormones. Without him, she would just have to be a spinster, thank you very much.

Without Magnus, she would be a lonely pathetic geek who never danced again. Where else would she find a man who would understand that she occasionally went catatonic and wouldn't die of it?

Where else would she find a man who wouldn't think she was crazy? She loved him for that, if nothing else.

But there were so very many reasons to love a man like Magnus—

And who was she to think she could have him? That he would want *her?*

Crap.

She cleaned up her salad and climbed into bed. She needed sleep or she really would be catatonic.

She listened to the shower stop and her heart pounded with expectation. Maybe she should get up and brush her teeth.

He was turning her into a gawky, self-conscious thirteen-year-old again.

She was better than that. Magnus had given every indication that he *wanted* her. He had shown appreciation of her mind and her ability. Either she'd been an easily fooled idiot—or something else was happening here.

She might still be a wuss but she was *not* helpless. Librarians found answers.

Politely wearing clean boxers and a t-shirt, Magnus left the shower room, hoping Nadine had gone to sleep. He didn't know how he would survive the next twenty-four hours, much less the days that followed when she went off to start a life without him.

She wasn't asleep, and his pulse escalated as he studied her warily. She occupied the center of the small bed like an angry elf, fuming, if her scowl was any indication. He picked up one of the pillows she'd discarded off the side of the bed. "I can sleep on the floor."

"Why?" she demanded, flinging a pillow at him. It hit him squarely in the head. "Have I worn out my usefulness? Is your next project rescuing some poor lonely nerd in Outer Mongolia? What the hell is wrong with you, Maximus Grandus?"

She kneeled and swung another pillow at him.

He caught the corner and yanked it from her hands. He couldn't help noticing that her cotton shirt clung to every unfettered curve. A cold shower hadn't cooled his engines. Combat sure the hell wouldn't either.

"I'm not a womanizer." He growled at the insult and flung the pillow across the room.

She bombarded him with small fluffy round pillows that he couldn't snatch from her grip. It was like being hit by marshmallows. Magnus located a bigger pillow and swatted her arm to halt her. She grabbed the other end and yanked.

"Then why?" she yelled senselessly, trying to extract the pillow from his grip in a futile tug-of-war. "Why sleep on the floor?"

"So you can get some rest?" he suggested, although even he was doubting his logic. He released the pillow and let her swat him with it.

She complied, swinging and hitting him upside the head. "Dolt! Idiot! You think you can just turn me on and off like a faucet?"

This was starting to sound a little too uncomfortably like a Diane argument. He almost walked away. Almost. But the image of Nadine bravely stunning a guard, racing from an institution with foil on her head, and unerringly finding his car reminded him forcefully that Nadine might act crazy, but only with purpose. Nadine had the brains and courage of a dozen Dianes.

She was trying to tell him something, if he could just learn to translate woman-speak.

He bent to gather all the marshmallow pillows. "I'd be an idiot if I wanted to turn you off. Is that what you think of me—that I'm as blind as the general? Then you're not as smart as you think you are." He flung the whole load at her, burying her up to her curvy hips.

Before she could retaliate, Magnus shoved her back against the pillows and sprawled on top of her, taking down her ammunition as well as her throwing arm. She felt like heaven, and he was having a damned hard time thinking straight. "Quit wiggling or I'll do what comes naturally and forget talking."

She quit wiggling and glared at him with suspicion. "Talking doesn't come naturally?"

"Not when I have you under me like this." He yanked her shirt up over her hips and cupped her bare ass, pulling her against his erection. "I've been damned well trying to turn *me* off, not you. I wanted to give you space. You've had a whole lot happen in a little bit of time and you need time to process."

"I don't need to process this." She grabbed his ears and dragged his head down to hers.

With a gasp of relief, Magnus quit thinking and shifted to action mode. He smothered her mouth with kisses. She returned to wriggling. Her shirt came off. So did his boxers. She kissed the place on his neck that shot him into overdrive. He teased her nipples until she dug her fingers into his arms and arched into him.

All the tension of the last twenty-four hours burst free. Magnus shoved her legs apart and nailed her in a single stroke. Nadine twisted her hips and nearly blew off the top of his head. They rocked together, both struggling for domination until nature took over. She groaned, threw back her head, and surrendered. Her climax wrung him dry at the speed of rocket propulsion.

"Only you," he muttered, rolling over and dragging her on top of him.

"Exactly," she murmured in what sounded like satisfaction. "Remember that."

The apricot gown fit perfectly. Nadine swung around in front of the full-length mirror and admired the way the gauzy panels added allure and concealed the excess pounds. There might possibly be less excess after this past stressful week. She couldn't be sure.

"I like that color on you," Magnus said, leaning over her shoulder to look in the mirror and straighten his tie. "It will look even better when you get rid of the brown dye." He wrapped one of her curls around his finger and kissed her.

"Ummm." She licked the sweetness of his lips. "Fortifying yourself with mangoes before dinner?"

"Pippa stocked the place with raw everything except steak. This rehearsal better not last long." He straightened and backed off so she could apply lipstick. "We still need to talk."

Reassured that he still wanted her, Nadine attempted to mimic his lifted-eyebrow look. "I believe I recall how the last discussion ended. Is *talk* a euphemism for sex?"

"Don't get cocky, woman. I'm having second and third thoughts. Are you ready? We're already late."

"Then stop thinking," she ordered. "I created a monster when I told you to think instead of act."

He opened the door for her, and they hurried into the chilly evening. Nadine clung to Max's arm so the tiny heeled sandals she wore didn't send her sprawling into the gravel.

"Maybe that's it. I should just heave you over my shoulder and haul you off to my cave," he countered, walking slowly so she wouldn't stumble.

"You don't have a cave. Ponder that for a while. Is the rehearsal being held in the pool?"

Nadine studied the myriad twinkle lights ahead with delight. Wrapped around palm tree trunks, dangling from plumeria, decorating hibiscus, they turned the heated pool garden into fairy land.

"Probably rehearsal for the wedding reception," Magnus said. "The whole town is invited tomorrow."

"Vera said Jack is bringing her up with more of his family. What about your family? Are there more than your brothers?"

"East coast contingent is staying at Oz's place in L.A. They'll be up tomorrow, too. Tonight should be just an intimate evening with the first hundred or two of Dorrie's family," he said dryly.

Seeing Francesca and several others with Dorrie's distinctive Asian features waiting on the terrace, Nadine giggled. "They're a fascinating family. I want to meet all of them, but I'll never remember their names."

"Frankie the psychic, Bo the navigator, Jack the bodybuilder... The bride's father is a big chap using a cane. Call him Irish Ryan Franklin."

She kissed his cheek. "Try introducing them that way and see what happens."

Her first night of freedom, without fear of the general or his expectations breathing down her neck. Nadine wanted to embrace it all, but she was on sensory overload. Too many people made her nervous. The brilliantly artistic décor kept her open-mouthed in wonder.

The stunningly handsome man at her side, wearing a deep blue suit and tie, held her awestruck. Magnus kept a possessive hand at her back while he shook hands and introduced her and her tongue froze. She needed to get her thinking cap back on. This crowd blocked her brain worse than wearing aluminum foil.

She had almost decided to pull out her phone and text Vera just so she could get words out when Pippa took her elbow and steered her away from Magnus.

"Dorrie's niece Alexis is bouncing off walls. I thought Mikala might calm her down, but Mikala is equally excited. She wants to talk to you. If you'll take Mikala in hand, I'll take Alexis. Then I hope you'll help me direct the crowd to the pergola so we can at least pretend to rehearse the ceremony. I knew that gown was perfect for you."

Her chatter carried them up the mansion's stairs and didn't require that Nadine do more than relax and admire her surroundings.

More quietly understated than the beach home she and Magnus had stayed in, the Oswin home featured light natural wood accents, warm southwestern colors, and windows that captured starlight. Despite its size, it felt like a home and not a showplace.

"Alexis is almost the same age as Mikala, so they're sharing a room." Pippa tapped lightly on a door. "Coming in!"

Dressed in long, flowered gowns, the girls guiltily dropped back to their trampled beds, but Mikala brightened at seeing Nadine. "I talked to Mama!"

"Did you now? And what did she say?" Relieved that her tongue was still operational, Nadine sat on the low twin bed beside Mikala.

"She said she has to find me another school." The child didn't seem happy about that. "She's going to England soon."

"Mikala's parents are in the diplomatic corps," Pippa explained. "Mikala apparently doesn't adapt well to strange places."

The child read minds, for pity's sake. She lived in a world of utter cacophony. Nadine bit her tongue, hard, then produced a smile for the child's sake. "Well, maybe we can find someone better to run your school. Did you like the teachers?"

"Some of them," Mikala said with a pout. "Some were real mean. I don't like oatmeal or the stupid tests."

"Oatmeal is good for you. What stupid tests?" Nadine asked, her mind suddenly whirling so fast that she feared it would come off its rims and blow out her ears.

"Looking at blank papers and telling teachers what number is behind them. Or color. That's just dumb. Can't I stay here?"

"You need a school where you can learn. Mrs. Oswin doesn't run a school. Why was the test dumb? Was it too easy?" Nadine didn't open her mind to let the child see what she was thinking, not until she was more sure of herself.

"They were looking right at the numbers!" Mikala cried, as if that made sense.

It did to Nadine. "So you saw the numbers in their heads?" Mikala nodded, pleased that she'd understood.

"Yeah," Nadine agreed, "that was way too easy. I'll find harder tests for you. We need to go down to the party, but we can talk again tomorrow."

They sent the little girls racing down the stairs ahead of them. Nadine was silent as she walked beside Pippa.

"We don't have teachers who can really help these kids," Pippa said when they reached the bottom. "Their parents need to be more understanding."

"If their parents are in any small way psychic or empathic, they may be more valuable in the diplomatic corps than as teachers," Nadine pointed out. "I've studied our genealogy, read the general's library. Hundreds of years ago, families stayed at home and helped each other. The world was a smaller place. We can't do that anymore."

"Maybe, we could each take a little time to visit the school?" Pippa asked tentatively, before a guest called to her from the kitchen, and she had to hurry away.

"Maybe," Nadine whispered to herself.

Thirty-three

Magnus stood under the bougainvillea-draped pergola with his brothers, watching the women emerge from the guest bungalow garden. The rehearsal might reduce the bride's wedding anxiety, but Conan was tensely jiggling coins in his pocket and shifting from foot to foot.

At Dorrie's arrival, the groom focused on his bride to the detriment of all else, but at least he finally stood still.

Oz continued giving clipped orders into his ear phone.

Restless, Magnus searched the guests for Nadine.

A cell phone emitted a discreet alarm. Dragged from his focus on his bride, Conan scowled. He rummaged in his pocket for the culprit, glanced at the screen, and handed it to Magnus. He returned to watching Dorrie give instructions to her flower girl niece.

Magnus didn't recognize the number on the screen but answered anyway.

"Oswin? This is Deputy Black with the sheriff's department. Do you know where we can find Miss Nadine Malcolm?"

That didn't sound promising. His stomach clenched while his gaze traveled across the crowd, hunting for a splash of apricot. "This is Magnus Oswin. I can give a message to Nadine." The man had called Conan, so presumably he knew the players here.

Deputy Black cleared his throat, stalling. A low voice in the background apparently spurred him on. "We have some bad news for Miss Malcolm. Perhaps it would be best if you can tell us where to find her."

"In El Padre, with all the rest of us, at a wedding party. Is this news that can wait until after the wedding tomorrow?" Magnus hadn't worked in war zones without recognizing the hesitation and the reason, so he prompted the speaker. "If it's about the general, you'd best tell me now so I can judge the best time."

"Joseph Adams died in the hospital an hour ago, after ingesting an unknown substance," Black replied. "The medical examiner has been called."

"*Friggin' son of a bitch bastard...*" Magnus searched his vast vocabulary of curse words but couldn't find appropriate ones to express emotions running the gamut from fury to regret. The damned general had found one final way to make Nadine suffer. "Suicide," he concluded. "Have you notified his sons?"

The deputy sounded almost relieved at his reaction. "I believe they're already consulting lawyers. I assure you, everything possible was done—"

"That's understood," Magnus responded instantly and curtly. "You're not to blame. I'll have Nadine call if she needs details. I assume his sons are making arrangements?"

Action, Magnus understood. He knew how to be a barrier between the introverted Librarian and the real world. He wanted to be her shield. He simply didn't know if she wanted him to step in.

Just trying to decipher his own reaction as he handed the phone back to Conan was too difficult. Oz glanced at him quizzically, but Magnus shook his head. He nodded at the women approaching to indicate now wasn't the time.

He searched for Nadine again and found her holding Mikala's hand at the edge of the crowd. She glowed like a candle flame in the twilight, outshining all Pippa's ridiculous twinkle lights.

Considering everything she'd been through, Nadine was stronger than a flame. She wouldn't flicker out in a wind. The news of the general's death would sadden her, but after the shock was over, she would realize that her stepfather couldn't have handled prison. Magnus hoped he was getting better at this understanding people business. Or at least, understanding Nadine.

Rather than slow the bride's procession from the cottage, Ryan Franklin had stationed himself near the pergola. He limped out now to lead Dorrie to the altar. The real estate magnate had apparently recovered sufficiently from his stroke to give his only daughter away.

Magnus didn't recognize the wizened old man acting as minister but appreciated his speed in explaining the ceremony. When the minister indicated it was time for the couple to depart down the red carpet serving as aisle, Conan kissed his bride instead. They didn't seem interested in stopping anytime soon.

Oz shrugged, took Pippa's arm, and started back to their guests, according to instruction.

Bo came to claim his ex-wife, Dorrie's other bridesmaid.

Duty done, Magnus made a straight line to where he'd last seen Nadine.

She wasn't there, of course. He contemplated a lifetime of tracking an elusive will-o'-the- wisp of a woman.

"Very impressive groomsmen," her familiar voice taunted behind him. "Will all of you remember to turn off your phones tomorrow?"

"Probably not." Magnus swung around and gathered her into his arms. "Is Pippa serving more than bean sprouts or should we go somewhere else to eat?"

"As I understand it, Conan insisted on real meat, so Oz has a barbecue chef preparing a he-man table. You should be fine."

"I was afraid the smoke was some family ritual for sacrificing small animals to the wedding gods. Glad to know that civilization and common sense still prevail."

She laughed. Magnus hated to dampen her spirits with the bad news. He led her in the side entrance and followed his nose to the buffet.

"Who was so important that you had to talk to them during rehearsal?" Nadine asked as they entered the crowded dining area.

Magnus grimaced. "Could we eat first?" Using his height, he located the table with real food and pushed her toward it.

Apparently sensing his mood, Nadine filled her plate and didn't waste time on chatter. Magnus appreciated her ability to give him time to formulate sentences. Once they had their food, he led her back to the terrace

Only a few guests had wandered from the crowded buffet to occupy the outdoor tables. Magnus steered Nadine toward a deserted corner near the bar.

"You're not too cold?" he asked, pulling out one of the bar chairs and helping her up. The overhead heater had been turned on.

She tugged a shawl around her. "I'm good." She sipped her wine, then met his gaze. "So, tell me."

"Eat." He pointed his fork at her plate.

"I'll have to use pool cushions to clobber you if you don't talk," she warned. "Is Vera okay?"

"Vera's fine. I wouldn't make you wait for that." When she seemed to accept his need to protect her from unpleasantness, he gave the conversation a more pleasant turn. "I promised to take you anywhere you wanted when this was over. Have you decided yet?"

"Everywhere. I want to go everywhere." Her eyes gleamed

mischievously over the sandwich she'd made of her roll.

"Yeah, I could get into that," he agreed, before injecting his real concern. "Especially if I'm allowed to go with you." He could see himself with Nadine in a bed on both tropical islands and snow-capped mountains. That worked real well in his head.

It was Nadine's head that worried him.

She licked sauce off her finger, and he nearly expired with the need to lick it for her. He shoved a forkful of beans into his mouth.

She seemed to be studying him with interest, not pummeling him with pool cushions. That had to be a good sign, so he kept his mouth shut and chewed. He wouldn't push her into what he wanted.

"I wouldn't mind the company," she agreed, to his relief. "But you have projects, a business of sorts, I guess. I don't want to stand in your way anymore."

He waved a chicken leg dismissively. "Where would we go first?" Because it had worked so well the first time, he shoved the drumstick in his mouth to keep from saying too much. She looked good enough to eat but he didn't think telling her that would help his cause.

"Australia?" she asked tentatively, still studying him over her wine. "I've traced some of our ancestors there. It would be fun to see if we have long lost relatives."

"I haven't been there. I'm game." She could have said Antarctica, and he'd have said the same. He had it bad. But he didn't want to influence her decisions by telling her how he felt. Damn, it was hard not taking the lead and grabbing what he wanted.

"Do you know what will happen to the academy?" she asked, even more uncertainly than she'd phrased the question about Australia.

"No clue. Want me to find out?"

She tightened her lips and stared over his shoulder. "No. I have to start doing things on my own. I'll talk to Chang tomorrow. He'll want to shut it down if he gets Jo-jo's power of attorney."

Here it was. He couldn't deny the opening. Magnus took a swig of his beer for fortification before speaking. "Chang won't need that," he said gruffly.

Nadine was poking at something filled with mushrooms. She cast him an inquiring look. "No?"

"The general must have kept a poison pill on him. He died

about an hour ago." More or less. Magnus froze, waiting for the hysterics.

Tears gleamed in Nadine's eyes. She stabbed a piece of meat without looking at it. "I should have guessed that. I should have told them to look for it, but I couldn't even stand to think of them putting him into a prison suit." She wiped her eyes with the back of her hand and spun the stool around to face the wall.

Magnus couldn't bear watching her whole body shake with sobs. Leaving his plate half empty, he slid off his stool. Wrapping his arms around her, he hauled her off the chair and against him, where she could cry on his shoulder . "He made his choices. You don't have to pay for them any longer."

She wept, drenching his suit lapel. He wished he knew how to comfort her, but that had never been his strength. He just held her and let her cry and wished he could have killed the general with his bare hands for doing this to her.

When the storm of tears seemed to be subsiding, he offered his handkerchief. "Do we need to leave? Just tell me what you want."

"I'm a mess. I'll go back to the studio. Why don't you stay and talk to your family?" She wiped her eyes and pulled back to let him go.

This was where he usually did as told and walked away in relief. He was lousy at tears. But the connection to Nadine was too strong. He felt her grief and couldn't abandon her.

"Everyone will still be around tomorrow. Want me to grab a bottle of wine or a tub of ice cream?"

She laughed a little and kissed his cheek. "You're a good man Magnus Oswin. Maybe I should reward you with whipped cream."

"You've been Googling sex, haven't you?" He lifted her over his shoulder and carried her down the garden path, while she laughed, cried, and beat at his back.

Their hostess was a vegetarian and didn't keep plastic whipped cream in her refrigerator. Since Magnus had so generously left without finishing his he-man dinner, Nadine rewarded him with dessert. She used jam.

Given the way he fell on her like a hungry lion, she had a feeling that Magnus didn't need enticement.

Confused at what to expect of the future, saddened by the unnecessary death of a brilliant mind, Nadine reveled in the mindless release of sex. She promptly fell asleep cuddled in the shelter of this courageous man's big arms, relieved that Magnus hadn't lost interest in her now that the job was done.

It remained to be seen whether he'd still be interested once she figured out how she would accomplish what she needed to do next. She didn't mean to test his patience. It just happened that way.

She woke early, in the gray light of dawn. Restlessly, she took a shower and donned the fluffy hotel robe Pippa had provided. She fixed tea for herself and coffee for Magnus. Sipping the hot brew, she studied the wardrobe Pippa had chosen. The lady had excellent taste.

Magnus rose from the bed, shedding covers like Neptune rising from the sea. He kissed her so thoroughly that she almost decided to go back to bed. But they had duties to attend. Reluctantly, he pulled away, grabbed his coffee, and headed for the shower.

Still in her robe, she stood in the open studio entrance, sipping her tea. It was a cool gray morning. From this valley, little was visible in the direction of the house, but she knew its location, knew what Mikala's room looked like. She opened her mind just a little, to see if she was awake.

The little girl's happiness spilled into her, although Nadine couldn't quite understand the jumble of thoughts. She sent a mental hug and returned inside again.

She needed to make a life of her own. She'd been dreaming of running away to exotic locales all her life—but that's what it would have been, running away. She'd had reason to run when the general had been alive. But now that he was out of the picture... She was not only bereft, but directionless.

She'd still like to travel, but after her recent experiences, she wanted something more tangible, more soul-satisfying. She wanted people in her life—people who weren't creeped out by her weirdness, people who didn't give her migraines with their angry thoughts.

People like Magnus, who blocked the constant low roar of mental activity around her. She studied him as he emerged from the shower wearing a man-sized blue robe.

"Wedding's not until noon," he told her, aware of her gaze, as always. "Want to just put on casual and go up to the house for a while?"

Her introversion screamed no. Her understanding of Magnus had her nodding yes. His Zorro complex carried to his brothers and their families. They needed his steadying influence on a tumultuous day like today.

"You're okay?" he asked, gathering her in his arms and enfolding her in the safety of his big chest.

"I'm okay. I'm kind of... disconnected. I've never not had a home. And my work and the general have been my life for years. It's very weird having nothing."

"You have me," he said with assurance.

She had *him*. That added a wealth of reassurance that she needed right now.

"And you have Vera," he continued, as if not realizing how much his declaration had meant to her. "And I promise, once the wedding distraction is over, you'll have entire families wanting to take you apart and blend you in. No worries for now. Today is for not thinking."

He was right—today was for just enjoying. So she hugged his promise close to her heart to keep her going forward.

Pippa was preparing pumpkin pancakes and apple syrup for the children. Dorrie supervised the toaster. She frowned a bit as Nadine picked up a butter knife to help with the toast. "Your chi is confused this morning. Is everything all right?"

"Confusion is my natural state," Nadine suggested, taking the toast from Dorrie and setting it on a plate for buttering. "Even confused, I can handle this. You must have bubble baths and hairdressers waiting for you."

Dorrie beamed. "No, I have a man to drag away from a computer. Thank you!" She danced off.

Pippa laughed and winked at Nadine. "The bread thanks you. We'll be cutting toast into hors d'oeurves as it is."

Absorbed into the community, Nadine slipped from task to task. She gathered that Magnus hadn't told anyone the news about the general yet. It would be a pity to spoil a beautiful day. It was her burden to bear, anyway, and she must be doing it well if perceptive Dorrie hadn't noticed.

Magnus disappeared inside the house with his brothers. Nadine took the children out to the heated pool after breakfast to work off some of their excess energy.

The small dignified grandmother Dorrie had introduced last night joined her underneath the pool awning. Wearing a rich floral silk floor-length gown wrapped with a contrasting gold sash, Ling Fai looked both traditionally Chinese and modern American businesswoman.

"Your family are teachers," Ling Fai said, after re-introducing herself. "You must see my charts. Very direct Malcolm descendants. Very rare. Your father could have been a great man if he had lived."

"He would have been a professor, like my mother," Nadine said, smiling at the correctness of Magnus's warning about the genealogy charts. "Professors are seldom great men."

The older woman looked indignant. "Professors are very great men. They shape the minds of our future. He would not have let you bury yourself as your stepfather did, may he rest in peace."

Nadine blinked. "You know Jo-jo is dead?"

Ling Fai waved a dismissive hand. "It is in all your thoughts, great sadness. You should not be sorry. He was in much pain, and now he is at rest. It is your future that matters. Consider it carefully."

The children started shouting for towels. By the time Nadine had supplied them, Ling Fai had disappeared.

Dorrie's grandmother had read her mind? And in more ways than about the general.

Her father had been a teacher, like her mother. The hurdle seemed impossibly high.

Thirty-four

Magnus admired the flowy turquoise skirt and short jacket that Nadine chose for the wedding. He was trapped in his tux—to which a turquoise cummerbund had been added. "Did you choose that outfit to match me?" He tugged at the bright band around his middle with discomfort. "Doesn't make me feel less like a dress dummy."

"Dorrie chose peach and turquoise as her wedding colors. I'm told the colors mark you as part of the wedding party. And since almost everything on this rack contains some shade of peach or turquoise, I'm assuming Pippa decided we should match." Nadine tugged on the bottom of her jacket and squirmed uncomfortably. "I hate jackets, but if I take this off, I'll look like a bimbo from outer space."

Happy to be given an excuse to look, Magnus opened the jacket and admired the cleavage-revealing silk top underneath. "I have a thing for alien bimbos. Best keep that hidden until we're alone."

She smacked his arm with affection. "Come on, dress dummy, we'll be late, and I want to find Vera before the ceremony starts."

"I take it we won't be sailing to Australia on a cruise ship requiring dress attire," he said amiably as they walked up the path to the main house.

"I hope not!" She sent him a hasty glance. "Sorry. I'm not used to sharing decisions. If that's the best way to go, then we need to explore the possibility."

He shook his head at her. "Don't retreat to the good general's daughter, please. I don't read minds. I need you to speak honestly. If there are reasons we ought to fly instead of cruise, we can discuss those reasons along with the fancy dress problem."

She pondered that for a while, then just before they reached the guest house, stood on her toes and kissed his cheek. "I have a lot to learn. Be patient."

She was plotting. Magnus hid his unease as he sent her off to join the guests while he tracked down his brothers.

Conan was pacing an office, phone in hand, wearing a shirt with the studs unfastened. His cummerbund had been discarded over a computer monitor. The boutonnieres were buried beneath an avalanche of file folders.

Magnus grabbed him in mid stride and began shoving studs into the shirt. Conan kept talking. Gathering Conan was speaking to the sheriff's department about the school, Magnus didn't interrupt.

Conan finally hit END and stuck the phone in his pocket. "The county is talking about shutting the school down and sending the kids home. I had social workers comb the place. They've found the facilities more than adequate. Someone needs to review the teachers and administrators. Nadine's stepbrothers aren't being helpful."

"The sheriff told you about the general?" Magnus handed over the studs.

Conan fastened his shirt without looking. "Poison in his tooth cap, added recently. The man was deteriorating fast. How's Nadine holding up?"

"Hard to say. She hero-worshipped the general for a long time. Made excuses for him probably longer than he deserved. She eventually recognized his paranoia, but he was the only father she ever really had. And now she's completely untethered. I'm crap at handling emotional women."

Magnus didn't really think Conan had any advice for him, but he was trying to learn to say what he thought.

"Don't handle her," Conan said with a shrug, picking up his white cummerbund and staring at in distaste. "She'll just bite your head off. Try asking her what she wants."

"She doesn't *know* what she wants. She's never been rootless before. Maybe I should talk to her stepbrothers about the school." Magnus liked the idea of that. He wanted to know what made the brothers tick. And bash Feng Jin's head through a wall. He was pretty certain that was the brother who had helped hold him hostage.

Conan shook his head. "You'd better take up mind reading if you're not going to ask Nadine what she wants. What time is it?" He tugged his phone from his pocket to check.

Magnus plucked the fancy gadget from his brother's hand and threw it on the bed. "Time to go downstairs. No phones at your wedding."

Conan scowled but obediently finished dressing. Magnus shoved a boutonniere at him before he escaped.

Magnus was as nervous as the bridegroom as they descended the stairs. He was pretty certain of the future he wanted—even if it scared hell out of him. Nadine was the question mark in the equation.

While guests gathered in the folding chairs in the garden, Nadine stayed in the background, thrilled to have the opportunity to talk with Vera. She'd introduced her sister to the few people she knew. Vera had introduced her to Jack's family.

Without Magnus, the cacophony of this many minds pushing thoughts into the universe soon had Nadine's head pounding. It was simpler to stand back.

The wedding was the loveliest event she'd ever experienced, and she embraced the love and joy despite the headache. Pippa sang one of her own creations, a paean to love and eternity that brought tears to every eye in the audience. She must have chosen the rest of the music, as well, because the guitars followed the emotional roller coaster of the ceremony to perfection. Even Nadine laughed and wiped tears from her eyes as the flower girls skipped to the music and flung blossoms at the audience instead of the carpet.

Under the brilliant blooms of bougainvillea, the bride and groom radiated love. Dorrie wore a tea-length white gown and carried a bouquet of blue and peach-colored flowers. Her short veil perched in her dark curls with the help of a spray of roses. Golden Conan wore his tux as if born to it. They held hands and beamed at each other throughout the ceremony, ignoring tradition.

Nadine could almost believe that love would last forever—unless parted by tragedy. That had been her experience. She'd never seen happy-forever-after.

So when her phone vibrated just as Oz produced the wedding rings, she stepped out of the crowd and behind the hedge.

"We've found Father's will," Chang reported without greeting. "His attorney assures us Father was in his right mind when he dictated the terms."

"That might be a matter of opinion," Nadine responded without thinking, then bit her tongue. "Sorry. I'm at a wedding. Can we talk later?"

She really didn't want to be disappointed yet again. She wanted to return to that scene of hope and joy.

"The authorities are raising a stink over that school. We need to do something now. Did you know the papers establishing it were fraudulent?"

"Learned that this past week." Her stomach sank to her feet. Here it came, the cutting of the one thread of hope she'd been clinging to these last hours.

"The state insists we dissolve the charter. My name and Jin's are on it. The school district and parents are screaming bloody murder. We're about to get our pants sued off."

"I'm sorry, Chang. I don't know what this has to do with me. My name wasn't on the charter. I assume Jo-jo left everything to you and your brothers. What am I supposed to do?"

"He made you executor," Chang said curtly, with obvious displeasure. "The school is part of his estate. It needs to be disposed of before we lose everything."

He was bullying her. He came by this performance naturally.

She had to develop that backbone she'd been missing. She took a deep breath and steeled herself for the explosion. "I'm not doing anything until tomorrow. And if you push me, I'll make it next week," she warned.

"I'll tell the judge you're not suited to be executor and have a new one appointed," he retorted.

"Then you'll have me suing you," she said without hesitation. "You need to back off and help me work this out, or I'll get an injunction against you." She didn't even know what an injunction was much less how to get one—but she'd figure it out.

Jo-jo had made her *executor*. Either he'd been seriously demented at the time, or he'd *trusted* her wisdom. Nadine turned her eyes to the brilliantly blue sky and tried to decide whether to sing hosannas or curses.

"Just *do* something," Chang insisted. "I have to run all his damned businesses. I don't have time for angry parents."

"I can't do anything right this minute. I'm not a lawyer." And then she remembered—the East Coast Oswins were judges and senators. She took a deep breath. "Let me talk to some people. I'll get back to you."

Feeling powerful, she hit END. Take that, big brother.

Executor. May all the heavens weep, what did an executor do?

Returning to the guests, she sought Magnus for assurance. He was already scanning the crowd for her. She smiled and waved. He looked relieved. Had he thought she'd run away?

She was confused, but she wasn't dumb. He was her rock. She wanted him in her life for as long as he would stay. But first, she needed a life.

The wedding photos took forever. Magnus couldn't get away until the photographer was done.

Complete strangers walked up and started talking to her, as if she were one of the family. Despite the increasing headache from all the thoughts bouncing around the party, she was enjoying herself, but she wasn't used to any of this.

Overwhelmed, she almost collapsed in exhaustion and relief when Magnus finally reached her. "What do you know about being executor of an estate?" she asked without preliminaries.

"Zilch. The general made you executor?" he asked, bending over to kiss her.

She luxuriated in the connection, and the headache almost receded. "That's what I love about you—you nail problems so succinctly and dismiss them with a kiss. Yes. I'm executor, and the estate is about to be sued over the school. I hate to ask but...help?"

"Zorro, at your service," he said solemnly. "Good to know you love something about me."

"I love everything about you," Nadine admitted in her weariness, "but I don't think I'm supposed to say that. So pretend you didn't hear it and steer me in the right direction."

Right in front of everyone, Magnus swept her into his arms and kissed her thoroughly. Breathless once he put her down, Nadine stared at him wide-eyed. "I didn't think you'd appreciate another burden. You'll give people ideas if you keep doing that."

He grinned. "Yeah. Let's go find the judge."

"Don't even kid me about that," she warned as he took her arm. "I could be standing in front of a court any minute now." Nadine let Magnus steer her through the crowd.

He hadn't run in the opposite direction, screaming, when she'd told him she loved him. He hadn't returned the sentiment, but her confidence grew another notch, and she felt a little less shaky.

"Considering what we've been doing lately, we both could be in front of a judge. Would you do anything differently?" he said in unconcern.

"Is that a rhetorical question, I hope? I can't answer anything else at this minute. You looked splendid up there in your fancy clothes." Nadine tried to see past the crowd of people to where he was taking her, but her heels weren't high enough. His family was tall.

Luckily, most of Dorrie's family was her size. She caught a glimpse of the stately older woman she'd been introduced to earlier talking to Pippa. Their hostess looked gorgeous in a peachy-colored silk gown with a full skirt that looked good on her slender figure and with her red hair. The judge in her gray, business-like suit...looked intimidating.

"Aunt Helena." Magnus intruded on their conversation. "We have a small problem. Pippa." He nodded at his sister-in-law. "We're about to steal a school. Keep Conan occupied or he'll abandon the honeymoon."

Pippa's generous mouth spread into a smile. "I like the way you think. You'll tell me what they're up to later, won't you, Helena?"

The judge tried to look stern, but one corner of her mouth lifted. "It's a good thing these boys are finally marrying. They'd all end up in jail otherwise. And don't think I was kidding you—you really ought to be on stage with that voice of yours. I'll talk to you later."

"I thought you were the sensible Oswin," Helena said, strolling toward the library. "Don't disappoint me."

"It's me, ma'am. I'm the one in trouble." Nadine hurried to keep up with her long strides. "Magnus keeps pulling me out. I have felons on my family tree, not judges."

Magnus made a rude noise. "That's the general's family tree, not yours. Just ask Grandmother Ling."

"Well, then, I was raised with felons. I don't think like a judge," Nadine retorted. "After what I've been through, I have a need to be perfectly honest."

"Honesty has its shortcomings." The judge entered Oz's library and closed the door after them. "Now, what is this all about that it couldn't wait until a better time?"

Nadine explained. Magnus and Helena listened.

"And this school... It's special because?" Helena finally asked, unerringly hitting the crux of the problem.

Nadine bit her lip, trying to think of some way a staid, east coast matron with a legal mind might accept the inexplicable. Unperturbed, Magnus leaned his hip against the library table, crossed his arms, and left the problem to her. That miraculously cleared her head.

"Have you met Mikala?" Nadine asked. "Have you had time to talk to Dorrie and her brother? How well do you really know Pippa?"

The judge frowned. With her immaculate salt-and-pepper coiffeur and designer suit, she could fit into any corporate boardroom. "I've not had time to really talk to anyone except Philippa. Why?"

"Because it makes it really hard to explain why the school is special unless you understand the children's difficulties. I can *tell* you, but you won't understand." Frustrated, Nadine tried to think of an example that might convince a no-nonsense legal type. It wasn't as if she was about to read a judge's mind.

"This doesn't go beyond this room," Magnus intervened with a warning. "Pippa has reason to believe she can kill people with her voice. We've seen and heard her do things that are implausible in the world as we know it. This is the reason she doesn't sing in public anymore. She tried to commit suicide at one point. She's been in mental institutions."

Nadine glanced at him in surprise. Pippa had seemed sane and grounded to her. Magnus stayed focused on his aunt.

"Dorrie's mother was murdered for her ability to manipulate what Dorrie calls chi energy," he continued. "Dorrie insists she killed Nadine's step-uncle with her ability to manipulate chi. I've *seen* her knock down grown men with nothing but a small rock and a mean look. Talk to Grandmother Ling if you don't believe me. I'm an engineer and know what Nadine tells me she can do is scientifically impossible. Yet she does it anyway. She found Mikala with her mind, by talking to her without phones or computers."

"I can see that you believe this," Helena said slowly. "Even if I accept what you say, what does this have to do with the school?"

Magnus turned to Nadine, leaving the floor open for her again. She loved his trust in her abilities.

"The children attending that school exhibit similar odd abilities," Nadine said carefully, finding her way. "It's impossible to explain how difficult it is for a mind-reader to fit into a general population. For one thing, people who scream their thoughts produce pounding migraines. And children are never quiet."

Nadine gestured at the door. "I'm having difficulty dealing with the wonderful crowd of guests out there. They're all highly intelligent, fascinating people, but one is terrified she's pregnant. Another has a bet on a ball game and is impatient to find a TV. Most of them are just thinking about the buffet or sex or they're picturing how to hang tin cans on Conan's car. If I'm having difficulty coping with this jumble at a party where I don't really have to do anything, just think what it does to a child who is trying to learn her alphabet and pay attention to a teacher."

"You just described Jo-lynn and George with the pregnancy and gambling," Helena said with a sniff. "Not that I believe you actually read their simple minds, but I understand what you're saying to some extent. The children in this school are more sensitive than others, the kind of children that are often bullied and misunderstood. Is that close enough?"

"Yes, if that's the description it takes to make you understand," Nadine agreed.

"So you want to keep the school open, but if you do, you're likely to be sued for fraud or by parents whose children were terrified by your stepfather's depredations?"

"Simply put, yes." Nadine clenched her hands together, realizing how desperately she wanted this. "My stepbrothers want to close the school and remove any possibility of further suit. Mostly, I think they want me to give them control of the estate as soon as possible."

"I have no jurisdiction here," Helena reminded her. "I'll need to talk with your estate lawyer and then with local authorities. If I'm right, there may be a way for you to set up the school anew, taking it outside the estate. Will that work for you?"

"If I can find financing," Nadine said cautiously. "Right now, Jo-jo's wealth is supporting it. I can't imagine tuition covers the cost."

"That will be your job, then," Helena said. "Let's return to the reception before they cut the cake."

Magnus squeezed Nadine's hand and kissed her forehead. "Courage. We'll do it."

He made her feel as if she could do anything. Holding his hand helped clear her head, though, so she wasn't about to let him go.

Thirty-five

Under the twinkle lights around the pool, the band played a sexy salsa number and the crowd danced.

Magnus thought his heart might thud right out of his chest as Nadine swung her hips and swept back her flirty skirt and stepped in time to his every gesture. She moved with him as if she were part of him—or read his mind.

She'd taken off the hated suit jacket. The cleavage revealed had him sweating despite the cool night air. He discarded his tux jacket, cummerbund, and tie. He spun her around just so he could bring those lush curves back into his arms again. Her hips rocked against his before she stepped back. Her eyes taunted him, laughingly, and he felt as if he'd been jolted with a thousand volts.

And then she flicked her gaze to the side, and Magnus realized they'd cleared the floor. Everyone had stepped aside to let them dance.

"Damn," he breathed into her ear, dipping her in one last move as the song reached its end. "I want you to myself, not as a spectacle for these clowns."

"I've never been a spectacle before— Oh, wait, yeah, the aluminum foil hat and Tweety-bird, but I meant a *good* spectacle. I kind of enjoyed this." She leaned against him as he escorted her to the darkest corner of the garden.

Magnus touched the healing cut on her temple. "People should make good spectacles of themselves more often, I guess. I just don't like sharing."

She laughed softly. "We'll see how long it takes before I wear out your patience. Until then, the crowd is breaking up. Conan and Dorrie are off to their butler-assisted hide-out. Do we need to slip away?"

Magnus closed his arms around her and swayed with the slow song the band struck up. Friends and family spilled out on the dance floor. Oz and Pippa had taken over center place. He smiled at their professional moves, and contented himself with the way Nadine melted into him.

"Yeah, let's call it a day to remember. How's your head?" He led her from the dance floor, down the garden path.

"Better. The music and you seem to block out the low roar. It's like having constant traffic in my head sometimes. I don't think I'll do well in a busy environment," she said sadly.

"It's the reason you clung to the safety of computers for so long, understood. I'm glad I can help, although I'm not sure what I'm doing right."

"You exist," she said with a happy sigh. "If you need scientific explanations, let the psychologist explain your Zorro complex. Maybe the answer is there."

He chuckled. "Okay, no explanations, but you're still young and have lots of time to explore options."

He just prayed those options continued to include him. He didn't know how people formed long term relationships, but he wanted what Oz and Conan had.

He knew how to work for what he wanted. And he wanted Nadine.

She had his shirt studs out by the time they reached the bottom of the hill. He yanked off her silk top the instant the studio door closed behind them. Nadine made love with the same uninhibited fervor with which she danced. He didn't have to restrain his needs—she encouraged them.

"For someone who turned herself into a machine, you sure know how to make a man feel wanted," Magnus declared, throwing her onto the bed.

Nadine yanked his shirt from his half-fastened trousers. "Once you take the top off the boiling pot, you get steam," she reminded him. "Just think of me as steam expanding your horizons like a hot air balloon."

He laughed. Her lack of restraint was what he'd been missing all these years. With utter fascination, Magnus stripped her of her finery. She pushed him over and climbed on top of him, claiming dominance. Her mouth was a sin in itself, teasing, taunting, caressing, and sucking until he had no choice but to flip her on her back and drive into her with a teenager's lack of finesse. And she laughed with the joy of the climax they reached.

He could handle her tears as long as he knew he'd eventually be rewarded with her laughter. Tucking her against his side, feeling her breathe, he accepted that he hadn't been whole until now.

He loved La Loca. Which made him as crazy as she was. He was good with that.

The next morning, with the house empty of most guests, Magnus left Nadine in his Aunt Helena's competent hands.

He knew he was asking for worse heartbreak than he'd already suffered. He was perfectly aware that Nadine was young and restless and not ready to settle down. She thought she loved him, but she didn't know what love was.

He wasn't entirely certain he did, either, but he knew how he felt, and losing her wasn't part of the equation. And he'd finally figured out what he had to do to show her what she meant to him.

So he called the sheriff, located Chang Adams, and drove his souped-up Camaro out of the mountains and into the desert to Palm Springs. The car's wireless computer—enhanced by Conan's devious software—had identified and hacked the general's security system before it reached the main gate.

The gates swung open, and he drove up to the front entry without being stopped. Or blown up. Perhaps Chang had dismantled any incendiary devices. The Camaro's systems didn't detect explosives.

Parking the Camaro at the bottom of the stairs, Magnus took the steps two at a time. The grandiose carved front doors looked old enough to have once adorned one of the state's original monasteries.

He could have unlocked the door and walked in, but he was trying to be polite. He rang the bell.

A startled Chang opened the portal. "How the hell did you get in here?"

Magnus pushed inside and studied the empty foyer to verify he didn't have machine guns aimed at him. "Magic," he said. "I told you I was coming. You live here alone?"

"My father fired most of the servants over the last months. I fired the rest. I want people I can trust. Is Nadine dissolving that school? I've had to hire someone to handle the damned reporters." Knowing what Magnus wanted, Chang led the way deeper into the mansion.

"She won't dissolve the school unless forced," Magnus told him as they took stairs down to the basement. "She'll take it out of your name, though. You might want to pay her to expedite it. She says she and her sister inherit nothing except what she'll earn in executor's fees. That's a thankless job."

"There isn't much cash. My father was a risk taker who invested everything he earned in his various enterprises. I'll sell off the businesses I'm not interested in, but his debts nearly equal his assets. Have her tell me how much she needs—just understand it better not be much." Chang unlocked a metal door.

"My family will help out," Magnus promised, now that he was getting what he wanted—respect for Nadine. "Someone with a head for numbers will run a budget and let you know. Nadine needs help, not bullying, keep that in mind. But as I told you, I'm here for a different purpose." Magnus stoically studied the room to which he'd been led.

"Yeah, books. Help yourself." Chang made a sweeping gesture to indicate the floor-to-ceiling metal shelves of the musty storage room. "The man was obsessive. He collected these, but I don't think I ever saw him read one."

"I'm betting your mother is the one who collected them. He was finding them for her." Magnus walked around the perimeter, examining old hand-written ledgers with no titles, more recent spiral bound notebooks, computer disks, and all the variations in between

"I've looked," Chang admitted. "My mother didn't write any of these. Some of them are in Latin. They're almost all handwritten, except these." He pointed at a collection of three-ring binders. "They've been printed on a computer from old CDs."

Magnus removed one of the binders and smiled. "*The Journals of Alicia Ives Malcolm*—Nadine's mother?"

"Probably." Chang shrugged. "I was out of the house by the time he married Nadine's mother."

"Do you want to keep any of them?" Magnus took down the rest of the blue binders with the computer documents and popped the CDs into his jacket pocket.

"I'll probably have to sell this place, so no, I don't need a collection of old diaries. If Nadine wants them, they're hers." Chang crossed his arms and looked defensive.

"I'll call someone to box them up. Once Nadine sees these, she'll probably do anything you ask. But give the school the money anyway. Your family owes her more than you'll ever be able to repay." Magnus found a box in a corner and stacked his valuable prizes inside.

"You can't prove that," Chang replied.

Magnus eyed him long enough to make the other man squirm. "I probably could. She worked as an unpaid flunky instead of the highly-trained professional she is for years. Don't make me push it. Try being a better person than your father, and maybe Nadine will be there for you when you need her. She's extremely handy to have on your side."

Chang scowled, but he nodded. "We give new meaning to the word *dysfunctional.* Tell Nadine I'll help where I can."

"That's all she asks. I'm sorry for your loss, and so is Nadine, probably more than either of us will ever know. But it's time to move on. Thanks for the books. They mean more to her than money." Magnus carried his box up the stairs.

"We have positions in Adams Engineering for men with your talent," Chang said as he escorted him to the door. "I'm not my father."

Magnus snorted at the offer but replied semi-politely. "For which the world gives thanks. I may have reason to hire your firm in the future. We'll stay in touch." Gravely, Magnus shook Chang's hand and walked into the desert sunshine with Nadine's past and future in his hands.

After spending the morning with the judge and lawyers and more legal documents than even her formidable brain could process, Nadine rewarded herself by accompanying the social worker when she took Mikala back to the school.

"You'll come visit?" Mikala demanded when they pulled down the long drive.

"I'll be here so often, you'll hate to see me coming," Nadine told her. "Today, you need to take me around and introduce me to everyone."

Having a purpose was far better than wandering rootless. Homelessness—now that was a different problem.

Oz's RV was parked on a concrete pad near the school's parking lot. One of Conan's drivers must have left it there after their little escapade the other night. Maybe... She let that thought tease at the back of her mind while she concentrated on the school.

Walking up the path to the sprawling, one-story adobe building, she admired the manzanita shrubbery and the succulent garden. Someone had been taking good care of the property. The open desert was easier on her mind than the population-clogged cities. She might be able to make a home out here.

She didn't know if Magnus could.

Inside, the building had high ceilings and lots of light, bright open space. Mikala was broadcasting her nervous eagerness with her fidgeting as much as her mind.

"Go find your friends," Nadine told her. "I'll be here for a few hours more if you need me."

Mikala sent a blinding mental *thank you* that resembled a rainbow in Crayola colors, then ran off down a corridor from which childish voices could be heard.

"Can you introduce me to the staff?" Nadine asked with a trace of trepidation. She was used to computers, not people. But Magnus had returned her confidence that she could learn anything.

Later that day, Magnus called to locate her and promised to swing by to pick her up. By the time the Camaro raised dust down the drive, Nadine had met all the teachers and most of the students and had been invited to share dinner with them.

She'd pretty much reached her limits of sociability and would rather share dinner with Magnus. She had so many things she wanted to talk about... And so many hopes she didn't dare consider until she understood what he wanted next.

Speaking with the school's administrator, Nadine waited for Magnus to come inside to get her. But the Camaro's dust settled without any sight of him. Puzzled, she excused herself and wandered out to see what had distracted him.

He was just hopping down from the camper. He looked like the football player he'd once been, with his shoulders straining his long-sleeved, charcoal, ribbed t-shirt and his narrow hips encased in black jeans. His hair had grown out just enough to promise dark curls in the future. He strode toward her with the supreme confidence of a man who had the whole world in the palm of his hand. Her heart fluttered like a trapped bird as she watched him.

The smile curving his chiseled lips released her anxiety, and she sashayed in his direction, flirting the skirt of another of Pippa's wardrobe selections. This one was a swirl of turquoises and darker blues. She wore a dark blue blazer over the halter top, but she had hopes the jacket would come off shortly.

His gaze fastened immediately on her cleavage. He slid his big hands beneath her jacket and lifted it from her shoulders, just as she'd hoped, inspecting the bare skin revealed. "Yeah, I like this one, too," he said with appreciation. "How did your day go?"

"Pretty well, I think," she said, almost shyly, uncertain if she'd accomplished as much as she thought. "It will take time and money and some persuasion, but I think once we apply for a proper charter, the school can be kept open."

"Good. Come see what I've brought you." He caught her arm and tugged her toward the RV with unusual enthusiasm.

"You brought me something? A surprise?" she asked with more excitement than she'd experienced in a long while. "No one has ever brought me a surprise."

"It's probably hard to surprise someone plugged into the universe," he said with his usual gravity, although he was still smiling. "I'm hoping this one surprise will last a lifetime."

"You brought me camping equipment?" she asked facetiously, stepping into the tin interior.

"It's not exactly the mansions we've been living in, granted, but the RV isn't what I'm talking about." He closed the door and switched on the lights.

"It has lights?" She glanced around at the various sconces in surprise, then at the table where he'd set plastic place settings for two. Steaming boxes of Chinese carry-out apparently constituted dinner. "No pizza?" she asked, laughing.

"I couldn't find pizza nearby, a definite downside to this set-up. There's a complete RV pad here, with water and everything. The original owner probably had a trailer here for guests." Magnus filled the tiny aisle as he steered her into the booth. "But that's not what I want you to see."

He took off her jacket and folded it over the driver's seat. He helped her into the booth and lit candles.

"I love this!" she cried in delight. "Can we do this often? Carry-out by candlelight, who can ask for anything more?"

His whole face crinkled when he smiled. "We could have carry-out by the sea next. The advantage of camping equipment is portability." He opened the storage under the couch and produced an enormous gift-wrapped box. "But this, I can only do once, so I'm trying to do it right."

Nadine covered her mouth and tears sprang to her eyes. Big blue ribbons covered the silver-foil paper, and she remembered happy holidays with her mother and sister. "You're making me cry," she whispered. "If you bring out a Christmas tree, I'll never stop crying."

He tipped her chin up and kissed her tears. "Christmas isn't for a few months. I'll bring you Rockefeller Center if you want it. But not today. This is a gift you've earned all on your own. Open it."

He handed her a pocket knife so she could slit the ribbon and tape without damaging the packaging. She folded the paper while studying the dusty, ordinary old UPS box beneath. "I'm afraid to look. There aren't any spiders in there, are there?"

He snorted and pulled back the cardboard tabs. "Maybe pressed and dried, along with eye of newt and all that."

She had to stand up to peer inside. The blue binders looked vaguely familiar. She lifted the top one, and the memories flashed back so vividly, that she nearly dropped her beautiful, beautiful gift.

"Mama!" she whispered, and tears rolled down her cheeks. "These are Mama's! Marvelous Max found Mama's diaries."

Weeping, she set the book down and flung her arms around his neck and covered his face in kisses. "I can't begin to thank you. I'd thought them lost forever. Vera will be ecstatic! It's a piece of the home we lost. I can't even begin to explain..." She was weeping too hard to talk more.

He squeezed her and let her cry. "I think I'm getting used to this," he murmured. "Especially if it means I can carry you to bed again."

She sobbed and hiccuped and laughed. "Yes, I think you definitely deserve a reward for putting up with my tears. And for bringing me the best gift ever. And just for being you. And because once I have my hands on you, I can't think of anything else."

"That might wear off someday, maybe in New Zealand. Or the Congo. When we're eighty or so." He carried her toward the back of the RV. "Until then, I vote we try as many beds as we can find until we find the perfect one."

"It doesn't have to be just beds," she reminded him. "There's sand and kitchen counters and Jacuzzis and..."

"We'll never run out, excellent." He deposited her on the covers and fell down beside her. "Our dinner will get cold."

"I know microwave," she informed him. "I am the world's best microwaver."

"No danger of starving, then," he said in satisfaction, trailing kisses down her throat, to the cleavage exposed by her halter.

"I'll keep you well-fed," she promised breathlessly as his mouth found a particularly succulent bite.

"I hear South American ants are tasty this time of year." He unfastened her bra and they both gave up on talking. Or thinking.

Sometimes, action was the only way to go.

Still glowing with pride that he'd found the way to his woman's heart, Magnus watched Nadine skim through her mother's journals while she speared chicken bits with her chopsticks. She'd put some kind of wash on her hair that had removed more of the brown dye and let the sunset color shine through. He hoped she would let it grow out again. He loved digging his hands into those soft curls. He loved the way her wide mouth curled upward when something pleased her. He loved... everything about her.

He produced a booklet and piece of paper from the shelf where he'd dropped them. "I checked with the DMV. You can use this address as your permanent address if you put the utility bills in your name. I think there's separate meters for the RV."

She tore her gaze from the journal to read the booklet title, and her whole face lit up. "I can get a driver's permit! Will you teach me?"

"Do you think anyone else could?" he asked wryly, remembering their discussions of having fits in the middle of traffic.

She flashed him a smile. "I'm a quick learner. Can I drive the Camaro?"

"About that..." He forked his chicken and waffled now that they were talking something resembling permanency in their relationship.

She raised her auburn eyebrows and waited expectantly—trustingly.

He loved that about her, too. She accepted him just as he was, without asking him to change. "The car is part of a security system I'm working on. It contains software that can hack keypads and interfere with wireless."

She looked alarmed, and he held up his hand to prevent the flood of questions.

"I'll probably sell it to the government when it's perfected. Drug honchos have impressive security systems, but my mechanics will fritz them out in ten seconds flat. But what I really want to do is build a hack-free system, so people like Oz can feel safe in their own homes, and businesses won't be easy prey for a new breed of thieves."

She nodded, wide-eyed with understanding. "And your infrared camera can detect paparazzi and probably thieves, too. You have a whole security industry in your head. I might even be able to help you with the hacking end."

He breathed a sigh of relief. "Exactly. Once I've worked out the mechanics, I'll have to travel to set up the systems, but I can have a home base anywhere. All you have to do is tell me where."

"Here, for now," she said without hesitation. "This school is what I want to do, at least until Vera graduates and has some experience and can take over. I want to leave her a solid foundation to build on."

"Ummm, we might have a minor problem with that." He dragged his chopsticks through his rice, looking for the best way to say this. "I kind of agreed to take on a pretty extensive library, one with some valuable old books that will probably need professional maintenance."

"That will require a real librarian?" she asked in delight. "What kind of library?"

"Your family's," he said with a shrug. "All the journals that Feng Po-po and her fellow scientists collected over decades, probably. Some of the books are so old, they're in Latin."

If it was possible, her eyes widened to fill her face. The candles illuminated the green to a fiery hue that was almost witch-like. That's when Magnus knew she'd grow her hair out to reach her shoulders—because this was who she was meant to be. The Malcolm

Librarian.

"We can build a temperature-controlled room right here," she murmured. "We can use it to help the children. And their parents. We'll be a world-wide resource..."

Magnus rose from the booth and pulled her out of her seat. She was wearing only a robe, and his hands slid beneath it easily, finding smooth skin. She purred and cat-like, licked his stubbly jaw.

"And you can copy all that information into computer archives for everyone to access—when you're not accompanying me in global adventures," he finished for her.

"Yeah, that, too." She stood on her toes and bit his ear lobe and they left the chicken to be microwaved again some other time.

Author Bio

With several million books in print and *New York Times* and *USA Today's* bestseller lists under her belt, former CPA Patricia Rice is one of romance's hottest authors. Her emotionally-charged contemporary and historical romances have won numerous awards, including the *RT Book Reviews* Reviewers Choice and Career Achievement Awards. Her books have been honored as Romance Writers of America RITA® finalists in the historical, regency and contemporary categories.

A firm believer in happily-ever-after, Patricia Rice is married to her high school sweetheart and has two children. A native of Kentucky and New York, a past resident of North Carolina and Missouri, she currently resides in Southern California, and now does accounting only for herself. She is a member of Romance Writers of America, the Authors Guild, and Novelists, Inc.

For further information, visit Patricia's network:
http://www.patriciarice.com
http://www.facebook.com/OfficialPatriciaRice
https://twitter.com/Patricia_Rice
http://patriciarice.blogspot.com/
http://www.wordwenches.com

CPSIA information can be obtained
at www.ICGtesting.com
Printed in the USA
LVOW13s1940121017
552169LV00031B/818/P

9 781611 383713